WHAT HAPPENS WHEN
AN INNOCENT ABROAD
PICKS THE DAZZLING
FLOWER OF JAPAN?

He took hold of her like the precious thing she was, and his hands touched only the softness of her skin. He let his fingers run down her back until he realized that she had come to him herself along, and he understood what that meant.

His consciousness lifted off the hard earth of reality and took to the sky . . .

"An admirable job of telling what happens when East meets West and each likes what it sees." —*Chicago Tribune*

Miss One Thousand Spring Blossoms

Books by John Ball

Last Plane Out
The First Team
The Fourteenth Point
Mark One: The Dummy
The Winds of Mitamura
Phase Three Alert
The Murder Children
A killing in the Market
The Kiwi Target
The Van: A Tale of Terror
Rescue Mission

Virgil Tibbs Mysteries

Five Pieces of Jade
The Eyes of Buddha
Then Came Violence
Singapore

Chief Jack Tallon Crime Novels

Police Chief
Trouble for Tallon
Chief Tallon and the S.O.R.

**For more exciting
Books, eBooks, Audiobooks and more visit us at**
www.speakingvolumes.us

Miss One Thousand Spring Blossoms

John Ball

SPEAKING VOLUMES, LLC
NAPLES, FLORIDA
2014

Miss One Thousand Spring Blossoms

ISBN 978-1-62815-012-4

For Minnie Herman
enduring friend

Author's Note

The preparation of a work of this kind requires help. Happily for the author, some very delightful ladies lent a hand, including Miss Asa Takizawa, and Miss Emiko Goto who, professionally, is the celebrated geisha Chyamaru. Very special thanks are due to Mr. G. Y. Sasaki whose contribution was major. And the whole thing would have been impossible without Japan's famous woman photographer, Miss Miyoko Sasaki, and Mr. Danny Tam Lung who, in private life, are husband and wife and the parents of my goddaughter.

Thanks are also extended to a lady whom I knew in Chicago, whose name I hesitate to use without permission, who first awakened my interest in a most remarkable and gifted people many years ago.

JOHN BALL

Chapter One

In the richly paneled, discreetly decorated sanctuary of his presidential office Basil Mercer tipped back in his executive chair, placed his fingertips carefully together, and contemplated the ceiling. For the third time in two days he proceeded to review, with the utmost care, a decision which he had already made, but which he had so far communicated to no one. He found it necessary to assure himself one more time that he was not being hasty, something which would have offended his New England conscience almost beyond repair. He paraded the pertinent facts before the mirror of his judgment and once more satisfied himself that what he was about to do was both conservative and sound. Then he resumed an upright posture and pressed one of the buttons mounted on the side of his mahogany desk.

Williamson came in. He was a dusty little man in a neat and correct business suit and a tie which was a model of decorum. He had been fifteen years with the firm, and for a relative newcomer was doing quite well; if he had not been, unfortunately, a Baptist, his rise might have been even spectacular. As presidential assistant he carried considerable authority, by proxy, a situation which he carefully preserved.

He stopped just short of the massive desk and waited.

"I have been considering the matter of the Matsumoto Company," Mercer declared.

Williamson knew that he meant he had at last made up his mind and was ready to announce his decision. He nodded that he understood.

"We are going to have to send someone over there," Mercer continued. "Largely because if we don't someone else will, and that could present complications."

Williamson nodded once more. The Matsumoto Company, while small, was a prime low-cost source for components of remarkable quality which had the added virtue of almost always being delivered on time. In fact, the current prosperity of his own firm was based, to a measurable degree, on the reliability of the Matsumoto production.

"I presume that with the present availability of jet transportation," Mercer went on, "Japan can be properly considered as being within a normal travel radius."

It was a weighty statement and Williamson knew it, in fact it approached the dimensions of a declaration of policy. To him Japan was an exotic, and therefore alien, land located on the far distant side of some other globe. Personal contact with the native population there was an innovation he would not himself have considered until after the most profound thought.

He realized that he was now expected to speak. If he agreed he was to say so; if not, he would be expected to damn with faint praise. Direct rebuttal, as such, was not to be considered.

"There are, of course, obstacles," he noted.

Mercer nodded. "I have considered them. The cost will be relatively high, although deductible. Whomever we send will be largely on his own for a considerable period, perhaps up to three weeks. And there will be language difficulties, although Mr. Matsumoto himself apparently speaks acceptable English judging from the letters which we have received."

"I would recommend that we engage a reliable interpreter if one is available," Williamson ventured. "We can hardly expect Mr. Matsumoto to assume that function personally and our man would be largely in contact with the firm's engineers."

2

"Quite correct," Mercer agreed. "We now come to the matter of whom to send. Considering all things, I believe it rests between Seaton and Fineman. Both are technically competent and fully acquainted with the Matsumoto products which we are now using. Of the two, Fineman is somewhat the more brilliant, I believe, if the term properly applies."

Williamson recognized the gambit. He raised his hand before his mouth and coughed very slightly. Mercer looked at him and nodded that he was to express himself.

"Fineman is very capable," Williamson declared cautiously. "I agree that in the technical area he is a shade better than Seaton."

He paused to look out of the window at the gentle roll of the Massachusetts hills. "While I can claim no acquaintance with the habits of the Japanese, it is my general understanding that they place great stress on deportment and courtesy."

That was precisely the response which Mercer had anticipated and he nodded his head slowly in agreement. "A very significant point."

"There is also the matter of family," Williamson continued. "Fineman is quite recently married, only a year or so ago I believe. Seaton is single, very much so. While the period of separation is not particularly significant, I have noted that matrimony does not seem to have eradicated completely certain inclinations which Fineman has been known to reveal in the past."

"He is, I believe, the person who slapped the telephone receptionist on her ass about three years ago."

"Precisely. Playfully, of course, and during the spring season, but if he should find the separation from his new bride a subject of difficulty, it must be considered possible . . ."

Basil Mercer made it clear he was not about to render a hurried decision. "You prefer Seaton, then?"

Williamson nodded slowly. "While he is fully competent, as you pointed out, he is a little less likely to—overshadow—the Matsumoto engineering people. I suspect they would be sensitive to that."

"I agree," said Mercer, "that his general conduct is a point in his favor. For a venture of this kind perhaps a little old-fashioned courtliness might be peculiarly appropriate."

Williamson cleared his throat. "At least we could probably

3

depend upon him to exhibit appropriate—biological restraint. I seriously doubt if he has ever been laid in his life. It is a very limited risk that he will slap any of the Japanese young ladies on their butts—presuming that they have them."

"Oh, I'm certain that they do," Mercer stated a bit more briskly. "The population over there, as you may know, is impressive."

There was a shift in the atmosphere to which Williamson was sensitive at once. "Do you wish to discuss this with him personally?" he asked.

It took Basil Mercer only a second or two to decide that his dignity would be better served if he delegated that chore. "Why don't you take care of that," he said. "Before he goes I'll have a word with him—the usual sort of thing."

Williamson nodded his approval. He had to restrain himself from overdoing it, because for him to dispatch someone to the far ends of the earth on company business would materially enhance his stature. The staff would know of it with a minimum lapse of time. His spine tingled in anticipation of the event.

"Have you a time frame in mind?" he inquired.

Mercer waved his hand. "All things being equal, I would say the sooner the better. Any unnecessary delay might open the door for someone else. That would be regrettable."

"Very. I'll attend to it immediately."

Satisfied with the outcome of the conversation, Mercer nodded for a final time. With that gesture he both terminated the interview and passed the ball to his subordinate who, he knew, would be off and running for yardage as soon as he was outside the door.

Williamson returned to his own office, sat down, and allowed himself almost four minutes of ego-satisfying contemplation. He planned with meticulous care how he would approach the subject and the exact manner in which he would deliver the shattering news. He then used the intercom on his desk to call his secretary. He said simply, "I would like to see Mr. Seaton."

He swiveled around and once more looked out the window. He saw the same familiar scene: the comforting stability of the landscape, the undisturbed beauty of the maples, the pleasant roll of the hills. In other parts of the world, he knew,

4

vast and terrible mountains soared with pagan power to dizzying heights which challenged the sky itself. He shuddered slightly and was grateful to Providence that he had been granted a more circumspect manner of life. He had, within the past month, been able to negotiate a loan on behalf of the company at a quarter of one percent under the going rate for such commitments. This was the sort of challenge he understood and which quickened the blood in his veins. He had no taste for the far side of either the moon or the planet on which he lived.

The intercom came to life and relayed the information that Mr. Seaton was outside and awaiting his pleasure.

"Send him in," he directed.

The door opened and his secretary ushered in his visitor. On most other occasions Williamson had found Seaton in his shirt sleeves either bent over a drafting table in the small engineering department or else out in the shop in conference with one of the production people. Now, of course, he had carefully put on his coat and had prepared himself for an appearance in the executive offices.

Seaton was tall, just over six feet, fairly thin, and had a prominent nose. Perched on it were a pair of glasses whose black plastic rims made him look notably like an owl. His sandy brown hair was neatly trimmed, his fingernails were short and clean, and his white no-iron shirt was entirely appropriate. Nonetheless, he managed to look slightly gawky, partly because of his stature, more particularly because of the manner in which he carried himself.

Before entering the office to which he had been summoned, he turned to the middle-aged secretary and bowed. "Thank you most kindly, Mrs. Herzog," he said. Then he faced the man who had required his presence. To the best of his own knowledge his work had been satisfactory, but the unexpected summons to the front office had him mildly concerned. It was most unusual.

With a careful nod copied from Mercer himself Williamson dismissed his secretary and motioned Seaton to a chair. When he indicated the one at the side of his desk Seaton was relieved; that was the chair of confidence. The one in front of the desk was more suited to reprimands and other unpleasant matters. He seated himself, carefully crossed his long legs,

5

folded his hands in his lap, and then looked up to indicate that he was ready.

Williamson took his time. Because he was a small man it was hard for him not to feel defensive in the presence of someone almost a foot taller. He could have saved himself the trouble; the aura of his position was established throughout the company.

"After very careful consideration," he began, "Mr. Mercer and I have decided to proceed with the development of the multipurpose tester. The performance of the mock-up prototype has been quite satisfactory."

Seaton gave a jerky little nod. "I'm very glad to hear that. I'm certain that there is a very good market for it."

"That is Mr. Mercer's opinion," Williamson said dryly, forever relieving Seaton from expressing himself on that subject again. "We have been giving some consideration," he added, "to possible sources of supply."

Seaton realized that he was expected to comment. "Some of the components we can do in house; the main case, VU meters, and other accessories we can get from our regular suppliers." He leaned forward and adjusted his glasses. "There is one very intricate unit which is the key to the whole assembly. It's quite sophisticated and needs very close quality control. If you concur, sir, I would like to suggest that we approach Matsumoto about producing it."

"Continue," Williamson said.

"Well, sir, if anyone can do that bit they are the people, and I don't believe that they would hold us up on the price. This is not like anything they have done for us before, but it should lie within their capability. The Japanese seem to be very clever in things of this kind, and Matsumoto's schedules of delivery dates have been proving reliable."

Williamson bounced his fingertips together. "Seaton, what would you say if I told you that we plan to do just that, and furthermore, we are planning to send a member of the firm to Japan to arrange the matter with the Matsumoto people?"

Seaton looked a little startled. "Is Mr. Mercer planning to make the trip personally?" he asked.

Williamson shook his head. "I said we were planning to send someone. Mr. Mercer's schedule wouldn't possibly permit it and I can't be spared either for such an extended trip. Actually we had thought of sending you."

Seaton reacted as though a sudden electric current had been discharged through his body.

"Me?" he asked.

Williamson did nothing.

"Japan, sir?" Seaton formed the words as though he were shaping them for ectoplasm.

"Japan," Williamson pronounced with full gravity.

Automatically Seaton reached again to adjust his glasses which had slipped down his nose. He struggled back to reality. "But it is a very long way, isn't it, sir?"

"Quite," Williamson agreed. "However, Mr. Mercer has expressed himself as wanting you to leave as soon as possible. I don't presume that you have a passport?"

"No, sir, actually I've never been out of the country. That is, I was in Canada once for a few hours, but there were minimum formalities about that."

"You will require a passport," Williamson said. "Also a visa, and I suspect that there are inoculations. I recommend that you contact a reliable travel agency and have them make the necessary reservations for, say, the end of this week. You will then be able to travel over the weekend and be in Tokyo in time for the start of business Monday morning."

"Tokyo," Seaton repeated, stunned.

"That is presuming that you can take care of all of the preliminary requirements in time. Come to think of it, there is some matter about the international date line—I would be interested to know how that affects interest rates."

He caught hold of himself. "Summarizing, the decision is definite that you are to visit the Matsumoto Company in Japan at the earliest date for which you can make convenient arrangements. I suggest that you clear your desk this afternoon and turn over whatever you are engaged in at the moment to Mr. Fineman. Spend tomorrow accomplishing as much as you can toward implementing your trip. Ask the agency to arrange a suitable hotel for you in Japan, a sensible business type. Not one of those, whch I understand they have, with built-in maids—one to each room."

7

Seaton looked shocked. "Sir," he said. He recovered himself enough to make his voice reasonably emphatic. "I can assure you that you need have no cause for concern in that direction."

Chapter Two

Richard Emmett Seaton went to the men's room and carefully soaked his head in cold water.

When he had finished, he blotted himself with paper towels and tried to bring what he had just been told into the focus of reality. He still could not believe it. He had an almost overpowering desire to tell someone about it, someone who would find a thrill of satisfaction in his news.

Unfortunately, there was no such person. He thought of a friend or two, but he sensed that their reaction would be one of polite interest and no more.

Still a little dazed, he returned to his corner of the engineering department, took one of the Matsumoto-produced components off the sample shelf, and examined it with a new interest. It was a finely made, beautifully finished product which clearly could not have come from the hands of barbarians. He knew almost nothing about Japan or the Japanese people except that they were very different and spoke an impossible language. But they could make very fine electronic equipment. Professionally he should be able to establish liaison; in fact he would have to, since that was the whole purpose of his trip.

He began to feel a growing sense of adventure. He had never been west of Chicago, now he was going to the Orient.

The Orient! The word was sheer magic to him. He realized how many had been there before him, tens of thousands of servicemen among others, but to him it was still a pioneering adventure. He would be an unofficial ambassador, an American abroad who would be a representative of his country. He gave silent thanks that he had been raised in the old tradition, that he understood courtesy and fine deportment. Perhaps, if he did exceptionally well, he might even come to the attention of the State Department.

The plant of Matsumoto and Company was located on the southern outskirts of Tokyo on a relatively small plot of ground which had cost a substantial sum. In front there was a tiny garden which had been created with cunning skill to suggest serenity in the midst of the industrial area. The architect had borrowed the hills in the background as part of his design, a trick which the Japanese use to perfection. There was even a miniature pond and the suggestion of a pathway, all in something less than a hundred and twenty square feet. By turning away from the inviting garden the visitor to the Matsumoto plant could look across to the tracks of the New Tokaido Line, the most advanced railway in the world.

Inside the plant, in his air-conditioned office, Mr. Tatsuo Matsumoto for the third time read through with greatest care the translation of the letter from MERCER & DOYLE, LABORATORY TEST EQUIPMENT, which had been placed before him. Mr. Matsumoto did not himself understand a single word of English; instead he relied on the capabilities of Miss Reiko Watanabe, who had studied that impossible and unpronounceable tongue for eight years and who could both read and write it with satisfactory skill.

When he had satisfied himself that the letter contained no information which he had not fully absorbed, he rose to his feet, opened the door to his outer office, and looked at the crowded ensemble of his clerical employees. There were at least twice as many as would have occupied the same area in an American company and who might have done substantially the same work. The overpopulation of Japan had made it

10

customary for employers to take on more people than were actually needed and to retain them on the payroll regardless of economic conditions unless some individual disgraced himself to the point where dismissal became mandatory.

The crammed room hummed with activity. Matsumoto had customers in six different countries, a circumstance which made necessary a great deal of paper work and translation. At one side of the office a girl was operating a Japanese typewriter, a cumbersome machine with three fonts and hundreds of individual characters. Miss Watanabe was bent over her desk checking invoices written in English. Everyone was busy.

Mr. Matsumoto indicated to his second-in-command, Mr. Shingiro Yamaguchi, that he wished to confer. The younger man came into the private office and Mr. Matsumoto shut the door.

"We are to have a visitor from Mercer and Doyle," he announced. (Actually in literal translation he said, "We from Mercer and Doyle a visitor to have are," using the proper Japanese word order, which puts the subject first, then the object, and finally the verb.)

"It will require hospitality," Mr. Yamaguchi said. "Do you wish me to establish a budget?"

"Yes, and plan on making yourself available when he arrives. I gather they are sending over their chief engineer to inspect our facilities. If he likes what he sees, then a new order may follow for the production of something quite intricate."

Mr. Yamaguchi sucked in his breath and pushed his own glasses higher on his nose. "I am glad now that I know some English. I will never learn it completely, I don't believe that anyone can, but I should be able to greet the man when he arrives and possibly answer some simple questions."

He shuddered at the thought; his knowledge of fundamental English grammar was acceptable, but his pronunciation was disastrous and he knew it. Of all of the linguistic accomplishments available to the human race, one of the most difficult is for a Japanese to speak good English. It can be done, but it usually requires extended residence in a foreign, English-speaking country.

"How much do we know about him?" he asked. "Is there anything about his age, or whether or not he is bringing his family with him?"

11

"Fortunately," Mr. Matsumoto replied, "there is no indication of any family. A wife from America, I have been told, might even expect to be entertained in our homes, which is, of course, impossible. Our visitor will be Mr. Richard Seaton."

The pronunciation of the name gave Mr. Matsumoto some difficulty; it was, in fact, quite unrecognizable in either language.

Mr. Yamaguchi sighed deeply. Foreigners from the Western world were strange people at best and their tastes were often extraordinary. It would clearly be his job to see that Seaton san enjoyed his visit and went home with a favorable impression of both the Matsumoto Company's competence and the manner in which he had been treated. It would not be an easy task. The language barrier was formidable, but even worse was the cultural gap—so few Americans had any training at all.

Precisely one week later Richard Seaton himself sat alone and gazed out at the lights of San Francisco from the Top-of-the-Mark. His left arm throbbed painfully from the second of the cholera shots his doctor had recommended, but his mind was fixed on other matters.

Once again he saw himself seated in the chair before the desk in Mr. Mercer's office receiving his final instructions from the president personally. On the surface it had been informal, but great weight had hung on every word which Mercer had chosen to speak. During the course of the conversation he had mentioned the Top-of-the-Mark and had advised Seaton to visit it while he was in San Francisco. Dutifully he was now carrying out this recommendation. On his own he would not have thought of coming here, but Mr. Mercer had made it compulsory.

It was imperative that he be able to describe this experience, if asked, upon his return. Failure to act on a presidential recommendation was unthinkable. But the drink he had ordered, he carefully decided, was a personal expense and would not appear on the accounting which he would give the company.

The experience of flying coast-to-coast nonstop on a jet-powered aircraft had been anything but routine for him. It seemed incredible that he was already almost three thousand

Miss One Thousand Spring Blossoms

miles from home. That was approximately one-eighth of the
way completely around the world. Yet his journey had hardly
begun. With a self-consciousness which he could not avoid he
crossed his long legs, wiped his glasses, and then carefully
finished his drink. The people who surrounded him in the
semidarkness of the cocktail lounge sat quietly or moved
about with an easy relaxed grace which had been denied him.
An extraordinarily attractive girl in a long dinner dress,
followed by her escort, walked past his table. For an accidental instant their eyes met, and Seaton was jolted when she
seemed to give him the shadow of a half-smile. When they
were past he rose to his own clumsy height and made his
escape back to the bank of elevators.

At the Matsumoto Company, Mr. Matsumoto himself was
waiting for someone to drop the third shoe.
First had come the news of the impending visit by the
American engineer. In a way this was not bad news, but many
preparations would have to be made. There was also the
unfortunate possibility that liaison would not be established
and the plum of the new order would go to some other firm.
There were plenty in Japan who could do first-class work at a
competitive price.
The following mail had brought a flat cancellation of a
valued order from a major customer in the Philippines. Since
disasters of this nature always occurred in threes, Mr. Matsumoto was waiting with fatalistic resignation for whatever
was to be his third misfortune. He would not know a restful
moment until it came.
Meanwhile Mr. Yamaguchi, his energetic and capable vice-
president, had proposed the name of Mr. Ichiro Futaba to be
his co-host during the period of Seaton san's visit. Mr. Futaba
spoke English, or at least thought that he did.
The suggestion was a reasonable one. A part of the compen-
sation of any salaryman, such as Mr. Futaba, was occasional participation in customer entertainment on an expense
account basis. Since Mr. Futaba was married and the father
of two, he had little left over after meeting his essential expenses for nights on the town or the Chinese-owned Pachinko
machines, the one-armed bandits of the Far East. He had not
been a co-host for at least ten months and it was fairly his

13

turn. Furthermore, he had the English—that accursed tongue which only the most profound *sensei* could master, and then largely on a theoretical basis.

Mr. Matsumoto weighed the matter and then gave his consent. He himself could hardly take the time which the job would require, and in his case the language barrier was absolute. Mr. Futaba received the joyous news with excellent spirit and hoped only that the American would know the rules and customs for being a good guest. In America, he had been told, business acquaintances were sometimes entertained in private homes, a shameful device for cutting down on the expenses.

The entertainment team was established as Yamaguchi and Futaba; jointly they swore that the American engineer would unfailingly discover the true worth of Japan in general and of the Matsumoto Company in particular. It was a reasonable promise, since not even the French can approach the Japanese capability for talking business. The date of Seaton san's arrival was circled in red.

Mr. Matsumoto issued a memorandum to the staff to do everything possible to see that Seaton san obtained a favorable view of the enterprise. Mr. Yamaguchi made several phone calls to central Tokyo to check that all preparations were complete. He did not intend to let anything slip at the last minute.

On the fateful morning it rained. The reduction of visibility was not enough to halt traffic at Tokyo International Airport, but it did impose instrument conditions and with them the need for incoming airliners to stack up on the holding ranges and wait. In the terminal building Mr. Yamaguchi nervously rehearsed his welcoming speech in his mind for the twenty-second time while Mr. Futaba began to have sinking second thoughts about his ability to converse in English. Actually, he had never tried. In his English class they had stammered sentences to each other, but conversation as such had never been attempted; the pronunciation was too difficult.

An announcement was made that the flight from San Francisco and Honolulu was overhead and waiting to land. It was already more than thirty minutes late on the ramp, but the fault was clearly that of the weather and not of Japan Air

Miss One Thousand Spring Blossoms

Lines. Left to his own resources Seaton undoubtedly would have chosen an American carrier such as Pan American or Northwest Orient, but the travel agent had felt that the Japanese airline would be a good introduction to what was to follow.

The mists lifted for a moment and the long sleek shape of the DC—8 could be seen, gear and flaps down, on its final approach to the runway. At precisely the proper moment the pilot flared, the nose of the long-range airliner rose appropriately, and the wheels threw up eddies of water as they touched the runway. Seaton san was in Japan.

Mr. Yamaguchi had an impelling urge to titter with nervous laughter—a sure sign of Japanese embarrassment. For all of his brave preparation he was entirely unaccustomed to Americans and had no idea how he would recognize the man he had been sent to greet in a language of strangling difficulty. As he waited with an even less confident Mr. Futaba outside the exit from the customs area, the problem began to assume nightmare proportions.

After the usual delays the passengers began to come out in single file into the general terminal area. Mercifully most of them were Japanese, which cut down on the number of possibilities. There were also some family groups, which, while not completely eliminated, represented a much reduced possibility. There remained an impossibly tall, obviously brainless American tourist who looked like a well-dressed scarecrow with glasses, and a total of three businessmen, all of whom appeared technically competent.

One of these eliminated himself at once by shaking hands with another foreigner who had come to meet him. Gathering his courage, Mr. Yamaguchi carefully approached the second.

"Mr. Seaton san, yes?" he inquired.

In fluent Japanese the American identified himself as a major in the U. S. Marine Corps.

It was now clearly Mr. Futaba's turn. Beholding his duty before him, he tried the third man with the fullest expectation of success.

"Anata wa Seaton san, yes?" he asked.

"I've already got a hotel," the foreigner answered shortly.

Yamaguchi and Futaba looked rapidly about them, but

15

there were no more businessmen to be seen. A hasty glance inside the customs area confirmed that there were no more waiting to have their baggage cleared. In that moment of distress help appeared in the form of an attractive stewardess who had been the last to pass through the crew baggage line. Mr. Yamaguchi rushed to make inquiry. After the necessary formal and polite bows had been exchanged and the proper greetings spoken, he asked if a Mr. Seaton san had been on the plane.

The stewardess replied affirmatively and nodded toward the awkward giant who was standing, totally baffled, before a Japanese telephone.

Horror engulfed Yamaguchi, both that he had failed his initial duty and at the prospect of what he now had to do. As quickly as possible he presented himself before the human caricature and made an exceptionally deep bow. Two paces to the rear and on his right flank Mr. Futaba reinforced his performance. The desire to laugh in embarrassment was now almost overwhelming, but with a massive effort Mr. Yamaguchi restrained himself.

"Mr. Seaton san it is, yes?" he asked. He desperately wanted to say "Dewa arimasen ka" at the finish, which would have meant, "This is Mr. Seaton, is it not?" in a most polite manner.

The American reached into his pocket and extracted a phrase book which he had been given on the aircraft. His brow clouded as he gathered his resources for a major effort.

"Wa taxi wa Richard Seaton desk," he pronounced carefully.

Mr. Yamaguchi reached the breaking point and giggled. The very first words which the honored guest and most important engineer had spoken to him in English had passed by without his understanding a single syllable! Then his mind cleared and he seemed to recall that in the midst of the gibberish he had caught the name Seaton or something to that effect. He was not sure, because he thought of it as "Setanu" despite the fact that "n" is the only consonant which a Japanese can tolerate and pronounce at the end of a word.

At this moment Mr. Futaba stepped forward. He bowed once more and spoke with great care.

16

"Matsumoto Company," he said.

Like a candle placed in a stone lantern, the American lit up.

"Mr. Matsumoto, how do you do," he said warmly. "I'm so glad to meet you. I know you speak English. I'm Dick Seaton." He thrust out his hand.

Mr. Futaba looked at Mr. Yamaguchi in helpless terror.

This time Mr. Yamaguchi showed the stuff of which *he* was made. He bowed once more, deeply, removed his wallet, and handed the towering American his name card. It was the proper and only thing to do.

The American accepted it politely and then looked at it blankly. He clearly could not read the Chinese characters, particularly since he had them upside down.

The stewardess approached and bowed. "May I be of help?" she asked.

The tall American actually displayed good breeding by bowing in return. He did it badly, but he bowed.

"Indeed so," he replied and explained the difficulty. So also did Mr. Yamaguchi and Mr. Futaba, both of whom produced name cards for her to read.

When they had finished she turned again to Seaton. "These gentlemen have come to meet you," she explained. "They are from the Matsumoto Company. This is Mr. Yamaguchi, the executive vice-president. May I also introduce Mr. Futaba of the customer relations department."

The two Japanese bowed furiously. "We make greeting," Mr. Futaba ventured.

Seaton became the perfect diplomat. "Gentlemen, how do you do," he greeted them with complete cordiality. He also shook hands, which was an excusable error. Then he turned and thanked the stewardess. "Where can I engage an interpreter?" he asked.

The young lady smiled gently. "These gentlemen both speak English," she said softly, preserving their faces. Then she bowed politely once more and carefully withdrew.

According to the clocks in the terminal it was now close to six in the evening. Because of his long and rapid flight westward Seaton was attuned to something closer to seven in the morning after a sleepless night. Nevertheless, he was prepared to do his duty beginning at once. He had shaved on

17

the plane and assured himself that his wash-and-wear shirt was still presentable. He was prepared to go directly to the Matsumoto offices, despite the fact that he could not quite believe that he was in Japan. The terminal building was very much like those with which he had become acquainted in the States and all about him were the names of familiar airlines posted in large letters.

Mr. Yamaguchi directed him toward the taxi area while Mr. Futaba insisted on handling the luggage. "You—make—sleep—now?" Mr. Yamaguchi asked.

Seaton understood him and their first direct communication was established. "Sleep, no thank you. But I would like to go to my hotel, if I may, and get a quick shower."

Mr. Yamaguchi did not comprehend all that, but he did catch the word "hotel." "We go hoteru," he said as soon as they reached the cabstand.

A very small taxi pulled up from the right, and the left rear door opened by means of a mechanical device. Seaton bent down and peered inside. It was exceedingly compact with wickerwork fastened over the seat cushions; he was not sure at first if he would be able to get in.

But he did, with a certain amount of slightly awkward folding up, while his luggage was piled in beside him. Necessarily he removed his hat and held it in his hand. When he looked ahead he noticed that the driver was sitting on the wrong side; all that was directly before him was the back of the front seat, the windshield, and a tiny spray of flowers in a miniature vase.

Mr. Yamaguchi leaned in and spoke directions in staccato Japanese. The driver nodded quickly, raced his engine for a bare moment, and then whiplashed away from the curb.

Within seconds Seaton was terrified. The taxi, seemingly piloted by a madman, burst into a stream of fast-moving traffic headed down the wrong side of the street and began to accelerate to breakneck speed. There were three normal lanes of traffic, the cab unhesitatingly created a fourth. When it seemed to Seaton that the ultimate limit had been reached, another cab bearing the Messieurs Yamaguchi and Futaba somehow managed to pass.

Stung, Seaton's driver rose to even more desperate action. He swung out of line and screamed past three other cars in second gear before he had to slow down to enter the tollway which leads from the airport to the center of the city. For the next twelve minutes Seaton lived on in numbed shock as the flow of traffic compelled the cab to observe a false restraint. As soon as the right exit ramp appeared the driver trod once more on the gas pedal and took off in full cry. He wedged his way between two cars in another lane which had been hardly twelve feet apart, passed a three-wheeled truck, and then spurted ahead after another lane change on the wrong side of the center line divider.

In fear of his life Seaton shouted in English to the driver, who flashed back a quick grin and pointed urgently ahead. He went around a corner with screaming tires in defiance of the well-known law that $F=MV^2$ and rammed his way into another solid line of traffic which miraculously gave way.

Seaton's forehead was wet, his knees quivered against the back of the front seat, and his heart was fluttering. The single guide to Japan which he had studiously withdrawn from the library had made no mention of the kamikaze cabs of Tokyo.

To divert his mind he tried to look at the scenery. Signs were around him in profusion, signs written in gibbering, tortured characters which gave not the remotest hints of their meaning. Weird-looking three-wheeled trucks were everywhere, bouncing over the pavement like berserk tripods. The whole mass of traffic was both jammed and fast-moving beyond anything he had experienced, and all of it flowed in the wrong direction.

He was convinced now that he was in a foreign land. The rain had been replaced by a damp heat. The cab screeched to a stop at an intersection and a solid phalanx of pedestrians blockaded the crosswalks. In that moment of respite he realized how astonishingly out of place he was. How in the world, he wondered, would he ever be able to discuss technical matters with these people.

The cab burst forward again; the baggage swayed and fell over as the tires recoiled from the pavement. A cab on the left came so close that there did not appear to be room to put a piece of paper between them, but they did not touch. A tall building loomed ahead, a huge neon sign on its face spelling out something in the same senseless characters and designs.

Seaton pressed his lips together and reminded himself of his duty. He was here now, in the fabulous, far-distant Orient, committed to a mission which he must accomplish. The cab swung around another terrorizing corner, but he merely shut his eyes and hung on. Cruelly his subconscious reminded him at that moment that the gentle, English-speaking hills of New England were now a hopeless nine thousand miles away.

Chapter Three

Standing in the lobby of his hotel Richard Seaton strove to regain his balance.

Everything which had happened to him since he had cleared through customs had somehow been upside down and backward. At a decently early hour in the morning, it was suddenly dinnertime. Furthermore, it was dinnertime *tomorrow*. Traffic was a mad whirl, all in the wrong direction. He had been jerked through it as though the Red Queen had had him by the hand and whenever he had attempted to protest, the driver had only been spurred on to more desperate efforts. Incomprehensible language had been jabbered at him and when he had introduced himself in that mad tongue, he had been ignored.

Some sanity prevailed at the hotel; the desk clerk spoke English. He had the reservation and was pleased to inform Seaton san that his room was ready and awaiting him. In the background the Messieurs Yamaguchi and Futaba were standing to one side.

When he had signed the register and had been relieved of his baggage, he began to feel better: the world was showing some signs of returning to its proper orbit. He turned toward the two executives who had gone to the trouble to meet him and tried his best to make him understood.

"Thank you for meeting me," he said, slowly and carefully.

Mr. Futaba lit up and bowed. "It makes us pleasure."

A near-universal custom suggested itself and Seaton acted on it. "Would you care for a drink," he said.

Mr. Yamaguchi, encouraged, tested his own powers. "You first make bath?"

Seaton was grateful for that consideration. "I could use a shower. I was on the plane for quite a while, all night in fact."

"We take you to bath," Mr. Futaba proposed.

"There ought to be one in my room," Seaton said with a sinking feeling. If they wished to take him to a bath, then perhaps he had assumed incorrectly. Anything was possible in this country.

"In Japan," Mr. Yamaguchi labored, "is hotsie bath. Verly best kind. Much refresh, very clean."

"You like try Japanese way?" Mr. Futaba inquired gently.

Fortunately, or perhaps unfortunately, Seaton had read *The Ugly American.* He was determined not to mimic the inconsiderate clods pictured in that work. He drew himself up, looked again at his hosts, and then slumped down again. "It will be my pleasure," he announced.

Immediately his two companions were transfixed with smiles. Seaton felt better himself since he had obviously said the right thing.

"Very close," Mr. Futaba said. "One block. You want taxi?"

Seaton did *not* want taxi. He never again wanted a taxi in this nation—not if he could avoid it. "Could he walk?" he proposed.

That settled the matter and they started out. For a long block he plowed his way through a congested mass of humanity with the uncomfortable feeling that he had suddenly added an additional four inches to his already ample height. Mr. Futaba, who was leading the way, seemed to be saying something which sounded like, "Go, men, aside," as he elbowed a pathway through the hopeless confusion. Directly behind him

Mr. Yamaguchi also ran interference. To Seaton the whole thing was a little unreal; he had never gone through such preliminaries in order to take a bath. Surely not all of the hotel's guests were compelled to do this!

At the moment when severe doubts had begun to pyramid in his mind, they arrived. His guides from the Matsumoto Company ushered him into a lobby and produced an attendant who spoke acceptable English. Seaton san could be accommodated at once. Since he was weary from travel, he would find the establishment perfectly suited to his requirements. Many Americans residing locally were regular patrons.

This last was reassuring. Ever since leaving the airport Seaton had felt himself badly adrift; he needed something stable to cling to—like the sight of a plate of Boston baked beans. If this was a place favored by Americans, then he was all for it.

From the interior of the place of business a young woman was summoned and Seaton san was made acquainted with Miss Sumiko. The lady, who was clad in a white smock, placed her hands on her knees and bowed most politely, an action which Seaton returned in kind. Once more he had obviously done the right thing—he was surrounded with faces beaming approval. While he considered it strange that a lady was permitted inside a gentlemen's bathhouse, he obediently followed her down a long corridor which was infused with the sanitary aroma of soap and steam. Then they stopped, Sumiko opened the door to a room, and motioned him to enter.

Now he understood: each client had a private facility, which was eminently proper. A recollection had flashed through his mind, gleaned from a forgotten issue of the National Geographic, that the Japanese frequently bathed together—an idea which his mind refused to admit. He was relieved to discover that the arrangements were proper and correct—but of course they would have to be if Americans came here regularly.

The room itself was of reasonable size and contained a steam cabinet of a reclining sort, an oversize sunken tub brimful of hot water, a stool, and a long table on which he could lie down and rest. The whole interior was spotlessly

23

clean and the tile floor had obviously been freshly washed. If this was a Japanese bathroom, then it had much to recommend it.

As he stood looking about he heard a noise behind him. Miss Sumiko had also entered the room and was now shutting the door from the inside. Rolling up her sleeve she tested the temperature of the bath water and insured that the long towel laid on the table was fresh and clean. Then from a little cabinet she produced a coat hanger and with a gracious gesture indicated that she would like him to remove his jacket.

Assuming that his wallet and passport would be safe, Seaton complied and saw his property carefully hung in the wardrobe. Then Miss Sumiko knelt on the floor before him and began to untie his shoes.

Not for as long as he could remember had anyone ever removed his shoes, except salesmen who were in the process of fitting him with a new pair. He was embarrassed to have a female serving him in this manner; it did not seem dignified. Remembering that he was, in a sense, an ambassador, he lifted his feet alternately while his shoes were carefully taken off and his socks pulled from his feet. Fortunately they were a new pair; the embarrassment of having an unexpected hole appear would have been acute.

When these had been placed in the cabinet, Miss Sumiko pointed to his tie.

Now that was going a little too far. He was certain that he was not in the wrong kind of establishment, but his tie was a symbol of the dignity expected of him. When at last he realized that he was compelled to comply, he carefully undid it and then graciously opened the door so that Miss Sumiko could leave.

Miss Sumiko giggled and pointed to his trousers.

"Those are my pants, dammit!" he said. He spoke louder than he had intended, but he considered her gesture to be obscene.

Sumiko considered the matter. Then she pointed to him, to the steam cabinet, to the bathtub, and then back to his trousers.

ズボンも、パンツも…
全部ぬいで下さい…
ないで、着ているものを
さあ、恥ずかしがら   she said.

Her meaning was slowly and painfully clear. Seaton stood there, frozen, unable either to say anything intelligent or to make up his mind what to do. At that moment he looked toward the door and saw the smart figure of a lieutenant colonel in the United States Air Force passing by. "Hi!" he called.

The colonel turned and pushed his head into the room. "Having trouble?" he asked.

Seaton turned toward him in gratitude. "I certainly am. This girl is trying to get me to take off my pants."

"Then why don't you?"

Seaton paused. "Is this a whorehouse?"

The colonel gave him a quick inspection. "No, and if it was I wouldn't be here, at least not at this hour. It's a hotsie bath. How long have you been in Japan?"

"Less than two hours."

The colonel relaxed. "Apparently you weren't briefed. The idea is simple: you get undressed and the girl gives you a bath. All very right and proper. That's the way it's done here."

"The girl . . . gives me a bath?" Seaton repeated, stunned.

"And a massage, that's her job. Actually that's Sumiko you've got there and she's the best masseuse in the whole place. You lucked out."

"She won't be shocked?" Seaton asked incredulously.

The colonel almost laughed at him. "Of course not! Where do you think you are, Boston? They're a lot more advanced over here. Have a nice bath." He lifted his hand in farewell and continued down the corridor.

Miss One Thousand Spring Blossoms

With the agony of a sheltered virgin forced to disrobe before a band of lecherous slave dealers, Seaton climbed out of his clothes. When at last he had surrendered his shorts and stood there entirely naked, Miss Sumiko hung them up and opened the steam cabinet panels. "Dozo," she said, and pointed.

Seaton climbed in as though it were the iron maiden. Efficiently Sumiko replaced the panels and turned on the steam valve. Softly she began to sing as she splashed fresh water over the stool and the surrounding floor. Her song was in a minor key—it gave the impression of being ages old and was utterly captivating. As the heat began to surround him Seaton listened.

Although he had been aware of them, and considered them to be quite proper in their way, Seaton had never visited a Turkish bath. Consequently he was entirely unfamiliar with the environment of a steam cabinet. He expected that he would perspire as indeed he did, but the lulling, soporific effect was new to him. He began to relax and as he did so Sumiko's song seemed to penetrate even farther into his spirit. The way she sang, softly and apparently almost unaware of what she was doing, erased from his mind any idea that she was concerned by the fact that she was isolated in the company of a totally nude male.

Presently the heat began to become uncomfortable. At almost the moment that he felt he had to speak, Sumiko wrung out a cloth in cold water and laid it across his forehead. At once he felt better, particularly when the girl proceeded to wash his face with smooth and expert motions. She smiled at him from close range and the heat in the cabinet seemed to rise an additional degree or two in response. Then she swung the panels open and pointed to the low stool.

Not since he had been an infant had Seaton ever permitted anyone to bathe him. He sat, slightly stunned, while this intimate service was performed without any omissions whatever. Several buckets of hot water, apparently only a few degrees below the boiling point, were poured over him. On direction he soaked in the violently hot tub, was toweled down, and stretched out flat, face down, on the massage table. Because he was a foreigner, and still had a slightly stupefied expression,

26

Miss Sumiko laid a towel across his middle to comfort him and then proceeded with her work.

Forty minutes later Seaton rose to his feet and discovered that he seemed to be floating some six inches above the floor. This peculiar feeling persisted while he dressed himself with discreet assistance from the lady, pressed a dollar bill into her hand in the hope that it was an appropriate expression of gratitude, and walked back down the corridor to the lobby. There the patiently waiting Messieurs Yamaguchi and Futaba sprang to their feet and irradiated him with happy smiles.

"Bath was good, heh?" Mr. Futaba inquired politely.

Seaton replied without his accustomed forethought. "Bath was damn good."

His guides accepted his remark as a compliment to the Japanese institution to which they had just introduced him and they were delighted. They escorted him back to the hotel through a lessened jam of foot traffic and then opened the subject of further plans for the evening.

This last generated several awkward problems in both etiquette and communications. The hotel desk clerk spoke good English, but to have enlisted his help, Seaton knew at once, would have been an indelicate reflection on the linguistic capabilities of his two mentors. He therefore resolved to understand and to make himself clear in return.

After almost ten minutes of frontal assault on the language barrier an agreement was reached: Seaton san would rest in his room until nine, when it would be the great pleasure of Matsumoto san himself to call upon him and take him to dinner. Since the distinguished Matsumoto san did not have the English or any part thereof, joyfully Messieurs Yamaguchi and Futaba would return to act as interpreters. Many bows.

Seaton san was himself thinking in terms of a light lunch, it still being morning to him, but to decline such an invitation made on behalf of the top man he had come to see was unthinkable. He thought of Basil Mercer and shuddered. After recovering he declared that the plans would suit him exactly, picked up his room key at the desk, and was bowed into the elevator.

His room proved to be agreeably familiar in furniture and arrangement. After satisfying himself that the bathroom was all that it should be, complete with shower, he hung his clothes in the closet and sat down to contemplate this remarkable city from the window.

Disappointingly, it looked like Cleveland. He was not familiar with Cleveland, but he could imagine it and Tokyo appeared to be the same thing. The traffic all flowed the wrong way, otherwise the familiar American municipal plan seemed to have been faithfully duplicated.

He rested his chin in his hand and confessed to himself a secret hope that in addition to the purely business aspects of his trip, he might have encountered a bit of the exotic—at a safe distance, of course. What he saw before him offered no such promise. He told himself that he was yielding to juvenile weakness, that the speed of the jet aircraft and near instantaneous communications had erased the boundaries which used to separate the peoples of the world. It was a good thing, of course, inside plumbing in every home, but it did destroy a great and wonderful illusion.

Take away the language difference and Tokyo might as well be Topeka. Larger, of course, and with the surprising bath girls, but otherwise. . . .

He lay down on the bed, folded his hands behind his head, and reminded himself that his mission was a technical one and no more. He remained quietly there, doing nothing at all, as night gathered over the city, as his room gradually grew darker and lonelier, and as his spirit relived the age-old battle between the ingrained quest for adventure and the rigid schooling of conformity.

Then the telephone rang.

With a surge of guilt that he had not prepared himself he answered and was informed in understandable English that Mr. Matsumoto awaited him in the lobby.

His first impulse was to stall by explaining that he was in the shower. After the hotsie bath such a gimmick would be absurd, he said instead that he was shaving and would be down as quickly as possible. Six minutes later he stepped from the elevator into the lobby. He pushed his glasses higher on his nose, looked about, and walked forward to where he saw Mr. Yamaguchi on his feet awaiting him.

As he approached the area of chairs and lounges two other men rose to greet him. One was Mr. Futaba, the other a short, stocky, balding Japanese whose smooth round face seemed to glisten with a metallic hardness. With courtly formality Mr. Yamaguchi did the honors. Mr. Matsumoto murmured something under his breath, bowed stiffly, and then with the air of an amateur attempting something for the first time held out his hand. Seaton took it, shook briefly, and then with inspired presence of mind bowed in return. That Mr. Matsumoto could understand; he signified that fact by bowing again in a manner which indicated clearly that this was the way in which things should be done without any of the handshaking monkey business. If he felt any discomfort because his visitor towered over him by almost a foot, he did not betray it. He seemed instead to grunt and then led the way out of the lobby.

At the curb a black car was waiting. It was slightly smaller than American luxury cars, but it had window curtains which suggested that it was on the upper level of executive transportation. In strict order of protocol Seaton was seated next to his host in back, Yamaguchi on the other side, and Mr. Futaba in front next to the driver. As soon as the doors were closed the car pulled away from the hotel entrance, the chauffeur obviously having been instructed. For one sick moment Seaton thought that he was in for another incredible ride, but this time he was driven with conservative decorum. It occurred to him that when they got to the restaurant he could play the part of the gracious guest by offering to buy the preliminary drinks.

After twenty minutes of comfortable motoring through streets which persisted in looking like Philadelphia without Billy Penn on city hall, the car turned and unexpectedly entered an alley. As soon as it did so Seaton discovered that he was in another world. The alley was not an alley at all, but a hidden street suddenly narrow and flanked by gentle wooden buildings which had softly glowing signs outside written in decorative ideograms. The car crept along at a slow pace; the harsh industrial city had vanished and this new, soft-focus delight had taken its place. This was indeed Japan!

When the car pulled up and stopped, Seaton was primed for adventure. He deduced correctly that the establishments on either side of the street were restaurants and their lack of ostentation suggested to him that they were of a class where some of the gourmet delights of the Orient could be sampled.

29

Miss One Thousand Spring Blossoms

For a moment he was reminded of hundred-year-old eggs and certain other dubious treats which were mentioned occasionally in the Western world, then he swiftly remembered that the Japanese were celebrated for their skills in preparing seafood. He was a true son of Boston clam chowder and the idea of a delicious shore dinner was most inviting.

In the company of his three hosts he was escorted to the door of what was obviously one of the finer establishments and was confronted by a stone slab on which were set several pairs of shoes. When Mr. Matsumoto himself bent over with some labor to remove his oxfords Seaton understood that following suit was essential. Carefully he undid his laces and for the second time that day was grateful that his socks were presentable.

When he finished and looked up he discovered that the hostess was receiving them at the door. She was a woman who appeared to be in her mid-fifties, her kimono was of a neat plain color and the obi somewhat above her waist was a model of circumspect good taste. Seaton was not conversant with Japanese dress, but he could sense at once that this lady was suitably attired. Furthermore, one careful look at her narrow and restrained face told him that she was not a person who would brook any frivolities in her establishment. His mind was now at ease and his palate began to savor the culinary adventure which lay ahead.

In his stocking feet he followed her into a hallway covered with thick straw mats; they had a slight give to them and were spotlessly clean. His hostess drew open a paper-covered sliding panel and indicated that he should enter the room.

Seaton found his first view of such an interior most interesting. The only furniture was a moderately large table which was only eighteen or twenty inches high. In one corner of the room there was an alcove which had been constructed in an unusual way. Its floor was elevated three or four inches, and on it there was a bowl containing a display of three flowers and some green branches arranged in a most artful manner. A vertical scroll which was hung on the back wall suggested a landscape which had been created by scarcely more than a half dozen strokes of the artist's brush. The only false note was Seaton himself, who sensed that with his height, despite the lack of his shoes, he was somewhat out of proportion.

30

Miss One Thousand Spring Blossoms

A serving girl, also in kimono, entered with an assortment of pillows and distributed them around the table. Then the gentlemen sat down. More accurately the three Japanese gentlemen sat down while Seaton became entangled in his legs. It was impossible for him to sit on his ankles as his companions did, he could not put his long limbs under the table for lack of room, and he could not curl them up beside himself like a caricature of Sir Joshua Reynold's *Age of Innocence.* He tried drawing his knees under his chin and finding that unsatisfactory, tried to sit like a Turkish tailor.

At that moment his anticipation of the evening to follow was somewhat dimmed.

The waitress reappeared with a serving tray and placed three small dishes in front of each of the diners. She also provided sets of new chopsticks still wrapped in their paper sheaths and then withdrew.

Seaton now had two difficulties to overcome, his decidedly uncomfortable posture and the chopsticks with which he was totally unfamiliar. To him they somehow went with Chinese laundrymen who were themselves a vanishing race because of the no-iron shirt. Still he had his obligations to fulfill, so he broke his chopsticks apart and allowed an enthusiastic Mr. Futaba to show him exactly how they were to be held.

With wavering and unsteady skill he attempted to sample one of the dishes before him, and succeeded, after some effort, in lifting a shred of food to his mouth. It proved to be cold spinach, but with a rich and nutty taste. He was savoring it when the door to the room was slid open; he looked up and was startled into immobility.

He saw there before him a young girl, not more than sixteen or seventeen, who looked like the Japanese dolls he had seen in cases. She was dressed in a rich dark kimono, her hair was piled high in an ancient classical style, and her face was chalk white, heavy with some sort of opaque makeup.

Seaton's mouth dropped open and he frankly stared. Mr. Futaba saw and explained. "Girl is maiko," he said. "Student."

Seaton was aware that many students in America favored strange garb, but this was different—it was pure exotica. He watched, fascinated, as the maiko entered with mincing steps and seated herself on the straw matting like an animated doll.

31

He was trying to untangle his legs when he noted that none of the other gentlemen seemed disposed to rise to their feet in honor of the lady; with a rare sense of diplomacy he suppressed his own desire to do so and remained on the floor.

Two minutes later another maiko appeared, an almost exact duplicate of the first, and seated herself also well away from the table. A new serving girl slid open the door and brought in a three-stringed musical instrument with a long neck and a small cigarbox-like sounding chamber at the bottom. She deposited it carefully on the straw mats and then closed the door behind her as she left.

Seaton looked at his companions and noted that they were all eating. Carefully he picked up his own chopsticks, fitted them into his fingers as he had just been shown, and had another go at the nut-flavored spinach. His hosts watched him without appearing to do so and when he finally managed to convey a reasonable mouthful without dropping most of it halfway, they gave nodded smiling approval.

Then, slowly, the door was slid open once more. The change in tempo gave Seaton time to adjust his glasses and focus his full attention; when he did so he could not credit his senses. Before him, like a heavenly apparition, was the most unbelievably beautiful female creature he had ever seen.

She was wrapped in a pink kimono covered with large white flowers woven into the fabric; her obi was a subtle shade of sandlewood richly brocaded with an exquisite design. Her hair, softly arranged in a contemporary manner, framed a face at once both clearly Japanese and a definitive example of the purest classical beauty. In her right hand she held a fan which was moving very gently to and fro.

Seaton was hypnotized.

Gently the fan continued to move as the lady carefully looked at each of the gentlemen present. Then, her mouth quirked into an impish wickedness, she entered the room. Her tiny steps were the rhythm of flowing poetry; she glided in like a spring breeze and with total grace sank onto an unoccupied pillow which, for the first time, Seaton realized had been placed by his side. She was inches from him now and he caught the scent of a tantalizing perfume.

He dared to look at her and saw with a sense of shock that she was looking back into his eyes—into and through them.

The rest of the room vanished, his companions remained suspended on some other plane. And then she smiled at him, a smile which came from centuries of heritage devoted to the study of pleasing men. She smiled with her lips, with a very slight flare of her nostrils, and with witchery in her eyes. The gentle sway of the fan added to the magnetic appeal which seemed to radiate from her features.

Mr. Yamaguchi waited until it was the proper moment to speak. Then with careful pride he announced, "Presenting Miss One Thousand Spring Blossoms, most first-class geisha of Tokyo!"

Chapter Four

During all of his adult life Dick Seaton had been aware that he lacked the gift of success with the ladies. He had attempted to compensate by studying the art of good manners, but it had not helped. He realized that he was tall, but many of the heroes of fiction were depicted as over six feet. Also he wore glasses, but so did many other men who seemed to find them no handicap whatever.

He had been advised many times that congenial young women could be found in bars, but he had rebelled against purchasing introductions. He did not believe that the mere fact of being a male entitled him to cut a wide swath, but that he did have the right to have one girl and to make his selection from a reasonable number of possible choices.

He was at times acutely aware that he was already well past the most popular years for matrimony and that so far not a single candidate had even remotely presented herself. His own approaches, which he had tried to make models of correct decorum, had inevitably failed. As a result he had come to the bitter conclusion that no girl wanted him, that no suitable one ever would.

Now he sat transfixed while the most devastatingly desirable girl he had ever imagined was lavishing on him her undivided attention. It mattered not one whit to him that she was Japanese, she could have been a Hottentot and he would not have been aware of it. Even the formidable fortress of the language barrier fell before this elementary communication between man and woman.

Biology was totally out of it—at least as far as biology is ever able to remove itself. The multiple layers of severely straight kimono took care of that. Instead it seemed to Seaton that here before him was the legendary princess from the simple stories he had read as a small boy. He had digested them many times and then had lain face down on his bed for hours imagining that such wonderful creatures as Ozma of Oz really existed and that somehow when he grew up he would claim one of them for his very own.

Now the long-forgotten, often-repeated dream came surging back with sharp clarity, for part of it had here and now come true.

She sat close beside him, ignoring the others with whom she could converse easily, to look at him with deep and wonderful understanding. At that moment he asked nothing more of life than to be permitted to sit, just as he was, and look at the miracle which was being wrought for his benefit.

Unfortunately, he had no understanding of the fact that she was a complete and absolute professional.

From out of the mundane world, so far removed, he was interrupted by a waitress who appeared with little covered bowls resting on a lacquer tray. With careful precision she set one of them in front of each of the men, but she did not so much as glance at the exquisite geisha or either of the maiko.

With infinite grace Miss One Thousand Spring Blossoms gestured with her hand toward the bowl, indicating that he should refresh himself. By way of showing him how, Mr. Futaba picked up his own bowl, removed the lid, and then drank from the rim. Since no spoons of any sort had been provided, Seaton understood at once that that was the proper and polite technique to be used.

However, one other matter was very much out of order and needed to be set right. It was incredible to him that the men had been served before the ladies, but that dull-witted blunder was one which he could at least in part correct. Carefully he lifted his bowl, steaming and hot, paused, and then as gracefully as he could manage, offered it to his companion.

One of the maiko so far forgot herself as to raise her fan and giggle; a single steely glance from Mr. Matsumoto hushed her on the spot.

With a little sidewise tip of her head the geisha motioned for him to go ahead. He understood her perfectly, but he also understood that there are some things which a gentleman simply cannot do. Trying almost desperately to overcome his ingrained awkwardness, he attempted to place the bowl in her empty hand.

There was an almost frozen quiet in the room. The geisha gently laid down her fan, accepted the bowl, touched it to her lips slightly and pretended to take a small sip. Then she handed it back.

From his early grammar school days Dick Seaton had had pounded into him the evils of the common drinking cup, until he had developed a complete fixation on the point. But this bowl was different—it had become a cup of honor and the idea that it could communicate disease was abhorrent. He placed it to his lips and drank.

The soup was water-thin, very hot, and flavored with an elusive taste of the sea. It was delicious. Before he had to face the awkward question of possibly re-offering it to his companion she relieved his embarrassment by picking up her fan and with it indicated that she wished no more.

Presently sake appeared and Seaton found himself accepting a tiny warm cupful from the gentle fingers of his companion. When he looked up to speak to his hosts, they smiled at him: somewhat uncertainly in the cases of Messieurs Yamaguchi and Futaba, definitely grimly in the case of Mr. Matsumoto. They made no effort to entertain him, the girl had been hired to do that.

The food, which continued to arrive, was in small dishes without any clue as to what was supposed to be the main course. It was all very different, but challenging. Much to his own surprise Seaton began to make some slight progress in handling his chopsticks. His body quivered when Miss One Thousand Spring Blossoms leaned over slightly and placed her hand on his to show him how. Nothing was served to the ladies, which led him to the belief that they had eaten just before their arrival. The tradition that a geisha ordinarily never touches food or drink at a party of this nature was unknown to him.

Presently the entertainment began, which for Seaton was a disappointment. The enchanting girl abandoned her position as though it was depriving her of the first true happiness of her life, retired to the other side of the room, and picked up her musical instrument. She tuned the samisen expertly, twanging the strings a few times, while the maiko got to their feet. Then, when everything was ready, she began to play an intricate, totally unfamiliar kind of music in very strict tempo while the maiko danced with careful precision, manipulating their fans and looking out from behind them from time to time.

At the end of the performance Seaton applauded; he was the only one to do so, but he was unable to restrain his enthusiasm. When he had subsided Mr. Matsumoto grunted his way to his feet, making it apparent that the party was over. The maiko backed away; Miss One Thousand Spring Blossoms placed her hands carefully on her knees and bowed.

Somewhere within his breast Seaton heard the long echoing voices of his Neanderthal ancestors, those primitive but notably direct persons who seldom stood on ceremony. When one of them saw a desirable female he bashed her efficiently over the head to keep her quiet and dragged her home. Across the span of the ages they told him to start the action.

He walked across to the wonderful girl to whom he could not speak a single word and produced one of his professional cards and a pen. Turning the card over to the blank side he handed the pen to the girl and indicated that she should write.

She beamed a smile which set his knees shaking, took the pen, and quickly lettered a little group of Chinese characters down one side.

That wouldn't do.

Seaton thought quickly, then he made a careful pantomime of trying to read the ideographs and shook his head that he could not understand. After that he handed the pen back to the geisha.

37

Miss One Thousand Spring Blossoms

She pressed her lips together and smiled again. While the men from the Matsumoto Company waited not too patiently, for the meter on the geisha's time was still running, she carefully block printed a short line. She offered the pen back to Seaton but he refused it, instead he raised his left hand and mimicked talking on the telephone.

For a moment the lovely girl laid her fingers against her cheek, then, apparently having made a decision, she wrote on the card once more.

Dick Seaton was hardly aware of the ride back to the hotel, or of the expressions of thanks he spoke in the lobby. He agreed to an appointment for the following morning and accepted the suggestion that he take a taxi to the plant. He was so far anesthetized that the word "taxi" failed to ring an alarm bell in his brain; he received the address and bowed his good-night.

In the privacy of his room, with the door securely locked, he examined the card. On its back, in addition to the Chinese characters, there was carefully lettered in almost a child's hand KANNO MASAYO. His whole being vibrated, for he understood that this was her real name. He sensed that he had been extraordinarily honored.

Below the name there were seven digits which could only be her telephone number.

Had he been isolated in some remote place far out of earshot of anyone, he would have burst forth with that ringing, resounding cry first heard from the lips of Tarzan of the Apes. He was denied that privilege, but he found a substitute. Abandoning his reserve he saw himself whisked back to his native habitat and, a few months hence, walking into some sophisticated place with that wonderful girl on his arm.

Richard Seaton, because of an early misfortune, had been raised largely by his mother. On certain subjects concerning manhood she had maintained a strong reticence; instead she had implanted the concept that women were ethereal creatures to be treated with the utmost respect, served unquestioningly, and regarded as spiritual rather than physical beings. He had dutifully tried to live by that code, but now he was beginning to doubt its validity.

His companion of the evening had been utterly chaste in

her conduct, except, perhaps, when she had looked at him so fixedly with her wonderful eyes. Her costume had been a model of propriety; he only failed to recognize that the kimono is the most provocative feminine garb devised by any civilized nation. Yet despite this evidence of proper restraint, there were stirrings in his interior which resolved themselves into a growing emotion. It was not a burning physical passion, but a reawakening of his latent instinct for agreeable female companionship. He wanted to have her with him, to walk with her, to talk with her, to share things with her.

The wonderful adaptability of the human mind swept aside the language barrier and the inconsequential one of racial heritage; he saw her beside him in a stunning gown laughing delightfully at some bright new sophisticated comedy. He saw himself with her afterward and felt the touch of her hand on his arm. With almost savage delight he savored the envy of those others who had always been slightly sorry for him where matters feminine were concerned.

He paused in the midst of his meditations and jerked himself back into reality—did he actually intend to *marry* her?

Prudence, with which he was amply supplied, told him that the question would be resolved in due time at some future date; it was not necessary to consider it now. He knew almost nothing about geisha, but it was his impression that most of them were single. He recalled again the gentle fingers which had rested on his and remembered distinctly that she had worn no wedding ring.

There was life—and by that token, hope. Her schedule was beyond his powers of deduction, but no one worked more than eight hours a day. Allowing eight more for sleep, that left some part of the eight remaining hours for him; it was now only necessary for him to find the right combination. She had given him her telephone number with the clearly implied permission to use it.

For one agonizing moment he wondered if she might have been leading him on, had given him any number at all to get rid of him. Then he remembered that girls had never had trouble refusing him before; by inductive reasoning the number was therefore genuine. As soon as he finished work the following afternoon, he decided, he would put it to the test.

That would be whenever the Matsumoto Company shut down for the day.

It never occurred to him that he might not be able to say one word that she could understand.

He went to bed a strangely happy man.

Chapter Five

𝕵t was not easy for Seaton to sleep. While it was admittedly dark outside, and he had had a notably full evening, he still could not separate himself from the sensation that it was some time in the late afternoon. He turned over and tried the other side, but his built-in clock, which had regulated his actions for all of his adult life, declined to be reset. He was a creature of habit and now he was paying the price.

As a device to induce sleep he began to relive the memorable evening. By intense concentration he tried to recall the scent of Miss One Thousand Spring Blossoms' perfume, but it eluded him. He got up, looked out of the window, and once more studied the city which, he knew now, harbored more than was visible on its Westernized exterior. At last he yawned and on that hopeful sign returned to his bed. Oblivion descended upon him and remained there until the ringing of the telephone beside his bed broke the spell. He was informed in acceptable English that the hour of 7 A.M. had arrived.

A little stiff in his leg joints, Seaton rose, showered, shaved, and dressed in a conservative business suit for the day's activities. Briefcase in hand, he descended to the lobby wondering if a suitable breakfast could be obtained in this alien land.

To his satisfaction, eggs were on the menu; he ordered them, some bacon, and coffee. As he waited for his meal to be served he remembered that he had forgotten to ask when Matsumoto and Company began its business day. He was horrified by the thought that he might arrive and find that the entire engineering staff had been awaiting him for an hour.

Then it came to him that a nation which dined at nine probably did not start work much before eight or eight-thirty. He would be through eating by seven forty-five; that should insure him from arriving at the Matsumoto plant at too disgraceful an hour. When he had consumed the last of the eggs and the bacon (which had a decidedly strange taste), he signed the check, left a quarter for the waitress, and repaired to the lobby.

The desk clerk advised him about transportation. Under normal circumstances he would have recommended the train, but he was not sure that the American possessed enough intelligence to avoid getting lost, besides which he could only gibber in a foreign tongue. He suggested a taxi and after examining one of the business cards which Seaton had been given the day before, wrote the directions down on a slip of paper in Japanese. Bravely Seaton crawled into another of the lethal Tokyo cabs, folded himself up so that the door could be closed, and resigned himself to what was to follow.

This driver, while clearly reckless, was not insanely so. Seaton looked out of the windows, took in the unending swarms of people, the pack-jam of the Tokyo population, and peered in the fronts of the many hundreds of shops which he was passing on his way to the suburbs. He did not see how anyone could ever keep it all straight and in that he was correct—no one can. At last the cabdriver, after asking directions twice at small police kiosks, pulled up in front of the Matsumoto plant and held out his hand for six hundred forty yen.

Seaton handed him seven hundred yen and attempted to wave away the rest. The taxi driver refused indignantly; carefully he counted out the exact change due and returned it to his passenger who might someday learn manners—though he doubted it.

The plant, Seaton found, was open and operating. He glanced at his watch and saw that it was almost eight-thirty—still, that was a respectable hour to be arriving; it allowed his hosts time to open their mail before they had to get down to the serious business of the new assembly required by Mercer and Doyle. He paused to admire the inviting miniature garden, then he pushed the door open and entered the lobby.

The young lady receptionist took one horrified look at Seaton, glanced desperately at the clock, and then would have fled had she been able. Unfortunately she was trapped in a tiny cubicle not designed for hasty retreats; all she could do, therefore, was to acknowledge the angular presence before her and receive him as best she could.

Once more Seaton resorted to the convenient phrase book and spoke as distinctly as he was able. "Wa taxi wa Richard Seaton desk."

The receptionist bowed her head before her ancestors and accepted what fate had done to her. "No Eengilishu/" she stammered.

"I'm not speaking English," Seaton said. "I mean—I wasn't." Then his carefully trained engineering intelligence came to his aid. He pointed to the girl to focus her attention and then said, very slowly and distinctly, "Wa taxi wa . . ." and waited for that much to sink in.

At once the girl brightened. She opened her mouth, hesitated, and then responded. "Wataksushi wa Shinagawa Chiyoko desu." Despite her concern she beamed; no one had ever asked her her name before; the American must, despite his ungainly appearance, be very polite indeed. She had a dear friend, O'Connell Yumiko, who had married an American and who now had two beautiful children in a place called Bernardino San.

Somehow it came through to Seaton that his Japanese lacked a certain element of clarity. He extracted his wallet, produced his business card, and tendered that.

It was the right thing to do, in Japan the name card being an essential accompaniment to every introduction, formal or otherwise.

Chiyoko turned it over and discovered that the printer had failed to supply the Japanese translation on the back, an inexcusable oversight. She rose, bowed, and wormed her way

43

out of the booth to see her friend Watanabe Reiko who was the English interpreter. When she reached her desk in the crowded office she laid down the card and explained the difficulty.

Dutifully Reiko rose to her feet. She was the English language expert for the company and the problem was therefore hers. She knew, of course, that Seaton san was coming; she had translated all of the correspondence, and had prepared herself for the ordeal of speaking with him in the fantastically difficult language which eight years of concentrated study had not enabled her to master more than superficially. She picked up her Japanese-English/English-Japanese dictionary, and made her way bravely to the lobby.

With a skill which no American could master after fifty years of diligent practice she bowed and then said, "Mr. Seaton, is it not?"

"Good morning," Seaton replied gravely. He attempted to bow, and as he did so Reiko realized immediately that while he might be awkward, he was not stupid, and that his inability to converse in Japanese was not the mark of a slow mind.

"Please to follow with me," she said, and held open the door. Seaton reached over her head, took the door, and motioned for her to go first. Embarrassed, but nonetheless pleased, Miss Watanabe led the way to Mr. Futaba's desk.

When that unfortunate gentleman looked up and saw his guest at that unthinkably early hour, he made a passive effort to control himself. Tea had not yet even been brewed, which meant that the situation was desperate.

He rose at once and bowed, shook hands because he thought that it was expected of him, and steered Seaton toward the corner conference room. It was a special facility which had been prepared for foreign visitors; there were chairs, a suitable table, and a rewarding view of the serene garden. Then he retreated to break the news to the others who were responsible for the American engineer's entertainment.

In the pleasant room Dick Seaton sat down, opened his briefcase, and removed the drawings for the assembly which Matsumoto and Company would be invited to produce—assuming that it lay within their capability. The drawings, he

44

knew, would be of great help since they represented a universal engineering language. The Japanese had proved that they could read similar ones several times in the past. All that was necessary now, after the plans had been examined, was a simple Yes or No answer and, if it was Yes, a price. The rest would be minor details.

When he had the papers laid out to his satisfaction he rose, walked over to the window, and studied the little garden, an engineering gem in its own right. He ignored the industrial landscape and concentrated his attention instead on the few square feet which had been made into something beautiful. There was a tiny pond inhabited by some goldfish; over it there arched a miniature bridge clearly intended for decoration only, but it was in exactly the proper scale.

It was a new kind of garden to the man from New England, but he recognized its exquisite design and was not deceived by the apparent casualness with which the stones were placed in odd-numbered groupings. He had the sudden desire to see the garden expanded until it covered several acres, then he would be able to walk through it, drinking in its beauties, and sharing them with the lovely creature on his arm. He had never really had such a girl on his arm at any time in his life; now he had an almost demanding urge to savor that privilege. And it was a possibility, in some other, larger garden, because he had her telephone number. Quietly to himself he repeated the digits from memory to reassure himself that he had not forgotten.

The door opened behind him and Mr. Yamaguchi appeared. So did Mr. Futaba, one more strange gentleman, and Miss Watanabe, who discreetly brought up the rear. There were introductions: the new man proved to be Mr. Fujihara, the chief engineer, who had no English whatsoever. That made the presence of the interpreter necessary without loss of face to anyone concerned, a brilliant solution to a most awkward problem. Mr. Matsumoto himself assumed that Messieurs Yamaguchi and Futaba had at least a minimum conversational command of English, because they had in essence told him so. To do them justice, they were themselves under that impression; they did not know their limitations in English because they had never really tried to speak it. Now

45

Miss One Thousand Spring Blossoms

Miss Watanabe would handle everything; translation would mercifully be necessary so that Mr. Fujihara could understand.

Everyone sat down, Reiko Watanabe on the front edge of her chair, her hands poised carefully on her knees. After a suitable interval Mr. Fujihara inquired through her if Seaton san had had a pleasant journey.

Dick Seaton nodded pleasantly, a little baffled by the delay. In an American company after brief introductions the drawings would have been pounced upon to discover what was proposed. These people did not seem to be the least concerned, the atmosphere so far was purely social despite the fact that it was a prime hour during the business day.

To break the impasse he picked up the first of the drawings; he was about to present it for consideration when the door opened and a young lady appeared carrying a tray of tea things. That made it necessary for Seaton to collect all of the drawings and put them safely back into his briefcase until the refreshments had been served and consumed.

With careful ceremony the young lady placed teacups around the table and then added a decorative box of bean curd confection in the center. She took her time and did everything with an unruffled calm which not even the presence of Basil Mercer himself would have disturbed. At that moment Dick Seaton could not help wondering what the reactions of that icy-blooded gentleman would have been had he been subjected to the charms of Miss One Thousand Spring Blossoms. Mercer was married, of course, but to a notorious battle-ax who was on the controlling committee of several women's clubs and political organizations.

At that a moment a second young woman appeared with another tray and more paraphernalia. She had two pots of steaming hot tea and a number of white towels twisted into miniature ropes and piled like cordwood in a bamboo holder. After setting her things down she passed the towels, serving Seaton first. Politely he took one and was about to spread it out on his lap when he became aware that it was both wet and almost too hot to hold. He did hold it until he knew what to do with it; Reiko sensed his distress; when she at last received hers she unfolded it and delicately wiped her face. Then she used it to wash her hands, being careful so that

46

the American guest could observe the proper use of an *oshibori*.

Grateful for the lesson, Seaton followed suit and at once approved of the custom. It was obviously work for someone to wring out all of the cloths in hot water, but the refreshments which they provided was worth it. Having prepared himself, he sampled his tea. It was green and unsweetened; furthermore no sugar or cream had been provided. Since no one else appeared to wish either of these refinements, he drank his just as it had been poured and decided that it was an acquired taste.

When the tea had been consumed there was another pause, then Seaton was asked if he would like to visit the factory. That was a reasonable enough suggestion, but matters did not end at that point. Following the tour there would be a lunch; after that a trip to Kamakura to visit the great Buddha was proposed. By unexpressed consent the party broke up for a few minutes, the implication being that Seaton san might wish to refresh himself before starting out on the next stage of his visit to the company.

With proper deportment Miss Watanabe waited for all of the men to leave the room first. Seaton noted this and took advantage of it: by contriving to be the last out he was able to have the interpreter to himself for a few moments.

"Will you explain something to me?" he asked.

She bowed slightly. "If I am able."

"I don't know your name."

"Reiko Watanabe, sir."

"May I call you Reiko?"

"Dozo-please."

"Reiko, when do these gentlemen intend to get down to business?"

"You are meaning to start on the work?"

"Yes."

"It is *possible* by tomorrow."

Seaton was shocked. "Not until then?"

Reiko relaxed a little, she was beginning to like this giant of a man whose heart, she decided, was good. "You are first time in Japan, Seaton san?"

Dick nodded. "I'm afraid so, it's all very strange to me."

"Then may I speak with open face?"

47

"I wish you would. What was that word you used—*dozo*?"

Reiko rewarded him with a smile. "Already you learning Japanese, you very smart man. I explain now Japanese custom: never talk the business right away. Always wait one day, maybe two, become acquainted. First know person, then when person is known, after that is the start of the work."

"I didn't know that," he said.

"You make pleasure today, become better to know this company. Tomorrow by afternoon perhaps you show plans for new pieces we make. They will ask you when the time has become."

"So that's it."

Reiko bowed. "Grateful to be of help," she said.

Seaton thought and then took a deep breath. "Reiko, would you do me a very great favor?"

"What is your wish?"

"Last night I met a young lady. I—I didn't know you at that time, so I more or less asked her out."

Reiko actually blushed; she had never known that a foreigner could be so polite, so considerate of others' feelings. They were not all untamed savages after all. "Has she the English?"

"I don't know that," Seaton confessed, "but I have her phone number."

"Ah so desuka, you wish me to make the telephoning for you?"

"Would it be asking too much?"

"A pleasure, Seaton san. What is it you wish of her for time?"

It took him a moment to unscramble that one, but he knew better than to let it show. "I'd like to take her to dinner if she's free," he said. With a slightly guilty feeling for no valid reason, he produced the little card he had been given the night before.

Reiko looked at it and her eyes opened in spite of herself. "She is geisha," she said. "You are aware this?"

He nodded, wondering at the same time if he were somehow missing something.

Reiko studied the card once more. "I will call for you. You wish in privateness, is it not?"

"If possible." He made up his mind that before he left he

48

would invite this girl out too on general principles. Never before in his life had he ever had two potential dates to choose between, although, unfortunately, Miss Watanabe was not in the same league with Miss One Thousand Spring Blossoms.

For the next two hours he allowed himself to be conducted on an exhaustive tour of the Matsumoto facilities. He saw rows of girls with cloths tied about their heads to hold back their hair, working on minute assemblies with apparently endless patience. He visited the design section and admired the work being done there. Well before the noon hour approached he was genuinely impressed with the visible technical competence of the Matsumoto organization.

Meanwhile, totally without his knowledge, certain intricate wheels were turning and Mr. Matsumoto himself was called upon to make a decision.

True to her promise Miss Watanabe called the number she had been given and found, considerably to her surprise, that it was indeed the personal telephone of Miss Kanno, who for some extraordinary reason had seen fit to give her her real name and home telephone number to the American. Reiko did not let this disturb her unduly. If Miss One Thousand Spring Blossoms chose to break tradition that was several hundred years old, from her position at the top level of the geisha ladder, than that was her business.

Reiko was only puzzled that the non-Japanese-speaking American, who was clearly not the man-about-town type, had been able to make such astonishing progress during the course of only one evening. He must have, she decided, hidden depths—extremely well hidden. She did not even dream that it hinged on as simple a matter as a bowl of soup.

With all the roundabout generalities with which the Japanese language abound, Reiko finally came close enough to the point to make it clear that Seaton san was extending an invitation for dinner that evening.

Despite the many years of her severe and unrelenting training, the geisha was oddly touched. It was not often that her attentions were through some mischance taken to be genuine, but she knew with complete feminine understanding that Setanu san, or whatever the strange foreigner's name was, had taken her at face value. Female blood still ran in her

49

veins and the thought of the compliment she was being paid stirred it a little.

Using a hundred words where ten would have done, she informed Watanabe san that she would call back. Immediately after hanging up, she phoned the geisha house and asked for instructions. The mamasan, who knew the value of Miss One Thousand Spring Blossoms' time as precisely as Dean Witter and Company knows the latest price on A.T. & T., called Mr. Matsumoto personally and informed him of Setanu san's invitation. Since he had first introduced the American, obviously Matsumoto san was responsible for any and all bills that he might run up. Because Matsumoto san was an old and valued customer, the geisha house did him the service of advising him what was up. It was not necessary, but it was a most considerate thing to do.

As Matsumoto received the news he had a strange foreboding that his third misfortune, which he had been expecting, was approaching rapidly. Face, however, had to be preserved at all costs; therefore he announced that he would, of course, honor the bill for Miss One Thousand Spring Blossoms' services for dinner and a reasonable evening if it came to that, but a pillow fee was excluded.

The reservation was a reasonable one, so reasonable that no loss of face was involved. Pillow service exceeded the normal bounds of hospitality and was properly the expense of the recipient of the pleasantness involved.

The geisha house reassured Matsumoto san that Miss One Thousand Spring Blossoms did not extend pillow service. Her virginity had been sold for a very high sum when she had been a maiko, but since that occasion, concerning which she had not been consulted, she had risen to such a level in her profession, and with such speed, that she had chosen not to offer this attraction. Since this was the position of the considerable majority of top-class geisha, the establishment which for all practical purposes owned her had never pressed the point.

At eleven-forty Reiko was notified by phone that Miss One Thousand Spring Blossoms was pleased to accept and would be accompanied by only one maiko. Reiko suggested the main dining room of the New Otani at seven, knowing that the bill of fare there was available in English and that American-style

50

food could be obtained. At that point Reiko wondered what it might be like to live in America.

Just before luncheon Dick Seaton excused himself and managed to pass Reiko san's desk on the way back from the washroom. She handed him a penciled note, no one in the crowded office thought this peculiar since Watanabe san was the English interpreter.

In the lobby, while he was momentarily waiting for Mr. Fujihara to complete his preparations in the gentlemen's room, Seaton was able to steal a moment to look at the brief communication.

The words he read sent the blood pounding through his veins. He looked at his watch and with excellent speed computed in his head precisely how many hours, minutes, and seconds remained before seven in the evening—Tokyo time.

Chapter Six

$\mathcal{N}$ow that the standard gambits
for opening a business discussion in Japan had been explained
to him, Dick Seaton determined to fit into them in a creditable
manner. It was not easy for him; he was aware how much it
was costing Mercer and Doyle to transport him and maintain
him here in Japan. But he could not overrun the established
customs of the country and his good sense told him so. Also
this was his life's first adventure and he was in no haste to see
it concluded.

At lunch he sat next to Miss Watanabe, who had again been
included for the sake of her knowledge of the English language. This time he was taken to a place where there were
tables and chairs and the welcome luxury of a knife and fork.
He hardly tasted the food: he was more interested in establish-
ing the necessary rapport with Mr. Fujihara who, despite the
language barrier, he could instinctively recognize as a fellow
engineer. He found that he was beginning to develop a
feeling for these people whose heritage was so different from
his own, and he hoped that his growing understanding of
them was reciprocated.

Following luncheon and a return to the plant, he was taken by a decidedly nervous Mr. Futaba to visit the seaside city of Kamakura. A company car was produced, a Toyopet which was provided with white linen seat covers and a gauze curtain for the rear window. Somehow these trimmings seemed to make the compact little vehicle considerably larger. Seaton managed to fold himself onto one side of the rear seat next to his host who, of course, would not do the driving; a lower level employee would be assigned to that responsibility. The man appeared almost at once and the trip began.

This time Seaton became more aware of the intense crowding of the countryside; every tiny bit of ground was being put to some kind of use. The roads were narrow and he still found it hard to adjust to riding on the left-hand side; then his concern with the mechanics of the excursion faded as his interest in what he was seeing took over. There were people everywhere, multitudes of faded, tiny wooden houses, and patches of garden ridiculously small. There was evidence of much modern engineering in the high-tension lines which crisscrossed the landscape, in some of the railway bridges, and in many of the buildings which they passed. It seemed to Dick that this was a country in transition, with clear evidence of the old mixed with the almost alien new.

After more than an hour they arrived at Kamakura. The driver threaded his way through the narrow streets and pulled up before the entrance to a peaceful small park. Mr. Futaba led the way inside, paid the admission fee, and escorted his guest up the mall at the head of which the great Buddha sat in immobile meditation.

For the second time Dick Seaton became sharply aware that he was in Japan, that this indeed was the Orient. As he approached the huge, seated bronze form he felt the aura of another civilization, another catechism of religious faith. He did not for an instant believe in the great image or the person whom it represented (actually not the Lord Buddha himself), but he could not escape its influence or the sense of awe which it inspired. There were many other persons there, practically all of them Japanese wearing cameras, but they were purely incidental. Seaton walked around the mighty figure, taking it in from many different visual angles, admitting to himself that it was a great work of art. At the souvenir stand he purchased a set of colored photographs and then looked once again at the almost overpowering statue itself.

Mr. Futaba was greatly pleased to observe Seaton san's obvious appreciation of the sacred image and considered it quite possible that he was a fellow Buddhist. If so, then that was a very good sign indeed. Encouraged, he led the way back to the car and instructed the driver to proceed to the Hase-Kannon, which has less exposure to the unending flow of tourist traffic. Happily Seaton followed him up the flights of steps to the modest temple and presently stood before the huge wooden image which projected the aura of ages past.

"Most beautiful," Mr. Futaba said.

"Yes," Seaton agreed, still thinking. It was not a kind of beauty to which he was accustomed, but he heard its voice. The thin wisps of smoke drifting upward from the burning incense formed a timeless veil, while the subtle pungent odor seemed almost to come from the goddess herself. When they went outside and stood for a few minutes looking over the calm Pacific, he felt sensations which he did not understand, but which told him that he was finding new corridors in his life, and that there were still others, as yet unrevealed, to follow.

New England was very, very far away as the Toyopet began to weave its way through the traffic back toward Tokyo. As it passed through the busy port city of Yokohama the very pressure of the Orient seemed to flow in through the open windows of the car. It was impossible for Seaton to isolate himself from all this, nor did he wish to do so. He saw men in neat Western-style business suits and he saw laborers who were human automata, men who traded the sweat of their bodies for brown hundred-yen notes decorated with the portrait of a heavily bewhiskered aristocrat of times past. Children were everywhere, and people carrying things wrapped in squares of purple cloth.

When he was at last deposited before the front door of his hotel, he felt that he had had the most memorable day of his life. He was jolted out of his meditation as he remembered that immediately before him he had the delicious prospect of dinner, and possibly an evening, in the intoxicating company of Miss One Thousand Spring Blossoms. He spoke a careful "thank you" for his entertainment and made an appointment for ten the following morning. Then he escaped inside and focused his entire attention on the evening ahead.

For a moment he contemplated a trip to the hotsie bath, but since it was already five, any undue delay there would press him to be ready on time.

In his room he bathed thoroughly, reshaved to be sure that his appearance would be as favorable as possible, and put on clean underwear. His thoughts refused to remain within bounds; they insisted on conjuring up vistas of impossible situations in which he was suddenly thrust into a hero's role. He was not a hero and he knew it, he was only an engineer from Massachusetts who had always been a failure with women, and who tonight was about to take out what must be the ranking beauty of the largest city on earth.

He only hoped that he would not disgrace himself.

For a long time he sat at the window of his room and looked out at the immense city, trying to sort out his thoughts and bring them into some kind of reasonable focus. When at last it was six he checked his appearance once more, pushed his black rimmed glasses up a little more securely on his nose, and then locked his room. He resolved to do his best and take things as they came.

The desk clerk in the lobby was most helpful. He assured Seaton that it was fifteen minutes by cab to the New Otani at the most and that he would be glad to instruct the driver where to go. He then reassured the American that under no circumstances would a black tie be expected in the dining doom despite the fact that the New Otani was a very fine, definitely first-class hotel.

Encouraged by this communication, Seaton put a question which had been troubling him all day. "I am having dinner with a lady named Kanno Masayo," he confided. "I'm not sure, is Kanno her first name or not?"

"Please?" the clerk asked.

Seaton saw the difficulty at once and applied a logical solution. "Which is her family name?"

That was understood. "Kanno is her family name, Masayo her given name. Opposite from English."

"Then I would call her Masayo when I know her well."

"Better 'Masayo san.' 'San' not like English, not mean

'Mister' or 'Missus.' More like 'honorable.' In Japanese 'Sato Sensei,' 'Sensei' is title, mean 'teacher'."

"Then if my young lady were a teacher, I would call her 'Kanno Masayo Sensei.' Is that right?"

The clerk smiled and bowed. "You learning Japanese very good. Very smart. Kanno san is teacher, yes?"

Seaton shook his head. "She is a geisha."

The clerk was suddenly impressed. "Ah, so you hire geisha!"

"Not at all. She accepted my social invitation to dinner."

The clerk was now wide-eyed. "Never happen!" he said.

"Well, it is happening. I just asked her and she accepted."

"She *personal* friend?"

"Yes."

"Seaton san, you some man, no doubt. But I think maybe not geisha; Kanno san not geisha-type name."

"Her geisha name is Miss One Thousand Spring Blossoms."

"*Fujikoma?* Seaton san you, knowing her for friend?"

"I'm taking her to dinner." Seaton leaned on the counter and let the indisputable proof sink in.

It did. "Seaton san, you like maybe bigger room? We have fine suite, suitable rich man like you. You know Fujikoma you real big shot; I fix you up better place."

"That will not be necessary, but thank you. I think I'll go over to the New Otani now."

"I call you cab. I no need say 'good luck' because you already have."

That statement Seaton had no intention of disputing. He collapsed into the rear seat of a Cedric cab and allowed himself to be driven, completely insulated from any sensation of terror, to the scene of his rendezvous.

The hotel at once met with his approval. It was obviously very new, beautifully planned and appointed, and might well have been the best available hostelry in any American city. He had arrived early, as he had intended; to have kept Miss One Thousand Spring Blossoms waiting was unthinkable. Like the good engineer that he was, he first located the dining room and quickly inspected the lay of the land. It was most impressive, ideal for his appointment; he made a careful mental note to thank Miss Watanabe for that. She had picked the perfect place. He stepped toward the headwaiter who was at once all attention.

"I would like to make a dinner reservation," he said. "I'm meeting a lady here at seven. My name is Seaton."

The headwaiter at once bowed, briefly but with complete poise. "I am most happy to inform you I already have your reservation, Mr. Seaton. It was phoned in by your office early this afternoon. Do you wish to be seated now, sir?"

Dick glanced at his watch, it was sixteen minutes to seven. For a moment he considered the possibility that his date would wait for him in the lobby, then he remembered that the main dining room had been specified.

"I believe I'll wait just outside if I may."

Again the headwaiter bowed. "Excellent, sir. Do you desire a cocktail waitress to serve you?"

"Perhaps later."

"Yes sir."

Just outside the entranceway Seaton tried to compose himself and at the same time savor the intoxicating fact that the fabulous beauty he had met only the night before would be joining him here, to be his companion, in a quarter of an hour or less. He dismissed as impossible the idea that she might elect to stand him up, but he did entertain the idea that Japanese ladies might, as a habit, be late for their appointments.

Then he wondered what she might be wearing. He tried to picture her in a Western dress and succeeded quite well. He pulled down the sleeves of his own very dark blue suit and adjusted the fit of the shoulders. He insured that his shirt was not loose and that there was no flaw in the adjustment of his trousers. He looked again at his watch; it was twelve minutes to seven.

Then the thought stunned him that perhaps she would be as helpless in English as he was in Japanese. If he could not speak to her, even to say "good evening," he would be lost.

He made an immediate decision: the Seatons were not quitters, they went down fighting. He walked the few steps into the dining room and readdressed himself to the headwaiter. "Excuse me," he said. "Would you be kind enough to tell me how to say 'good evening' in Japanese?"

"It is very easy, Mr. Seaton: konban wa."

"Konban wa," Seaton repeated.

"Exactly correct."

This time Seaton bowed, not well, but with admirable tact. His gesture was immediately returned with obvious appreciation. He returned to the corridor with the stimulating sensation that he might indeed someday become a man of the world. He was confident for the first time that it did not lie beyond his powers. As the connection between Mercer & Doyle and the Matsumoto Company continued to develop, it would of course be necessary for him to come to Tokyo quite frequently to supervise the production of various new assemblies. By becoming the only Japanese-speaking member of the firm, his position in this respect would be entirely secure.

He could say "good evening" in Japanese and he was willing to bet a month's salary that not even Basil Mercer could do that.

He was about to look at his watch once more when his attention was caught and riveted. Two ladies were approaching and one of them was Miss One Thousand Spring Blossoms. She was in kimono, a very different one this time, but even at a moderate distance a stunning garment. With her there was what appeared to be a teen-ager in a conventional blue and white dress. Seaton barely noticed her, the approach of his date was such a symphony of graceful and gentle movement. He had hoped that he would not be disillusioned by seeing her a second time; that fear took wings as he discovered that she was even more wonderful than he had remembered. His good fortune almost overwhelmed him as he saw her beautifully arranged hair, the rich brocade of her magnificent obi, and the zori which she wore on her feet.

She looked at him and dazzled him with a radiant smile.

Forcing his limbs to move Seaton walked to meet her, conscious of his height, aware how awkward he must look to her. When he was close enough to do so he bowed as best he was able and recited carefully, "Konban wa."

The exquisite geisha bent her knees, tipped her head slightly to one side, and returned his bow with a grace it had taken generations to develop.

"Konban wa, Setanu san," she answered. Her voice was like

58

a perfume that is heard rather than inhaled. If Circe had been able to match it, Odysseus would never have gotten home.

The girl in the blue and white dress turned a pleasant, pretty Japanese face toward Seaton. "I'm Peggy," she announced. She had an accent, but her tone suggested at once that English came easily to her, "I'm a maiko, a student geisha. I came along because Miss Fujikoma's English is a little shaky."

"Yours isn't," Seaton said.

"When you take out first-class geisha, not in a regular geisha restaurant, then a couple of maiko usually come along. I hope you don't mind—too much."

"An extra dividend."

"Dividend I don't know."

"That's money you get from a company in which you hold stock."

"Thank you. I'll try not to bother. I can always get lost."

Marveling at the girl's knowledge of his language and her American usage, Seaton stepped beside the lady who had filled his thoughts during the past few hours. As he walked up to the door of the dining room and the waiting host, it came to him that part of his exotic daydream of the night before was at this moment coming true. He *was* entering a very elegant public place with the fabulous Miss One Thousand Spring Blossoms on his arm. She *was* his date and the presence of the unexpected Peggy could not detract from it to the slightest degree. Furthermore she was in kimono and since this was Japan, it was completely appropriate.

Seaton had to put his feet all the way down to be sure that they reached the ground. He could not believe what was happening to him. He, Richard Emmett Seaton, Seaton the gawky, Seaton the awkward, Seaton the unmarried because no girl had ever cared to cultivate him, was escorting a celebrated beauty and taking her in to dinner. If the devil had appeared at that moment at his elbow and had said, 'Okay, homely boy, I set this all up for you. Sign here," he would have reached for his pen. Of course he would have done no such thing in his right mind, but that was a state which he had for the moment misplaced.

The headwaiter received them with dignity and skill; at a

59

suitably slow pace so that the lady in kimono would not be forced to take more than short steps, he showed them to a choice table where the lighting and the view of the city were beyond improvement. The geisha seated herself in a chair as gracefully as if she had been doing it all her life, folded her hands, and looked like the consummation of every boyhood dream Seaton had ever known.

Peggy sat at the end of the table, allowing Seaton to be opposite his principal guest. She was aware that within minutes as far as Seaton was concerned she would cease to exist—even if she spoke to him and he answered.

Only one thing troubled her; she could not understand why in the world Miss One Thousand Spring Blossoms, with her reputation, had chosen to entertain a foreigner. She needed new clients like Tokyo needed another two million citizens. Yet here she was, far off the regular geisha beat, pouring out her art before a man who couldn't begin to appreciate her wonderful skills as a conversationalist. Then she looked at Seaton again and awoke to the fact that conversation was not of great concern at the moment.

A waiter materialized, placed a set of wrapped chopsticks at the right hand of each of the ladies and then stepped back to wait until his services would be desired. Seaton was only vaguely aware of his presence.

"Miss Kanno," he asked, "do you speak English?"

The geisha smiled and displayed her perfect teeth. "Sukoshi," she answered and held up her right hand with the first finger and thumb a scant inch apart. "Little bit."

"Then I will have to learn Japanese," Seaton said gravely.

When it was clear he had not been understood Peggy translated swiftly. The geisha smiled, but this time she pressed her lips significantly and looked at him through lowered lashes. Seaton saw it; he would have sensed it if he had been stone blind, and his blood pressure rose dangerously. *No* woman had *ever* looked at him like that before!

When he had recovered to the point where his head had ceased to swim, he nodded to the waiter and said, "Cocktails?"

The ladies both declined. Miss One Thousand Spring Blossoms continued to inspect him with what appeared to be

60

freshly awakened interest; she took the menu mechanically when it was handed to her and waited a few seconds before she opened it.

The waiter turned to Seaton first for his order. Since he was apparently expected to set the pace, he ordered a steak, aware that a little red meat would do him good. He did not know what his guests chose; they placed their orders in Japanese following which the waiter bowed and withdrew. Then, for a few moments, there was an awkward silence. He forced himself to concentrate on his duties as a host and turned to the maiko. "How did you ever get the name of Peggy? I mean, that doesn't seem Japanese to me."

The girl giggled once more. "My boyfriend gave it to me, he also teached me my English. Airman First Class Willis Millsup, U. S. Air Force. We crazy about each other."

"Are you engaged?" Seaton asked, and then wondered if he had been unforgivably rude.

"I can't, not in the geisha business," Peggy answered. "Geisha have to stay single, you know." She saw the tall, bespectacled man grow pale and in that moment she began to understand. She quickly drew breath. "Unless she wants to quit to get married."

Seaton controlled himself with great care. "Do many do that?"

"Oh, quite a few," Peggy lied at once. "Some become second wives, but that isn't exactly the same thing. They can go on being geisha, but I don't like it so much."

Seaton did not know what a second wife was, but he could guess.

"Airman Millsup must be a good teacher. Your English is very good."

"Oh, I have eight years in school before I meet Willie. I studying it hard for long time."

"Have you ever been to the United States?"

"No, but I'm going."

For a moment Seaton was puzzled, then he saw the explanation. "You're going to take a holiday and see my country," he suggested.

Peggy smiled at him. "Not quite. I've got different idea. I read long time ago that there aren't geisha in the United States, no geisha houses anywhere."

Miss One Thousand Spring Blossoms

The man from the strict soil of New England felt a pang of regret. "That's right," he admitted.

"Then, like Willie says, the field wide open. I'm in training now, but in a few years I'll be geisha with my own name and my rank. When that happen, I'm going get some other girls who graduated too and can speak some English; together with Willie we're going to open up first geisha house in the U.S.A. It should be a smash."

Seaton took several seconds to digest that staggering idea. He quickly reviewed his slender knowledge of the law on the basic assumption that whatever was any real fun, other than going to the baseball game, was almost automatically illegal. At least in Boston if nowhere else.

"Have you any idea where you would locate?" he asked, to make conversation.

"Willie says in East. People there are more needing for fun."

Seaton nodded gravely. "That could be, you have a point there. But the East is pretty big you know."

Peggy nodded with calm assurance. "Willie knows. He think hard and pick best spot. I'm sure he right."

"And what was his choice?"

"He say Fifty-first and Broadway."

Chapter Seven

Dick Seaton was not disposed at that moment to spend his time speculating on the prospect of a geisha house in the heart of New York; there were more important matters at hand. He looked again at the near-perfect creature who sat across the table from him, but close enough that her tantalizing perfume drifted to him with a message so subtle he did not dare to believe its meaning. Because he knew that small talk was out of the question, he laid his long, slightly bony hand on the table toward her as a symbol that his whole interest lay in her direction.

She smiled at him, lifted her own left hand from her lap, and laid her tapered fingers on top of his own.

The physical contact, modest as it was, sent electric waves up and down his spine. He looked into her face and studied her almond eyes. They were beautiful, smooth without an upper eyelid wrinkle, and warm with understanding. Her hair was jet black, of course, but it served to set off the cream-colored loveliness of her complexion. Her features were unmistakably Japanese, but he could not fault them in any way. He considered the idea that she was a Mongolian, a representative of a different segment of humanity. He found that the very idea, despite its validity, was repugnant to him. She was a beautiful woman, the most beautiful he had ever seen, and his companion of the evening.

Despite the brief time that he had known her, he was convinced that the man who married Miss One Thousand Spring Blossoms would dwell in the Elysian Fields forever.

With a severe effort he pulled himself back and made room for the fruit cocktail which was being placed before him. His guests were being served something else, a white food cut into attractive squares and served on finely shredded greens. He studied the dish as he unfolded his napkin. "What is it?" he asked.

Kanno san answered him; with her beautiful liquid voice she said, "Sashimi."

"It looks very good," Seaton said, probing to discover how much English she understood.

For answer the geisha broke her chopsticks apart, delicately picked up a piece, and offered it to him. It was a problem to accept it gracefully, but he did his best. He chewed it experimentally, but exact identification eluded him.

"Raw fish," Peggy said.

Seaton stopped his jaws and tears came into his eyes. An almost compulsive urge demanded that he get the uncooked stuff out of his mouth and fast, but he shut his eyes and swallowed.

"Shall we order you some?" Peggy asked.

With massive self-control Seaton kept himself in hand. "No, thank you," he replied. He managed to suggest that he had considered the matter before declining; it was a triumph of mind over palate. When enough interval had passed to permit him to change the subject, he put a very important question. "Are you ladies," he hesitated, almost afraid to go on, "free after dinner?"

Peggy reshaped the words into Japanese and waited for the verdict of her superior.

The geisha picked up another piece of sashimi with her chopsticks and held it delicately poised in the air. "If you wish," she answered, a touch of pride showing in her face that she had managed the reply in English.

"I most certainly do wish!" Seaton proclaimed. Then he

64

realized that he had no idea what to suggest for entertainment. For a moment panic touched him, then his reasoning powers showed him a way out. He excused himself and located the headwaiter.

"I have just learned that the ladies with me will be free for the evening. Can you suggest where we might go after dinner? I'm not familiar with your city."

The headwaiter understood perfectly and without delay. "I would suggest the Nichigeki," he said. "Not the music hall, that is a nude show, but the main theater. The stage show is very elaborate and beautiful. I may be able to arrange tickets for you; the hotel may have a few left."

Seaton slipped out his wallet and extracted a thousand-yen note. The headwaiter raised his hand to decline. "It is my pleasure, Mr. Seaton, sir. I will look into the matter of reservations immediately." He turned toward the telephone.

Baffled to find himself in a nation where hard cash was not the only measurement of human intercourse, he returned to his table and for the next hour reveled in the company which had been granted to him. He disposed of a magnificent Kobe steak without grasping its quality. Toward the end of the dessert course, when his concern had mounted as the meal neared its conclusion, the headwaiter reappeared.

"The arrangements have been completed, Mr. Seaton," he reported. "I regret the delay, there were some minor difficulties. The tickets are in your name at the box office."

"I am deeply grateful to you, sir," Seaton responded.

The headwaiter bowed, recognizing the contact between gentlemen. Then he conversed briefly with Seaton's guests in Japanese. "The ladies are most pleased with the dinner you have given them," he said. "And they are delighted that you have invited them to the Nichigeki."

That made everything close to perfect. Ten minutes later, with more aplomb than he thought that he possessed, Seaton paid the check and escorted his guests through the lobby to the cabstand. He noted with satisfaction that Miss One Thousand Spring Blossoms in her magnificent kimono was attracting considerable favorable notice. He was really living for the first time in his life.

The cab ride to the theater was short and the tickets were

indeed waiting. Inside, the theater was pack-jammed with standees around all of the walls, but the seats they had been given proved to be in a prime location. On the screen a vividly photographed Japanese movie was obviously approaching its climax. When Seaton had settled himself between his two guests and had tucked his long legs away under his seat, Miss One Thousand Spring Blossoms laid her hand on the armrest and by that action invited him to take it. He did and then settled back, dizzy with the aura of success.

The huge and elaborate stage show was the best he had ever seen; equal or better than any similar theater anywhere. Every little while he glanced at his companions to reassure himself that this was indeed reality. His good fortune overwhelmed him.

When it was over and he was escorting them through the lobby, Peggy told him that they would take a cab home. There was no need for him to inconvenience himself, they were quite used to being out in the evening on their own.

Actually Seaton had been incubating a little dream that he might see his lady home and possibly meet her parents, but that was now clearly out of the question. He paused at the curb, hesitated, and then plunged. "May I see you tomorrow?" he asked.

Peggy obligingly translated in case her superior had not clearly understood. The geisha was for a moment at a loss herself, a very rare event in her life. "Do you wish?" she asked.

"Of course," Seaton answered. Peggy rewarded him with a bright smile, she had had no idea he was so rich! Being an American he was of course wealthy, but to be able to invite a top geisha three days running was something.

"Maybe I must work," Miss One Thousand Spring Blossoms said, pronouncing the words with great care.

Seaton did not give up. "Suppose I call you when I'm through at the plant. Then if you have some time, I would very much like to spend it with you."

Peggy put it into Japanese and waited, bursting to hear the answer.

It took a minute, then the kimono-clad beauty looked at him with a wisp of a smile. "You call," she said, and turned toward a cab which had just pulled up.

66

Miss One Thousand Spring Blossoms

At a few minutes after nine the following morning this restrained and entirely polite conversation was the subject of a very heated discussion in Mr. Matsumoto's executive office. Despite the early hour the geisha house had already phoned and the worst was known. Since Japanese is an indirect language at the best, exact translation is perilous, but the state of mind of Messieurs Yamaguchi and Futaba was in no doubt whatever. The same was also true of Matsumoto san himself—only more so.

Mr. Futaba had the floor; freed of the restrictions imposed by the English language he was considerably more articulate. "The entertainment budget is already all but exhausted," he said almost as directly as that. "I am of the opinion that we should get down to business at once, get rid of this reckless-spending idiot at the earliest possible moment, and put him on a plane for home. Let him run up geisha bills in his own country."

Mr. Yamaguchi was thinking a little more deeply. "They don't have geisha in America yet," he informed his colleague. "It's a new country and socially they're still primitive. I'm sure he doesn't understand. However, if we get rid of him promptly as you propose, then we stand to lose the Mercer and Doyle account."

"It was understood," Mr. Matsumoto interjected not too happily, "that Seaton san was to be with us for about two weeks. Until we could produce a satisfactory prototype under his direction and check it out. If we send him back without it, they're going to smell sashimi. You've got to think of something else."

"A cheaper geisha?" Mr. Futaba suggested.

No one saluted that idea.

"We could possibly find him a nice girl who speaks some English," Mr. Matsumoto said. "One who might be happy just to be taken out to nice places. How about Norigami Suzuko? She speaks English, she can even write it a little."

Mr. Matsumoto's opinion, like Basil Mercer's, automatically was regarded with respect.

"Possibly even an American girl," Yamaguchi proposed.

Matsumoto disagreed. "Can you think of anyone who would want an untrained American girl when there are Japanese ones available? We ought to be able to find somebody."

"Just how much is the bill right now?" Yamaguchi asked.

"Well, the first evening doesn't count, that was expected. Last night for the two it was about one hundred fifty thousand yen. If that was the end of it we could swallow it, but he very definitely invited the girl again for today."

Since one hundred fifty thousand yen is in the ballpark of four hundred dollars, Matsumoto san's concern was justified.

"One thing," Yamaguchi pointed out, "Seaton san isn't just interested in feminine company. Being childlike in the matter of the geisha profession, he is hooked on this particular girl who just happens to be one of the most expensive in the whole stable."

"That's my fault," Matsumoto conceded. "I knew she was good when I hired her, I just didn't allow for the naïvete of our guest. I never ran into this before. Furthermore, I don't blame Reiko for making his phone calls for him; she did the only thing she could and she reported the facts promptly."

These last few words were lost on Mr. Yamaguchi; he had suddenly departed from the conversation despite his physical presence. He was deep in a clearly distracting thought. Matsumoto realized it and waited for his second-in-command, who was highly intelligent, to speak.

"I will give it until five tonight and no longer," he said slowly, "before Sakamoto George learns about all this. He will also know precisely why Seaton is here."

That was a profoundly sobering thought. Before the minds of each of the three men there rose the image of the extremely alert, highly competitive, English-speaking manufacturer who, because of his remarkable language capability and penetrating knowledge of the U.S.A., was fearfully competent in taking business away from less fortunately placed contemporaries. If Sakamoto san got on the trail of Seaton san, then it would call for every exertion to hang on to the Mercer and Doyle account, let alone get the contract for the intricate new component. Sakamoto san was in almost as many businesses as Mitsubishi and he could sniff a profitable deal from a hundred miles away with the wind in the wrong direction.

"Could we get Fujikoma on a weekly rate?" Mr. Futaba asked without much hope.

"It was all I could do to avoid a surcharge for a foreigner,"

Matsumoto answered him. "The only break we've gotten so far is that Seaton san hasn't proposed pillow service."

"If he got the bill for *that,* he might get the message," Yamaguchi said. "But I don't think he will. Reiko told me that he is as awkward as sin around women, but he is also that almost impossible combination, a foreigner and a gentleman at the same time. It's hard to believe, but it's true."

"What about today?" Futaba asked. "It's easy enough to have the geisha otherwise engaged."

"No," Yamaguchi answered. "If that happens, Seaton san will go back to his hotel in his misery and be right there to receive Sakamoto George's call. And he'll call, you know that."

Matsumoto made his decision. "Let it ride for today. Get him out of the plant about two or two-thirty and have the girl meet him about an hour later for a walk in the park. Maybe his feet will hurt, his shoes look tight. He'll undoubtedly ask her to have dinner with him; have her turn that down. After we get her report, we can decide what to do."

As the meeting broke up Mr. Futaba was most unhappy. It was only about once in eight or ten months that he had his turn to be a co-host and now this selfish American was spending every cent and more on himself. What was worse, the poor fool didn't even know.

Chapter Eight

𝓕orewarned this time, Chiyoko Shinagawa sat in her little reception cubicle and with some inner fluttering awaited the arrival of Setanu san, the American. She knew, from her friend Reiko, that he had personally invited a very high-priced geisha for the evening and had taken her out at the company's expense. Extremely rich people, like Americans, did that sort of thing apparently without giving it a second thought. For the first time she wished that she had gone ahead with an English course when she was in high school.

Promptly at ten the tall foreigner entered the lobby and bowed a good-morning greeting to her. At once she bowed in return, which, considering the size of her tiny cubicle and the fact that she was sitting down, was an achievement. She plugged in a cord and informed Reiko that Setanu san had arrived.

When Miss Watanabe appeared, Seaton greeted her cordially and then detained her for a moment. "How do you say 'good morning' in Japanese?" he asked.

Reiko was flattered. "Ohayoo gozaimasu," she replied. "Not very hard. Say just like state of Ohio, then go-zai-mas."

Miss One Thousand Spring Blossoms

Seaton tried. "Ohio. Go-sigh-mash."

"Go-*zai*-mas," Reiko corrected, before she realized what she was doing.

To her great relief the American, if anything, seemed pleased. "Ohayoo gozaimasu, Reiko san," he tried. His pronunciation was quite acceptable.

The girl was delighted. "Ohayoo gozaimasu, Setanu san. The gentlemen await you now. Very splendid you learn Japanese, everyone will be made happy." She led the way to the conference room where the tea things were already in place. Messieurs Yamaguchi and Fujihara were there on their feet to greet him; there was not a hint of chill in the air.

Seaton entered, took a breath, and plunged into his effort. "Ohayoo gozaimasu, Yamaguchi san," he recited. "Ohayoo gozaimasu, Fujihara san." Then he waited to see the effect, if any, of his performance.

It was a minor triumph; a glow of appreciation filled the room. Yamaguchi at once reciprocated by holding out his hand; if the American could make such an effort, so could he. When they all sat down for tea, a new rapport had been established. Seaton still did not care for the beverage, but he remembered his enchanting date of the night before and drank it in her honor. Then something was said about the drawings for the new assembly; happily Seaton opened his briefcase and prepared to get down to business.

During the next two hours much was accomplished. In the Matsumoto engineering department Seaton discovered that his Japanese counterparts could read the drawings prepared in the northeastern United States with perception and clarity. Various research and development personnel were summoned and with Miss Watanabe's valiant help details were examined and the first steps toward the construction of a prototype were taken. The atmosphere was charged with the feeling of engineering under way; with his coat off Seaton was in his element, his pencil poised and a log log duplex slide rule close at hand. His awkwardness vanished as he immersed himself in his work and shared ideas with Fujihara, who was at least his equal in electronic technology. By the time the noon hour had arrived a great weight had been lifted from his shoulders, all of his lingering doubt concerning his ability to work with the Matsumoto technical people had vanished and

71

the thing he had come to Japan to do was already well under way. He made a mental note to write from his hotel that evening and report this encouraging fact to Williamson, who would be waiting for word of some progress.

He went to lunch with the engineering staff and ate with chopsticks—this time a little more easily. He was ready to admit now that this system of conveying food to the mouth might be a satisfactory solution just as long as he was not confronted with a hot fudge sundae. Five minutes later a dish of the snow-white Japanese ice cream made from skimmed milk was set before him and a spoon was furnished for its consumption. As he ate Seaton remembered his tentative appointment and was at once torn between his enthusiasm for his work and the possibility of another date with the fascinating Miss Kanno. If he worked too late at the plant, he might have to forego seeing her and she had half-accepted his invitation the night before.

As if by magic the difficulty was resolved. Not long after two in the afternoon Mr. Fujihara offered the opinion, via Miss Watanabe's translation, that he needed to study the drawings in detail before he went further and would appreciate some time for the purpose. Difficulties disappeared as though the Green Bay Packers were running interference. Seaton left a set of the prints with the Matsumoto engineering department, returned to the front office, and was met by Matsumoto san himself, who extended personal greetings. He hoped that Setanu san would have a pleasant afternoon.

"In your beautiful country," Seaton said, "nothing else is possible."

When that remark had been translated by the efficient Miss Watanabe, Matsumoto san grunted and grudgingly allowed to himself that in some respects his expensive visitor had points of merit. If he had had the advantages of a Japanese upbringing, he might well have been a superior individual. Matsumoto san made some sort of appropriate reply which impressed Seaton as the utmost in courtesy, and then withdrew.

Feeling a little guilty to be using an unattached young lady for such a purpose, Dick turned to the patiently waiting Reiko and asked her quietly if she would care to make another phone call for him. She smiled her willingness, led the way to the privacy of the conference room, and dialed from memory. She did not bother to ask whom she was to call, that question would have been ridiculous. Also, for some strange reason, she did not seem to require any instructions from Seaton as to what she was to say.

The American engineer listened, frustrated, as the phone was answered and the conversation began. Reiko flashed him a bright smile to indicate that it was indeed Miss One Thousand Spring Blossoms on the line—and then, using her head, lifted her eyebrows in inquiry.

"Ask her if she has any time free today," Seaton instructed.

Staccato Japanese flowed back and forth through the circuitry for almost a full minute, then Reiko supplied a translation. "Miss Fujikoma on such nice afternoon like to walk in park. She ask if you like to join her."

"Just ask her when and where. Be sure to allow me enough time to get there," Dick instructed.

Reiko completed the conversation with all of the necessary expressions of formal courtesy and then passed the glad tidings on to her guest. "She happy meet you at half behind three at entrance to park. I call you a taxi and give driver instructions."

"One more thing, Miss Watanabe," he said, pushing his glasses up higher on his nose. "May I have the pleasure of your company for lunch tomorrow? I understand there is quite a nice place close by."

That was unexpected; Reiko had to do some fast thinking. Her lunch hour was brief and not suitable for social engagements, but it took her only a second or two to decide that management would want her to give a favorable answer. Plus which she would like it that way herself—naturally a lesser consideration.

"With greatest pleasure," she responded.

"We have a date then."

Reiko bowed. "I shall look forward."

Feeling that at long last he was beginning to get a grasp on the social graces, Seaton allowed himself to be guided out of the plant and into an easily hailed taxi. Unfortunately Reiko told the man to hurry, an exceedingly dangerous thing to do to any cabdriver within a fifty-mile radius of Tokyo. He took off in a burst of burning rubber and revealed extraordinary virtuosity at the wheel for almost forty minutes. At the end of

73

that time he had reduced his passenger to a state of numbed shock. Only the fact that he was on his way to meet the intoxicating Miss Kanno enabled him to preserve his sanity.

He paid the driver the exact fare this time, accepted the man's grateful thanks, and then walked in through the ancient formal entranceway to the park. He knew that he was early, which allowed him a little time to sit down and recover his composure.

He was still sitting, bent over in self-communication, when a pair of shapely well-nyloned legs appeared in his limited range of vision. He looked up and discovered that there close before him, neatly turned out in an attractive blue and white Western dress, was an extremely pretty girl. As he rose automatically to his feet he looked again and saw the same magnetic eyes, the same enigmatic lips, the same flawless complexion. Furthermore there was no one else nearby; apparently this time she was alone.

It was a startling change. She was no more a kimonoed creature of the evening, but a lovely girl dressed in a frock just like anyone else. He looked at her, sucked in his breath a little, and realized that not even the mercilessly revealing sun could find anything to fault.

"Good afternoon," Seaton said. He had forgotten to ask someone to teach him how to say it in Japanese.

"Good afatanoon." She paused and seemed to be collecting her limited supply of English words. Then she took the fabric of her skirt between her fingers. "You like?"

He beamed and offered her his arm. "Beautiful," he answered, knowing that he must keep his remarks simple.

She understood and smiled, then looked at his extended arm not knowing what to do. He took her right hand and gently placed it just above his elbow.

"Ah, so!" She was a bit uncomfortable, but willing to try it his way. Together they started slowly down the finely graveled path which led to the interior of the park. Before them there was a full-grown tree which had its trunk and main branches protected by a carefully wrought covering of straw securely wrapped and precisely tied. There were several more such trees, all with their fitted suits of handmade covers; everything about the park spoke of the most meticulous care.

Presently they reached a series of outdoor tables on which

74

there were a variety of unusual plants. "Bonsai," the girl said, hoping that he would understand about the miniature trees. Indeed he did. He looked at them all carefully and marveled how they were living in lilliputian grandeur with all of the dignity and grace of forest giants. Totally happy, he let his companion gently guide him down another, narrower path until they reached the shore of a small lake.

Despite the fact that the lady by his side was a good nine inches shorter than himself, Seaton discovered that they were walking together with the mutual relaxed ease of those who are contented and who have no certain objective that they must reach by a stated time. When they had gradually made their way halfway around the placid shoreline they came to a little pavilion not much more than six feet square which opened onto the water and where they could sit in the quiet shade. By common consent they crossed the stepping-stones and settled down on a wooden bench which offered them privacy and the chance to talk.

He hung his head for a moment, wishing that the Lord had seen fit to make him handsome. Then he accepted things as they were and determined to do his best regardless.

"Fujikoma," he began.

"Hai?"

"Miss Kanno—may I call you Masayo?"

She squeezed his arm a trifle. "Dozo. Please yes."

Much to his surprise she opened her purse and after a moment of fumbling produced one of his business cards. He did not recall that he had given it to her. She studied it carefully and then tried her best. "Ri-ka-du," she attempted, letting each syllable stand alone.

"Richard," Seaton said gently. "My friends say 'Dick.' "

"Diku san."

"No, just plain 'Dick.' "

It was quite a moment while she thought. When the words had been assembled in her mind, she pronounced them. "You have babies?"

For a moment Seaton clamped his teeth and then faced the truth. "I don't have a wife," he said.

Compassion swept his companion's features. "She die?"

Again he shook his head, then he spread his palms upward to indicate the painful truth.

Miss One Thousand Spring Blossoms

She understood, but the idea itself eluded her. "Not want?" she asked. Her eyebrows were like gentle question marks.

He could not trust himself to sit there any longer, he stood up knowing how ungainly tall he must seem to her. Afraid that with her poor English she had offended him, she rose too and searched his face. A professional who was devoting her life to the art of entertaining men, she was suddenly fearful that she had failed. Also she felt a tug of compassion for the overgrown foreigner who had hired her and whose feelings she had unintentionally hurt.

She had been schooled for years *never* to intrude into personal matters; now she had done so and disaster was the result. She was ashamed of her stupidity.

Then he turned to her. "Yes, I would like to have a nice girl. Very much."

As daybreak had brought the miracle of Enlightenment to the Lord Buddha as he sat under the bodhi tree, at last she understood. It came to her in that moment of understanding that this man had never found his fulfillment—that no girl had wanted him. And he had not been able to find solace because as yet, for some unexplained reason, they had no geisha houses in America.

Despite her utmost efforts to control herself, the disgrace of a tear crept out of the corner of her eye.

Seaton saw it and blamed himself for his blasted clumsiness. He took out his handkerchief, placed his left hand under her chin to hold her still, and lifted the tear away.

Japan is an ancient and mystic land whose cloud-shrouded mountains have stood guard over its traditions for all of the ages of its existence. It is a place set apart from the great land masses of the rest of the world, a haven where the shades of past glories may remain in peace, respected and allowed to roam where they will amidst the Shinto shrines and the great forests on the steep sides of slumbering volcanos. It is a nation by its very nature close to the nether world with many silken threads reaching from one plane to the next.

In that moment when his presence could have been useful there might have come a certain vaporous spirit who had been known in life, many centuries before, as Sir Giles Seaton the

Miss One Thousand Spring Blossoms

Lesser. In his day he had rescued no less than eight damsels in distress and had amassed the notable score of three dragons confirmed slain, plus one probable. Of the eight maidens he had saved from a fate worse than death, he had sent all of them home joyously happy, seven, as was subsequently learned, with child. This stalwart performance had made his name known in the land as one found fit for the king's service at a time when the standards which prevailed were of a more vigorous and earthy nature than those which are favored today.

It cannot be proved that Sir Giles was indeed there on that peaceful day in the Happo-En Garden, but it seemed to his only living male descendent (a quite remarkable distinction in view of the known facts) that he could hear Sir Giles's voice floating ethereally into his ear.

"You clod!" his illustrious ancestor transmitted across the chasm. "You've got her chin in your hand and you're inches away. Get on with it!"

After careful reflection it must be assumed that Sir Giles *was* there, for there is no other explanation for what Seaton did. He did not think, he did not consider, he simply tipped her face up toward his and kissed her, thoroughly, making up in intent what he lacked in skill. It was electric; the touch of her lips intoxicated him so that he gathered her to him, and did it again with his arms tight around her.

Had there been a gifted medium present, that person might have detected the aura of a once-famous samurai lifting his sword in salute to a British knight who was bowing in return. But there was no such bridge to eternity, only a man who was suddenly engulfed with the fear that he had ruined everything by going too far too soon, and a highly trained young woman who was not used to foreigners.

Seaton released his hold on the girl, trying his utmost not to look guilty as he did so. He was ashamed now; he had overpowered her and that, no matter how sincere his intent, was inexcusable. Then he stepped back to look at her and read what his fate was to be.

She raised her hand slowly and touched her lips. "You kiss me," she said as though she were trying to bring that fact into focus.

77

"Yes, I did," Seaton admitted.

She looked at him for several seconds, studying his features. "First time," she told him.

It seemed incredible, she was so utterly desirable. He opened his mouth and spoke without thinking. "But you're a geisha aren't you?"

For a few terrible seconds more she stood perfectly still and merely looked at him. Her eyes were not the same now, the depth that had been in them was gone as though invisible shutters had been drawn. "Yes, I am geisha," she answered him. Then she contrived to look at her watch without appearing to do so, but visibly enough so that he would detect it.

Seaton had very limited experience with women, but he knew then that the verdict was in and that he had been found wanting. As he guided her over the stepping-stones and back onto the pathway he knew two things: that he had undone himself with one careless remark and that there was nothing he could say or do now to repair the damage.

Trying to maintain the pretext that all was still well he saw her back to the entrance. Too late he remembered the tea house restaurant he had noted while they had been inspecting the bonzai trees. He put her into a cab and had the presence of mind to hand the driver three hundred-yen notes. After she was seated, he bent over so that he could look in the open window. "Thank you very much," he said.

She nodded and smiled, quite professionally. Seaton knew that he was defeated, his brain refused to supply him with the words he needed even after she was gone. He climbed into a cab and managed to make the driver understand the name of his hotel. He remembered nothing of the ride, it seemed to him that he ought to be walking about with a veil over his head, ringing a handbell and crying out "Unclean! Unclean!" When he had been deposited he paid the driver and then hesitated before going inside. He pondered for a moment and then, turning left, walked the block to the hotsie bath.

The same lobby attendant was on duty; the man recognized him at once and beamed a cordial welcome. "You wish Miss Sumiko, yes?" he inquired.

"If she's free," Seaton replied.

"Maybe ten minutes she come."

"Okay."

He sat down and let the few minutes pass until the bath girl bowed out her client and then turned toward him with an agreeable smile. "Konnichi wa," she said.

That, of course, would be the way to say "good afternoon." Seaton repeated it and then followed the tiny girl down the corridor to the room where she presided.

An hour later he *did* seem better, at least the feeling of being soiled by his own ill deeds had been washed away. He walked back to the hotel and paused at the desk to see if there was any mail. No one had written to him, but there was a message. A Mr. George Sakamoto had called. If Mr. Seaton had no conflicting plans, he would like very much to take him to dinner at seven that evening.

Seaton did not know any George Sakamoto, but if he were trying to reach him, he must have something to do with the Matsumoto company. He asked the clerk to phone and accept; a business talk might help to break the mood of solid gloom which had settled over him and would not be dissipated. The clerk nodded his willingness to oblige; it was a reasonable request since the American did not speak Japanese.

Seaton went up to his room.

Chapter Nine

"*M*r. Seaton, how do you do, I'm delighted to make your acquaintance!" George Sakamoto waved his arm around the hotel lobby. "I so hope you are enjoying your stay here."

With a gesture which had long been part of his life, Dick Seaton pushed his glasses up higher on his nose and surveyed his visitor through the lenses. "You are an ... ah ... American?" he inquired.

The shorter, but definitely muscular man before him smiled.

"No, I'm Japanese, but I've spent a good deal of time in your country on business trips." He turned to an attractive girl at his side. "Norma, this is Mr. Seaton. Miss Scott is my English language secretary; I took the liberty of inviting her to join us."

Seaton took one careful look at Miss Norma Scott and knew immediately, from long and painful experience, that she was the kind of young lady he could not have. She radiated a confidence and self-possession he would have sold his soul to possess, but even at that price those assets were beyond his reach. She was a good five feet five and almost as darkly brunette as the Japanese. Her hair, however, lacked the midnight blackness common to all of the Far East, it was rather a very dark brown and seemed to delight in being fashioned into artful hairdos. At the moment it was in an evening upsweep which was faintly familiar, then he remembered the very stunning girl whose eyes had met his for just a moment atop the Mark Hopkins in San Francisco. This was not the same girl, of course, but she was a variation of the basic design. The patent was worth millions.

"It's very kind of you to invite me, Mr. Sakamoto," Seaton said, "but I'm not quite clear. Are you connected with the Matsumoto company?"

Sakamoto laughed easily. "Not at the present time, though of course Mr. Matsumoto himself is one of my oldest and best friends. I know a most interesting and unusual restaurant, Mr. Seaton; if you like Japanese food I think I can guarantee you a new dining experience. Would you care to try it?"

Seaton was confused. "You're most generous, sir, though I don't quite understand. . . ." Another thought intruded and he yielded to it. "Am I to have the pleasure of meeting Mrs. Sakamoto there?"

For a moment a startled look crossed the normally smooth features of the Japanese executive. "Why, of course not. That is . . . you must excuse me, it had slipped my mind for a moment that you are new here. Mrs. Sakamoto is engaged this evening, I believe she is having some friends in."

With polished dispatch he ushered Seaton toward the outer door where a car very nearly the duplicate of Mr. Matsumoto's was waiting. Before he quite knew what he was doing he found himself seated in the rear seat next to his host while Norma climbed in the front next to the driver.

"Now please tell me," Sakamoto began, "what are your first impressions of Japan?"

Seaton considered his answer as the car pulled away from the curb and slipped into the traffic stream. "It's very modern," he said, cautiously, "and I must say that the ladies over here are very beautiful."

Norma Scott turned around in the front seat. "I don't know whether to take that as a compliment or not," she commented.

"Most certainly," he assured her.

"I consider myself fortunate to have Norma with me," Sakamoto interjected. "She is here on a study program which leaves her free during most of the business day. My previous English language secretary left me and I really needed someone to take her place."

The car wound evenly though the streets for several quiet minutes, then it turned into another of those narrow, half-hidden lanes which Seaton now knew led to fascinating areas screened from the ordinary sightseer. At reduced speed it rolled for half a block and then pulled up before an unprepossessing doorway in which three people materialized at once and began bowing a welcome. George Sakamoto acknowledged the reception and with appropriate gusto led the way inside.

The place proved to be very small and did not resemble any restaurant that Dick had ever seen before, in fact for a moment he wondered if he were being led into some sort of an elaborate trap. After following his host down a short passageway he found himself looking into a kitchen presided over by a gratifyingly fat cook who was bending his generous middle in as much of a bow as he could comfortably manage. Facing the kitchen and separated from it by a low partition was a narrow table at which four people could be seated along one side. Sakamoto motioned for Seaton to go first.

Bending over, Seaton edged his way down to the end and maneuvered himself into position as the tantalizing Miss Scott settled herself at his side. George Sakamoto completed the threesome.

"As you can see," he explained, "this is a very small place. It is operated for gourmets and only one party is entertained each evening. All of the food will be prepared as you watch, so you'll have a chance to see how it's done."

"What are we having?" Seaton asked, trying his best to keep a natural suspicion of the unknown out of his voice.

"That's up to the chef," Sakomoto replied. "He goes down to the market, personally selects what he considers the best, and that's it. You place yourself in his hands."

Smiling with bland contentment the rotund cook accepted a bucket of boiling water from a subordinate and sloshed it across an immense chopping block before him. Then he laid out three or four wickedly sharp knives, produced a variety of foodstuffs from a refrigerator behind him, and began to demonstrate his art. With a chopping cleaver which would have been suitable for the Lord High Executioner he cut wedges of lettuce into almost hair-like shreds, bringing the blade down smartly and rapidly a tiny fraction of an inch ahead of his fingers. Then he fitted the finely cut lettuce into three glass cups.

"I'm fascinated," Norma said.

The chef picked up a fish, split it expertly, and tossed the bottom half away, He skinned the remaining part with almost uncanny skill, boned it, and then cut it into wafer-thin strips. He arranged the slices with an artist's hand on top of the shredded lettuce and passed the completed offering over to his guests.

"Sashimi," George explained.

"I know." Seaton pushed his glasses up and prepared himself for the inevitable; under the watchful eye of the master chef refusal was out of the question. He picked up his chopsticks, fitted them into his fingers and gathered his will-power.

"I know what you're thinking," Norma said. "But it's really quite good when you get used to it."

Seaton managed a mouthful and then looked across at the happy chef who was already at work with odd-appearing vegetables and something which might have been part of an octopus.

"Japan is an unique country," George began as though he were starting a speech. "We carefully preserve our traditions which go back centuries while at the same time our technical capabilities are outstanding. In many areas of industry we lead the world. Shipbuilding, optics and camera manufacture, industrial design. We are also very strong in electronics."

Seaton lifted his arm so that a diminutive waitress who had appeared from somewhere could place a sake service at his right hand. "I know what you can do," he acknowledged. "Take the Matsumoto people; despite a language difficulty they understand our requirements very well and I'm sure they can produce what we want."

Sakamoto nodded agreement. "They're very good. I'm glad

you're working with them because they lost a major account in the Philippines recently and they've had some other troubles. Your business will help, and they'll do well for you."

"What kind of troubles?" Seaton asked.

Sakamoto waved his hand to suggest that the matter was minor. "I understand that they sank a good deal of working capital into an R-and-D program which didn't pan out for them."

"What's R-and-D?" Norma asked.

"Research and development," Seaton said. "We got caught on one like that ourselves about five years ago, so I know what you mean."

The chef, blandly innocent of the language was diluting the proper appreciation of his food, passed two more sets of dishes across the serving counter as the waitress returned with a dark-colored sauce and fresh flasks of warmed sake.

"Actually," Sakamoto went on, "while you are here you might want to check into a possible alternative source of supply just in case Matsumoto dries up for any reason. I don't expect them to, but as an engineer you know the value of a back-up if you should ever need one."

"Do you believe that the Matsumoto people are in any serious difficulties?"

"No, certainly not. Even if I thought that, I wouldn't say so, but I don't. I've heard that they have a price increase in the works, but that's fairly common right now. My thought was simply and only that you might like to have a safety valve in the form of second source of established capability when you go back. If that were the case, I might be able to help you. That's all."

Seaton could not argue with that, instead he tried one of the new dishes and found it unexpectedly delicious. "I certainly appreciate your bringing me here."

"Entirely my pleasure. We like our visitors to see something besides the standard stuff on the rubberneck tours."

Seaton tried another tiny cupful of the warm sake and found it had a decidedly relaxing effect. No one drink had any visible potency, but the cumulative effect was considerable. He turned to the girl beside him. "What are you studying, design?"

She shook her head. "I'm a judoka," she answered, and dug her chopsticks into a fresh offering which the chef had just placed before her.

Seaton looked blank. "A judoka?"

"A judo player. You know, the fine art of self-defense. I can't very well say 'manly art,' can I?"

"You do that? You wrestle and throw people over your shoulder? That sort of thing?"

She nodded. "Sometimes I make throws, as you say, and sometimes I go flying on my own can. It's part of the game."

Seaton stared at her, astounded at her frankness of speech and trying to accept the idea that this beautifully groomed, sophisticated creature practiced hand-to-hand combat!

At least he thought she did.

"Have you been doing this for long?" he ventured.

She ate another mouthful before she answered, and downed another cupful of sake. "About six years."

"Have you progressed well with your . . . studies?"

She laughed. "I've taken my ten thousand falls. So far I've made shodan, but that isn't very much."

"Shodan?"

"Black belt, first degree. It's only a start really. What I'm trying for is third; until you get that far, it doesn't really count."

The chef caught their attention and passed over still more small dishes of food, each one an individual serving. Most of the tastes and textures were new to Seaton, but he willingly absorbed them, making them a part of his whole Japanese experience. He was free of language restrictions now, free of the need to be professionally alert.

He was not free of the still fresh memory of a certain face, one which was indelibly part of this quadrant of the Orient. He kept hearing the echo of the words, "Yes, I am geisha." Not even the potency of the sake could erase the consciousness of his incredible clumsiness.

He told himself almost savagely to forget the geisha and to concentrate instead on the wickedly attractive American girl who was so close he could feel the warmth of her body. At any other time he would have been paralyzed by his good fortune.

Norma Scott was gorgeous—he knew that. She was being very nice to him. But his mind was preoccupied with the raw memory of how stupid he had been.

George Sakamoto kept the party going. Before Seaton realized it he was engaged in engineering talk with his host while Norma sat in the middle and seemed to be amused by it all. It quickly became apparent that despite his lack of an engineering degree Sakamoto was very well informed concerning the electronics industry. As the rapport between the two men developed, Seaton found himself wishing that he had been commissioned to work with this obviously highly intelligent, completely bilingual gentleman rather than with the slightly toadlike Mr. Matsumoto who had not taken the trouble to learn even one word of English. Then he remembered that the Matsumoto people were doing their best and he had no justifiable reason to complain of their efforts.

Presently the chef smiled even more broadly and thereby indicated that the dinner was over. There was a ceremony of exchanging drinks of sake in honor of his culinary achievement, much additional bowing on the part of all present, and the business of taking departure. No check was presented. When they were outside on the narrow, intimate little street two cars were found to be waiting, each equipped with a patient driver with apparently endless time at his disposal.

"I don't like to be a poor host," Sakamoto said, "but I do have a business conference this evening with some gentlemen from the Philippines. In Japan, Mr. Seaton, business is discussed at all hours, even in the bath—you may have discovered this already."

"To some degree," Seaton said.

"Then you will understand. This was a prior commitment and I have to honor it. I have another car here; the driver has been instructed to take you and Norma on a little sight-seeing tour if you find that suggestion acceptable."

"Very much so, if Miss Scott has the time."

"I'm certain that she does, just don't let her get any judo holds on you. I foolishly challenged her once, playfully of course, and she deposited me with a complete loss of my dignity onto the floor of my office."

"I'll be careful."

"Good. Then I'll leave you with genuine anticipation of

86

our next meeting. I trust it will be soon. Norma, he's all yours."

"How nice," the girl said.

A few moments later Dick Seaton felt perspiration on his brow. He was seated with unaccustomed luxury in the back of the white slipcovered car, protected from outsiders by gauze curtains at the windows, and with a stunning girl who, easily and naturally, had snuggled herself against him. She had assumed that he was used to that sort of thing and had chosen to sit close beside him, with his outstretched arm across her shoulder, as though they had known each other well for years.

Seaton felt that there was a mist on his glasses and he wanted to push them up his nose. He managed with his free arm and wondered, for the first time in many years, why he could not have been gifted with normally keen eyesight. He wondered if he had been endowed with any gifts at all. Meanwhile his pulse was throbbing and he felt himself disastrously off balance. The car began to swing around a corner; instinctively he took hold of his companion to protect her and found that his left hand was in contact with an extremely soft and yielding part of her body.

"Well!" Norma said.

In horror Seaton detached himself, stricken with the engulfing thought that he had done it again. He looked into Norma's face to receive her scorn, and found that she was smiling instead.

"I ... I ..." Seaton lost the power of speech.

"You should become a judo man," she said. "That was a pretty good mat hold." Deliberately she lifted his arm and placed it back across her shoulders. "Don't worry so much, after six years in the dojos I'm pretty used to being handled. Besides, it was nice of you to protect me from being thrown on the floor."

The car slid up to the curb and stopped. Anxious to escape from a situation which was more than he could handle, Seaton almost leapt out and then cautiously assisted his companion to her feet. Facing them was a massive wooden entranceway and beyond it a long roofed mall.

"Come on," Norma invited. She took his hand with easy informality and led him up to one side of the portal where, in

87

an alcove, a bug-eyed creature with violently ferocious features glared down his hostility. "What do you think?" she asked.

"It could be acute dyspepsia."

She giggled. "Actually he and his companion on the other side are gentle and friendly. They look like that to frighten away the evil spirits. Come on, I'll show you the temple."

They walked together down the long mall, looking into the dozens of little shops which offered varieties of merchandise— almost all of it at tourist prices. At the end the overhead roofing ceased and the vast bulk of a great wooden Buddhist temple loomed against the darkened sky. Although the doors were closed, a handful of people were in prayer before the oblong offering box. They chanted their petitions, ignoring those who stood about and looked at them.

Seaton was moved. The familiar gibbous moon overhead seemed different now, as though it too had yielded to the echoing centuries of tradition which infused this land. He laid his arm across Norma's shoulder. Finally he turned reluctantly away and remembered the earthier world of solid state technology.

When they were almost back to where the car was waiting, Norma had a suggestion. "Tokyo rolls up the sidewalks officially around ten," she said. "It isn't like New York or Los Angeles. But there is action until dawn around some parts of the Ginza. I have to go to work tomorrow and so do you, but how about some coffee first? I know a nice place, typically Japanese."

"Why not," Seaton replied. His unconscious familiarity had been forgiven if not forgotten, and from it he had learned a little.

The car took them through the near-silent streets into the labyrinth of tiny byways which surrounds the central shopping area and the huge department stores. Here the lights were still on and the many small restaurants displayed their wares in the form of wax models in the little showcases. The car stopped. Once more Seaton got out, helped his date to her feet, and then listened with some surprise when she dismissed the driver in effortless Japanese. Before he could ponder the matter she steered him almost literally to the entrance to a small cafe. Once inside they went down a staircase to find themselves in a medium-sized dining room fitted out in Western style with tables and chairs.

They were promptly shown to a small booth but Norma remained on her feet. "I'd like to wash up if you don't mind," she declared.

"Certainly." Seaton had to stop himself from bowing.

"Coming along?"

"What?"

"There's only one john—it's for everybody. Boys and girls together."

Seaton was thunderstruck. "No, I'm sorry ..." he protested. In fact he had been hoping that his companion would excuse herself so that he could seek out the gentlemen's facility, but a coeducational latrine was something he could not conceive.

At the price of discomfort he would manage.

While Norma was gone he surveyed the number of brown hundred-yen notes in his wallet and the comforting green of good solid American money. He would have parted with a ten dollar bill for the temporary possession of a strictly private toilet facility, but his conscience was unrelenting. He looked up and saw a girl who reminded him of Masayo.

They chatted over coffee and some badly baked cake while Seaton adjusted himself to the fact that he was actually out on a date with a stunningly attractive girl. He wished, vainly but with warming satisfaction, that a few of the people he knew around the plant at home could see him now. Clearly they wouldn't believe it. Dick Seaton did not rate beautiful women, at least not in his own country. But he was not in his own country now.

He was amazed how relaxed, how unimpressed with herself, Norma was. He responded to it and found that he could talk to her without straining. It was a new sensation and it lifted his spirit. Then he remembered his manners.

"I'll get a cab to see you home," he said when she stood up to leave.

"Don't bother, Dick, I'm used to going alone. It's way out of your way."

"I don't mind."

She reached up and patted his cheek. "I know that, it's nice of you." She paused and surveyed him up and down for a moment. She didn't want to take advantage of him, but the chance to tease him a little was too good to pass by.

"What if I suggested that we drop by your hotel? What would you say to that?"

Seaton struggled to find the proper and polite answer. "I believe I'd invite you in for a drink."

Norma nodded her approval. "That's a good beginning," she said.

Chapter Ten

*W*hile he was shaving the following morning, Dick Seaton realized that Japan was beginning to reveal a remarkable personality. In this never-never land on the far side of the globe, through some unexplained alchemy, he was able to get on with attractive young women. The thought so enthralled him he almost cut himself.

Norma Scott, who would have been a clear first prize in almost any debutante raffle anywhere, had parted from him with the potent words, "Call me." And the matchless Masayo had accepted his company twice on a social basis, or so he thought, before his disastrous blunder had brought things to an end. He winced at the pain of that thought and *did* cut himself.

While applying a patch of moist paper to stop the bleeding, he remembered that he had a luncheon date with Miss Reiko Watanabe. The pleasant little interpreter in a less spectacular way also merited attention. In considering his pending engagement Seaton thought about her quite warmly, for the moment forgetting entirely that she was Japanese.

At the plant the morning passed quickly. The first bits and pieces of intricate circuitry began to flow in from the development section. Tiny gemlike creations made of plastic, wire, and semiconducting materials, they manifested a high level of fine workmanship and technical skill. He took each one of them lovingly into his hands, appreciating what they were designed to do and how they would all fit together to form the prototype it was his responsibility to see produced. This was a world which he understood, and one in which he felt he belonged.

When at last he took time to look at a clock it was twelve-fifteen. Regretfully he excused himself, washed, and then presented himself at Miss Watanabe's desk. She greeted him with a smile and at once rose to her feet. Ten minutes later they were facing each other across the top of a small, Western-style table—one of a half-dozen which were all that the compact little restaurant could hold.

As he surveyed his third date within twenty-four hours Seaton decided that in her own unpretentious way Miss Watanabe too had much to offer. She was not a beauty, but her features were pleasant and flawed only by a small dark spot high on one cheek. Her shining black hair was tastefully arranged to frame her face without drawing too much attention to itself in the process. Like most Japanese girls her figure was slender and her curvatures restrained, but she had about her an appealing charm.

Despite the pleasant appearance which she made, Reiko san herself was somewhat ill at ease. She was acutely aware of being with the giant foreigner whose goodwill and approval meant so much to her company. She was also concerned over her limitations in the English language, which was compounded by her lack of understanding of the customs and manners of these round-eyed people. She was anxious to do her best and hoped, with a certain tightness, that she would not be found too much wanting.

The limited menu was in Japanese, of course, which broke the ice for her. After a quick glance at the Chinese characters she explained what was available and dared to offer a recommendation. To her delight the man from America ignored her breach of manners and accepted her suggestion. Shortly thereafter large bowls of noodles were set before them and the meal began.

"Do you know Mr. George Sakamoto?" Seaton asked.

Miss One Thousand Spring Blossoms

Poor Reiko, who had been caught with her chopsticks in the corner of her mouth, almost choked on the hot noodles. She bent her head down to hide her shame while tears of embarrassment glistened in the corners of her eyes. When she had recovered she managed to say "Sakamoto san is famous man. He many companies own." For the moment she forgot to insert the article, which is nonexistent in the Japanese language, and reverted to the word order most familiar to her.

Seaton apparently failed to notice the confusion in her speech. "I had dinner with Mr. Sakamoto last night. I understood when I accepted his invitation that he was connected with your company."

"No," Reiko answered; it was all she could do to keep her voice soft and quiet as politeness demanded.

"Anyhow," Seaton went on, "he had his secretary with him. A very nice girl, just like yourself. Her name is Norma Scott. Perhaps you know her."

For a few fervent seconds Reiko san appealed to her ancestors for help. "I do not have that pleasure," she carefully recited from her advanced phrase book. "Mr. Futaba, he is I think know Miss Scott. Most beautiful girl. Mr. Futaba make practice with her playing judo at Kodokan. For a moment he divert attention to admire and she catch him in Seoi-nage hold. Mr. Futaba not expecting and he make big splash on tatami when he hit. For one week he walk a little crooked I think."

Seaton pondered this information, comparing in his mind the beautifully proportioned Norma Scott and the chunky solidarity of Mr. Futaba. The idea of a man and a woman engaging together in physical combat was repugnant to him, but his concern was tempered by the obvious fact that Miss Scott could protect herself as required. When the silence became a trifle awkward, Reiko welcomed the opportunity to change the subject. "You have nice time together with Miss Kanno? It is very nice in park—in the park—this time."

It was Seaton's turn to feel embarrassment. He looked into the friendly eyes of the girl opposite him, and yielded to the temptation to confess. "I had a very nice time," he began slowly. "Then, Reiko, I did an awful thing. I kissed her."

"She allow?" Reiko asked.

93

"Yes, I think so."

"Then is okay." Reiko, despite her carefully schooled exterior, had an enormous, unfulfilled romantic temperament which had been whetted by a steady diet of tragic Japanese movies.

"No, it isn't okay," Seaton admitted. "I did a terrible thing, Reiko, and I'm afraid I killed myself with her permanently."

Reiko's eyes went wide with fright. *"You kill self?"* she gasped.

"No, no, not literally," he said hastily. He reached out and took her hand in his. "What I meant was, I'm afraid she doesn't want to see me any more."

Reiko drew breath; she was about to say, "She have no choice," but caught herself. She could think of only one thing. "You bite?"

That idea did not even penetrate—Seaton was too concerned with the painful recall. "She told me that it was the first time for her," he said.

Reiko nodded. "Japanese girl not much kiss. Maybe true."

Seaton looked at her, anguish in his eyes and the tight corners of his mouth. "Then, Reiko, I said to her, 'But you're a geisha, aren't you?' Just like that."

"You insult," Reiko said firmly. "She first-class geisha, no make love customers. Only friends. She kiss you, you special rate. Seaton san, you fine gentleman, but you no understand Japanese women."

"I don't understand any women," he confessed bitterly. "If I told you the truth about myself, you wouldn't believe it."

Reiko was thinking. She had never imagined for a moment that this towering man from another world could or ever would be hers, but she felt for him now and if it had been within her power to comfort him with the few resources she had to offer, she would have done so. She looked up at him.

"You want me to fix?" she asked softly.

Seaton looked at her with new eyes. A feeling of guilt touched him: Reiko was a very nice girl. He sensed that she would gladly have accepted another invitation from him.

"Could you?"

94

Reiko looked at him. "I shall try."

Seaton squeezed her hand, which he still held, until there was sharp pain in her fingers. She smiled in return, for she felt only the warm reassurance of a man's regard for her, and there was room for a great deal of that in her life.

Despite the fact that both his appearance and his manner suggested an autocrat shaped like a pile of mashed potatoes, Matsumoto san was a man of feeling and sensitivity. It was a weakness which he tried to his best to conceal in the ruthless arena of business, but at times he could not help himself. Occasionally he asked nothing more of life than being allowed to sit in silent meditation, contemplating the Zen perfection of a Japanese garden. As a devout patriot he considered Western business methods to be a temporarily necessary evil, an expendable veneer laid over the rich and seasoned core of true Japanese culture. Someday it could all be cast aside and the exquisite order of things which had been evolved over the centuries would be restored to its proper place. He was not at all impressed by the Tokyo Tower. On the other hand he regarded the stone garden of the Zuiho-in Temple at Kyoto, with considerable justification, as one of the great art treasures of the world.

At times, in secret, he wrote poetry.

It troubled Matsumoto san, then, to have to call in Watanabe Reiko and ask her how things had gone during her lunch date with the American client. It had been an essentially private engagement with a good possibility that intimate personal matters had been on the agenda—after all, the American had been away from home for some days now. On the other hand essential business intelligence might have been involved and if so it could not be neglected. As soon as he was certain that Seaton san was safely back in the R-and-D section of the plant, Matsumoto san pressed the proper button and issued his instructions.

Reiko was waiting. When she walked into the large corner office Matsumoto took one look at her downcast features, feared the worst, and sent at once for Messieurs Yamaguchi and Futaba.

When the full party had been assembled he turned to his

interpreter and asked with careful tact, "Was there any part of your luncheon conversation with Seaton san which would be of interest to us?"

Freed of the curse of the impossible and completely inconsistent English grammar, Miss Watanabe became almost eloquent. She came right to the point which, for a Japanese, was nothing less that startling.

"Seaton san was entertained last night by Sakamoto George. He had with him Miss Scott Norma. Afterward Seaton san and Miss Scott went off by themselves for coffee on the Ginza."

"I wonder . . ." Matsumoto began, and paused.

"Undoubtedly," Mr. Futaba supplied. "In the judo dojo Miss Scott is sometimes troublesome to throw onto her back. Under other circumstances it is not nearly as difficult."

"You know her then?" Matsumoto said.

"Sometimes to my sorrow."

"You must excuse me," Matsumoto continued, "but how well are you acquainted?"

"I am not one of those whom she has honored with her intimate affection. I therefore consider myself one of the minority."

Matsumoto sat more erect in his chair and for a moment wished that his abdomen was a little less generously proportioned. "It must be considered, then, that Seaton san has been to bed with Miss Scott and that Sakamoto George has scored in the first inning."

Reiko bowed very deeply and by that most respectful gesture succeeded in capturing her president's attention. "I do not believe that this is true," she said.

An unhappy suspicion dawned in Mr. Yamaguchi's mind. "He does not like girls?"

"I'm sure that he does," Reiko said, her eyes downcast. "It is just that he does not know what to do with them. Or how. Since you are paying the bill for her services, I must tell you that Seaton san did not have a good time with Miss Fujikoma in the park yesterday afternoon."

Matsumoto looked surprised. "You astonish me. She is an excellent geisha and well schooled, that's why her rate is so high. What in the world did she do wrong?"

Reiko hesitated; a sense of betrayal was overcoming her, for the conversation had been presumably a private one. Only the fact that the welfare of her company was at stake and that her superiors by reason of cash investment were entitled to the facts, overcame her reticence. She told the simple story with appropriate restraint but also a well-developed sense of romantic drama. This was not an easy combination, but she managed it quite well. When she had finished she looked up and was astounded to see that the great Matsumoto san was showing some slight signs of emotional concern.

Everyone waited for the head of the business to speak.

"It is to the credit of Setanu san," he began, "that in the short time he has been here he has become aware of the infinite superiority of Japanese womanhood. I am touched that he was so deeply moved by his attachment for Miss Fujikoma that he felt himself unable to perform in bed with the readily available Miss Scott Norma. I have seen her in Sakamoto san's company and she is better put together than the best tape recorder Sony ever made."

Everyone present was moved by this eloquent tribute.

"It is now clear to me," Yamaguchi said with a hushed voice, "that if Setanu san had enjoyed himself properly last night, he would not today be so concerned over his remark to the geisha. He does not understand the nature of her profession, of course, so his disturbance is undoubtedly genuine."

"Most certainly," Futaba agreed.

Like the dog in the nighttime,* Reiko did nothing and remained silent, the only possible line of conduct she could follow.

Matsumoto san was thinking. In his mind figures were dropping into position, probabilities were being evaluated, and the overall financial welfare of Matsumoto and Company reappraised. When all this had been done in an aura of respectful silence, he again took notice of his employees present and announced his decision.

"At the moment we have the pole position," he summarized, "but with Sakamoto George on the prowl and Miss Scott

---

* "Is there any other point to which you would wish to draw my attention?"
"To the curious incident of the dog in the night-time."
"The dog did nothing in the night-time."
"That was the curious incident," remarked Sherlock Holmes.
—John H. Watson, M.D. "Silver Blaze."

Norma for bait, our situation is hazardous. I consider a
further investment in the geisha to be necessary, in fact
essential."

He turned toward Reiko. "Most unfortunately, the young
lady was guilty of a serious breach of her training, but it is
possible we may turn it to our advantage. Please call her for
an appointment and then go and see her as soon as possible.
Before four o'clock if you can make it. Explain the situation.
Hire her on an open basis and ask her to call Seaton san here
at the factory. I suspect that if he receives a phone call from
her, he may be less concerned with the temptations to which
Miss Scott is subjecting him."

Again Reiko bowed. "Great wisdom," she murmured in true
admiration. At once Messieurs Yamaguchi and Futaba echoed
her sentiments.

The little interpreter backed a step or two toward the
door, slipped out of the room, and hurried toward a telephone. It was Friday and the better geisha were being swiftly
booked for the weekend. She dialed from memory, conversed
briefly, and then left the plant without even stopping to pat
her hair into place. She hailed a cab and was gone.

It was a few minutes after four when Mr. Fujihara, the
chief engineer, tapped Seaton on the shoulder and indicated a
telephone which was waiting off the hook.

"For me?" he asked in surprise.

Fujihara nodded.

In the few steps that it took him to reach the instrument
Seaton decided that it would be George Sakamoto calling with
another invitation. This time he would decline, his natural
prudence telling him not to get involved too deeply until he
knew the full score. He picked up the phone and said, "This
is Mr. Seaton."

For a second or two there was silence on the line, then a
quiet, liquid voice said, "Setanu san?"

Instantly he knew who it was. He did not believe it, but he
was overwhelmed by it. Was it possible that he was forgiven?

"Yes, yes," he answered. "This is Dick Seaton."

"I am Masayo," the voice came over the wire. The words
were slow and labored, straining against the inertia of the
unfamiliar language.

98

For a paralyzed moment he could not think of anything to say. A half-dozen possible remarks whipped through his mind and were pushed aside as unsuitable, too complicated, or inadequate. Then he gathered himself and said, very slowly, "I am very glad to hear from you."

There was another pause. He was tingling now, knowing that he had a chance to see her again. He would ask for a date as soon as he could bring the cautious conversation to that point.

"You mad?" came the hesitant question.

"No. No," he repeated. Then he added, "I want to see you. May I?"

By an apparent miracle of good chance Reiko appeared at his side. At once he handed her the instrument. "It's Miss Kanno. Please ask her if I can see her."

Reiko, who was still a little breathless from rushing back to the plant as fast as possible, took the phone and exchanged polite phrases for a good half-minute. Actually she told the geisha that she had just barely gotten back and that they had almost missed connections, then she relayed the query Seaton had entrusted to her.

The geisha most politely asked about the time. When was she wanted and for how long.

Still off balance because the geisha had called too soon, Reiko relayed the question almost literally. She did not stop to think.

Seaton shut his eyes and took a deep breath. "Ask her if she is free for the weekend."

The impact of that request hit Reiko with stunning force. The expense would be astronomical if the geisha accepted, but worse than that, her image of Seaton as a gallant gentleman whose animal instincts had been refined to the point of complete control went crashing to the ground. Numbly she repeated the message literally in translation. She heard the geisha draw her breath sharply at the other end of the line. It had hit her too.

Dick Seaton was tapping Reiko urgently on the shoulder. "Look, please don't let her misunderstand. If she is free this weekend, I would love to see some of Japan in her company. But under proper circumstances—do you understand? Don't let her think . . ."

99

Reiko's English was still very labored, but that she understood. Swiftly she translated that Seaton san desired to take her somewhere in Japan to admire the scenery, but that was all. She added that he was terrified that she would misunderstand. Then, realizing that the facts might as well be stated plainly, she added her own comment—that in her opinion his intentions were lamentably, almost unbelievably, honorable.

Miss Fujikoma had already been instructed to accept Seaton san's invitation, even if it was to the ball game. The directions had been explicit and no reservations had been included. She asked to speak to the foreigner directly.

Reiko passed over the hand set. Seaton took it, shaking, to hear his fate.

"Setanu san."

"Yes."

"I come weekend. You want see Kyoto?"

Seaton did not know where Kyoto was, but he would have gone there if he had had to pay Charon the boatman on the way. "Yes!" he answered.

"I come."

He handed the telephone back to Reiko. She set the time and promised to call back when she had made the reservations on the New Tokaido Line.

It was all over in ten minutes. Reiko booked two first-class seats on the 9 A.M. super express, wrote out the time and place in English on a slip for Seaton, and then, with complete humility, informed Matsumoto san of what had taken place.

Poor Mr. Matsumoto, who had still been hoping for some small measure of profit from the Mercer and Doyle account, saw the abacus beads sliding madly in his mind, adding up to the inexorable total he would have to pay. An entire weekend with a first-class geisha was a staggering commitment. Before it was over there would probably be pillow service which would more than double the total. But even that was not the end—the prototype was far from finished and before it was finally completed, checked out, and delivered, there might be nothing left of Matsumoto and Company to accept a production contract if one were offered.

He very nearly wept.

Chapter Eleven

𝔍t was on the following morning that Richard Seaton, solid son of rock-ribbed New England, pushed his glasses once more higher on the bridge of his nose and for the first time began to cross into the real Japan. He was unaware of the transition during its beginnings, he only sensed that something of an unexpected nature seemed to be overshadowing his activities.

During his early morning preparations he was somewhat concerned. He was not at all experienced in taking proper care of young ladies even for a few hours—now he was to have a superb one on his hands for the entire weekend. He was not disturbed by the cost, but he was most anxious to be sure that he conducted himself properly and did not repeat his disastrous error of two days before.

While tying his tie he squared his shoulders and told himself that a combination of genuine interest in his companion, basic good manners, and unassailably honorable intentions would see him through. With a fresh sense of adventure, he picked up his overnight bag and took a taxi to the Tokyo railway station.

He found it staggering. Up until then Grand Central in

New York had been his standard for an illustration of scurrying humanity; now that image was eclipsed by the surging mass which crammed the Tokyo Central Station. He had never seen so many people hurrying in so many different directions; a vast human flow pressed together until it almost became one homogeneous sea of mankind en route to a thousand different destinations.

Most of the signs were in Chinese characters, a kind of jabberwocky with no Humpty Dumpty to explain it. Seaton looked about him and found that he was staring into a long latrine where urinating males were in plain sight of all who passed by; he jerked his attention away and discovered a small sign in English which pointed out the way to the New Tokaido Line. Feeling once again that he was at least four inches taller than his normal stature, he allowed himself to be carried along by the human tide until he saw ahead of him the stairway he wanted and managed to maneuver in that direction.

On the upper level there was only a partial respite from the crush of travelers below, each of the many platforms was still heavily crowded with an unvarying pattern of dark suits on the men, blue and white dresses on the women. Electric trains, made up of long strings of cars packed to bulging with still more people, snaked in and out, all running in what was clearly a masterpiece of scheduling and precise timing. As an engineering project it was a spectacle of near-saturation movement of people and equipment, an ordered confusion in which everything came out precisely right because the tactical planners had done their job to perfection.

The platform was marked where each car of the train would stop; with the aid of small numerals which he could read Seaton found the proper place to wait for car five. He was concerned that there was no sign of Masayo, but a glance at his watch reassured him—he was almost fifteen minutes early.

A thousand irritating needles began to prick him. He might be stood up. He did not know his intended companion very well. She might well have misunderstood his invitation. Certainly she must be popular with other men who would be equally anxious for her company. He had once been kept waiting miserably for a date who had never appeared and the painful embarrassment had not left him for weeks.

As the minutes snipped off their tiny allotments of time and then vanished, he watched the trains coming in and pulling out, each one accommodating hundreds of people who surged in and out of the cars. Then with streamlined perfection the superexpress came gliding into the station, ready to take on its load of passengers for Kyoto and other points south. The cars stopped precisely where the entrances were marked, so smoothly it seemed to be no more than a happy accident. The doors were opened and waiting people began to pass inside. Seaton joined them with the thought in his mind that he could always get off at the last minute if his date had not appeared. He took his assigned first-class seat and allowed himself to admire the beautifully designed interior of the car.

His watch told him that there were still eight minutes to go.

For three of them he cursed himself for being a stupid fool. He should have asked her to a movie, that would have been much more reasonable and far less susceptible to misunderstanding. He had no business being on this deluxe train which shortly would depart on its sensational hundred-and-twenty-mile-an-hour run down the interior of Japan. He was in a strange foreign nation where he was completely adrift and couldn't even begin to understand the language. Perspiration began to annoy him despite the efficient air conditioning; the bridge of his nose became moist and his glasses slipped down.

Then a gentle hand was laid on his shoulder, and he turned to look up into her face.

He was on his feet at once, to place her small overnight bag on the rack, to offer her the seat next to the window, and to show her how grateful he was that she had placed her safety and her honor in his hands.

She was in street attire, a blue blouselike affair with a white pleated skirt which was totally becoming. Everyone in the car could see at once that she was a beauty.

"Ohayoo gozaimasu," she said, pronouncing the words carefully.

103

Glorious satisfaction flushed Seaton's features, for he had done his homework. "Okayoo gazaimasu, Masayo san," he replied and was rewarded with a delightful smile. It was more than just that, it was a final forgiveness for his blunder in the park; he was being given another chance.

For the next three hours he lived as he had never lived before. He was in the company of the most enchanting girl he had ever seen, she was close beside him, and best of all, she seemed to find his companionship very much to her taste. As she relaxed and the rapport between them grew, her English became less rigid and she revealed a wider vocabulary than he had suspected that she possessed.

They ate together in the dining car, facing sideways toward the unfolding scenery and drinking in the majestic perfection of mighty Fujiyama. A speedometer at the end of the car showed in large figures that they were traveling at a hundred and twenty miles an hour. When he could divert his attention from his companion long enough to do so Seaton gave whole-hearted admiration to the Japanese engineers who had planned and built this magnificent rail line. It was indeed the finest in the world and nothing in the United States could compare with it.

A little after noon they slid into the station at Kyoto, on time to the second, to find that they were expected. The efficient Reiko Watanabe was twenty-seven years of age and sufficiently experienced in the business world to know what to do when matters were entrusted to her hands. She had, therefore, called the unrelentingly capable Japan Travel Service and made certain practical arrangements which she was well aware Seaton san would not be able to handle on his own.

As Seaton emerged onto the platform, carrying his own overnight bag in one hand and his companion's in the other, he was immediately approached by an energetic young man who bowed with quick precision and at once relieved him of the light luggage.

"Japan Travel Service, Mr. Seaton," he announced in definitely good English. "Welcome to Kyoto. Your arrangements have all been made, the car is waiting to take you to your inn." He turned to lead the way apparently without ever noticing that a lady was also present. He had been dispatched to receive the American and receive the American he did. He was, as a matter of fact, completely aware of the attractive Miss Kanno and he knew that she was a geisha. It was beyond him why anyone would want to bring a geisha to Kyoto, which is the center of the girl-training industry, but one did not expect Americans to be logical. Only rich. And any man who could hire his favorite for the entire weekend was obviously far beyond having to consider the expense.

He escorted his customer to the front entranceway and placed the luggage in the trunk of a waiting hire car. Seaton san was not expected to ride in an ordinary taxicab. He saw both passengers inside, spoke a rapid instruction to the driver in Japanese, and wished them a pleasant stay in the city.

Almost before the car had left the curb Seaton realized that Reiko Watanabe had set this all up for him. He had a surge of respect for her, for she had relieved him of what could have been an awkward dilemma and had certainly made him look better in the eyes of his beautiful companion.

For fifteen minutes the car wove through traffic at a dignified pace, then it entered a narrow, all-but-invisible street and pulled up before an establishment which had no sign of any kind on display outside.

At once a smiling, stocky Japanese man of uncertain age appeared to take the luggage. Confident that Miss Watanabe had not made any mistakes, Dick climbed out and then helped his guest to her feet. Beaming contentment the amiable porter led them into a stone entranceway and then indicated that they should remove their shoes. He pointed to a long row of waiting slippers perfectly lined up at the front door and with happy gestures invited them to enter the premises.

With Masayo beside him Seaton did so and discovered that he was in the lobby of what appeared to be a small inn. It was a charming place, vastly different from the commercial reception areas of conventional hotels. The bare wooden floor had a rich patina created by thousands of pairs of stockinged and slippered feet. The walls and ceiling were also wood, constructed with notable simplicity but clearly revealing the hand of a skilled designer. There was a modest reception desk and toward it Seaton turned in search of further enlightenment.

Two women in kimono and a man in a business suit were

there to receive him; with a gesture the man handed him the pen and invited him to register. "Seaton san, hai? Irasshaimase," he said.

Despite this strong evidence that English was not too well understood here, Dick Seaton prepared to make himself clear in the only language that he knew.

"Have—you—a—reservation?" he asked, pausing after each word.

"Reservation, hai. Dozo." Once again the man proffered the pen.

Seaton took it and registered, block printing the letters of his name so that the Japanese could read them. Then he handed the pen to Masayo and turning to the clerk once more said most clearly, "Two rooms, please." He underlined it by holding up two fingers.

The geisha took the pen and drew quick characters next to his name on the same card. Seaton's attention was distracted at that point by the happy little porter who was trying to fit a pair of slippers onto his feet despite the fact that the largest ones available were at least four sizes too small. One of the ladies in kimono appeared, bowed, and began to lead the way down a corridor which actually went over a tiny bridge. Then she slid open a panel and indicated that they should enter.

The room was delightful. The straw-matted floor had the usual low black table, but there was an alcove with two Western-style chairs, a small table between them, and a picture window which opened onto a miniature private garden. A trickle of water flowing from the end of a bamboo pipe added its music to the scene. The tokanoma was enriched not only by the usual scroll and flower arrangement, but also a modern television set.

The hostess hoped that they would be very comfortable and happy, an obvious sentiment as she attempted to back out of the room and leave them alone. At that precise moment the beaming porter appeared carrying their overnight bags which he carefully deposited in the corner.

Seaton was violently embarrassed. Not for himself, but because through an appalling blunder Reiko had failed to specify two separate rooms and Miss One Thousand Spring Blossoms at that moment must be thinking the very worst of him. The fact that Miss Watanabe might be of a practical turn of mind, or even a fatalistic one, did not concern him. He picked up his overnight bag, swept his hand in a wide gesture to indicate that the room was entirely his guest's, and retreated.

In the lobby he confronted the gentleman behind the desk who was immediately concerned. He had given Seaton san one of his very best rooms and if it would not do, it was beyond his power to improve the arrangements. His guest, however, was visibly upset.

There was a partial impasse; because in his whole life Seaton had never encountered the language problem, he had somehow assumed that everyone spoke or at least understood English. It was the essential civilized language. Now, face-to-face with the hard reality, he was uncertain how to proceed.

Sign language might prove to be the answer; the man behind the desk looked intelligent. Carefully Seaton got his attention and then raised his forefinger and pointed to it with his other hand.

"One," he said.

"Yubi," the man responded, trying his best. If his guest wanted to know how to say "finger" in Japanese, he was happy to oblige.

Seaton raised two fingers and pointed to the pair.

"Yubi," the man said once more, there being no plural form in his language.

Clearly that wasn't working, furthermore the issue was compounded by the arrival of Miss One Thousand Spring Blossoms who was wondering if her client was in some kind of difficulty.

"I'm trying to get two rooms," Seaton said to her. In his tension he spoke rapidly and she did not understand; she only knew that he was upset and getting more so by the second. In gentle Japanese she spoke to the man at the desk.

In response he looked his gratitude at her, motioned to Seaton to wait, and swiftly dialed a telephone. When he had his number he spoke for a moment at apparent breakneck speed and then passed the instrument to his guest.

"Hello," Seaton said.

"Mr. Seaton, this is Japan Travel Service," a voice said in wonderful, glorious, understandable English. "Please state to me the problem and I shall translate for you."

"Thank you, sir," Seaton said warmly. "I have just arrived at this inn with a lady who is my guest. We are not married."

"I believe, sir, that the management will not create for you any embarrassment."

"I didn't make myself clear. I very much respect this lady. I do not wish to sleep with her."

"As you wish, sir."

Seaton was about ready to give up—now he couldn't express himself in English!

"I beg your pardon," he tried again, "I did not speak clearly. I wish to have two rooms, one for the lady, one for myself."

"Ah, so!"

"Precisely. My intentions are honorable, do you understand?"

There was a brief pause. "I think so, sir."

"Good. Please tell the manager here that I would like to have a separate room."

"Seaton san, it shall be as you wish, but in Japanese inn dinner and again breakfast are served to you in your room. Waitress will be present."

"This is quite proper for unmarried couples?"

"Oh yes, sir. Done all the time. Especially by Americans, sir."

"Then I will have dinner with the lady, but wish a separate room to sleep."

"Separate room, yes, sir."

"Good, now you've got it. I know many Americans do differently, but if I sleep with a girl, I will marry her first, understand?"

"Ah, yes, Seaton san—most admirable. My compliments, sir."

That was more like it, Seaton let the tension go out of his body and his shoulders relaxed. "You are a great help to me, sir."

"It is my pleasure. Allow me to speak to the manager, please. I shall instruct him what to do."

In silent satisfaction Seaton passed over the telephone—the way had been found. He turned to his charming companion and with a smile indicated his appreciation of her clever thought. Clearly the few words she had spoken had resulted in this satisfactory solution.

For almost half a minute the manager conferred with the man from the Japan Travel Service on the phone. He expressed some surprise, a considerable relief, and much satisfaction. At last he hung up and in his most eloquent manner, which was considerable in his own tongue, congratulated Miss One Thousand Spring Blossoms on the fact that the American gentleman was about to marry her immediately. He beamed his approval of this happy fact. A suitable party would, of course, be arranged.

In any language known to mankind the giesha was, for the first time in her adult life, completely speechless.

Chapter Twelve

$\mathcal{M}$iss One Thousand Spring Blossoms née Kanno Masayo, was extremely well schooled in her profession. At the parties which it was her duty to attend sake usually flowed liberally, a circumstance which quite often brought about a regrettable lack of restraint on the part of the honored guests. Under such circumstances she could have fluttered her fan and held off the Notre Dame backfield, individually or en masse, but she had had no experience in sidestepping matrimony.

Apparently Americans were in the habit of hauling any girl they happened to like off to the Shinto shrine and marrying her without a second thought. And Kyoto was world-famous for its great number of shrines and temples.

At once she contemplated the idea of flight. She could get her shoes back and somehow make her escape, the geisha house would understand despite the loss of a magnificent fee. At least she hoped they would, since the other alternative might be even less acceptable to them. "Welcome back, Masayo san, how was Kyoto and your client?"

"Kyoto was beautiful as always; the client is now my husband."

110

She could hear the mamasan screaming, "What! *Without paying?*"

Before making a decision she cast a quick glance at Seaton and concluded that if she knew anything at all about men (which she most emphatically did), he would never willingly place her in a position of such embarrassment. He was at that moment trying to arrange for a second room; logic told her that if it was his intention to marry her that afternoon, he would not be so engaged. There had to be a mistake somewhere.

There was. A second call to the obliging interpreter at the Japan Travel Service was necessary after which all was understood. The disappointed manager wished them a pleasant tour of the city and had the porter call a cab.

While these matters were being attended to, the careful Miss Kanno was given some additional thought to the man whom it was her obligation to entertain. He was certainly not handsome, but he had about him an honesty which she recognized and respected. The way in which he had been treating her had made one thing clear—he was not aware that her time was being sold by the hour and that for every minute which she spent in his company someone would have to pay.

She decided that it would be much better for him if he found a nice girl who was not in the geisha business. His manners were not those of the usual patrons of the *mizu shobai,* Japan's vast and sometimes overpowering entertainment industry. Not once had he taken her for granted. For one fragile moment she wished that she herself were not committed as she was, so that she could be his honest and truly girlfriend—then the rigid fetters of her training asserted themselves and she remembered that she must not be a person—only a property.

As she climbed into the cab she tried to run over in her mind any girls she knew who might be suitable for him, but the only one who could be right at all was a cabaret hostess and she sold her time too. Then, remembering her duty, she gave the driver an address.

To Seaton the cab ride was a long one. The little vehicle went on and on until it reached the suburbs, crossed a concrete bridge, and began to weave through a near-rural

111

area. Then it pulled up and stopped before a modest gateway.

Masayo looked bright anticipation at her client. "Moss
garden," she said, "Very most beautiful."

It had been Seaton's intention upon arrival to engage a
guide to show them around the city, now it was clearly
apparent that this step would have been unnecessary. Because
his Japanese vocabulary consisted of approximately ten words,
he was unaware that during the conversations with the representative of the Japan Travel Service over the telephone a
guide had been proposed and declined. Miss One Thousand
Spring Blossoms had made it clear that she was well acquainted with Kyoto and had been here many times. She was visiting
it again because it was her customer's wish.

At the entrance gate Seaton paid a small fee, passed
through an unprepossessing entrance, and found himself in a
transformed world. It was an enchanted garden, a garden so
far removed from the mundane that only the genius of
Maurice Ravel could have captured its spirit. There were no
formal paths or clipped rose hedges, but what might have
been Eden itself—unspoiled, timeless, and so exquisitely designed that the work of its architects had been rendered all
but invisible.

Undisturbed trees cast rich deep shade over the gently
rolling earth which was blanketed with a thick green carpet of
moss in every direction. There was a simple footpath which,
like the garden itself, appeared simply to have happened.
Through the shadows and between the trees there was visible
the shoreline of a wandering little lake.

It was wonderland. A never-never world restful and beautiful. Its spell was hypnotic. It was worth the whole trip just to
stand and drink in this incredible scene which seemed to have
been placed here by the Creator himself.

Slowly, almost worshipfully, Seaton walked down the path,
so taken with the sheer beauty all around him that he did not
realize that his companion was by choice following behind.
When he turned a little bend and saw a large flat rock,
precisely where there should have been a large flat rock, he
paused and then sat down to try and comprehend what he was
beholding.

From the ample bag which she was carrying the geisha

removed a small but expensive camera and raised it to eye level. Realizing that he was to be the subject, Seaton pushed up his glasses and then self-consciously looked toward the lens. After he heard the click of the mechanism he rose to his feet, asked for the camera with a gesture, and then pointed toward the rock. Obligingly his companion seated herself and tipping her head slightly sidewise, offered him a winning smile. He pushed the plunger and then paused to take stock of himself.

To his surprise the girl motioned for him to come closer. He did so, stopping obediently before her as she stood up on the rock so that her face was very nearly on a level with his. Without taking the camera which he offered to her, she reached up and instead gently lifted off his glasses. Then, mistily before him, she studied his features, even placing one hand under his chin to turn his face slightly from side to side.

"Do you like garden?"

"Yes."

"So beautiful."

"Yes. When *you* are in it."

She understood, which made it very hard for her. She forced herself to remember that he was a client, simply another customer with enough money to command the services of a geisha of her rank. For one mad moment she did not want to be a geisha any more; she wanted to lay aside the mantle of Miss One Thousand Spring Blossoms to become just a girl free to go where she chose in the company of anyone who pleased her.

Perhaps the magical beauty of the garden reached the poetry ingrained in her even more deeply than the years of schooling she had undergone. She was, after all, Japanese, and the sensitivity of things beautiful was therefore almost part of her bloodstream.

She had just received the most gentle and exquisite compliment that had ever been paid her. It had been a compliment not for a famous geisha, but for Masayo Kanno. She had also discovered something in this big ungainly man, something she had not thought that any foreigner could possess. Without his glasses, his face, while lacking the classic lines of Oriental features, was strong and honest.

113

"You are very handsome," she lied, but only a little.

For a moment Seaton's eyes crinkled shut, then he slowly shook his head.

She understood, understood perfectly. Still holding his glasses in her hands she slipped her fingers gently behind his neck and drew him to her. At that moment she did not care one whit for the fact that in Japan kissing someone in public is an obscenity, or that she had never been intimate with a man except under compulsion; she wanted to try it again and there was no one to see.

He stood very still, afraid to speak for fear he would again say some unthinking and disastrous thing. Without his glasses he was in a blurred world, a world so far removed from reality that a lovely girl had just called him handsome.

"I think," Masayo struggled for the words she needed, "better you not wear glasses."

"I'm sorry," Seaton answered carefully, "I don't want to. But I must."

Even with his handicapped vision he could see her shaking her head. Once more she battled the language problem and again she emerged victorious.

"Contact lenses."

When they had absorbed the beauties of the moss garden they returned to the other world of Japan and hailed a cab, something which he had now learned to accept as a normal hazard of living in the Orient. As he helped Masayo inside she gave the driver some brief instructions. Fifteen minutes later he pulled up before an imposing wooden building which was very clearly a religious edifice of some kind. Seaton paid the cab fare and another small admission charge, and then learned that once more he was expected to remove his shoes.

As he bent far over to perform this duty it occurred to him that there was considerable logic to the idea of not tracking street dirt all over well-maintained indoor premises.

Masayo took his hand and led him inside. They turned left and walked down a wooden corridor floored with polished boards which might have been there for centuries, then they turned right and looked down a very long narrow hall.

To the left there was a walkway ten or twelve feet wide; to the right, on a series of gradually rising steps, in silent rows

114

were hundreds upon hundreds of carved, life-sized figures. They stood there, mute and inert, as though some vast court spectacle had been frozen into immobility at a climactic moment uncounted generations ago. All of them faced forward, a phalanx of deities many rows deep, which defied time and all that the destructive forces of evil might do to move them from their appointed positions.

"One thousand images," the girl said. It was a statement, an explanation, and also a question; she looked up into his face to see if he understood.

At first of course he did not. He was astonished at the display of sheer numbers, but the figures themselves, as individuals, left him unmoved. Following his companion he walked very slowly down the long passageway, looking up into the vast parade of unseeing faces which seemed to be fixed on some objective which it was beyond the powers of mortal man to discern.

Halfway down the great hall the girl paused and looked up at a majestic image of the Lord Buddha which sat in silent meditation, ready to receive in audience those who came in search of His presence. Then, allowing herself the luxury of forgetting for a few moments that she was on duty, she pressed her palms together and bent her head in prayer.

It had never occurred to Seaton that she might not be an Episcopalian. Now with a sense of shock he saw her as she stood, in an attitude of humble supplication, before the image of a pagan god about whom he knew almost nothing whatever. Vaguely he had heard the word Buddha, but only in the context of a squatting idol. Never in his lifetime had he been made aware of The Enlightened One, the Prince Gautama Siddhartha of India who, six centuries before the birth of the Savior, had renounced his royal heritage in order to seek enlightenment and the betterment of all humanity. He saw only a great candlelit figure of an Oriental personage he took to be the result of some sculptor's imaginings.

He had no conception of even the basic simplicity of the Eight-fold Path, and he did not dream of the tens of thousands of volumes of profound thought which over the centuries had been prepared to illuminate and expound the teachings of the royal sage who had influenced the world more than any other mortal who had ever lived. The shadow of the legendary Arminta Buddha had never once been cast across his path, and the great Buddha yet to come was totally unknown to him.

For that matter he would not have known whether to take off, or put on, his hat upon entering a synagogue. He only knew that seeing the girl who had grown so significant in his eyes making her devotions before the graven image of a strange and non-Christian deity was an abrupt and shocking revelation. It opened the first gulf between them and he was vastly disturbed by it.

He completed the tour of the temple, walking past the remaining five hundred images on the other side of the main statue and returning by a corridor which took him past carved wooden figures in frightening, distorted postures which increased the uneasiness he felt. As he put his shoes back on he realized, and reminded himself, that he was in a country not akin to his own and that he must therefore be on his guard.

His lovely companion looked at her watch and then turned inquiringly toward him. "One more place?"

No matter what, he could not refuse her. "Please."

Once more they boarded a cab and set out across the city. When they had been riding a few minutes Seaton began to sense that Miss One Thousand Spring Blossoms was in deep and somewhat worried thought. He waited for her to speak and at last she did.

"Dicku san, where we go now you maybe no understand."

"Where are we going?"

"Garden."

"I like gardens very much," he said. "Almost all kinds of gardens. And all kinds of flowers."

She shook her head. "No flowers this garden, Dicku san, no trees."

That was puzzling, but he wisely decided to wait and see. He had just made that decision when the cab pulled up and he paid the modest fare.

This time they were apparently at a park; there were quiet paths which led inside. For a few minutes they strolled, the geisha abandoning her carefully practiced enticing walk to simply be herself on this most agreeable afternoon. Only she knew the words she had spoken to the Lord Buddha as he sat enthroned in the overwhelming bliss of Nirvana, and she would never tell anyone what they were.

Presently the inevitable temple appeared. Once more Seaton purchased two tickets for a tiny donation and then allowed himself to be guided inside. For just a moment the lady beside him stopped to study his features as if trying to read something there, and then she slipped out of her shoes with practiced ease and led the way into a severely plain building.

Seaton followed, came out upon a long wooden veranda, and discovered before him a garden totally unlike anything he had ever seen before.

Strictly speaking it was not a garden because almost nothing grew there. A long narrow rectangle of space was covered instead with fine white gravel almost dazzling to the eye. From it there rose a few sparse clusters of large rocks, their stark severity broken by wisps of moss which fought for existence around their bases. It was a still and frozen eternity.

Masayo sat down, rested her chin in her hands, and responded to the spectacle of the rock garden. Seaton sat beside her, looking too at the strange sight—the few weathered boulders, the minute fragments of moss, and the wide area of flawless gravel which had been raked to give it a surface texture and a pattern which swirled with timeless rightness around the bases of the rock islands.

For fifteen minutes they sat there, silently, looking at the motionless, almost lifeless garden. Then Seaton began to perceive certain things. Possibly because of his engineering training, he sensed a kind of abstract balance of the kind to be found in a Mondriaan painting. The stark white gravel began to resolve itself into a vast and limitless ocean with islands thrust up through its surface by the unguided force of raw nature. Yet there was an organization about it all. It was not on the surface, it was not visible, but the more he looked the more he began to see in that enigmatic unchanging scene before him. It became hypnotic; the wooden fence in the background ceased to be evident, only the gravel, the rocks, and the careful, intricate pattern of the raking commanded his attention.

Then he had the odd feeling that he did not want to move,

117

that he wanted simply to remain and look at this mystic spectacle for an indefinite period. His mind told him that there was a challenge here and he wanted to understand it.

"You like?" Her voice startled him out of his reverie.

"Magnificent," he said. He did not shape the word, it came of its own accord.

She looked at him and her features glowed.

"Oh Dicku san," she said. "I so glad."

"Because I like this unusual garden?" He did not understand her sudden change of mood.

"Because, Dicku san, I not know before you Buddhist!"

When they returned to the inn the happy little porter seemed to outdo himself. He took their shoes with great energy and then sprung his surprise: he had somehow obtained a pair of slippers much larger than any of the others for Seaton to try. He insisted on fitting them on and was overjoyed to discover that they would do. Seaton himself was slightly less ebullient; the only way he could keep them on was to shuffle gingerly without even once lifting his feet to move them forward. Even then it was marginal—they seemed determined to slip off if given the slightest opportunity to do so.

With a great show of accommodating his exact, if somewhat irrational desires, the manager showed Seaton to a second room, across the corridor from the first, and pointed out that his overnight bag had been properly installed in the corner. Seaton was at once pleased and showed it by bowing as he had now learned to do. When he was alone he shut the door, unpacked a few of his things, and stroked his chin to determine if it would be desirable to shave again before dinner. He explored the bathroom and found a conventional (to him) toilet fixture and a square wooden box which might conceivably be considered to be the bathtub. There was no shower so his plan to refresh himself properly had to be set aside.

He had his shirt off and was washing when there was a scratching at his door. He opened it in his undershirt expecting the manager and found to his embarrassment that his companion was standing outside. Furthermore she was wearing a kimono, not one of the elaborate beautifully decorated ones which were part of her professional wardrobe, but a plain blue and white cotton garment which had been freshly laundered and starched. In it she looked adorable and Seaton caught himself staring.

Without invitation she came in, kicking off her slippers as she did so, and surveyed the room with an expert eye. In one corner she found what she wanted, a tray with a black and white yukata folded into a compact flat bundle. She picked it up, pulled apart the starched surfaces, and reclaimed the tying strip from one of the sleeves. When it was ready to her satisfaction she insisted that Seaton put it on.

He did so, feeling very foolish, but comforted by the thought that his lack of a proper shirt was now no longer evident. His assurance was short-lived; the girl who had suddenly taken charge pinched the crease of his trousers between her fingers and said, "Not wear with kimono. Make off."

One glance downward assured him that the strange long garment he had on covered him almost to his ankles. Then, to please her, he turned his back and slipped out of his pants as discreetly as he was able. He would never have done it if he had not been conditioned by the efficient Miss Sumiko at the hotsie bath who had demanded that and much more besides. When he had complied he lapped the yukata carefully closed over his underwear and tied it shut with the piece of fabric which had been provided. He noted how the long sleeves hung down and was embarrassed by them. He felt as though he were being taken to a fancy dress ball.

The geisha seemed to think otherwise. She gave him a quick approving glance and then literally led him by the hand down to the room they had been originally given. Without pausing she took him to the little alcove next to the garden and motioned him toward one of the low Western-style chairs. Then she took the other and sat facing him, a tantalizing smile playing about her lips.

From the open window the sound of the trickling water in the miniature garden offered its sense of repose. Seaton leaned back a little, took hold of the arms of the chair, and was suddenly engulfed by the thought that at that moment he *was* truly a man of the world. He heard the music of the water and felt the serenity of the charming little garden. Then he turned and looked at the girl across from him. Despite himself his heart leaped, she was too attractive to be believed. As he watched her, she reached to the back of her head and began to remove hairpins. She took out almost a dozen with no visible effect, then, after one more, she shook her head and a cascade of shining jet black hair fell down onto her shoulders. She brushed it back with her fingers and then looked at her client, her very special client, with complete feminine witchery.

At that moment he could no more have moved, or have spoken, than could the Sphinx. With her hair down her beauty was startlingly intensified. Seaton looked at her and wanted her—wanted her so desperately that he could not believe the pounding new emotion which had taken hold of him. He had a drastic, surging desire to spring to his feet and to sweep her into his arms—he might have done so had not a maid at that moment knocked, slid open the door, and appeared inside with two bottles of ice-cold beer on a lacquer tray.

With a mighty effort he recovered himself and waited while the beverage was served. It was in a way providential; when he lifted the glass to his lips and the cool flow of the excellent Japanese beer went down his throat he remembered what at least theoretically separates civilized men from the savages and gave his inhibitions an opportunity to recover themselves.

Presently their dinner was served. Trays were set out on the center table each with several small dishes and the inevitable chopsticks. In addition he had been provided with an incongruous knife and fork. He took proper pride in ignoring them; by now he was able to handle chopsticks with some measure of skill and his newly discovered talent added to his enjoyment of the food.

It was the most delightful dinner he had ever had. Sitting on the floor was still decidedly uncomfortable, but he had learned to live with it. He felt reckless, a nonconformist in his yukata, and alive as he had never been before. For one guilty instant he wished that he had not been so insistent about the matter of separate rooms, what might have been his destiny otherwise was so incredible an aspiration he did not permit his mind to form it into a definite image.

He did allow himself one release—he cursed the code of manners which had deprived him of what might have been the

Himalayan summit of his life—the unattainable that might have been his. He reviled the code and tore it to shreds in a few moments of savage fury at what he had been refused because of its prissiness. He was a man, Goddammit, and he was entitled to inherit man's estate. It was here before him and it might have been his for the taking.

They went out for a little walk afterward through the arcade area near the inn. The colorful shops were all open and seemed to reach for blocks in every direction. He bought her some candy to please her, but when he began to explore the possibilities of a more elaborate gift, she surprised him by firmly declining. A beautiful leather handbag which might have been appropriate she would not let him even consider. He had carefully redonned his coat and trousers, but she had kept her kimono and in it she was completely and utterly Japanese. He loved her for it and walked proudly with her, a man who had for the moment partway conquered himself.

When they returned to the inn the room had been prepared for them. Twin futons, Japanese on-the-floor beds, had been laid out side by side and the light had been turned very low.

What Seaton did not know was that his companion had read his every thought since the moment she had let her hair down purely for comfort and knew in complete detail the struggle going on within him. She had never known a man so determined to regard her as an important person and not merely as a paid companion. She was not sure whether he was in love with her, but she knew with clear certainty that he had never had intercourse with any girl or woman in his life.

When at last he stood just outside the door of the room which had been prepared for them, swallowed very hard, and wished her good night with tears in his eyes, she pushed her own manners aside and held him very close for just a moment. Then she offered herself to be kissed and gave more than she received. As she slid the door shut and was alone at last, she was acutely aware that she had never had a client like this before and that some of the things she had been told about Americans were, in his case at least, patently untrue.

121

Chapter Thirteen

*W*hen Richard Seaton arrived for work on Monday morning, the Matsumoto Company was already braced for the shock. He strode through the lobby with a quick pleasant smile for little Chiyoko Shinagawa in her tiny cubicle, brushed open the door, and entered the crowded premises of the general business office. Reiko Watanabe looked up and satisfied herself in one glance that Seaton san had had a fine weekend. It would cost the company dearly, particularly for the pillow service, but the thing which had happened was now a thing of the past. Apart from the expense to her firm, her only real regret was that it never seemed to happen to her.

There were too many girls in Japan and not enough men; since she had little to offer other than herself, she had become one of the victims of this imbalance. It was too bad because she desperately wanted a home of her own and dearly loved children.

To her surprise the American visitor came directly to her desk as though she were actually an important personage.

"Good morning, Reiko," he began, "Ohayoo gozaimasu."

"Ohayoo gozaimasu, Seaton san. You are having nice weekend?" The words were hard for her to say, but she got them out without faltering.

"Yes, Reiko, I had a very fine weekend. Did you make all those arrangements for me?"

"Yes, I make. Is all right?" She was very worried at that moment because she had taken a great deal on herself; he might not have liked the Japanese inn despite the fact that the one she had chosen was equipped with Western-style toilets and was therefore particularly recommended for foreigners.

"Could we step into the conference room?" Seaton asked. He realized that the many other employees who crowded the working area did not understand English, but they could still be adept at catching the drift.

Reiko was now thoroughly frightened; if the American wished to speak to her privately, total disaster could quickly follow. It was much too early for him to want her to call the geisha for him. Head bowed, she followed him to the corner room and waited for her fate to be pronounced.

Seaton shut the door behind them.

"First Rieko, thank you very much for everything. Arigato gozaimasu."

She looked up, not daring to believe that she had been reprieved.

"I liked the inn very much and if you had not made reservations for me, I might have been in trouble. I did not think well enough ahead."

Reiko bowed her head to hide her face.

"Just one thing," Seaton went on, "the inn had reserved only one room. I had trouble making them understand that I wanted two."

"Two rooms?" Reiko echoed, not believing what she had just heard.

"Two rooms. Do you understand?"

"You not like futon?" It was the only thing she could think of.

"Of course I liked the futon, it was the first bed I've had in Japan where I could stretch out."

Reiko looked at his face, question marks in her eyes.

"Reiko san, let me put it this way." He tried very hard to

123

make himself understood without sounding like a stick-in-the-mud in the process. "I respect Masayo san very much—do you understand?" Reiko tried. "You mean you like."

"Yes, I like. Now maybe in Japan everybody sleeps with his girlfriend . . ."

"Same all over world."

"Yes, but in my country there are still some of us left who believe that you should marry the girl first."

"But Masayo san not marry, she geisha. You can buy maybe . . ."

"Look, Reiko, let me be very frank. If a girl is going to have a baby, she should also have a husband."

Reiko could have supplied an answer to that, but she refrained because she did not fully understand foreigners. She also considered the possibility that events had not transpired at the geisha's request. Even girls in that business had their periodic problems and if Kanno san had been indisposed, that would explain matters right there.

At that precise moment Matsumoto san was receiving similar news and finding it equally hard to believe. The always efficient geisha house had phoned to inform him of the amount of his indebtedness for the weekend. Although it was a staggering sum, it was still somewhat under the worst that the unhappy manufacturer had anticipated. Always honorable in its dealings, particularly with old and valued customers, the geisha house reported that pillow service had not been requested by Setanu san. Furthermore, he had treated the valuable property, Miss One Thousand Spring Blossoms, with notable consideration.

Astonished as he was, Matsumoto san recovered himself brilliantly and suggested almost at once that since Setanu san was such a superior client, and because the wear and tear had been less than anticipated, perhaps a somewhat lower rate might be considered for the remainder of his stay.

The mamasan, who was also in business, agreed at once that the request was reasonable, but most unfortunately Miss One Thousand Spring Blossoms was her most popular attraction and always in great demand at her regular fees. However, in view of the circumstances, one thing would be arranged: she would be made available whenever desired to entertain Setanu san who henceforth would have priority.

Faced with a Mexican standoff Matsumoto san grunted and hung up. He had already implored his ancestors to have the scintillating Miss Kanno break her leg or encounter some similar fortunate accident, but such a happy event was clearly improbable. He would have to think of something else. Already he had briefed Mr. Futaba to invite the American engineer for dinner and the theater that evening—which would make his employee happy and save one geisha fee at least.

In the R-and-D section, Seaton himself, his coat off, was once more immersed in the project before him. With the aid of the very capable Mr. Fujihara, the chief engineer, he was constructing a bench mock-up which would be ready to check out the intricate component when the first prototype had been completed.

In the course of his labors Mr. Futaba appeared and managed with profound effort to suggest dinner and the Nichigeki Music Hall afterward. To his great pleasure and relief Seaton accepted at once. Perhaps after the American had seen what Japan had to offer in the way of beautiful girls not given to too much in the way of costumes, he might even think twice about spending so much time with an expensive and possibly uncooperative geisha. There were much faster and better methods with a successful outcome practically guaranteed.

The day was made up of winged hours, lunch hardly seemed over when it was time for the plant to close. The work was at a good stage: the testing rig was all but completed and the parts for the component assembly were ready to be fitted together in the morning.

In the company of Mr. Futaba who at last was having his chance to be a co-host in the proper manner, Seaton enjoyed an excellent dinner at the Imperial Hotel new wing. Conversation was a bit strained, so the food was largely consumed in silence while Futaba san struggled with the knife and fork and tried to remember to change hands each time he conveyed a portion to his mouth. Nevertheless they got along and Seaton began to sense a genuine personality bricked up behind the wall of language.

125

When the meal was almost over, Mr. Futaba became fraternally confidential. "You like Japanese girls?" he asked, unaware that for the first time he had managed a sentence in reasonably accurate English.

Seaton nodded. "Of course. I find them fascinating." He was rather proud of that, it was a neatly phrased tribute to the ladies of this exotic nation.

Encouraged by the positive response Mr. Futaba plunged a little deeper. "You like brewtiful girls?"

On the surface that considerably enlarged the field, but it was intended to limit it. To Mr. Futaba all beautiful girls were automatically Japanese, even despite his painful acquaintance with the, in many ways, potent Miss Norma Scott.

"Of course."

"Is to Nichigeki Music Hall one block. We are walking, yes?"

"We are walking," Seaton agreed, glad that he had sense enough not to correct his host's English.

Futaba beamed. "You liking brewtiful girls, seeing prenty tonight. No clothes."

When they reached the small entranceway of the upstairs theater fifteen minutes later Seaton saw from the lobby display that his companion's statement had been exaggerated—but not very much. He had never been to any performance where the female members of the cast were not fully clad according to traditional requirements. For a moment he feared a possible police raid, then reason told him that the large, brilliantly colored transparencies on display guaranteed that there was nothing clandestine about the theater or its operation. He therefore rode up the crowded elevator as a good guest should and was shown to his seat in the second row of the small auditorium.

Presently the performance began. When the first of the bare-breasted girls entered he felt a distinct heat under his collar, particularly since they were all indeed beautiful and one, at whom he scarcely dared to look, bore a definite resemblance to the lady who was filling a great many of his thoughts.

He had to admit that it was a good show, well staged and with attractive settings. After a while he began to adjust to the pert and shapely bosoms on frank and uninhibited display.

126

He remembered the time when, as a small boy, he had come downstairs unseen on Christmas Eve and had peeked at the dazzling Christmas tree he was not supposed to see before morning. He had dreamed about it all that night, savoring the forbidden fruit which would become commonplace the next day. It was the same way now, he had been forbidden by strict convention to behold this much of feminine shapeliness, but he was doing so anyway and he found it pleasurable. As a man of the world he was supposed to accept all experiences with uniform urbanity.

Toward the end of the show an American girl appeared, danced, and then deftly discarded the upper half of her costume. "Always one foreigner," Mr. Futaba said, sotto voce. "Big liking."

The American dancer did have breasts notably larger than her Japanese colleagues, but they did not seem to encumber her in the least. She was so unconcerned that when she spotted Seaton, towering above all the others despite the fact that he was sitting down, she winked at him just before making her exit down a stage elevator.

Seaton wiped his brow, wondered what his mother would think, and then drew a measure of comfort from the fact that she had passed to her reward before entertainments of this nature had invaded her world. For the first time he realized that he now was called upon not only to lead his own life, but also to set and adjust his own standards of behavior and morality.

When the full ensemble of pretty girls came on for the finale, he admired them frankly and regretted that the show was over. The phrase "strip tease" had never appealed to him, but this was something different and he found it most enjoyable.

When he returned to his hotel there was a message that Miss Scott had called and would like him to ring her back any time before midnight. After saying the proper things to his host he retired to his room and picked up the phone. It gave him a subdued tingle of satisfaction to do so—in this country he was contacting young women, very attractive young women, with as much savoir faire as if he had been the fabled James Bond himself.

Norma's voice on the phone was intimate and almost

127

indecently feminine. "Dick, I have an idea. Have you ever seen sumo?"

"Some kind of wrestling, isn't it?"

"Yes, but it's a lot more than that. It's a sort of ceremonial with centuries of tradition behind it. Anyhow, I've got two tickets for tomorrow night and I wondered if I could talk you into escorting me. You'll have to sit on the floor."

"I'm getting used to that."

"Good. Suppose you pick me up at the Kodokan around six. I'll treat you to dinner at a little place I know and then we'll see the matches."

It began to dawn on Seaton that a young lady was inviting him to take her out—it was wonderful! "It's a deal," he said warmly, "except for the fact that the dinner must be on me. I'd very much like to see sumo in your company."

"Well, it's all set then. See you tomorrow. Good night." The last phrase throbbed over the wire like a caress.

"Good night." Seaton produced the words from somewhere down in his throat and hung up. He had intended to call Masayo in the morning to invite *her* out, but reason told him that waiting an extra day might be to his advantage. Furthermore, he would be spending the evening in very agreeable company.

For a moment he stretched out on the bed, on his back, folded his hands behind his head, and reflected on what was happening to him. A month ago there had not been a girl in the world he could have called up for a date. Now he had found an exotic beauty so much a fulfillment of his dreams he could hardly believe it. In addition, there was no question concerning the desirability of Norma Scott—she clearly had everything and had it in spades. For some incomprehensible reason she seemed to like him and didn't appear to find him awkward at all. She was wickedly attractive and he had a date with her in less than twenty-four hours. Even little Reiko Watanabe, the patient interpreter, had accepted his luncheon invitation, and she too could be called an appealing girl.

Foreign travel was supposed to broaden a man—in his case it was exceeding its advertised advantages. Besides which Norma was an American, completely suitable, and totally free of the annoying language problem.

He came to one conclusion—when he returned home he

would look on himself in a new light: perhaps he was not such an impossible gargoyle after all.

At three o'clock in the afternoon on the following day Matsumoto san began to feel the cooling winds of deliverance. Two glorious days had all but passed without his American visitor once mentioning the delightful but disastrously expensive geisha with whom he had spent the whole past weekend at the company's expense. To do the stocky little manufacturer justice he was neither parsimonious nor inhospitable; he was merely facing bankruptcy. In order to clarify his thinking, he summoned his executive vice-president and sat down with him to reevaluate the situation.

"I have been imploring my ancestors," he began, "to divert the attention of Setanu san from the geisha Fujikoma. They responded with Miss Scott Norma which is unfair competition; she can speak his language."

"Both vertically and horizontally," Mr. Yamaguchi observed.

"And Miss Scott Norma is securely attached to the establishment of Sakamoto George, which is a potential disaster."

"Is there any hope that the Philippine contract may be reconsidered?" Yamaguchi asked.

The unhappy Mr. Matsumoto shook his head. "For reasons known only to themselves and to their gods, the people down there have decided to seek another source of supply. It has been reported to me that Sakamoto san is right now on his way to the Philippines; he must be strongly motivated since he has left town just before the start of the sumo tournament which he has never been known to miss."

"He is a very powerful fan," Mr. Yamaguchi concurred. "He has a season box."

"Then we must assume he is after the business with the same degree of certainty with which we regard death and taxes."

Mr. Yamaguchi pondered briefly. "He does have considerable lumber interests down there, and I believe that he is also in the prefabricated schoolhouse business."

"Trees are seldom impatient," Matsumoto san observed. "They are quite willing to wait until after major sumo tournaments have been completed."

129

"I will assume the blame," Mr. Yamaguchi stated. "When we received the Philippine commitment I considerably enlarged the staff to handle the new business. Good electronics assemblers and similar people are now hard to find."

"You did the right thing," Matsumoto conceded. "You could not foresee the disaster that awaited us."

"I could have consulted authorities. At any rate we are now stuck with these people; it is impossible to dismiss them unless we wish to degrade ourselves to the American system and simply tell them to go home."

Matsumoto san banged his fist down onto his desk. "Never! Remember Yokosuka and what happened there? Due to the orders of some barbarian in Washington the commander was forced to dismiss two or three hundred of his faithful and competent employees. The American face was shattered into ten million pieces. The order to hire them all back again did nothing to restore it. Even now good shipyard men fear to permit themselves to work for the Americans with their high pay and many benefits. They once laid off good employees, and men who will do that will do anything."

Yamaguchi hung his head. "True. New business is our only hope; the people I hired are all young and we can expect that they will be with us for twenty-five or thirty years, barring accidental deaths and things like that."

"How much will the Mercer and Doyle account help?" Matsumoto san knew the answer to that, but he hoped for a more optimistic estimate from his subordinate.

"There is a single ray of light," Yamaguchi answered. "This is Tuesday and neither yesterday or so far today has Setanu san even mentioned the costly Miss One Thousand Spring Blossoms."

At that moment the phone rang and Matsumoto gave it his attention. The geisha house was calling: they had an urgent request for Fujikoma that evening, but they would not commit her until it was determined if her services would be required to entertain Setanu san.

With great happiness Matsumoto assured the geisha house that it would be all right to release the geisha to other clients. That saved more than a month's pay for at least two of the office employees and relieved the strain to some degree.

"While you were phoning, an idea came to me," Yamaguchi

said. "Our honored guest apparently enjoyed his visit to Kyoto very much; he has spoken of the magnificent temples and shrines."

"I did not expect that he would appreciate them," Matsumoto san responded. "Is it even remotely possible that he has seen the Path of Enlightenment?"

"I doubt that, but the absence of a pillow fee, or any attempt on his part to incur one, leads me to the opinion that the attractions of the city were not wholly feminine. He seems honestly to possess some taste and discernment."

"What is your suggestion?"

"There are also magnificent holy buildings at Nikko. What other countries of the world have the scenic attractions of Japan?"

"None—of course."

"Then why not propose to our distinguished guest that we would like him to see more of our country while he is favoring us with his presence. We can ship him off to Miyajima, and of course he will want to see Hiroshima while he is down there. We can arrange things easily and the whole deal won't cost as much as an hour or two of the geisha's time. You know what her rates are."

Matsumoto knew an inspiration when he saw one. "Go out into the shop and propose it immediately. Tell him if necessary that the arrangements have already been made. In another week he will be going home, so we may get out of this thing with a relatively whole skin yet."

As he hurried back toward the development section the energetic vice-president was proud of his Japan tour idea. It would keep the American engineer close to the countryside and far from the geisha house for the entire weekend, which would include Friday afternoon if he managed things properly.

He found Seaton, in his shirt-sleeves, working with great diligence on the check-out rig which he had so carefully constructed during the past several days. It was a very complicated-looking apparatus and awoke in Mr. Yamaguchi a frank respect for the man who had been able to develop it and put it together. The Americans obviously were people who could boast of a superior technical culture if nothing more.

Discreetly Reiko Watanabe appeared in case her services

might be required. Directly in part, but largely through the interpreter, Mr. Yamaguchi outlined the proposition and extended the invitation.

"Why that's a wonderful idea, Mr. Yamaguchi," Seaton acknowledged with genuine enthusiasm. "Nothing would please me more than to see some more of your wonderful country. It's a great opportunity. I'm afraid, though, that if I accepted I'd be putting the company to far too much expense."

Through Reiko, Yamaguchi almost fervently assured his guest that the cost to the company was not to be considered. As a means of diverting attention from this critical point he acted on impulse and asked what plans, if any, Setanu san had for that evening.

"I'm so sorry, Mr. Yamaguchi," Seaton answered. "I didn't anticipate that I might have the pleasure of your company. I've made a date to have dinner with an American lady and then to escort her to the sumo matches."

Sudden agony engulfed the young Japanese executive. He knew precisely who the American lady was, he even knew exactly where she and his American visitor would be sitting in the sumo hall. The pit of Sheol loomed beneath his feet.

The situation was at once acute and called for drastic action. Miss One Thousand Spring Blossoms, regardless of her shattering fees, would have to be summoned again at once.

Chapter Fourteen

Despite the incredible jam of Tokyo traffic during the rush hour, Seaton arrived at the Kodokan a half hour early. He paid the cabdriver the exact fare, looked once carefully at the modern building which is the world headquarters of judo, and then entered the lobby. There was a reception desk on the left-hand side where he went to inquire. Unfortunately his English was incomprehensible to the receptionist on duty, but by now he was beginning to learn how to overcome this difficulty.

"Norma Scott," he said slowly. "Scott san." Then to underline the statement he drew the universal pattern of a female in the air with his hands.

At once the receptionist brightened and motioned him toward a stairway. Seaton bowed his thanks, went where he had been directed, and climbed several flights before he encountered an exit. When he did he found that he was in a spectators' gallery overlooking a spacious gymnasium floor, a floor which was completely covered with thick tatami mats. Seated on them were a number of men and women in two parallel rows facing each other; in the middle two partici-

133

pants were wrestling with a referee hovering close by. All of the players on the floor were dressed in uniform white cotton garments tied at the waist with belts of purple, brown, and black.

A bell sounded once and the match in progress stopped. As he sank into one of the many empty seats Seaton spotted Norma, sitting on her heels like all the others, as erect and motionless as an image of some Buddhist deity, but with her American features conspicuous among so many others of different endowment.

An official seated at a small table toward the end of the floor called out two names. In response two players arose, one from each side of the center area, and formally bowed to each other. Then, at a word of command, they stepped forward and each took hold of the front of his opponent's heavy cloth jacket. For approximately half a minute they maneuvered with what was obviously both speed and skill. They side-stepped, watched each other's feet, and occasionally turned their bodies sharply toward one another. Suddenly without warning one of the players was swept off his feet, whirled across his opponent's hip, and whacked solidly onto the mat.

"Ippon," the referee announced, and extended his arm in the direction of the man who had been victorious. There was more formal bowing before the defeated man sat down.

"Scott."

Seaton was jolted. He fully accepted the fact that Norma played this rough game and that she was good at it, but women simply did not contest with men except in mixed-doubles tennis and polite contests of that sort. The sheer brutality of body-to-body combat was acceptable in the prize ring, perhaps, but a man versus a woman was unthinkable.

Obviously this opinion was not held on the playing floor. Norma got easily to her feet, stepped forward to face the well-muscled victor of the previous contest, and exchanged a formal bow. Then she advanced into the combat area as though she were unaware of the privilege of her sex to decline such engagements.

The man seized hold of her jacket as she took his. From the gallery Seaton could see that she was wearing a black belt with a thin white line through it, but if anything it served to emphasize the slenderness of her waist—her physical unsuitability for a brute-force contest with a grown male.

Despite the knowledge that it was his place to keep quiet and do nothing, he half rose to his feet as though it were in some way his chivalrous duty to protest this gross mismatch. From that position he had an excellent view as Norma, moving like a flash of feminine lightning, spun her body, bent sharply, and sent her heavier opponent cleanly over her head. He landed with a sharp impact as the word *Ippon* echoed in the air.

When Seaton had seen her handily dispose of another challenger he was at least partially convinced that she could, if necessary, protect herself and would not cower in the background like a cringing movie heroine while the man in the white hat did her fighting for her.

The third man to face her was slightly older and obviously experienced. The two locked in combat after the usual formalities and for perhaps half a minute Norma appeared to be holding her own. Then the powerful man with flashing speed whirled on her and to his horror Seaton saw Norma's body swung through the air in a wide arc over her opponent's head. She landed with a smashing impact on the hard-appearing mat, but she still managed to regain her feet and to bow as the word *Ippon* was pronounced against her.

Seaton was struck by the thought that almost any normal female called upon to take a fall like that would probably be crippled for life. His mother had pounded into him the delicacy of womanhood, but the fragility she had depicted did not seem to apply to Norma Scott, who was undeniably a member of the gentler sex.

Abruptly the formal gathering broke up; Norma walked gracefully off the floor conversing pleasantly with the powerful brute who had just defeated her. Seaton went down the long stairs to the lobby and waited there, wrapped in thought, until Norma appeared, neat and fresh, looking very chic in an expensively styled dress.

"Hello there," she greeted him as she slipped her arm through his. "Did you have any trouble finding the place?"

"No," he answered, and then voiced his concern. "Are you all right?"

"Of course I'm all right, what did you expect?"

135

"I was sitting in the balcony and I saw you . . ."

She laughed. "Oh that. I got flipped, but Shig is a third-degree black belt, so I don't have to feel too bad about it. You can't win all the time, you know."

"Yes, but the fall you took; I was afraid . . ."

She tightened the pressure on his arm. "Nice of you to be concerned, but I took several thousand of those before I got my black belt. They teach you how. Now are you ready for something to eat?"

The place to which she took him was a tiny, out-of-the-way restaurant which could accommodate only a handful of patrons at a time. It was tucked in on one of the little back streets in the catacombs of the world's most confusing city. They shared an intimate little table which violated the Japanese sense of proportion by being more than three feet high and equipped with chairs in the hope that some foreigners might thereby be attracted.

"Do you like tempura?" Norma asked.

"I don't know what it is," Seaton confessed.

"Do you enjoy seafood?"

"Oh yes, certainly."

"Then you'll like tempura. I'll order some; this is one of the best places to get it in the city."

When the order had been placed Seaton remained silent for a bit while he attempted to arrange his thoughts into order. "Do you really enjoy that sort of physical combat?" he ventured at last, trying hard not to sound too conservative or stuffy.

"Well now, wrestling with a man can be a lot of fun if you go about it in the right way," Norma answered him. Her mouth quirked in amusement. "But I know what you mean. However, there isn't any reason at all that a girl shouldn't play judo and get a lot of benefit out of it. I usually stay off the mat when I'm menstruating and of course it's not the thing to do when you're pregnant, but hundreds and hundreds of girls do judo and love it. It's wonderful fun and marvelous exercise. Have you ever tried it?"

Seaton shook his head. "I've never been any good at sports. I'm not built for it, I don't seem to have any talent, and of course I have to wear glasses."

"You might be very good at basketball; you're tall and you've got a nice build."

Mercifully the waiter interrupted the conversation. He set little dishes of Japanese pickles on the table and provided chopsticks. Seaton broke them apart and fitted them properly into his fingers. "How's Mr. Sakamoto?" he asked.

"Just fine. He's out of the country right now on a business trip. He likes you a lot, by the way; he thinks you have much more ability than many people may have recognized."

Seaton dug his chopsticks into the shredded pickles, lowering his face a little to hide his embarrassment. The more or less studied order which had controlled his life for so long was now hopelessly out of gear. Everything was different in Japan. Here he was suddenly a man of promise, a man invited out by stunningly attractive girls, a man who, for the first time in his life, had been evaluated as an athlete.

"How do you like this country?" he asked. He knew that the question sounded inane, but he wanted to know.

Norma visibly reacted. "It's a wonderful place—so refreshingly different from some of the stuffiness back home. I love my own country of course, but I get awfully fed up at times with all the 'thou shalt nots.' The only thing I think is wrong is deliberately harming someone else—someone innocent, of course. Do you like it here?"

It was a surprise question for which he had no ready-made answer; he hadn't really thought about it in those terms. Then he remembered the moment when Masayo had kissed him in the moss garden. "I've never been so happy," he confessed.

Norma reached out a hand and laid it on his for a moment. "You know, Dick, I think that in some ways you've just been afraid to live. Maybe I shouldn't say that, but you're really quite nice. Take off those Boston blinders and you'll have the girls fighting over you." She gave him an impudent wink. "I fight pretty good myself for a female. Who knows?"

The waiter appeared with the tempura and a number of other dishes on a tray. Carefully he ladled paddles of white rice into small bowls, set the deep-fried shrimp in the middle of the table, and poured two minute cupfuls of green tea.

Under Norma's tutelage Seaton dipped the batter-covered pieces of tempura into the dark brown sauce and then bit off

137

small sections while he held them in his chopsticks. She had been right—the taste was wonderful and he enjoyed every bit of the meal—even the unsweetened tea which seemed to refresh his palate every time he took a sip. He tried to tell himself that he was now completely divorced from the life he had known up to now, that he was living in a new way in a remote part of the world.

Certainly his success here with women was an unexpected blessing. He looked frankly into Norma's face and saw a beauty who would never have given him a second glance at home; if he had asked her out she might have laughed at him. Yet here he was, in her company, at her invitation, eating exotic food in a tiny gourmet restaurant of the Far East.

Suddenly he felt himself a new man. He was the Saint, Colonel Hugh North, Handsome West, all come to life in the person of himself—Richard Emmett Seaton. Only one thing was missing—according to the standard plot three desperate thugs should enter at any moment and assault his beautiful companion. It would then be his role to go into instant, unpremeditated action and to dispose of them in thirty seconds or so with lethal karate skill. That he knew he could not do; he had never taken a boxing lesson in his life.

It struck him that in the manly art of self-defense his delightful companion was almost indecently capable—probably even more so than himself. It was a biting thought; he overcame it by telling himself that she probably couldn't design even a simple transformer if her life depended upon it.

When the meal was over he paid two thousand yen for all they had eaten and then hailed a cab with newfound skill. They wove through the traffic, Norma sitting close beside him as though it pleased her to be there, until they reached the sumo hall.

It was a large auditorium charged with the atmosphere which always precedes a major sporting event. They were shown to a small private area close to ringside where there were no chairs, only a straw mat on which to sit. Seaton got down and contorted himself into the least objectionable posture he could manage while Norma seated herself on her heels, Japanese style, with ease. She looked very charming that way, with her skirt spread about her almost as though she were a life-sized animated doll. For a moment he had a

138

Miss One Thousand Spring Blossoms

sudden surge of feeling about her, a crazy desire to take her into his arms.

The mood passed almost as suddenly as it had come, as people flowed in a steady stream into the huge hall and seated themselves where they could watch the action to follow. Presently the first of the contestants appeared, wearing astonishingly brief trunks which failed to conceal their bare buttocks, and all attention turned to the small ring where an ornately dressed referee was gesturing with his fan.

As a wrestling exhibition Seaton found sumo to be a disappointment. There seemed to be far too many ceremonial preliminaries, false starts, and scatterings of salt to purify the ring. When at last the real action began, it was all over in a matter of seconds. Then two more performers appeared and the whole opening ritual had to be repeated in full. One or two of the contests did offer a little excitement, but the premium was clearly on huge size and pure weight.

When the evening was almost over, a gigantic wrestler appeared who wore an apron embroidered with the words "Go For Broke" in English.

"That's Jesse," Norma told him. "He's an American, from Hawaii. He's a big favorite despite the fact that he's a foreigner; the Japanese are proud that he is following their traditions. Watch him."

Seaton did watch and saw him handily dispose of an equally massive opponent in perhaps a half-minute of action. When the match was concluded Norma laid a hand on his arm. "If you've seen enough, let's go," she suggested. "I know it isn't comfortable for you sitting that way and sumo, like sashimi, is an acquired taste. How about a good cup of coffee?"

For answer Seaton untangled himself and got to his feet, helping his date up in the process. They slipped out quietly during the next set of foot-pounding challenges and escaped into the open air. This time Norma raised her hand for a cab and when they were inside supplied the driver with an address in effortless Japanese.

"You speak the language well," Seaton told her in honest admiration.

She shrugged it off. "Just enough to get by. Actually it's not hard when you get on to it. In many ways it's simpler than English."

139

"Isn't everything?" he asked.

"I think so. We're going up to my place, do you mind?"

"Of course not."

As Norma unlocked the door of her apartment without expecting her escort to do it for her, Seaton realized that this would be the first time that he had crossed a private threshold in Japan. As his hostess pushed upon the door and flicked on the light inside, he was genuinely interested to see what sort of an interior would be revealed. It was also the first time in his memory that he had entered a young woman's private quarters, particularly late in the evening.

The room in which he found himself was small, but artfully designed to make the most of its dimensions. The furniture was Western in type but Eastern in design, so that it was both suited to its owner and an integral part of the exotic culture in which she had chosen to live.

"It's warm," Norma said. "Park your briefcase, take off your coat and shoes, and be comfortable. I'm going to change."

Hoping that it was the right thing to do, Seaton complied while his companion absented herself through a sliding panel doorway which quite obviously led to her bedroom. She was gone only briefly when she reappeared wearing a long white silk garment with the characteristic oversize sleeves of a kimono. It was nothing like the elaborate garments Miss One Thousand Spring Blossoms wore; it was instead casual in the extreme without sacrificing an iota of the dignity of Japanese traditional design. As Norma walked over to a small wooden bar and raised the lid, Seaton became aware, despite himself, that underneath the cool and comfortable garment she was wearing nothing else at all.

She did not ask him his preference, instead she mixed two cocktails, poured them into double-size glasses, and then came over to sit beside him.

"Tired?" she asked after she had sipped her drink.

He sampled his before replying and found it different. He did not know what was in it, but it pleased him with its lingering taste. "Yes," he confessed. "But we're making good progress; I'll be able to go home in a few more days' time."

Norma turned her body until she was facing him, one foot tucked underneath her. "Want to?"

Seaton rolled his glass between his hands while he debated

140

his answer. "No," he admitted finally, "I should say that I'm anxious to get back to the things I'm used to, to the life I've laid out for myself, but I honestly can't. I can't speak the language here, I don't understand most of the customs, but ..." He turned and looked at her squarely. "Maybe I've been leading too dull a life."

Norma consulted her drink. "I'm sure of it. When we first met, you were stiff as a board. Maybe that's a bad choice of words; I mean that you were, let's say, unrelaxed."

Seaton nodded. "I'm not used to being with girls ... as beautiful as you."

Norma set her glass down carefully, then slid over to him and offered herself to be kissed. She looked once quickly at his face and then said, "Shut your eyes."

He obeyed, and then felt Norma's warm body almost next to his own. One or two layers of thin fabric was all that kept them apart. She pressed warm wet lips against his own for a full three seconds and then, after a pause, gently drew herself away. "Tell me what you're doing," she invited, her voice clearly making it a change of subject. "I understand it's some sort of new product."

Seaton took out his folded handkerchief and carefully wiped his brow. Then he readjusted his glasses and searched for his composure.

"Yes, it's a rather intricate assembly for a new kind of tester we're planning on building."

Norma curled up easily, beside him but still far enough away to let him recover himself.

"Is Matsumoto the only company developing it for you?"

"At present, yes."

Norma picked up her drink again. "I'm going to tell you something: George Sakamoto is one of the most successful men in Japan. Among other things he owns an electronics company. You ought to get a bid from him."

Seaton tried his own drink once more and decided that he liked it very much. "I'd like to, but we've pretty much promised the business to the Matsumoto people and they've been very cooperative."

"That isn't what I meant." Norma's voice and manner were both relaxed. "George is completely ethical in everything he does, by both Western and Japanese standards; he isn't after

141

Matsumoto's customers. But if Matsumoto had a fire or something like that, then it might be weeks before they could get back into production. In a case like that it could be a big help to you to have George to turn to."

Seaton leaned back and let his tired brain relax its control of his every thought and movement. "If I gave you a set of the blueprints, could you pass them on to him?"

"Of course, if you'd like me to."

"All right." He reached over for his briefcase, opened it, and pulled out a manila envelope. "Then give this to him. You say he's to be trusted?"

"Absolutely." Norma raised her right hand, palm toward him, and then dropped it back into her lap.

"Then tell him I'd appreciate a cost estimate per unit in lots of one hundred."

Norma took the envelope and laid it casually aside. "Dick, you're dead on your feet, I can see it. I'm going to draw a hot bath for you and I want you to take it. Then, when you've soaked out all the cares of the day, or better yet—I may join you."

Seaton looked at her blankly. "In the bathtub?" he inquired.

She looked level eyes at him across the top of her cocktail glass. "It's quite the thing over here. It's one of the nice things about the country. Let's make it a night, shall we?"

With the impact of a multi-car collision three ideas smashed themselves together in his brain. The first was the utter desirability of Norma and the incredible fact that she was offering herself to him. The second was the formidable lifetime of conditioning which unfurled the word *immoral* before him like a sacred banner that no one dare defile. The third, and the most powerful of all, was the acute and sensitive memory of the moment when he had bid Masayo Kanno good-night when he might, perhaps, have soared to the summit of Olympus instead.

He reached out his arm and very slowly let his fingers take hold of the fabric of his coat. Then he hung his head while tears came into his eyes. He would have to go home.

Five minutes or so later Norma kissed him good-night with passionless friendliness at her door and whispered something pleasant in Japanese. Hardly aware of what he was doing he

142

went down the small elevator, hailed a passing empty cab, and rode back to his hotel. Mechanically he undressed and fell onto his bed, hating every bone, muscle, and conditioned response in his body. He wanted desperately to be a man and he was afraid to become one.

Chapter Fifteen

By half past three the following afternoon the gloom which hung over the Matsumoto Company was thick enough to have been cut into strips and sold for viewing eclipses. Every possible misfortune which could or could not have been anticipated seemed to have either already occurred or to be waiting in the wings.

It had actually all begun the day before. The disastrous news that Setanu san was to spend the evening, probably until a most advanced hour, in the company of Miss Norma Scott was not underestimated by any member of the organization acquainted with her. In the morning it became Mr. Yamaguchi's painful duty to inform his superior that Setanu san had indeed attended the sumo tournament with Miss Scott and he had been seen with her sitting in the box normally occupied by George Sakamoto. Furthermore, immediately after the American star had appeared, they had been seen leaving together with Setanu san still carrying his briefcase.

This made it necessary to phone the geisha house and launch a counterattack at full list price plus expenses. This single step was enough to erase the last hope for even a modest profit from the Mercer and Doyle account for at least the next two years—many many components would have to be built and shipped before the geisha fees already incurred would be recovered.

For the first time Matsumoto san began to understand, in a vague way, why they did not have geisha in America: they couldn't afford them.

Then, in midafternoon there came a piece of news which made Matsumoto san, the secret poet, bury his face in his hands and wonder if it would not be best to don the white kimono and end it all in the traditional way of honor. An ashen-faced Mr. Fujihara had appeared, leaned on the desk, and stammered out the disastrous tidings—the new component would not check out.

In this desperate crisis Matsumoto made his way to the engineering department to view the catastrophe with his own eyes. He himself had a very limited knowledge of electronics— he depended upon his technical staff, headed by Mr. Fujihara, for that. He was a businessman, the executive manager of the enterprise which bore his name, but he could not permit everything he had worked for to shatter into fragments without at least seeing the cause of it all.

There in the developmental section was the complicated piece of apparatus which Seaton had constructed to test the new product. There, when it was pointed out to him, he saw the beautifully constructed assembly which his workers had produced. Gathered about were two or three of his most capable engineering people who looked as though they had just seen an *obake*. An obake, it needs to be added here, is a Japanese ghost considerably more frightening than some of the venerable practitioners who ply their trade in the mustier mansions of England.

There was Setanu san, the man who had to be pleased, patiently at work tracing out a key circuit one more time. The results were forewritten—the Matsumoto component was defective. In the awful stillness of that terrible moment Reiko Watanabe ventured to intrude to announce that Setanu san was desired by the telephone. Miss Kanno Masayo was calling.

As the American engineer left to answer the summons, Mr. Fujihara supplied a brief rundown of the situation. "It must be one of three things," he explained carefully. "First, the basic design could be wrong, in which case the Americans are to blame. Secondly, the testing device could be at fault, but this I doubt because I worked with Setanu san on it and I find nothing whatever to criticize in the work he did; he is a very fine engineer. Lastly, and this I fear to be the truth, something is seriously incorrect in our product. But it is a fact that the assembly will not work."

"It could perhaps be a small thing?" Mr. Matsumoto asked hopefully.

"If our work contains an insect, as the Americans say, we shall locate it and it will be removed. But I cannot promise you that it will be that simple. It will be necessary to go back to the blueprints and study them from the beginning—perhaps there the trouble may be found."

"Has Setanu san a duplicate set of the prints?" Matsumoto asked. "If so, then we should apply our utmost efforts to both sets in order to find out where the trouble lies."

Mr. Fujihara recalled the messengers of ancient times who, when they brought bad news, were often slain on the spot for thus disturbing the tranquility of their masters.

"He did have a set, sir, but he told me that last evening he entrusted them to Miss Scott Norma—I believe you know the rest."

"I am leaving for the day," Mr. Matsumoto announced. "I am going to the temple to meditate. You are authorized to do whatever is necessary until I return. If I fail to do so, a copy of my will is located in the upper left-hand drawer of my desk. Sayonara."

Meanwhile Seaton had been trying to straighten out his own thoughts without distinguished success. The coming of morning had brought with it a sharpened realization of exactly what he had done and what he had not done the night before. He asked himself one harsh and pointed question: if he chose to push aside Norma Scott's offered companionship and intimacy, then precisely what was it he was waiting for? She was a genuine beauty, enormously appealing, intelligent, and she appeared to like him.

He slashed his razor across his face hoping that he might cut himself as punishment for incredible stupidity and stuffiness. The prim and parochial voice of conscience told him that first

146

must come marriage, that other matters could follow only after that essential step had been taken first.

"And how in the hell," Seaton had demanded of his conscience, "am I supposed to find a bride if I continue to insult the most desirable girls I could possibly imagine?" There was no other word for it—turning down a lady's favor when it was freely offered was insulting, patronizing, and—probably—unforgivable.

If Norma Scott never looked at him again in his lifetime, he deserved it. To punish himself, he imagined, for just a few seconds, that he had accepted the gift which had been so generously offered. He pictured himself lying in a soft bed, with just a thin sheet covering him and with Norma there beside him, her warm, intimate inspiring body next to his. There was no shame in this, no peekabooing at forbidden anatomy, but only a man and a woman together as they were created to be.

The image was so sharp in his mind, so charged with the frustration of "it could have been," he had to grit his teeth to control himself. He had sold his birthright for a mess of outdated moral pottage—he could not view it any other way. He had been denied too long; his manhood refused to be confined any more. He had always lived a so-called moral life because he would not have the crime of seduction laid against his name, and he had an instinctive distaste for the services of a professional prostitute. Such a public woman would be akin to going into a restaurant and eating his meal off the unwashed plate of some unknown person who had preceded him. But Normal Norma who embodied everything desirable, whose kiss had stunned him so he had been literally unable to move.

He had thought of grabbing the telephone to tell her at once how he felt—then he realized that he had no idea where or how to reach her. It had been a preposterous idea anyway, what he had done he could not undo now. All he could do was to hate himself for being Richard Emmett Seaton, the mother-raised imbecile. . . . He stopped and tried to take hold of himself. Consciously he thought about Masayo and let the image of her lovely presence float before his mind. He saw himself waiting for her, holding himself back so that she should be the one. As he dressed he tried with fierce concentration to conjure up again the touch of her lips in the moss garden, the slender unspectacular figure she made as she stood on the flat rock and gave him something of herself.

In that way he kept his sanity and came to work to begin the checking out of the new component. It was not until one o'clock that he had learned that something was wrong, not until three that he had satisfied himself that it was not merely a simple open connection or some other easily remedied fault. Then he almost lost control of himself; when poor little Reiko Watanabe tried to talk to him he was almost savage with her. Reiko knew, of course, that he had had a date with Norma the night before, but to her the American's terrifying displeasure was probably the result of the failure of Norma san to entertain him as he had hoped and wanted. Of course there could have been the usual reason, but even then she need not have left him in a state of such bitter agitation.

Now, over the telephone, came the cool sea breeze of restoration—the voice of Masayo Kanno. She spoke for herself this time, in hesitant English, but he did not require grammar and syntax from her—only the sounds which came from between her lips.

He asked her out for that evening before she had a chance to advance the excuse for her call. When he went back to the engineering department the clouds were still gathered heavily over his head, but there were breaks in the overcast and crepuscular rays of sunshine slanted down to form patterns of brightness.

On the following morning, when Seaton arrived for work earlier than usual, he found a hollow-eyed Mr. Fujihara already bent over the equipment, testing one of the minor circuits. Almost at once Reiko appeared with tea; while she was serving it she informed Seaton that Fujihara san had not left the plant until three in the morning and that he had had only about two hours' sleep.

A strong sense of guilt hit Seaton; he had spent the evening taking his delectable date to an American movie while his colleague had been driving himself to solve their common problem. He stripped off his coat, took his tea while he worked, and plunged into the job with all the energy and

148

capability that he could muster. Since the checking was largely a one-man job, he advised Fujihara to go into the conference room and get some rest while he took over. This the Japanese engineer refused to do, but he accepted with appreciation Setanu san's good wishes.

Working together, by early afternoon they had the answer—the original design prepared in the United States was at fault. Through Reiko the matter was discussed, something which almost drove the willing little interpreter out of her mind. She did not know the technical terms they attempted to use and they were not in her dictionary. Time after time Mr. Fujihara drew characters on a piece of paper for her to read, but the language of electronics at this level of technicality was totally beyond her. Gradually, by simplifying his questions, the Japanese engineer managed to get through but it was not easy.

"Do you have a working prototype back in the United States?" he asked.

"Yes," Seaton answered, "but it doesn't contain this assembly. We breadboarded a mock-up to check out the concept and then designed this afterward."

In swift Japanese Fujihara asked Reiko if Seaton's initials were on the blueprints as either designer or draftsman. She glanced at the plans and told him that this was not the case—whoever had made the mistake, it was not Seaton san.

"I am greatly grieved to say this," Fujihara began and had his words translated, "but I must offer the opinion that whatever is wrong is most likely in the original design. I have myself checked your testing equipment and find it in perfect order. I have four times gone over every part of our assembly and it is made as specified."

It took Reiko almost five minutes to render this into English with the proper degree of diplomatic restraint. When she had finished, Seaton nodded. "I agree, Mr. Fujihara; you are, in my opinion, correct. I have also checked your product and it is exactly as designed. The testing equipment seems to be in order. The fault is entirely ours."

When this was made clear to him, Fujihara rested his hands against the workbench. "Then let us redesign it together," he proposed. "I am sure that we can if we combine our efforts."

Seaton felt a stronger bond between himself and this smaller

149

man with jet black hair whose intelligence he had come to respect and whose companionship he valued and enjoyed. "We will do it together," he echoed, "and when we finish, it will be better than it would have been if it had worked the first time."

Silently Fujihara offered his hand. "The last time I faced such a problem I failed. The cost to our company was very great—I tried to do something which cannot be done. Now, in a small way, I shall try to redeem myself."

Seaton turned to the interpreter. "Reiko san, will you do me a favor? Please tell Mr. Yamaguchi that it will be impossible for me to accept his kind invitation to tour some of the beauty spots of Japan this weekend. If he has made any reservations, cancel them. You can explain why."

Reiko disappeared to discharge her errand; as soon as she had left, another girl appeared with fresh tea and a cold, milky Japanese drink on a beautiful lacquer tray. With many bows she offered the refreshment and withdrew.

In silence, because they could not speak each other's language, the two engineers sat together and enjoyed the interval of rest and relaxation. But they communicated nonetheless in the empathy which exists between human beings who like and respect each other, in Seaton's mind was the thought that it would be wonderful if the capable Japanese engineer might come and work for Mercer and Doyle. He would have to learn English, but he would be a wonderful addition to the staff in every respect. He thrust out of his mind the possible reaction of Messieurs Mercer and Williamson to the thought of a foreigner in their engineering department—that matter could be considered later.

They did not leave the plant until after eight that evening and only then because Seaton realized that his colleague was almost literally out on his feet from fatigue and continuous mental exertion. At that hour Reiko Watanabe was still standing by, her well-worn dictionary clutched in her left hand, wondering how much longer she would be able to keep up with the task of translation which was normally well beyond her powers.

When at last they agreed to call it a day, Seaton hustled Reiko outside and informed her that he was about to buy her dinner. She protested at once that she was not hungry and would eat at home, but in part making up for his lack of decision the night before, he took her by the arm and hailed a cab.

Once free of the plant and of the need to translate the intricate jargon of electronics, Reiko began to relax and Seaton found that she was an appealing feminine companion. She was enthusiastic about his improving skill with chopsticks, and with justice—he handled them now with easy assurance. They were no good for eating a steak or ice cream, but when it came to characteristic Japanese food, which was served in small pieces, he did very well indeed. Reiko asked many questions about the United States and jotted down several words which she wanted to add to her English vocabulary.

Toward the close of the meal, when they had each had enough sake to loosen things up a bit, he suddenly asked, "Reiko, are you married? I don't know if it is Miss or Mrs. Watanabe."

"Miss," Reiko answered, not too easily. "I come from a poor family, Seaton san, and I do not have enough to offer to become a good man's wife."

Seaton leaned toward her. "Reiko, listen—I want to tell you something. The man who marries you will be very, very lucky. You are a very fine person, you are certainly intelligent, and you are also very lovely." He felt that in this last statement he was exaggerating a little, but while Reiko lacked the magic of Masayo Kanno, or the pure facial beauty of Norma Scott, her features were decidedly agreeable and any man who would not enjoy looking at them would have to have something wrong with him.

Reiko buried her chin on her chest and began to cry.

Seaton produced a handkerchief, took her face into his hands, and wiped her tears away. "Another thing," he said. "My name is Dick. Now you can speak English, so you can say it without it coming out 'Diku.' Let's hear it."

With moist eyes Reiko looked at him. "Dick," she managed.

"That's right—from now on you're to call me that all the time, understand? No more Seaton san, not even if Mr. Matsumoto himself is around."

151

When they had finished eating she begged to be excused. When Seaton insisted that he see her home, she confessed that her neighborhood was far too humble for him to visit.

With a new sense of decision, Seaton hailed a kamikaze and held Reiko under his outstretched arm during the wild ride that followed. At last they were deposited at the head of an unpaved alley-street which had a benjo ditch down one side. The houses were all small, wooden, completely Japanese structures, each with a small stone outside on which the residents and guests could leave their shoes before entering.

They walked down a block and turned a narrow corner, then Reiko paused. "It is here that I live, Dick san, together with my mother."

"May I have the pleasure of meeting her?" Seaton asked.

"If that is your wish, but we are very humble people." She pushed open a gate and entered a front yard which was hardly five feet square. Then she slipped out of her shoes, knocked on the doorframe, and called inside in softly accented Japanese.

After perhaps a minute an elderly woman appeared, stooped from hard work, her face a maze of wrinkles. She bowed profusely several times without stopping, an action which accentuated the severely plain black kimono she wore.

"Dick san, this is my mother," Reiko said. Then she spoke again to the elderly woman. Her words set off another cycle of bowing which was almost embarrassing in its intensity. "Please to come in," Reiko said.

Seaton bent down and loosened the ties of his shoes. When he had stepped out of them Reiko motioned that he was to go first, that he must precede her into the house. Stooping slightly to avoid hitting his head on the low doorframe he walked in and found himself in a very plain little room floored with a half-dozen tatami mats. A picture hung on a wall and there was a tiny tokanoma with the usual flower arrangement and a scroll. Beyond that there was little else and the house itself was so small there did not seem to be any space for bedrooms or very much in the way of a storage area.

Reiko dropped to her knees and sat down Japanese style on

152

the tatami; Seaton was about to do the same when Mrs. Watanabe appeared hurrying with tiny steps to bring in a cushion. He accepted it as gracefully as he could manage and sat down, curling his legs beside himself as he had learned to do. It was not the Japanese way, but the standard heel-sitting position he had found almost impossible to master.

Again Mrs. Watanabe hurried in, carrying a small low table which she set in the middle of the floor. With a swish of her slippers she again vanished, leaving Seaton with the feeling that by accepting the invitation to come in he was putting his hostess to a great deal of trouble. He could think of nothing intelligent or appropriate to say—he could hardly compliment the room since there was nothing in it to discuss, nor could he praise the house as he would have done automatically at home. He remained strangely tongue-tied while Reiko sat quietly and without movement. Here in her own home she was a traditional daughter, which meant that she was forbidden to speak until a remark was addressed to her.

Mrs. Watanabe returned again, this time carrying a tray. She set it down and removed three tiny tea services of decorated china which she arranged on the table.

"Please," Seaton said, "she's going to too much trouble. It isn't at all necessary."

"If she does not serve tea," Reiko explained, "she will utterly lose face. She is from the old style."

The shuffling feet of the tiny elderly woman sounded again on the tatamis, this time she had the teapot and a small plate of Japanese cookies. She sank to her knees before the table, poured the tea with a shaking hand, and then offered the cookies to Seaton almost as though she were placing an offering on some temple altar.

The American accepted one, embarrassed now to be the center of so much attention and trouble. When the moment seemed appropriate he picked up his teacup, touched it to his lips, and then said, "Oishii." He did not remember where he had learned that word, but he was somehow aware that it was the proper thing to say when offered food or refreshment.

At once Mrs. Watanabe bowed three more times from her sitting position and spoke to her daughter.

Reiko translated. "My mother says that you do us great

153

honor. For two hundred years this house has been builded, for the first time you are foreigner who come in through the door."

It was almost impossible for Seaton to bow while sitting, but he attempted it anyway. "Please tell your mother that it is I who am honored. It is a great pleasure for me to meet her."

When Reiko had put this into Japanese her mother outdid herself in still more bowing, then she spoke briefly.

"She much regrets that our home is so humble."

"The house is small," he replied, "but the hearts are very great and good."

Although he did not know it, that speech, when put into Japanese, lifted from his elderly hostess the terror which had clutched her from the first moment she had become aware she was to entertain the great Setanu san from America. She knew nothing of foreigners and was afraid of them. This one, while a giant, was gentle in his manner. The words which her daughter spoke were almost like a haiku poem—a sign of the highest culture and learning. Clearly Setanu san was a *sensei,* a very great man, and she was overwhelmed by his presence.

When the tea had been drunk Seaton rose to go. He expressed his warm thanks through Reiko and made his way to the door. "Dick san," Reiko said, "to go back to your hoteru it is best you take the train. I will show." Deftly she slipped into her shoes and waited for him to tie his. When at last he was ready he bowed once more to his hostess and then turned to let Reiko guide him toward the station.

It was a brief walk, but a revelation to him. The modern complexity of Tokyo was completely gone, instead he might have been in some remote village. The people they passed were largely in kimono, and for the first time he heard the clatter of geta on the hard ground. Tiny little open-front shops lined each side of the roadway, which was hardly more than eight feet wide. In the dimly lit interiors all sorts of merchandise was on display with sometimes all-but-invisible attendants behind the counters or at the side of the stall.

Presently they reached the little plaza where the train station was located. Reiko took him up to the ticket window, pushed a coin underneath the wicket, and spoke in Japanese. She got back a bit of cardboard and a tiny aluminum coin, one yen. At the gateway she spoke to the attendant, who nodded and let her pass through to escort Seaton onto the platform. "This train take you to Tokyo station," she explained. "There you make taxi to hoteru."

Seaton turned to her. "Thank you, Reiko. Thank you for your company at dinner, and for the visit to your home."

She bowed to him. "It has made my mother and I much happy."

He looked quickly and saw that the platform was all but deserted. He took her hands, bent down, and kissed her gently. Two days before he would not have done that, but he was learning.

Reiko was startled. "For me, Dick san?" she asked, remembering that for him a kiss in public was not the same as it was for her.

"For you. Thank you again for everything."

"Sayonara," Reiko said.

"Sayonara."

The following morning, which was Friday, brought with it rain, something which suited Mr. Matsumoto's mood perfectly. In one sense he was greatly relieved, the failure of the component to operate properly lay in its faulty design, therefore his company was not responsible. This single blessing was more than offset by a number of other considerations, all of which were on the negative side. He had already been informed that Sakamoto san had returned from the Philippines and therefore was presumably ready to go to work on Setanu san to get the Mercer and Doyle account. He had a duplicate set of the blueprints. He also had Miss Scott Norma who was exceedingly effective and who did not charge by the hour for her companionship.

The bill from the geisha house lay on his desk and would have to be met very promptly to avoid loss of face. Immediately beside it lay the neatly piled payroll vouchers which could not be delayed under any circumstances.

Lastly, the need for perhaps considerable redesign effort meant that Setanu san would not be returning home as soon as otherwise might have been the case. It was a choice of leaving him open to skilled attack by Sakamoto san, or else running the bill at the geisha house higher still. The morning

155

mail, in fact the mail all week, had contained no new business—not even any reorders. The rain continued to patter down and trace psychedelic pathways on the window panes.

The intercom box on his desk came alive for a moment or two; Mr. Yamaguchi asked if it was a convenient time to come in. Half a minute later he was comfortably seated and ready to discuss matters with his chief.

"I will begin with pleasant news," he said. "Yesterday evening our distinguished guest from America worked here quite late. He then took Reiko san to dinner and later visited her home. This means he was both well separated from Miss Scott Norma and from the attractions of the geisha house as well. We lucked out."

Matsumoto was impressed. "Shingiro, do you think that there is the slightest hope that Setanu san might transfer his affections to our English interpreter? If so, I would gladly raise her salary to cover any inconveniences."

Yamaguchi pondered that. "Reiko san is a very nice girl," he allowed. "She is well trained, can comprehend English, and being Japanese automatically outclasses Scott san."

"We must entertain the possibility that Setanu san might not see it in that light. Being American himself, he may not be able to distinguish the fine points which make the difference. Scott Norma is not to be underestimated."

"True. She has just been promoted to Nidan at the Kodokan; second-degree black belts are not awarded to barbarians."

Mr. Matsumoto thought for a moment. "Reiko san is a very desirable young person," he allowed. "It is possible to describe her as attractive. But to stack her up against the geisha Fujikoma is like asking a good bush-league pitcher to face both Nagashima and Oh with the bases full and nobody out."

Yamaguchi nodded. "I am forced to agree; I respect Setanu san for being so nice to our young lady when he has experienced the headier wines. He is a gentleman and has greatly improved my opinion of Americans."

"Mine also," Matsumoto agreed. "Apart from the expense he represents, I am in no hurry to see him go home."

"Which brings us to the crux of the matter: the weekend is

156

before us. Setanu san has declined the offer of a trip to Miyajima, I suspect to save us money."

That thought so shook good Mr. Matsumoto that he forgot himself and took the name of Lord Buddha in vain. "Have you observed any lessening of his interest in Fujikoma?" he asked when he had recovered himself.

"Only the fact that he has seen her only once this week, and that for a comparatively short time. But he has been busy: it would not surprise me if he has her very much on his mind for this weekend."

"The weekend!" Matsumoto groaned.

Yamaguchi raised a cautioning hand. "I know, but consider this: he does not seek pillow service, which is a major economy. The bill this past week has been comparatively moderate. He insists on paying all of the expenses himself, since he believes that he is entertaining the lady and does not imagine that it is the other way around."

"True," Matsumoto agreed.

"And if he does not see our beautiful candidate for his attentions, I can without hesitation name another young lady he might seek out who could be vastly more expensive for us. At least Fujikoma only charges by the hour."

Mr. Matsumoto shifted in his chair. "Instruct Fujihara that Setanu san is to be discouraged from working here this weekend. Call the geisha house and engage the grl to entertain Setanu san as before. See if you can get a favorable rate—though I doubt it. Suggest to Setanu san that he take her somewhere not within convenient range of Sakamoto George and the potentially diastrous female in his employ. He does not know Japan and will require guidance."

"Atami is a nice romantic place," Mr. Yamaguchi suggested.

Mr. Matsumoto shut his eyes tightly for a moment. "It most certainly is," he agreed.

Chapter Sixteen

S aturday was a picture postcard day. A thin haze hung in the air, but the rain, which had lasted through most of the night, was gone and the sun was out blessing the land. On the beautiful coast highway below Kamakura a sleek, comfortable, air-conditioned sight-seeing bus purred along in midmorning, offering to the tourists on board a fine view of the Pacific and of the Picture Island which was one of the advertised attractions of the trip.

Inside the bus the seats were all oversize and set farther apart than is usual in Japanese vehicles, for the benefit of the larger-sized people they had been designed to accommodate. The driver bent over his wheel and the safety girl in her neat uniform perched beside him on her jump seat, while the tour conductor, microphone in hand, called attention to the points of interest along the way.

Halfway back on the right-hand side Dick Seaton leaned back and tried to convince himself that this was all reality. He had expected to spend the weekend hard at work at the Matsumoto plant, but as Friday afternoon reached the midpoint and the tea break, Mr. Fujihara had been struck by an inspiration. He insisted that he take the plans home for the next two days in order to put his theory to the test. If he was right, then it was entirely possible the difficulty they faced might be resolved quickly and easily.

After that things had moved with remarkable smoothness. He had hoped to call Masayo if possible; now he was suddenly free to do so. He was still turning over in his mind exactly what he would say when Reiko appeared at his elbow on some minor errand and, after discharging it, asked if she could be of any help to him.

Together they went into the conference room and placed the call. Fortunately Masayo was at home: after the usual polite preliminaries Seaton inquired through the interpreter if she had any time free during the weekend.

The geisha replied that she had been working very hard and would welcome a holiday in his company.

Seaton was not familiar with the Oriental concept of total bliss which is Nirvana, but if anyone had tried to explain it to him at that moment, he would have understood perfectly. He asked Reiko to find out if there was any particular place Miss Kanno would like to visit, anything she would like to see.

The seashore resort of Atami was suggested and of course accepted. Reiko promised to make all the arrangements and did so while Seaton was back conferring with Mr. Fujihara. She remembered that the New Tokaido Line went to Atami, but she herself would have much preferred the beautiful ride through the mountains by bus. She therefore made the appropriate reservations, set them up for lunch at the picturesque Hakone Hotel, and booked them into the Onoya Inn for dinner and the night. After she had done all that she took a deep breath, allowed herself to wish for moment that it might have been she, and then remembered that she had been trained as an interpreter, not as a beautifully schooled professional companion. Atami was a lovely dream; someday, perhaps, she might go there too.

Presently the bus left the shoreline road and began to enter the mountain region where the air had a clarity which suggested that the world had only just been born. As the driver shifted gears to begin the long steady climb Seaton turned his head and looked once again at his companion. She smiled back at him and touched the back of his hand with her

159

fingers. It was not a professional smile she gave him, but an honest and truthful one. Then she turned to look out the wide window at the unfolding scenery.

Seaton studied her profile; he found it even more attractive than the panorama gradually being revealed as the bus climbed higher. Her nose was small, but well formed and without a hint of flattening. Her lips were all but perfect; she wore only light makeup which suited her perfectly—there was no need to gild the lily. Her forehead had a gentle curve which was well set off by the simple but tasteful hair arrangement she wore. Like all Japanese, her hair was raven black, but even if it had been dark brown like Norma's, it would not have suited her as well.

Her eyes, of course, were different—different if you studied them. They were smooth at the inner corners betraying her Mongolian ancestors, and there was a slight arch to them which added to her beauty. After almost two weeks in Japan Seaton had adjusted completely to this minor alteration of appearance. As he noted again her almost perfect complexion he realized that apart from the tiny difference in the shape of her eyes, she might well have been any one of the famed beauties whose exploits adorned the pages of European history. If Napoleon had seen this gorgeous creature, it might well have been to hell with Josephine.

A little self-consciously he noted her trim and gently molded figure. She was feminine but not in the least obtrusive, something which won his unqualified approval. Since his evening with Mr. Futaba at the Nichigeki Music Hall he had become somewhat more aware of what is politely known as curves; on his scale of values his companion swung the needle over until it hit the pin. He was grateful that she was not overendowed and therefore conspicuous.

The tour conductor interrupted his thoughts with the announcement that they were about to enter Fuji-Hakone National Park. Presently the party would leave the bus to cross Lake Hakone by catamaran to Kojiri. There those who wished to do so would be able to ride down on the spectacular cable tramway across the volcanic areas to the vicinity of the hotel where luncheon would be served.

The trip was delightful. The boat ride across the lake

Miss One Thousand Spring Blossoms

brought a fresh inviting breeze, and the descent on the high-swung cable car seemed dangerous enough to provide a blood-quickening sense of adventure. The hotel lunch, while typical tourist fare, was good and well served. The meal was just concluding when the tour conductor came to their table to inform them that a private car was waiting to take them on into Atami. Everything had been taken care of by the Japan Travel Service, which seemed incapable of making a mistake.

They had ridden only a little way in the car, which was furnished with both a driver and a guide, when a turn in the road brought a breathtaking view of mighty Fujiyama. Automatically the driver stopped.

Standing in the open air close to the high roadway Seaton studied the propositions of the incomparable mountain which seemed to be the special gift of the Creator to this land of so many artists, poets, and designers.

"Nothing, anywhere, can be as magnificent as this," he said. He wondered if any human being could ever fully appreciate this sublime sight.

"Fujisan is great pride of Japan," Masayo said. "My geisha name, it is part from him. You understand?"

He took her hand. "Yes, and you deserve it. I have heard of Fujiyama all my life, but I never imagined that it was so splendid."

They stood there together for several minutes absorbing the magic of the unrivaled mountain and sensing the near-eternity that it represented. When at last they could take in no more, they turned back to continue the drive. The guide was pleased that they were both so impressed with Japan's finest spectacle; in better than passable English he chatted with Seaton and exchanged views about the scenic charm of the country. The car wove its way down steadily until the sparkling ocean swept into view and the buildings of Atami clustered together against the foothills.

The Onoya Inn was beautiful. It lay close to the ocean in a parklike garden; it was a sizable structure of many floors, but still designed with Japanese simplicity. As the car pulled into the driveway bellboys were immediately on hand to take care of the luggage.

161

Miss One Thousand Spring Blossoms

The only real difference in entering the ample modern lobby as compared with Western-style hotels was the need to take off street shoes and substitute slippers, dozens of pairs of which waited in immaculate rows. There were even some of large size so this time Seaton was fitted without delay. He registered at the desk where their reservations were in order.

"It is our understanding that you wish one separate sleeping room," the desk clerk said. "We have assigned you one large room with the best view for eating and resting. The extra sleeping room is smaller, but close by. Is that satisfactory?"

"Very much so," Seaton agreed. "I appreciate the trouble you have taken."

"It is no trouble at all, sir. Your room awaits you, I trust you will find it to your taste."

In slippered feet they followed the bellboy as he led them up a flight of stairs, down a short corridor, past a miniature indoor garden, up another flight, and then down a hallway where he unlocked a door. Automatically Masayo waited for Seaton to go first, then she remembered that he was a foreigner and she enjoyed the luxury of leading the way.

The room was perfection itself. It was large and airy, covered with immaculate fresh tatami mats, and had the usual little alcove in front of the huge picture window with a Western-style table and two comfortable low chairs. In the corner an electric refrigerator hummed softly; when Seaton looked inside he found that it was liberally stocked with cans of cold beer, soft drinks, and a variety of cheeses and other delicacies. One look out of the window took in the town itself, the majestic ocean, and the rich green hills which seemed to be piled up on one another as far as the eye could see. Below was the attractive garden—nothing whatever detracted from the sheer beauty of the scene.

"You like?" Masayo asked.

"Yes, yes indeed! It's wonderful." He had never seen anything to compare with it, he only wished that he was beginning a two-week vacation in this very spot. In the midst of his total happiness an odd thought hit him: he remembered Mr. Williamson, the dusty little assistant to Basil Mercer, who had regarded Japan as a land of near-savages. He was older than Seaton by quite a bit, but obviously he had yet to discover what real living was like. A genuine pity for him touched Seaton—he was missing so much.

When they were alone in this private paradise, Seaton turned to look at Masayo, drank in her loveliness, and tried to realize the incredible change which had come over his life. Silently his lips formed the words, "Thank you, dear God."

Then he realized something: there was no bed in the room as there are none in any Japanese inn, which removed the suggestion of intimacy that might otherwise have been present. It was a sitting room, a parlor, complete with a tokanoma and all of the other features necessary to a fine Japanese room. The low table stood where it should in the middle of the floor.

From a tray in one corner Masayo picked up two heavily starched yukatas and straightened them out. One of them, darkly patterned in deep blue and white, she handed to Seaton. "You put on, dozo," she said, then took the other and disappeared into the bathroom.

For a few moments he hesitated, then to please her he complied. He took off his shirt, hastily donned the yukata, and then turned his back while he slipped out of his trousers, just in case his companion returned a few seconds too soon. He tied the sash as best he could and then waited, regretting even these few minutes that he was denied her companionship.

She came back presently, looking breathtaking in her simple robe. She had let her hair down as she had once before in his presence; he took one careful look at her and was almost numb.

She seemed unaware of his frank admiration. Instead she walked up to him, surveyed his appearance and then retied his sash in quite a different manner. "Socks must off," she said, and bent down to remove them for him herself.

Since he had no real choice Seaton let her perform this service, thanking his lucky stars that he had bathed thoroughly that morning. Giving her offense in any way was a disaster he could not face, his feeling of pure happiness had never soared so high.

"So nice here," she said.

163

He suddenly and urgently wanted to kiss her, but refrained because he knew better. He put it into words instead. "You are so beautiful, I cannot believe it."

"And you are ... *yoi tomodachi.*"

He did not understand her Japanese, but he knew that she was saying something nice about him. He tried to remember the sounds of the words so that he could have them translated when he returned.

She took his hand. "We go out," she suggested.

"Dressed like this?"

She laughed lightly. "Of course, you Japan now. Most suitable. You ashamed?"

"Of course not." He answered the challenge. "Make this thing out of asbestos and I'll walk with you straight through hell." She did not understand that, but she grasped his willingness. Gaily she turned to him, took his hand, and pulled him gently toward the door. He put his bare feet into the oversize slippers, and followed her out into the corridor. There he met a Japanese couple, also in yukata, who bowed. He returned the gesture at once, wondering how it was that Masayo could do it with such exquisite grace when all she was really doing was bending over.

Three more times they bowed to others on the way to the lobby. The last couple were Americans who ignored them, and the lack of courtesy hit Seaton. Anyone who could insult the spectacular beauty he was escorting was not fit to be seen overseas.

In the front lobby their yukatas attracted no attention. He followed Masayo to the wide entrance where a porter promptly produced two pairs of geta and fitted them onto their feet.

If there was anything Seaton did not feel the need of, it was additional height. Furthermore, the wooden shoes with the two heavy cleats on the bottom seemed to incorporate a built-in invitation to pitch over forward. He was not at all sure that he could walk in them with any success at all.

Masayo understood completely; she took his hand and encouraged him to try. The first ten steps were hopelessly awkward, but by the time they had passed through the garden he felt that he could manage it after all.

Then a change came over him that he could no more

control than he could alter the landscape that surrounded them. He did not feel at all Japanese, but he felt that he had absorbed some fraction of Japan. The hard sound of his geta against the pavement put it into something audible, the people around them who did not stare at his garb underlined it, and the presence of the girl at his side made it a wonderful thing. He felt a new and stronger kinship with her, for now, in costume at least, he matched her and they were a couple, a man and a woman who had something more than just the bond of casual friendship.

The feeling of unity with her grew, gently, as they walked together past small shops, looking into the windows, discovering things together. He caught her admiring a jade bracelet and had an impulsive desire to buy it for her. She restrained him, holding his arm back when he turned to enter the store.

It occurred to him that some people might misunderstand their relationship. With a freshly discovered sense of freedom he found that he did not care what they thought—he was above such petty considerations. He was just glad that he was alive and that he had by some miracle been granted the company of this wonderful girl.

By the time they strolled back to the hotel he had mastered the geta to the point where he walked in them without fear. The yukata rested comfortably on his shoulders and he had lost the initial feeling that he was walking around in a bathrobe and his underwear. He even forgot that his glasses were, as ever, perched on his nose. He had cast off the endless need to conform; he was now a man who could adjust to new things and one who could win the companionship of a beautiful woman.

At that moment life had nothing more to offer him.

When they had reentered the lobby and had exchanged the wooden geta for indoor slippers, Masayo spoke for a moment with the clerk at the desk. Whatever she was saying, he indicated his approval and pointed politely to his right.

It gave Seaton a thrill just to see Masayo walk toward him; she moved with such grace.

"Dick san," she said. "You like Japanese things?"

He could have made a speech at that point, but he restrained himself and simply said, "Yes."

She took his arm and gently guided him in the direction the clerk had indicated. "Dick, this place have most lovely bath. You come see?"

"A steam bath?" he asked, remembering the establishment in Tokyo.

"No, not steam bath. You ... will ... like." She struggled with the future tense.

He was not sure what she meant, but he trusted her and the complete respectability of the hotel was beyond question; it was a luxury resort of the highest class.

They came to a corridor which led off to the left and down a few steps. He managed them decently well in his slippers and then walked calmly with her, refusing to let anything intrude into the complete contentment he felt.

At the end of the corridor she allowed him to push open a door and they were inside a sort of room. Behind a small counter a smiling elderly attendant immediately handed them two towels and gestured toward one wall. There were benches there and a rack of medium-sized wire baskets.

At that moment from a door opposite a nude Japanese man entered the room. Masayo did not appear to notice him, nor he her. He turned the opposite way and took a yukata out of a wire basket. Then Seaton understood.

"Masayo san, is this a community bath?" He had heard of them, but it was his understanding that all of them were long extinct; they had ceased to exist about the time that Edo was renamed Tokyo.

She looked at him. "Most good. Make famous this inn. You come with me?"

The appeal of those last four words was compelling. "You come with me?" They would not go away.

He turned to her and said, "Masayo, you are beautiful. I am not."

She did not answer; instead she lifted one of the baskets out of the rack and handed it to him. "Dozo," she said, using the potent word which means so much more than just "please."

A sudden sharp fear surged through him which had nothing to do with either timidity or cowardice. He could not possibly, under any circumstances, mention it to her, but he felt compelled to say one thing.

166

First he made sure. "Masayo, you mean all clothes off? Everything?"

A little quirk appeared at the corners of her mouth. "Very best way for bath," she said.

"I've never been with ... that is, seen ... a girl ..."

She gave him a little mock bow. "Then I am so honor."

With those words spoken she turned to the rack, pulled out a basket next to the one she had chosen for him. When he saw that she was untying the sash of her yukata he turned his back and realized that he had no honorable escape. Then he remembered again the steam bath in Tokyo and the fact that he had been able to undress there in front of a young lady who took it quite as a matter of course. And there had been no disastrous involuntary reactions.

Bending over he took off his slippers and dropped them into the basket. He released the knot which Masayo had tied for him, took off his yukata, folded it, and placed it carefully on top of the slippers. Then, closing his mind to what he was doing, he slipped off his shorts and concealed them in the folds of the yukata.

"Remember towel," Masayo said. In sudden gratitude he remembered the blessed towel—if he hung it across his arm, perhaps spread it out a little bit ...

He had to turn to pick it up. As he did so he saw Masayo putting the basket with her clothing back on to the rack. Her back was turned to him; but in a single glance he could not avoid, he saw that she was completely nude, and that she was also quite relaxed. Aware that he could not allow her to wait on him, he took his own basket and pushed it into place beside hers.

She picked up her towel casually with one hand and walked toward the door from which the man had emerged a little while before. He reached out to open it for her, waited while she passed through, and then cautiously followed.

He found himself in a huge circular natatorium which could have been transported intact from ancient Rome. In the center there was a round pool of water which seemed to be at least fifty feet across. Completely around the rim there was a wide tiled area with several smaller alcoves which also contained pools of water. At one side a classical piece of sculp-

167

ture served as a fountain to flow more water into the center pool. The whole interior was very warm and had about it an almost sybaritic feeling of exalted living. The several obviously nude people who were in the water or resting around the rim completed the illusion of an unreal setting from a long past age—the pleasure palace of some barbarian potentate.

Close to the door three elderly Japanese ladies beheld Seaton and clustered together in mutual fright. They slipped out at once through the glass-paneled double doors, fleeing not from the nude man, but from the giant foreigner with the curiously white skin.

Masayo turned to the right and led him to a row of low-set faucets which obviously provided hot and cold water. There were soap dishes and a cluster of little low stools similar to the ones used in the Tokyo steam bath. There were also some small plastic buckets.

For a sickening moment Seaton wondered if Masayo proposed giving him a bath in public. He could accept that service now from a professional like Sumiko, the little Tokyo attendant, but only in the strictest privacy—his mind recoiled at the thought of the beautiful girl who had brought him here taking over such an intimate function. He watched as she put her towel conveniently aside and filled two of the buckets with water, adjusting the temperature to her satisfaction. Then she turned to him and he felt the shock of her full nudity. "First we wash ourselves," she explained, and smiled at him as if to say that she understood that this was all new to him—but that he would learn.

She handed him one of the buckets of water. "Dozo," she said. Then she sat down on one of the little stools, held her hair up on top of her head with her hands, and bent slightly over. Obediently he took the bucket of water and poured it carefully over her. When he saw that it had not wetted her completely he took the second one and splashed it across her shoulders.

She smiled her thanks, reached for a piece of soap, and began to bathe herself. No one appeared to pay her the slightest attention. Seaton refilled the buckets, poured the water over himself, and then turned to face the wall a few inches away while he applied the soap. By keeping his eyes fixed on the pattern of the tilework he was able to accomplish a mild form

168

of self-hypnosis and dilute the reality of the situation in
which he found himself. One quick glance informed him
that Masayo was not watching him; reassured, he performed
the most essential, and at the same time most intimate, part of
his ablutions.

When he had worked his way down his long legs and was
soaping the tops of his feet, he became aware that his companion was filling more buckets with water. When he at last
forced himself to turn he saw her holding a full bucket in one
hand and motioning for him to sit down with the other. He
folded himself like a jackknife and perched on one of the
little low stools, determined to undergo his ordeal like a man.
A moment later a flow of very warm water flooded down his
back; he heard her pick up another bucket and before he
could draw a deep breath the water came down this time over
his chest.

She laughed—softly, gaily, cocked her head a little on the
side, and smiled at him with bewitching charm.

For the first time he dared to look at her, for just a quick
fraction of a second. She was covered with soap and her skin
was wet, but the sight of her was totally intoxicating. Like the
girls at the Nichigeki she had breasts, but they were beautifully formed—dainty, poised, exquisitely proportioned to her
figure. The rest of her was a quick flash of wonderful symme-
try, of gently flowing curvatures, of physical perfection. He
had always thought of her as beautiful, but now the revelation
of her whole person staggered him and he drew a quick sharp
breath to steady himself. Paris had awarded the golden apple
to Venus, but that had been because Masayo Kanno had not
been present and competing. She was a goddess and he could
not believe that he was in her presence.

She sat down and turned her face up to him. "Water?" she
asked. He quickly filled three buckets and tested the temperature of their contents with his hand to be sure that they would
provide a pleasant and agreeable sensation to her body. Then
he rinsed her off as carefully as if she had been the irreplaceable lens of some great telescope. When he had performed that
service she rose to her feet, a living sculpture, and drew more
water to splash over her feet and ankles. Seaton followed her
example until the last of the soap had been washed away.
Then she reached out and took his hand.

169

"Water hot," she warned. "We make slow."

It was a wise warning; the temperature of the main center pool was just below the point of being bearable. There were railings to hold on to while entering the water; Seaton clutched one firmly while he gradually accustomed himself to the almost steaming heat. After perhaps five minutes he had progressed to the point where he was at last standing on the bottom in a depth of about four feet.

"Feel okay?" Masayo asked.

"I guess so. I've never been in such hot water. At least not literally."

She did not understand the last part, but she led him forward toward the center; the depth increased very slowly as they advanced. Presently they were almost at the center with other heads and shoulders spread throughout the very large pool.

Then the entrance door was pushed open and a whole family came through, five children of varying ages and their parents, all quite nude and unconcerned. The three smallest turned quickly left and even on the wet tile floor ran to one of the alcoves which was filled with water and several pieces of playground equipment all made out of tile and cement. Indulgently their parents followed, chose bathing stools, and prepared to wash themselves.

"You like community bath?" Masayo asked.

He looked at her and saw a quizzical smile playing about her lips.

Since he was safely more than waist deep in water, he nodded his head in agreement. "Very much. Something new and different."

"Not' new," Masayo answered. "Very long time idea, also very good."

"Hot water and all?"

"Yes." She paused to try and find the words she needed. "Japanese farmer, maybe fisherman so hard work. Body very sore. Hot water make soft, give rest ... understand?"

"Yes, I understand. Masayo, I feel a little faint, could we go out?" To make himself clear he wiped one hand across his perspiring forehead.

She glanced at his face and at once turned toward the steps; he waded just behind her and climbed out of the hot pool

170

with a great sense of relief. Masayo quickly soaked a towel with cold water and with it washed his face, giving him immediate relief from the sense of suffocation he had felt. He was momentarily quite unaware that he did not have a stitch to his back, and neither did she; it did not seem to matter. She stood close enough for him to have put his arms around her easily, but the sensation of her physical presence did not disturb him at all.

When she had finished cooling off his face she motioned him to a stool and a few seconds later poured a bucket of moderately cool water down his body. The reviving effect was marvelous, he felt as though he could have gone right back into the hot pool once more and stayed much longer this time.

"We go room now," she proposed. "Maybe more bath tonight."

"Okay," he answered, remembering she knew that idiom. They went through the double doors together and reclaimed their clothes from the rack. This time Seaton noticed, to his surprise, that she had not been wearing any intimate feminine underthings; her yukata and slippers made up her entire ensemble. When she was dressed again he looked at her once more, thoroughly this time, and saw much more than the lovely face and flowing hair. He saw instead a whole and complete person with an intimacy which he had never before experienced. It was not because he had seen her entire body, but because he saw her with perhaps a greater depth of understanding. He thought he could put a name to it in his own mind, but he did not dare.

She tied his yukata for him again and adjusted the belt not at waist level, but further down on his hips. Then she handed their towels to the attendant and they returned, at an easy pace, to the lobby.

At the top of the stairs they were approached by one of the desk clerks who happened to be walking by. "Excuse me," he said to Seaton with a polite half bow, then he turned to Masayo and addressed her in Japanese. They conversed for a half minute or so, then the clerk turned to include Seaton once more. "I trust, sir, that you enjoyed our fine bath. We are very proud of it."

"You have every right to be," he replied. Then a happy

171

thought struck him and he added, "I've never seen one like it."

The clerk bowed his appreciation. "We are most flattered when our guests from other countries try our customs and find them good. I am myself a great fan of baseball."

This time Seaton bowed. "I am most happy that we have come to your hotel." It took another minute to break away since after that remark more bows had to be exchanged and polite phrases recited in Japanese. Then at last they were threading their way back through the corridors and up the steps which led to their room. When they reached the door Seaton fished in his sleeve for the key, found it, and unlocked their private haven which seemed almost to be awaiting their return.

Masayo produced a brush, sat down in a chair before the picture window, and began to smooth out her hair. Seaton went to the refrigerator, looked inside, and then turned toward his companion. "We have beer, Coke, and several other kinds of soft drinks. What would you like?"

"Coka Cora," she answered.

He uncapped a bottle for her, put ice in a glass, and served her proudly. Then he fixed himself one and sat down opposite her and watched while she continued brushing.

"You have lovely hair," he said.

"Every day must do this. Long time. Today, not so long." She smiled. "Not must work."

"Good, we are on holiday." He realized that that might be hard for her and rephrased it. "I am free too."

She took a dozen more strokes and then put the brush down. She turned her head toward the window and looked out for several seconds at the mountains which rose behind them and the ocean which lay at their feet. "Brewtiful Japan," she said.

He reached across, took her face gently between his hands and looked directly into her eyes. "Beautiful Japan," he repeated.

She lifted her shoulder and rubbed it against his hand. Carefully he released her and sat back in his chair, thinking of a certain word which seemed to be forming itself in his mind and on his lips. He did not allow it to be born, instead he tried to impress himself with the fact that he had known her

172

for less than two weeks. He had no reservations about her in his mind, but the habits of a lifetime dictated caution. He decided to humor his inhibitions and to let them have their way, perhaps for just a little while. They had taken an awful beating in the community bath and were entitled to a little time in which to recover.

So they sat together, sipped their drinks, and absorbed the wonderful view, peaceful and serene, which seemed to have been created for their special benefit. Masayo relaxed in her chair, almost like a little girl, her feet tucked up beneath her. Seaton was content just to sit quietly, his long legs stretched under the table, taking in the view so very different from New England, and looking at Masayo, so different from everyone. They were interrupted by a discreet tap on the door.

Masayo answered in Japanese without moving from her chair. In response a girl in kimono came in, bowed pleasantly, and then began to arrange the low table for dinner. She placed two cushions at opposite sides, set some small dishes in the center, then went outside and returned with two large lacquered trays which she placed carefully on the table. When everything was ready she withdrew and closed the door behind her.

The meal was superb. There were a number of small dishes, extra sauces, and three different varieties of Japanese pickles. Seaton was still not comfortable sitting on the floor, despite the substantial pillow which had been provided, but the chopsticks were no longer a problem.

"Masayo," he said. "I like this, eating together. It is a nice custom."

She smiled happily. "I like too, Dick san."

He ate the mouthful of food he already had in his chopsticks and then spoke to her again. "Masayo, I know 'Dick san' is the polite Japanese way to say my name, but will you call me just 'Dick,' dozo?"

She did not quite understand. "You not want me say 'Dick san'?"

"Dick."

"Ah, so. All light—Dick."

"Fine, now what do you want to do after dinner?"

"Walk little maybe. Sit in garden."

When they had finished she excused herself easily and

173

visited the bathroom. When she returned she gestured with her hand to indicate that it was now his turn, then with a mirror she began to apply light makeup to her face.

While he was absent from her Seaton reflected on the way that the Japanese people accepted things, like the need for a toilet, without making a production out of it. By giving it so little attention they succeeded in de-emphasizing it as his own people had never been able to do.

Masayo had difficulty pronouncing the sound of "r," and her English was hesitant and faulty, but she did better in his language than he did in hers—which gave him a little idea how he must look to the Japanese. When he returned to her she flashed him a quick smile and rose to her feet to join him.

Then evening air, which had cooled from the heat of the day, was almost intoxicating. The sounds of the ocean blended with it to recreate an invitation to visit faraway places and seek adventure on distant shores. But this *was* a remote land, the Far East—the Orient—and the girl beside him was a living symbol of that reality. And this *was* adventure as he had never known it before.

The simple act of being with a lovely girl along the shoreline, but what magic there was in it! He held her hand gently in his own—apparently she had put it there—and walked with her with a growing sense of pride. The yukata felt comfortable and cool, he sensed that he looked well in it as she did in hers. The geta were still a little awkward, but they were a vast relief from the tight close leather of conventional shoes. He was male and she was female, but they matched each other in dress and manner, they were a pair. He drew in a deep breath of satisfaction, looked at her, and his heart swelled with pride.

When they returned to the hotel they turned into the garden and sat in one of the lawn swings which dotted the grounds. Seaton did not want to speak, he had nothing to say and he did not want to break the mood which had settled over them both. He gave no matter to Mercer and Doyle, to the problem facing him at the Matsumoto plant, to any of the other matters of the workaday world. He was content just to sit where he was, and to look at Masayo. She, in turn, seemed to find his company agreeable and he could ask no more than

174

that. He even forgot that she was a geisha, the Miss One Thousand Spring Blossoms who had entertained him so charmingly on his first evening in Tokyo. That glamorous image had faded to be replaced by the living presence of Masayo Kanno. She was just herself now, and that was the way he wanted her.

He looked up to see that a middle-aged man and his wife were hesitantly approaching them. They were both also dressed in yukata which established, automatically, a certain small bond of unity. When they seemed to pause before quite daring to venture too close Masayo smiled at them and spoke a phrase in Japanese. Encouraged, they advanced and bowed.

"Good evening, sir," the man said. "May I make introduced myself, I am Mr. Otsuki. This is my wife Aiko."

Seaton stood up and shook hands, "I'm Dick Seaton, this is my friend, Miss Kanno."

This called for certain bowing and the exchange of polite phrases between the ladies; the men waited until they finished.

"I did not wishing to disturb you," Mr. Otsuki said. "I am high school teacher of the English. Would you honor me by giving me practice for perhaps very briefly?"

"Of course. Please sit down, there's plenty of room."

"I am great admirer of American country," the teacher said. "Someday it is my ambition to behold it; until then I read and observe the pictures."

"You will be a very welcome guest," Seaton said.

The man bowed his thanks. "Please, if I am making the mistake, have the great kindness to correct me. It is the way I attempt to perfect myself."

The conversation lasted for more than an hour. The language teacher was almost pathetically anxious to learn and repeatedly asked to be corrected if and when he made a mistake. This imposed a diplomatic problem which was solved when they got onto the subject of idioms. Here grammar was no longer an issue and Seaton was able to help with several expressions which Mr. Otsuki was anxious to learn. When the Japanese couple realized that they had taken quite a bit of time, they withdrew with apologies.

"Please, it was my pleasure," Seaton informed his guest. "You have added to our evening."

"Your kindness is the same size as the greatness of your country," he was assured in return. "I shall speak of you to my students."

Darkness had settled now and the garden of the inn glowed with soft lights. There were others enjoying it too, but the many little quiet places to sit were carefully separated. Each minute now was precious to Seaton, because in a little while he would have to excuse himself and go to his own room. He would see her again in the morning, of course, but then they would have to return by train to Tokyo and separate. He forced from his mind the realization that within a very few days he would be leaving Japan and that once he was gone, he might never see her again. She was too lovely, too utterly desirable, not to be immensely popular, and sad experience had taught him that girls of her caliber did not remain unmarried very long.

He looked at her now and when she smiled quietly back he wanted to stretch each minute into an hour, the evening itself into a decade.

Presently she stepped out of the swing and held out her hand. "Maybe we go now room?" she suggested. The open clear look which she gave him told him that he was trusted, that she had no fear he would attempt to take advantage of her invitation.

"For a little while it would be nice," he said. He knew that if she understood his remark she would also grasp its meaning. Together they returned to the lobby and once more exchanged their geta for the comfortable backless slippers which were always ready and waiting at the entranceway.

The room, when they reached it, had been considerably changed. The dinner things had been cleared away, the center table had been removed and stood up in a corner, and dim nightlights had been turned on close to the surface of the tatami mats which made up the floor. In the middle of the room two futons had been carefully laid out for sleeping, side by side. What had been their sitting room and dining area had been converted to something else, a sense of intimacy now replaced the openness which had been present before dinner.

At the doorsill Seaton hesitated when he saw what had been

176

done; he was not at all sure it would now be suitable to come in. Masayo resolved the matter for him by tipping her head and speaking the single word, "Dozo."

Since it could not be much after nine, he accepted her permission to enter for a little while. He stepped over the waiting futons, and went directly to the refrigerator. "What would you enjoy?" he asked.

She came to join him and bent down to look inside. Then she removed two bottles of Kiren beer and looked a question at him.

"Fine," he said.

This time she poured the drinks, put them on the little table between the two chairs, and sat down to look at the lights of the small city, the outlines of the hills, and the stars which gave proof of eternity overhead. Seaton, opposite her, drank his beer, and refused to think of the day when he would have to leave for home.

For more than a half hour they remained in silence. There was no need to speak. He was content to look at her, and the longer he studied her features, the more he marveled at their classic perfection. She was beautiful in a way which ignored any question of racial heritage or from what part of the world her forebears had come. She was not limited to mere good looks or a pert attractiveness; she was in the deepest and fullest sense of the term a true beauty whose perfection came from much more than a flawless complexion and the shaping of her facial structure. It lay deep within her, it was an integral part of her character and her very being.

That thought was still in his mind when she sat up a little and said, "Dick, I want to talk with you."

He was startled a little by the unexpected sound of her voice and the accident of her correct grammar. Then he realized what it was she had said and a sense of foreboding touched him.

"Dozo," he said, using the Japanese word because it more accurately conveyed his feelings.

"Come." She rose to her feet with the liquid grace that never left her, took his hand, and led him to the center of the room. Then she dropped easily onto one of the futons and stretched out on her side, her head on the pillow, her hair

177

lying where it fell against the white linen. With her hand she indicated the other futon and that it was her wish that he lie down as she had done.

Very carefully he complied, making sure that the distance between them was not encroached upon in any way. He laid his head on the cool pillow and waited for her to speak.

"English is for me much hard," she began, but with such evident sincerity he did not even notice her lapse of grammar. "You are ... first foreigner ... I ever meet. I see sometimes, but speak no."

When she paused he nodded to indicate that he understood her perfectly so far. "You are man of great goodness, so I tell you now best you forget me. I am not girl, I am geisha, do you know?"

This was not as clear, but he was determined to hear her out.

"For you must be girl to have like Scott Norma san."

The words jolted him hard; he had had no idea she even knew of Norma's existence. He raised himself on one elbow the better to look at her.

"I have seen Norma Scott twice," he said. "She is a very nice person. That is all." He hoped anxiously that the exact meaning of his words would get through to her, that she would understand precisely what he meant.

"I know," she answered, her voice low, even, and quiet. "You take her to sumo, many geisha see you there."

"I did," Seaton admitted. "She invited me and I accepted." He hoped that did not sound like an excuse; he had not intended it that way—he had only wanted to speak the exact truth.

With her forefinger Masayo traced an invisible pattern slowly on the tatami mat. "You go early," she continued, almost impersonally. "I think you go her room."

"Yes, I did."

She stopped tracing and drew her hand back to the edge of her pillow. "I understan', do not make worry. Men live life different, I know." Then she raised her head, turned her face directly toward him and fixed her eyes on him. In the dimmed room the pupils had enlarged and they were compelling. "I am geisha, but I try to be your friend. Tradition say 'no,' but

178

I try. I think now tradition best." She sank back and lay still.

He forced himself to say the thing he feared most. "You mean no more dates?"

For a moment she did nothing, then she rolled her head just a little from side to side.

"Why?" he asked.

She did not move or say a thing, she just looked at him.

He waited a long time for an answer and when it did not come he asked again. *"Why?"*

Once more she gave him no reply. For a full minute he remained entirely silent and motionless, waiting for her to pick her time. When he was sure she would not, he tried a third time. "Why?" he asked again.

After a few seconds she turned onto her stomach so that she would not have to look at his face.

"I take you to community bath," she said.

"Did I do wrong there?" he asked.

She shook her head; he saw only the back of it, the silken black hair which was a part of her.

He thought he knew now what it was. "Masayo, I tried awfully hard not to look at you—you understand. I did once, yes, for just a second, I couldn't help it. I . . ." He could not think what to say after that, he had confessed and then there was really nothing more.

"Of course," she said. "I not mind."

He could contain himself no longer, he physically took hold of her and turned her over until her face was inches from his own.

"Then what did I do wrong?" He pronounced each of the words separately and distinctly, determined that she should understand them. He did not realize how hard he was gripping her shoulder, but the fierceness of his anxiety was in his fingers.

"You tell me not truth." Once she had said the words she had tried to avoid, the tears in her eyes would be denied no longer.

He looked hard at her, his teeth clenched together. "Never!" Then he repeated himself. "I have never done that."

He felt her body relax as though it could no longer sustain

179

the tension in which it had been held. "You say ..." She stopped.

"Go on."

"You say to me ..."

"Yes—dozo!"

"You say . . . you never see girl before."

"That is true," he affirmed.

She appeared not to hear him.

"I not care, I expect. But I not want you tell me not true." She covered her face with her hands.

"Masayo, that was true. Believe me. When I was a little boy once ..." He stopped as a long-buried memory came back to haunt him. A confession of that episode would be meaningless now, and probably not understood. The fat little girl in the neighborhood who had liked to be admired disappeared back into limbo.

She took her hands away and spoke to him calmly. "You tell me just now you go home to Norma san. I know who is Norma, she work Sakamoto san. And you go her home."

"Yes, but that's all."

She did not quite understand.

"Dozo?"

He put it into basic words. "I did not stay. I did not sleep with Norma san."

"Why?" she demanded.

"Because I'm in love with you!"

Now he had said it. It had been in his mind and close to his lips all day, but he had been afraid—never of her, only of himself.

"You say love?" She looked at him.

"Yes, dammit, *love*. Don't you understand? I turned down Norma Scott because I wanted you!"

On the instant he realized the terrible thing he had done. He had not meant it, but the words were spoken and they were forever gone from him.

He fell back, emotionally blinded by the horror of his blunder. He knew her sensitivity, he had learned it painfully the first time he had insulted her. This was infinitely worse. The only question in his mind was whether to attempt to say something to her before he left, or just to go away and hide himself from her.

180

Then he thought he felt her fingers against his cheek. He turned, looked at her, and saw that both her arms were out toward him.

He reached out and gathered her in. He held her tightly to him, and felt her lips against his. Madness took control of him and he did not care. He kissed her throat, her cheeks, her eyes to take the tears away and held her, resolved never to let go.

Then from somewhere back in his determined mind came a demand and he made one mighty effort. "Masayo, I ..." He relaxed his arms and shut his eyes to her face so that she could escape from his physical strength, so that he need not forever revile himself for having overpowered her.

When he had done so she moved gently, almost tenderly away from his reach. He sensed that—perhaps she understood. He heard a slight sound, and then she spoke his name.

He was afraid to do anything, one more look at her and what slender control he still had left would be gone. Then he felt the pressure of her body on his arm again as she quietly, very quietly, returned to his embrace once more.

He took hold of her again like the precious thing she was, and his hands touched only the softness of her skin. He let his fingers run down her back until he realized that she had come to him herself alone, and he understood what that meant.

His consciousness lifted off the hard earth of reality and took to the sky. Then he found himself floating on a vast ocean where there was no light, and no darkness, where there was only the totality of fulfillment and everything else had ceased to exist. Very slowly he began turning on the surface of the directionless ocean until it came to him that he was on the rim of a great whirlpool.

He began to slide down its side as the speed of revolution gradually increased and the horizon vanished. The world shrank and he held his own life tightly locked against himself aware only that without it, without her, there was only instant destruction. He clung to her as the sky began to turn faster and faster overhead, until he felt the power of the vortex, and plunged downward into another eternity.

181

Chapter Seventeen

Dr. Oda leaned forward and carefully studied the face of his patient. "Do you feel any discomfort?" he asked.

Seaton blinked before he answered. "No, doctor, it doesn't seem to bother me at all. I'm aware that they're there, but I don't feel any pain or smarting."

"You are very fortunate," the doctor told him. "Some people have had considerable difficulty adjusting to contact lenses and there are a few who cannot wear them at all."

Seaton turned his head to look into the mirror, and what he saw he found it difficult to believe. For as long as he could remember he had either seen his own face with his glasses on, or else, without them, as a blurred image which he could never quite bring into focus. Now he looked and saw his own features clearly and distinctly, and without the slightest evidence of the new lenses he was wearing.

"I not only can see as well as with my old glasses," he reported, "I seem to see over a wider range."

"That is quite true, Mr. Seaton. When you wear conventional glasses, the rims are always somewhere in your field of vision. With them gone you naturally see more."

"Where did you learn your perfect English, sir, if I may ask?"

"In your country. I studied there for three years."

"Do you fit many Americans?"

"Quite a few, yes. Most of the better hotels have sent me patients, and the various travel agencies. There are many excellent men in practice here, but not all of them can speak English."

"May I wear these when I leave?"

"Yes, of course, but for a month at least I would suggest that you restrict the hours that you use them. Carry your old glasses with you and take out your contact lenses at the first sign of increased discomfort. Try to wear them a little longer each time, but if they do not settle in properly for you, I would like to see you immediately. In any event, please come in after one week's time."

"I will certainly see you before I leave," Seaton promised. "I may not be here for another week; I'm not certain of my plans."

An hour later he was back at the Matsumoto plant for another conference with Mr. Fujihara. When he walked in through the lobby he had the satisfaction of hearing a startled little gasp from Chiyoko Shinagawa, the receptionist. When he went directly to Reiko's desk to ask her to come back and translate for him, she took a long, careful look at him and then stood up.

"I am so happy," she said. "You now wear inside eyeglasses, yes?"

"That's right—do you like them?"

"Oh, Dick, so much better, I like very much. I think maybe Kanno san, she will like too."

"She suggested it and my hotel gave me the name of a good eye man. So I thought I'd give it a try."

"Much handsome," Reiko said.

He put his hand affectionately on her shoulder. "That isn't so, but thank you anyway. Now let's see how things are going in back."

Things were going well. Thanks to a weekend of intense work, Mr. Fujihara had a new approach to the problem and a most ingenious possible solution. Once again Seaton was hit by the idea of what a great asset this fine engineer would be

183

to the Mercer and Doyle technical staff. It would be cruel to the Matsumoto Company to take him away, but it might represent a real opportunity. If Williamson would buy it, which was the stumbling block. Williamson was fussy and could be depended upon to bring up questions such as lack of citizenship and the absence of fluent English.

They worked together for almost two hours before the American had to excuse himself and remove the contact lenses. With his old glasses back in position, he resumed work, but he looked forward to the day when he might be emancipated from them forever. Dr. Oda had not only tested his eyes and checked the prescription of his conventional lenses, he also had had the contact replacements in stock. He had a considerable amount of tourist business and knew that transients could not normally wait two or three days for a laboratory to deliver what was actually a stock item anyway.

A little after four Seaton was called to the telephone. His heart sang within him, because it might be Masayo. Happily he picked up the instrument and was met by the voice of George Sakamoto. "I hope I'm not inconveniencing you by calling you at work, Mr. Seaton, but I was most anxious to reach you. Would it be at all possible for us to get together for a few minutes this evening at your convenience? I have something for you in which I believe you will be most interested."

Seaton remembered that he had requested cost estimates; now he was honor bound to accept them—and he was also indebted to Sakamoto for a fine dinner. But what if Masayo called? He had hoped to take her somewhere for a quiet meal together if she were free. Time was precious now and he wanted to make the very most of it.

Perhaps he could do both. "Would you be free around nine or a little after? I have a pending dinner engagement I'm not sure of yet."

"Nine would be excellent. Suppose I send my car for you and we'll have a drink together."

The conversation concluded, he went back to the shop. He had asked Masayo for dinner, in fact he had asked to see her every day that he remained in Japan, but she had, with considerable hesitation, reminded him that she too had a profession and had to work most evenings. If she were not on

184

the job Monday night, the water at the geisha house would be hotter than the community bath at Atami. They had left it that if she could squeeze time out for a dinner together she would call.

By six-thirty Seaton was convinced of two things—that Masayo had had to work and would not be calling, and that Mr. Fujihara had overcome the problem in the component design. His solution was brilliant, the word properly applied, but it required that the actual layout and manufacturing work would have to be done over again from the beginning. He secretly was rather happy about this—it would almost certainly prolong his stay in Japan and every day meant an additional possible opportunity to see Masayo. He thought now about her more than all other things combined, or so it seemed. He recognized, admitted, and was proud of the fact that he was in love with her—he would tell anyone who asked. Reiko Watanabe did not need to ask—she knew. She also surmised certain other things, was very happy for Dick san, and had one great and terrible fear.

When he left the plant at seven, for the first time in many years Seaton felt like whistling—just to pour out some of the music that was in his heart. He hailed a cab, folded up inside, and thought about Masayo. He refused to visualize her in her kimono and full regalia attending a party and being the gay companion and performer for some Japanese businessman who was being entertained on an expense account. She had a right to make her living, of course, but that necessity might be over very soon. He had definite thoughts and plans in that direction.

He arrived at his hotel to find a letter from the home office enclosing his salary check and reminding him that he was incurring a great deal of expense for which definite and early results were expected. He contemplated writing back to inform Williamson that there had been a flaw in the design which the Matsumoto Company was brilliantly correcting, but then he realized that to do that would put Herb Fineman murderously on the spot. Herb had made the design and if by an honest mistake he had put Mercer and Doyle to any extra expense, and they knew it, Williamson would have his gizzard. Back at the home office you made your mistakes, if any, at home and on your own time.

185

Miss One Thousand Spring Blossoms

Dinner in the hotel dining room was good, but a strangely lonely affair. There was no wonderful face across the table, no presence of an irreplaceable person. A little before nine he went up to his room and put in the contact lenses once more. There was a possiblity that he might run into Norma during the course of the evening and it would be nice to try out his new appearance on her. It was not that important to him now, but it might, in a small way, help him to recover the face he had lost the last time he had seen her.

On time to the minute George Sakamoto's chauffeur arrived and took him away. They drove through the city in a direction he could not determine and eventually turned down one of the half-hidden little sub-streets which held so much that was not immediately visible. It struck him that Tokyo was a little like an iceberg—by far the smaller part was on the surface despite the fact that the surface itself was vast, complex, and almost totally bewildering. There could be no other city like it anywhere.

The car pulled up before a quiet wooden building with a glowing lantern outside. For a moment he was afraid that it was a geisha house; he did not want to meet any more geisha and he did not want to have Masayo engaged to entertain him. She was something different now, different and very precious, and he would not have her degraded.

He took off his shoes mechanically at the door, bowed to the mamasan in response to her greeting, and allowed himself to be led down a short tami-floored corridor. A door was slid open and there was George Sakamoto getting to his feet to greet him. Otherwise, the room was empty.

Sakmoto shook his hand warmly. "I'm so very happy to see you again, Mr. Seaton, I do hope that I haven't inconvenienced you."

"Certainly not," Seaton answered. "I'm delighted to meet with you. If the bar is open, may I have the pleasure of buying the first round?"

Sakamoto gave him a careful second look. "I presume, Mr. Seaton, that you are wearing contact lenses, though I can't see them. If so, let me congratulate you on your success in making the change-over."

"I'm just starting, to be honest about it, but so far they seem to be working out well."

"May I say that in my opinion it considerably improves your appearance. Not that I am casting any aspersions, you understand."

"Of course not. What is your pleasure?"

"Suntory and water; if you haven't tried our Japanese whiskey, I can genuinely recommend it."

"Make it two then."

When the beverages had been ordered and produced, the small talk ceased and the agenda turned to business. "In accordance with your instructions," Sakamoto began, "Norma turned over to me a set of blueprints which you left with her for that purpose. Incidently, she spoke of you in the highest terms as a gentleman—perhaps I should offer congratulations on that point also."

"I would be hesitant to accept them," Seaton answered. "Have you had a chance to look over the design?"

Sakamoto sipped his drink. "Yes, I turned the blueprints over to my engineering staff who studied them quite carefully. In fact, they took a considerable liberty which I hope will meet with your approval."

From a box beside him he lifted out a component and set it on the table. "Fast reaction time is one of our major assets. Quite frankly, Mr. Seaton, we receive quite a bit of business based on our ability to do something both rapidly and well when the occasion demands. This is not intended as a demonstration of speed, but only as an indication of how we do things. It was quite simple to make up a prototype and we did so for your examination."

Seaton leaned forward and picked up the assembly. He could see almost at a glance that it was a very close duplicate of the original Matsumoto product, also finely made, and obviously the work of a sophisticated concern. He turned it over several times in his fingers and studied it carefully. The clear evidence of fine workmanship was unmistakable, but there was also a strong possibility that it would not work. The fault in that case, of course, would not be Sakamoto's. But if his engineers had caught the fatal flaw—then he would have to consider the matter in the light of what would be best for Mercer and Doyle.

He hated that thought. He saw before him the faces of Mr. Matsumoto himself, of Messieurs Yamaguchi and Futaba who

187

had met him at the airport, of little Reiko Watanabe who tried so hard to translate technical jargon from one language into another, of her elderly mother whom she was undoubtedly supporting, of Fujihara, the exceptionally capable engineer whom he so liked and respected.

"I didn't expect you to do this," he began. "When I left the plans with Norma it was to request a cost estimate and nothing more."

George Sakamoto waved a hand through the air. "That is fully understood. In order to give you as accurate an estimate as possible we made one up, that is all. In addition, it seemed to our engineering people that to ask you to take us on faith alone, even as an alternate source, would be unreasonable. Please understand that this sample is part of our estimate; it is yours with no cost and absolutely no obligation whatever."

"In that case I will certainly show it to our management back home. In all fairness I should tell you . . . let me put it this way: did your people have an opportunity to check this out in any way?"

"No, but they did look the design over very carefully and were satisfied that they had executed it with precision. Would it be reasonable now for me to ask you in what general price bracket you are procuring these from Matsumoto?"

Seaton thought for a moment before he replied. He wanted to play fair with Sakamoto, but he did not want either to betray the Matsumoto Company or confess the error made by Mercer and Doyle. "About fifty-five dollars each in production quantities," he said after he had made up his mind.

From a briefcase also laid beside him George took out a typewritten sheet. "I asked you that," he explained, "because if their price was better than ours, obviously the matter would rest there. This is what we can do for you, should you have occasion to use our services."

Seaton took the estimate sheet and studied it for several seconds. "Forty-eight dollars each," he commented.

"That's right, and of course that was made up before I had any knowledge of your price arrangements with Matsumoto." He paused and finished his drink. "Now there is something I would like to make very clear to you, Mr. Seaton, so there will be no misunderstanding. We are in business, of course, and

188

we have certain expansion goals in mind, but we adhere to very strict ethics in all of our dealings. I personally insist on it. So I want you to consider our offer in the light of a second source and as a primary one only if something happens so that you can no longer procure your requirements from the Matsumoto people. Is that fully understood."

"Yes, sir, it is," Seaton answered, "and let me add that I certainly respect your putting it that way. I feel a definite obligation to the Matsumoto firm as I'm sure you understand."

"Of course. By the way, I'll either keep your blueprints on file at our offices or return them to your hotel, whichever you prefer."

This time it was Seaton's turn, he felt, to play fair. "I suggest that you return them, Mr. Sakamoto, not because of any lack of confidence in you, but because we are contemplating a major change in the design. We think it can be improved."

"Very good, let's do it that way. Now that the matter is settled, may I say that I admire the way in which you are supporting Matsumoto's effort. They have had some very difficult problems lately and I'm honestly glad to see them getting this piece of business. They deserve it and I know that they have been fine hosts to you."

Seaton picked up his glass and drank a silent toast to Masayo. "In every way," he agreed. "And I am also indebted to Mr. Matsumoto for an introduction to a remarkable girl. As well as to yourself," he added quickly.

Sakamoto nodded. "I believe that I know her. The geisha Fujikoma."

"You certainly keep up with things, don't you?"

Sakamoto laughed. "Well, not with any intention of spying, I can assure you of that. I only heard about it when I tried to get her for a party and was told that the Matsumoto Company had engaged her almost exclusively for your entertainment."

Seaton did not understand. "Would you say that again, please?" he asked.

Sakamoto looked at him sharply. "Perhaps it would be best if we changed the subject," he suggested. "How did you enjoy the sumo matches?"

Seaton leaned forward. "You said that the Matsumoto Company had 'engaged' Miss Kanno. Would you explain that a little further."

Sakamoto shifted his position. "Mr. Seaton, in general terms the geisha system is something which is not only nonexistent in the Western world, it is also very frequently misunderstood. I don't think it would serve any useful purpose for me to try and explain it to you in detail here and now. I would like to assure you, though, that Fujikoma is a geisha of the first class, she has an excellent reputation, and in making her available to you the Matsumoto Company has given you of the very best. She is a charming companion and I am delighted that you have found her company agreeable."

Seaton waited several seconds before he spoke, keeping the subject in his mind in the realm of an abstract engineering matter. It was the only way he could block out his emotions until he made sure of the facts. "Mr. Sakamoto, on my first evening in Tokyo I was entertained at a restaurant very like this one. Miss Kanno was present as a geisha and of course I understand that she was paid for her services."

"Certainly, but you appreciated that this is her business."

"Of course. Now subsequently I have seen her several times socially. We had dinner together at the New Otani, we went for a walk in the park, and there were other occasions. In your opinion was she paid professionally for her time ..." Despite the tight rein he was holding on himself, he was unable to finish the sentence.

This time George waited, embarrassment visible on his otherwise well-controlled features. "Mr. Seaton, I profoundly regret that this subject came up at all. I had no idea that you were not aware of certain considerations and if I have caused you any discomfort, please let me offer you my complete apology. And I want to add this; Fujikoma is a splendid young woman, she is strikingly beautiful, and her character is above all question. Anywhere that you were seen with her, it was to your credit."

"But she was paid," Seaton persisted.

"Bluntly put, yes, but there is another consideration, and a very important one. She is immensely popular and can select her clients to her own taste. The fact that she chose your company is most significant and I suggest that you view it in that light."

190

Seaton picked up the component, the cost sheet, and finished his drink to avoid embarrassing his host. Then he got to his feet. "Mr. Sakamoto, thank you very much for your company and your hospitality. I hope I may have the pleasure of seeing you again soon. "As the Japanese executive quickly got to his feet Seaton shook hands, hurried down the short corridor, got into his shoes without bothering to tie them and ran to the corner to hail a cab. He ran because he did not want to let anyone see his face.

He went through the lobby of his hotel without pausing. For the first time he did not inquire at the desk for any messages. He held himself together by a sheer effort of will until he was safely inside his room. Then he kicked off his shoes, fell across the bed, and felt the irritation of the new lenses in his eyes. He removed them and for a moment contemplated smashing them under his feet. Then, unwilling to take even that action, he let them fall into an ashtray, lay across the bed, and buried his face in his arms so that it would be hidden even from the unseeing walls.

191

Chapter Eighteen

*W*hen his phone rang to awaken him he was not asleep. He had turned over and once he had gotten up to go to the bathroom, otherwise he had lain on the bed all night, wide awake, while the world had disintegrated piece by piece around him.

He answered the phone and then proceeded to discharge his obligations. He took off the clothes he still had on, shaved, showered, and dressed in fresh things for the day. He put his old glasses back on as before, pushed a handkerchief into his pocket, and went down to the lobby. In the clearer light of morning his mind was beginning to function again with a certain computerlike precision and in so doing it shut out everything else. He did not stop for breakfast, which startled the headwaiter who knew now how he liked his bacon and eggs and had them already prepared and waiting.

He climbed into a cab, gave the address of the Matsumoto Company in understandable Japanese, and settled back to ride. He did not look out of the windows; he paid no attention to the driving. His mind was completely focused on a single thing and it refused to be diverted for any reason.

When he reached the plant he went immediately to Reiko and stopped by her desk. "May I see you," he asked.

Reiko looked into his face, saw the glasses he was wearing, and knew at that moment that the thing she had most feared had somehow happened. She got to her feet and followed him to the conference room, hardly daring to breathe.

Seaton motioned to her to sit down, then he took a chair opposite her. "Reiko san," he began. "I trust you completely. I want to ask you some things and I want complete and truthful answers—is that clear?"

It was clear, but Reiko was terrified.

"Each time that I have been going out with the geisha Fujikoma the Matsumoto Company has been paying the bill, is that right?"

It was a fearful thing to ask her, because it forced her to make a decision which might well be disastrous. But she knew it would be useless to lie.

"Yes," she said.

"Who is the bookkeeper?"

"Shizu."

"You know her well?"

"Yes."

"I want you to go right now, without telling anybody, and get the bill. It's here, isn't it."

Reiko nodded. "You sure?"

"I am very sure," he answered her, and there was steel in his words.

She had no choice, quietly she left the room and presently returned, a little group of papers in her hand.

Seaton pulled out a pen and picked up a memo pad. "The first night I was in Tokyo," he said.

Reiko dared to defy him. "That private," she answered.

He saw the point and for the moment let it pass. "Dinner at the New Otani."

The tears in her eyes blurred the figures on the slip of paper.

"In yen, one hundred fifty-five thousand." She tried to make it sound casual.

Seaton produced his slide rule and consulted it quickly. "About four hundred and ten dollars," he said very factually.

193

Miss One Thousand Spring Blossoms

"I'll work out the exact figure later. The walk in the park."
"Yen thirty thousand," Reiko answered miserably.
He looked at his slide rule again. "Ninety-four dollars. Thank you. The weekened in Kyoto."
She did not want to tell him. When he understood that he took the paper from her and read the figure himself. "Yen five hundred thousand. Let me see, half a million yen . . ." He read from the rule. "In round figures eighteen hundred dollars—that's quite a lot, but I presume she charged for her time overnight as well."
"Not she, geisha house," Reiko dared too interject.
Seaton ignored her. "Last Wednesday I took her to the movie."
Reiko bowed her head. "Yen forty thousand."
Seaton continued to add with careful precision. "A hundred and forty-four dollars." He stopped, and the fierce control under which he was holding himself almost gave way. "The weekend at Atami."
He knew that would include the fee for her intimate services—the wages of the professional prostitute.
"Bill not come yet."
"Reiko, don't hold out on me!"
She recoiled, but held her ground. "I tell you fact, Dick, no bill yet. Not yet come. Maybe today."
With his lips a thin line he added the figures before him. "Two thousand four hundred and forty-eight dollars," he announced. "When the bill comes in for Atami I'll add it on and work out the exact cents. Meanwhile . . ." With businesslike precision he took out a blank check, filled it in, and signed his name. "Will you please ask Mr. Matsumoto if I may see him—now if possible. I'll have to ask you to come along to translate."
"I shall see," she said carefully and fled. She ran first to Mr. Yamaguchi and told him the news, quickly so as not to take too much time. Then she presented herself at Matsumoto san's office, stated that Seaton san wished to see him, and told him why.
By the time Reiko went back to inform Seaton that the president awaited him, the disastrous news had spread through the office. Mr. Fujihara back in the engineering department, who perhaps knew Seaton best of all, understood the frame of

194

mind that his colleague must be in and desperately wished he could speak English.

When Reiko ushered the American into Matsumoto's office, Mr. Yamaguchi was also there, apparently in casual conference over a paper in his hand. He politely offered to leave, but Seaton indicated that he should stay.

The conference began on a note of stiff formality. "Mr. Matsumoto, last night I learned for the first time that my supposed social engagements with the geisha Fujikoma were in fact professional appointments. May I first of all apologize to you for my lack of understanding of the geisha system and for my unwitting gross abuse of your hospitality."

With greatest care Reiko consulted her dictionary twice and then put the words into Japanese.

"It has given us the greatest pleasure to do so," Matsumoto answered. The fact that it was not entirely responsive told Seaton that there was a flaw in the interpreting, but his meaning had obviously gotten through.

"In Japan I know that face is very important," he continued. "In my country honor is equally so."

"It is the same thing," Matsumoto san said. "Only the name is different."

"Thank you. It is my understanding that during my first evening in Japan you wished to entertain me; I accept that hospitality with gratitude. On the other occasions when I have seen Fujikoma the initiative was mine." He produced his check and laid it on the desk. "This represents the approx-imate amount of Miss Fujikoma's charges up to the time when we left together for last weekend in Atami. I understand that that bill has not yet come; when it does, I shall insist on the privilege of covering it. I expect that it will be quite high—higher than the one for the previous weekend in Kyoto."

All three persons in the room understood him perfectly, Reiko at once, the other two as soon as she had completed her translation.

"The check at this moment is not good," Seaton admitted without blinking. "You will note that I have dated it ahead. I will be returning home as quickly as possible at which time I will transfer funds from my savings account and the check will be valid. Normally I don't carry a checking balance of that amount. I hope you understand."

Reiko struggled to do him justice. When she had finished Matsumoto glanced at Yamaguchi, a question subtly shading his face. It was invisible to Seaton as was Yamaguchi's answering nod.

"Mr. Setanu san," Matsumoto began, his Japanese slightly clouded by emotion. "You are a man of the greatest honor; your name deserves to be written alongside those of the forty-seven ronin. I refuse your check, but I shall always cherish the spirit in which it was offered."

"If you wish to preserve my honor," Seaton answered him, "you must accept it. Otherwise my position will be intolerable."

The secret poet behind the massive desk took the slip of paper which Seaton had given to him and carefully placed it in the top center drawer. Then he rose to his feet, came forward, and held out his hand. It was a major concession not to bow, but the man he wished to honor had earned his fullest respect.

He was therefore not at his desk when the phone at that moment rang. Reiko picked it up for him. As soon as she understood the nature of the call she did her best to make her face a blank. To avoid using a proper name which might be recognized, she stated that the foreign visitor was indeed at that moment in Matsumoto san's office, but he was in a most important conference and could not be interrupted to speak to anyone. Then she glanced up quickly, saw that no one was paying her close attention, and in the language she knew that Seaton could not understand informed Masayo what had happened. Of necessity she put it into a very few words and then hung up.

"What was it?" Matsumoto asked her.

"I will explain later," she replied.

Matsumoto made an immediate and accurate guess. "Good girl," he said. He made a decision at that moment to raise her salary.

The purpose of the interview concluded, Seaton excused himself and returned to the engineering department. A highly sympathetic Mr. Fujihara met him there, but he did not betray the fact that he knew of his colleague's disillusionment. Instead he plunged at once into engineering talk and pointed

196

out a minor difficulty to which he already had the solution in his own mind. Mechanically Seaton looked at the problem, but his mind would not function. He toyed with it during the rest of the morning and for most of the afternoon, but the evident way out did not suggest itself to him. During much of the time he simply sat still and stared.

Sometime around six Seaton roused himself, looked at his colleague who was still quietly working, at the patiently waiting interpreter, and said, "Shig, are you planning to be here this evening?"

"For a little while. I'll sleep better when this is fixed."

"Then I guess I'll go out and get some dinner. I skipped lunch."

"I know. By all means go and eat." He started to ask if his colleague would like his company, then thought better of it and told Reiko to say nothing. Seaton disappeared from the plant, and set out on foot. Walking perhaps, would clear his mind. He was numb with pain and although he had not eaten for twenty-four hours, he still did not feel any sensation of hunger.

When he was not back by seven-thirty, Reiko and Fujihara looked at each other and wondered. Cautiously they discussed the situation and tried to think of something they could do. Neither wanted to go home; the American had said that he would return and they would have to be there—if for no other reason, to see that he was turned around and sent back to his hotel.

The minutes dragged on in the quiet plant, empty now except for themselves, and there was still no sound of someone coming in the front door. When it was eight-thirty Fujihara rose to his feet. "Reiko, I'm going out to look for him," he said. "If you don't mind and aren't afraid, I suggest that you stay here and wait. If he comes, see him to his hotel; if I come back and find you aren't here, I'll know what happened."

"It is the best plan," she agreed.

At the front door to the plant Fujihara hesitated, trying to decide where Seaton might be, in which direction he might have gone. He finally struck out toward a small area where there were a number of little restaurants and bars. There were two places there which catered in some degree to foreigners and where he knew Seaton had eaten before. He walked three blocks and then began looking into one small interior after another. In each one he asked if a tall foreigner had been seen, and received the same negative answer. For almost an hour he kept trying, working his way in a big circle around the plant. He had reasoned that his colleague must be close by, because if he had gone back to his hotel or done anything like that, he would have had the courtesy to call the plant and let him know. Seaton san was always polite; it was one of his best virtues.

He pushed his head into one more place, a small bar, and asked the same question.

"Dozo," the proprietor said, and nodded his head toward the inside.

There were six bar stools and one small table in the back. Seaton was sprawled across it, his arms reaching out over the edge, his head turned to one side. He was barely conscious. "I was about to call the police," the owner said.

"That will not be necessary," Fujihara answered. "He has totally exhausted himself with immense exertions. Is his bill in order?"

The man behind the bar nodded. "If you want to get a taxi, I'll help you to put him inside. I would like very much to have him removed."

Fujihara went outside, ran to the corner, and after two or three minutes found a cab that was free. He came back in it to the bar, managed to get Seaton inside with the aid of the manager, and then gave the address of the plant.

When they arrived there Fujihara ran inside and got Reiko. He snapped the night latch shut on the door after them and put her in the front seat beside the driver. "I think we ought to take him back to his hotel," Fujihara said. "Even though it will create a scene in the lobby."

"No," Reiko said. "He cannot be permitted to lose face like that."

"I would take him to my home," Fujihara offered, "but my parents live with us and there's no room for another futon anywhere. We will go to another hotel; have you any suggestions?"

"No hotel," Reiko shook her head. "It would destroy him. I will take him to my home where we have room. My mother

198

can sleep next door. Please to come, because I cannot handle him alone."

"I am very strong," the driver offered. "And I have had experience. I will be glad to help."

Fujihara was thinking. "Fine, then this is the plan. I will phone his hotel and inform them that Seaton san has accepted an overnight invitation and will require some of his things. A messenger will call for them. I will then go and collect what he will need and bring everything to your house. I will need your address."

Reiko gave it to him on a slip of paper together with a quickly drawn map to indicate where the house was located. The cabdriver dropped Fujihara off at the nearest railroad station and then followed Reiko's directions to her home. When he reached the immediate vicinity he maneuvered his small vehicle down the narrow dirt street and around the almost impossibly tight corner until he was directly in front of her door. Then he waited while the girl ran inside and informed her mother of the circumstances.

It was not easy to get Seaton into the tiny house, he was almost entirely a dead weight and even the capable taxi driver had considerable trouble. At last he was laid out on the floor of the main room, his shoes were pulled off, and a pillow was put underneath his head. Then Reiko paid the cabman who, as would be expected, declined a tip for the extra service he had given. She bowed her thanks very low and expressed her great appreciation for his help; when he had driven off she turned her attention to the man who lay in a stupor in the middle of the floor.

With patience and much of her physical strength she removed his coat and folded it neatly in the corner. She took off his socks and undid his tie so that it would be easier for him to breathe. After that she got a basin of water and carefully washed his face, putting his glasses into a coat pocket. She released the buttons at the cuffs of his sleeve and at his neck. Then she sat down and gently held his hand.

She was still sitting that way when Fujihara quietly arrived. He placed a traveling case in the room against the wall, then while Reiko made up a futon he relieved Seaton of his shirt and trousers. Leaving him dressed only in his shorts he helped to get him into the futon and carefully covered him. When he

199

had done all that he could he whispered to Reiko not to be in any hurry to come in in the morning—he would advise Matsumoto san privately of the circumstances. Assured that he could do no more for the present, he slipped out and walked back toward the train station.

Like a thin animate shadow Mrs. Watanabe appeared to see if tea could be offered. Gently her daughter told her that everything had been arranged for the best and not to trouble herself further. With her futon tucked under her arm the elderly woman toddled out to sleep with her next-door neighbor who knew enough not to speak of things which were not her concern.

With a small night light burning Reiko slipped out and undressed. Then she put on a comfortable yukata, tied it, and returned to Seaton. She sat down on her heels, quietly so as not to disturb him, and remained there all but inanimate. He might rest comfortably all night, but if he did wake up and did not know where he was, he might be very alarmed. Against that possibility she kept her vigil.

After two hours she shifted her position and sat against the wall to give her legs a little rest. She was there when Seaton came to, raised himself up on one elbow, and tried to look after him. "I'm lost," he said simply, his mind still struggling against the effects of the alcohol.

Reiko came to him. "You are not lost, Dick. This is Reiko. You are now a guest in my home."

"How did I get here?" he asked.

"You collapsed from overwork. It was too far to your hotel, so Mr. Fujihara and I took the great liberty of bringing you here."

"I got drunk," he said. "I got drunk. I never did that before."

"Please to rest yourself," she said, and smoothed her hand against his forehead.

"Reiko, I made a fool of myself." Self-contempt touched his voice.

"Not possible. You most perfect gentleman."

"I wanted so much to have someone to love," he said.

"You need love?"

"Terribly."

200

She came and sat close beside him. Then she folded her hands and looked down at them so she would not see his face. "Dick, if it is that you need the love, I will make love with you. It is too little to offer, no experience. But I willing to try."

"Reiko, you mean that?"

"Yes, Dick san. I am past the age to make marry, but I would becoming so proud if I have great honor to have your baby. I so much love children."

He was fully awake now. "Reiko, teach me something in Japanese. What do you call someone when you like them very much? What is the word for 'dear'?"

"Do not have such word in Japanese, Dick, but when you much like someone, you say not Seaton san, but Seaton *chan.* It is different."

"Reiko chan, I have met three girls in Japan, in my life if you like, and you are the pick of the lot. You are the best. Will you marry me?"

She bowed her head and then looked at him. "You give me greatest honor I ever have," she answered, "but not best. I not good enough for you."

"Yes you are, you're good enough for anybody."

"Dick chan, I thank you from the completeness of my heart. I cannot accept, but I forget never."

"Then will you at least kiss me good-night?"

She leaned over and pressed her lips against his for as long as she dared. Then she sat up again and said, "Please now to sleep. Tomorrow we talk."

"Good night, Reiko chan."

"Good night, Dick chan.

She remained there, sitting without movement, until his deep and steady breathing told her that he was now truly and naturally asleep. Then she slid backward a few feet and listened further until she was sure that consciousness had left him for many hours to come. When that was certain, she placed her hands on the mat before her, pointed inward so that the tips of her fingers touched. In that formal position she bowed until her forehead touched the space between her wrists. In a very soft voice, so as not possibly to disturb him, she spoke in English.

201

"Dick chan, it is with the greatest honor that I accept your propose of marriage. I will become your wife and serve you always."

She remained in that position, living her dream, until she knew that it was over. Then she went back to the side of the room and lay down. There was no spare futon, but she did not mind. If he needed her before morning, she would be close by to help him.

Chapter Nineteen

*W*hen Shig Fujihara arrived for work the following morning, he let it be known that Seaton san was out checking on component suppliers and that Reiko san had accompanied him as interpreter. Only Mr. Matsumoto knew any differently and because his own problems were so severe, he both understood perfectly and sympathized deeply. Otherwise business went forward as usual.

Seaton and Reiko appeared as soon as the lunch hour was over. The American engineer looked fresh and well groomed, but his face was set as solidly as it had been the day before and the cheerful manner which everyone had come to expect of him was entirely gone. He sat on a stool in the development section across the bench from Fujihara and said, "Give me something to do."

"The component redesign is now completed," Shig told him. "I am certain that it will work properly. The parts are now being made."

"Then what else is there—I don't care what it is. I must do something. You're doing my job, let me take on one of yours."

Shig was embarrassed. "Do not misunderstand me in what I

203

tell you now—there is no work in the shop. We have received no new business, except yours, for many weeks. We have nothing under development, our R-and-D funds are exhausted."

"I don't understand," Seaton said.

The Japanese engineer stopped his work and looked at his friend even though his words would have to be interpreted. "Since you are now finding out certain painful truths, perhaps I should tell you about our company. In Japan very much is decided by face—by reputation. Is this understood?"

"Yes it is," Seaton answered.

"Very well. It is a second truth that it is a great loss of face for any Japanese company to have to admit that it cannot do something which is supposed to be in its line of work. A grocer will not refuse an order for strawberries because they are out of season. He will always state that he will get them. If you ask later, he will say that they are on the way. Three months later, when they are in season, he will inform you that they have arrived."

"What has this to do with Matsumoto and Company?"

"Simply this, Dick san. A few months ago we were asked if we could produce something for the U. S. Air Forces. Something new to be used in side-looking radar. Several American firms had turned it down because it was not within the state of the art, but when we were approached, honor required that we say that we could do it."

"To Americans?"

"To anyone. We are an electronics house, therefore we cannot confess publicly that there is anything in electronics that we cannot do. I know that this sounds strange to you, but it is our way and on the whole it works."

"What if someone asked you for, say, television sets—would you tool up and produce them?"

"No; in that case we would probably buy them from Sony and make delivery. The customer must always be served."

An anguishing memory bit into Seaton and for a few seconds he was back in Atami.

"Go on," he said.

"We tried our utmost to fill the order. I worked as I have never worked before, so did everyone on our staff. But it was impossible, the specifications could not be met. But it was not possible either for us to announce failure. After all of our R-and-D funds had been used up, we drew on the general fund until we had nothing left with which to work."

"What is the present status of this job?"

"We have informed the U. S. Air Force that we are still at work on it. Meanwhile every other company in our area knows that we have failed. Therefore they do not give us their additional business. We lost a very big customer in the Philippines because the manager there lost confidence in our ability."

"Is there any hope that the problem may be eventually solved?"

"At some future time by someone else—yes. But we cannot do it as of now. That is why I have nothing to put before you."

"Is Matsumoto and Company in any danger?"

Fujihara shook his head. "I honestly don't know. All I can tell you is that the orders are not coming in. We are reasonably busy at present, but it is almost all old business. I should not tell you this, you are a customer, but it is best, I think, that you know."

Seaton gave up and simply sat there, his fingers locked together, looking at nothing. Presently Reiko slipped a cup of tea onto the table next to him. He hardly saw her.

"I want to go home," he said at last.

Fujihara looked at him. "I can check out the assembly and then send it on to you," he offered.

"I'm expected to bring it back with me," Seaton said. "In America our ways are sometimes tradition-bound too. My company is very conservative, and it costs them money. Only they don't know it."

"Why don't you go somewhere and have a good time. I can make some suggestions."

"I've been, thank you," Seaton answered with frozen words. Then he realized. "I'm sorry, please forgive me."

"I understand."

For half an hour there was no more conversation. Reiko slipped away and reported to Yamaguchi that there was no change in the situation. Then she dared to make a suggestion—if the bill from the geisha house had come in for the Atami weekend, it should be promptly lost.

Yamaguchi agreed, the matter would be handled with discretion and Setanu san would not be allowed to pay. There was no present intention of cashing his check, even though the funds would be very welcome.

Back in the engineering department Seaton still sat, zombielike, letting his mind torture him. How much had she charged to take off her clothes in front of him in the community bath? Had she made an additional fool of him in order to put that surcharge on the bill? Quite probably the answer was yes.

To hell with Japan! To hell with the exotic, the unusual, the different! To hell with foreigners, every damn blasted one of them!! His body jerked in a spasm of acute mental pain. To hell with Reiko? No. To hell with Shig? No. To hell with Mr. Matsumoto? No. But to hell with every damn, black-haired, jibbering, bowing leech who preyed on Americans and made fools of them every time they turned around! He did not know how much longer he could stand it.

Fujihara called to one of his staff and spoke to him in Japanese. The man nodded and disappeared. When he returned his arms were filled with blueprints neatly tied together with ribbon. Carefully Shig unrolled them until he found the specification sheet he wanted. He was not a medical man, but he was willing to attempt possible first aid.

He came around the table and spread the work sheet out before Seaton. "This is what we were asked to do," he explained. "Technically it isn't classified since no Japanese can be given a security clearance for lack of a national espionage law. But the understanding is that the requirements are not to be shown to any unnecessary people. I consider that you are now a necessary person."

Seaton bent over the blueprint and studied it without interruption for a little less than an hour.

"You were crazy to take this on," he said finally. "It's well beyond what can be done. Custom or no custom, you should have ducked it."

When the remark had been translated Fujihara nodded his agreement. "I would have been too busy with pressing orders to give it proper attention," he said. "But Mr. Matsumoto is not an engineer and he is a gentleman of the old school. He accepted the order."

Seaton slowly shook his head, reached for his slide rule and checked a minor point. "How did you attack it?" he asked.

For answer Fujihara nodded toward the pile of rolled blueprints which rested on the table. "We all did our utmost," he said.

At six o'clock, when Reiko rested a hand on his shoulder, Seaton waved her away. He was holding his head in his hands and staring at the complex blueprint before him. The lettering was in Japanese, but the schematics were in the international language of engineering and required no interpretation.

Reiko withdrew and waited half an hour. Then, when she saw how things were, she slipped out of the plant, walked to a nearby restaurant, and bought a box lunch. It was sushi, but they had nothing available for foreigners. Carrying it carefully she returned to the plant and put the lunch beside Seaton. She laid a pair of fresh unbroken chopsticks on top so that he would understand that it was food, and then sat quietly in a corner, looking at Seaton as he sat under the single bright light suspended above his head.

"Reiko chan." She came quickly forward to answer his summons.

"Yes, Dick chan?"

"Go home."

"But you may need ..."

"Go home."

She bowed her obedience.

He looked at her and realized that he had been rude. "Come here," he said.

He kissed her good night, then he squeezed her hard for a moment before he let her go. "Remember me to your mother," he said.

She bowed again and left him. After she went out the plant was quiet and still.

In the morning he was still there. His tie was loose now and twisted to one side, his hair was disarranged, and his chin dark with stubble. Beside him there were three broken pencils, a stack of paper, and a confusion of fragmentary drawings and sketches. As the department began to fill up, he apparently took no notice of anyone. Beside him the box of sushi was half empty with the chopsticks stuck in the side.

Miss One Thousand Spring Blossoms

As soon as he saw him, Shig Fujihara quietly and unobtrusively cleared the department. Then he put a sign on the door, hastily brushed on a sheet of white paper, that no one was to enter. Reiko was summoned to stand by, otherwise Seaton san was to be left entirely alone.

As though he were isolated on another plane known only to topology, that strange realm of mathematics which deals with impossibles, Seaton remained locked on to the work before him with total intensity. His mind anesthetized itself against every outside impression; the plant might have burned down without his feeling the flames until they touched the worksheet before him. He continued to make notes, to draw diagrams, like a man demented but unaware of his own affliction. The world now to him was the drawings before him, the paper at his elbow, the immediate basic tools of his profession. He worked on, ignoring everyone and everything, in total combat with the treacherous problem before him. It was a quicksand in which he was trapped, which was slowly engulfing him, but to which he refused to yield.

Fujihara brought him a lunch on a plate and he ate some of it mechanically while he worked. Quietly the Japanese engineer kept him shadowy company, assembling the parts of the Mercer and Doyle component as they came in from the shop.

As the afternoon wore on, Seaton's concentration seemed to become even more intense; he bent over like a man in a frenzy and his breath became uneven and forced. Reiko was alarmed and slipped out to notify Mr. Yamaguchi. In Matsumoto's san's office there was a brief conference and the advisability of calling a doctor was discussed, but it was decided to let things stand for the moment.

Toward four o'clock Seaton tossed a piece of paper at Fujihara and spoke the first words he had said all day. "Make that, please."

His colleague looked at it and saw that whatever it was, it was rational. He took it and went quickly to the experimental bench. Fujihara understood that whatever level his mind was now on, Seaton could no longer make himself understood through the interpreter—he was going it alone.

It was close to evening when the American got up, helped himself to a large piece of drawing paper, thumbtacked it down, and began to make a layout. After he had been at work for some time Fujihara dared to walk quietly behind him and look over his shoulder. He stayed there for almost half an hour, then noiselessly he left.

Most of the employees had already left the plant. Mr. Matsumoto had remained, knowing that something would have to be done—Setanu san could not be left for another night. Yamaguchi was also there, the problem of the American visitor shrouding his every movement. Without formality Fujihara walked into Matsumoto's office, nodding to Yamaguchi to join him on the way. When the door had been safely shut, he spoke.

"Seaton san was hurt far more deeply by the episode of Fujikoma than I dreamed; he is now like a man possessed."

The two others nodded that they understood.

"He did the most sensible thing—he went out and got plastered. Reiko took care of him last night."

"To what extent?" Yamaguchi asked, because it had a bearing.

Fujihara shook his head. "No," he said, "—not that. In order to distract his mind from its intense pain, I showed him the job we attempted to do: I had nothing else which might engage him."

Matsumoto nodded. "Probably very wise," he said.

"I called Dr. Uyehara, and he said for the time being to leave him alone—to let him work it off," Yamaguchi contributed.

Fujihara spoke again. "When men come up against something that is too much for them, they sometimes give up and jump into volcanos. Others go out and try to do desperate things. Seaton san is different." He stopped while the others waited. "I have just looked at what he is doing. I do not understand it, it is frankly over my head, but I can tell you this—it is not the work of a madman. It is something I have never seen before, perhaps no one ever has."

"I heard once of a pianist," Matsumoto said, "who faced an enormous grief. He went to his instrument and produced music of sublime inspiration; unfortunately no one was there to write it down."

"I think we have the same thing here," Fujihara said. "You gentlemen are neither one engineers, but I can tell you that

209

in this discipline the mind is frequently trained to a very high degree. It acquires the ability at times to exceed itself."

"What do you want us to do?" Yamaguchi asked.

"Leave him alone."

Shig Fujihara was the first to come to work in the morning, as was his intention. He unlocked the front door and passed through the silent offices to the back. There he found Seaton, lying on the floor, his head pillowed on his arm, utterly asleep. His chest lifted and fell with a steady rhythm, and there was peace in it. At the table where he had been working there was a vast and complex drawing; laid on top of it was a slip of paper with something written in English.

Shig sat and waited, cursing his lack of a proper language education. When Reiko came in, and she too was very early, he handed it silently to her. She read it quickly and then translated.

> *Dear Shig:*
> *Here it is.*
> *Dick.*

The department was kept closed. For an entire hour Fujihara pored over the drawing, trying to grasp the startling concept that it revealed. When he had seen enough he took it and left the room. He gave the drawing to his second-in-command with instructions that it was to be built, exactly as shown, with the utmost speed.

He heard a noise and turned around to find an anxious Mr. Matsumoto standing behind him. "Is he all right," he asked.

Fujihara did not answer that question, instead he spoke what was on his mind. "I think he's done it," he said.

210

Chapter Twenty

𝕵t was not until after eleven that Seaton began to stir. His long legs twitched convulsively once or twice, then he awoke, sat up on the floor, and rubbed his face with his hands. Reiko came and knelt beside him, waiting for him to speak to her.

"I'm sorry," he said, his voice huskier and more labored than usual.

She did not bother to answer him; instead, with Shig Fujihara's help she got him to his feet and pointed toward the washroom. There was a separate small facility in the engineering department; when Seaton stumbled inside he saw that his shaving things had been laid out neatly on a little glass shelf. He did not bother to wonder how they had gotten there, he concentrated instead on trying to bring himself back into the land of the living. His body ached cruelly from lying on the hard floor and there was an anvil chorus inside his skull.

After he had used the toilet he drew water in the basin and began to make himself at least presentable. It was a slow and torturous process accompanied by the pounding in his head which gave a measure of agony to every breath he drew. He looked inside the built-in medicine cabinet to see if there was any aspirin, but the few items on the shelves were all labeled in Japanese and he was in no mood to take any chances.

When he had shaved and doused his face with cold water, he felt a little better. He did the best he could to make his well-rumpled shirt appear neat and retied his tie so that the knot would be properly formed and in the correct position. Finally he wet his comb and did what he could with his hair. When he had finished all this, apart from the cursed headache, he felt more like himself.

Reiko had tea ready and waiting for him. He sat down on one of the drawing stools across from Shig and sipped the hot beverage. "Do you have any aspirin?" he asked.

Reiko literally ran to supply his need; she returned within seconds with a bottle and a paper cup of water. When he had taken the medicine he turned to his colleague and spoke with a voice still charged with weariness. "Shig, I finished up that job you gave me."

"I found it," Fujihara answered. "Thank you very much."

"Don't thank me, thank you for giving me something to do. By the way, I want one thing understood: that design, if you decide to use it, is by the Matsumoto Company, is that clear? It came out of your shop."

"I insist on using your initials as the designer," Shig said.

"All right, but don't point out who did it. It'll work, I'm almost certain of that. But it's a Matsumoto effort and I won't have it any other way."

Reiko interrupted her role as interpreter to say something on her own. "Dick chan, I think you best now go your *hoteru* and rest. Maybe take steam bath to fix muscles. But you need to be making sleep in bed."

"Can you get along without me for a while?"

Fujihara smiled. "Come back in the morning. Not too early."

Ten minutes later Seaton was in a cab and on his way back to his hotel, his overnight bag beside him. Halfway there he remembered the steam bath. Unfortunately it was Sumiko's day off, but the young lady who took her place was efficient and most pleasant. An hour after he had gone in Seaton emerged feeling much better; the headache had left him and life again approached the endurable.

At the desk there were a number of messages for him. He picked them up in a bunch and rode up to his room. Once inside he stripped off his clothes, put on a cool dressing gown which was as close to a yukata as anything he owned, and sat down to see what had happened in his absence.

The first was from a Japanese man whose name he did not recognize. He picked up the phone and asked the operator to get him on the line. Presently the struggling voice of a Japanese trying his utmost to speak grammatically good English came over the wire. He introduced himself as a reporter for the trade press; he was preparing a little item about Setanu san's visit to the Matsumoto Company and would like the American's opinion of the Japanese electronics industry as he had seen it.

Seaton spoke the appropriate words of praise and added a special one for Shig Fujihara.

"Your business, it is now I believe the principal concern of the Matsumoto Company, is it not?"

Publicity and public relations was not his field, but just having been briefed on the company's position, he automatically knew what to do. "No, I don't think so," he responded. "They have just completed the design of something very intricate for the United States Air Force. You had better get the details from them, but I have the impression it's a most important contract."

The reporter, who knew his business, smelled the hot story at once. "Did you saying, sir, that they have *completed* the design?"

"That's right, they're building the prototype right now, at least so I understand."

The reporter sucked in his breath. "Most interesting. I thank you, sir, most very much."

"My pleasure," Seaton acknowledged and hung up. That ought to get the monkey off Matsumoto's back when it appeared in print.

The next message was from the Japan Travel Service; did Mr. Seaton desire any arrangements for the coming weekend? He crumpled that one up and shot it into the wastebasket.

Mr. George Sakamoto had called, that could be taken care of later.

Miss Norma Scott had called, according to the dating on the slip the day before. She had left the message that she had delivered the material as requested.

Miss Kanno had called.

That brought the whole sickening thing back like a dagger thrust. Last week such a message would have sent his whole body tingling; now he could not bear to hold it in his hand.

The final message stated that Miss Hazama had called. She had left her number and had asked that her call be returned as soon as convenient.

Seaton had never heard of her and had no idea what it was that she wanted. She could wait. He pulled down the window shades, asked the operator to hold his calls, took off his robe, and climbed into bed.

Four hours later he awoke and realized that he was hungry. He could not remember when he had eaten his last full meal, it must have been days ago. He got out clean underwear, a fresh shirt, and a different suit from the wardrobe which substituted for a closet. He was tying his tie when he remembered the call from Miss Hazama, whoever she was. He called the operator, gave her the number and asked her to get the woman on the line. Then he began to put on his shoes.

His phone rang in about forty seconds and he picked it up. "Mr. Seaton?" a youthful-sounding feminine voice asked. "Is very important, I think, that I am seeing you."

"What about?"

"You remember me, don't you—I'm Peggy."

"I remember you," he answered, his voice frigid. "We had dinner together at the New Otani."

"Yes. When will you be free? Tomorrow?"

"Tomorrow I expect to be very busy."

"I kid you not, this is important," the girl persisted. "Nobody knows I call you except my boyfriend, Airman Millsup, I told you about him."

"I remember."

"Then please I see you."

"How much does a maiko charge per hour?" he asked. It was cruel, but fresh wounds had been opened in his mind and the pain was renewed.

"For maiko not much, I lucky to get ten dollars hour."

"Very well; I have now learned about the geisha system and that you do not see a member of your profession without paying for the privilege. I will therefore hire you for one hour this evening—you and no one else, is that clear?"

"Seaton san, you want *hire* me?"

"I believe that is the usual arrangement. Give me the address of the proper restaurant. I do not want to meet anyone else, *is that clear?*" he repeated.

"I not square, I understan'. If you want this way, all right. What time you like?"

"Have you a booking open at nine o'clock?"

She ignored the savage thrust, instead she offered a practical suggestion. "You let me talk to desk, I tell him place and he write in Japanese for taximan."

"Very well. I will see you at nine." He hung up the phone and almost at once was convinced that he had made a fool of himself again. If he didn't know enough to stay away from geisha and everything about them by this time, then he didn't have brains enough to put on his own pants.

He reached for the phone again to call her back and cancel the arrangements, but he saw in time that to do that would only compound the blunder. If Masayo showed up, he would tell her that he had already paid as much for her company as he could afford and then walk out. He gulped hard for just a moment, then remembered. Two thousand four hundred and forty-four dollars; plus, of course the weekend in Atami and the prostitution fee. He had no idea what that would be, but high on the scale certainly. When he had run that tape through his mind and had read it off with fresh and bitter sharpness, his rigidity of thought returned, and whatever was to happen he was protected now from any worse and deeper hurt.

He went down to the dining room and took his time over an excellent dinner which he did his best to enjoy. He did not notice that he was consuming every scrap of food placed before him, even to the last of the bread and butter.

At fifteen minutes to nine he hailed a cab and handed the driver the slip of paper which had been prepared for him at the desk. The man studied it for a moment, nodded his head

215

quickly to show that he understood, and took off. Where he was going or by what route Seaton neither knew nor cared; he had once resolved to learn his way around Tokyo, but that starry-eyed thought was now dead and buried.

After some minutes the cab turned into one of the little alleylike hidden streets, rolled slowly down a long block, and then halted. The driver looked again at the slip of paper and then pointed to one of the many establishments in a long row. Seaton paid him and looked at his watch. It was two minutes after nine.

Without emotion he walked up to the door and was taking off his shoes when it was opened from the inside. It was a new place—he had not been here before, and the hostess welcoming him was bowing in the usual style. He returned it formally and stepped inside to be confronted by a white-faced, doll-like maiko; her hair was piled in an elaborate upsweep arrangement and held in place by long ornaments which stuck out and were tipped by tiny hanging pendants. Her black flowered kimono was of the standard pattern, her face a blank behind the heavy, pastelike coating of stark white which hid every bit of natural flesh.

"I have an appointment," Seaton said. "Miss Hazama is to meet me here."

"She doesn't dig English," the maiko said. "Don't you recognize me?"

For a moment he was startled to hear his own language coming from the totally foreign animate object he saw before him. Then he remembered that he was a gentleman. "I'm sorry if I kept you waiting," he said. "And please excuse me for not recognizing you."

Before the maiko could reply the hostess showed them to a room equipped with the usual small table, two cushions, a tokanoma alcove, and a musical instrument laid out on the floor. They sat down formally opposite each other and then Peggy bowed low. Seaton could not think of her by that name, it was too violent a contrast with her appearance.

"Thank you for coming," she said. "You didn't need hire me, but you make a sensation at geisha house. No one ever ask for a maiko by name before."

"You gained face?"

216

"Up to the sky. I ordered for you, some light Japanese food. Okay?"

"Okay?"

"Since you hire me, I'm ready to play, sing, and dance for you before we talk. May I please?"

"If you like."

She picked up the shamisen, adjusted the tuning, and then began a simple, fragile melody. When she had played enough to establish a mood she began to sing, not in a pip-squeeky thin voice, but with clear, soprano tones which were as clean and pure as a mountain stream, Seaton did not want to be entertained, he had no wish to hear a Japanese song, but the spell of the music was magical and he found himself enjoying every note.

When she had finished he applauded her quietly. In answer she twanged the strings of her odd instrument and then began something which soared like an invisible bird high in the night sky. Her voice too took wings and when she had finished Seaton knew that his mood had been a little softened and that the tightness within him had been slackened off.

"You sing beautifully," he said. "What was it?"

"The first one in English is name 'Moon Shining on the Ruined Castle.' The other one no translation, its name 'Kuriku Kuriku.' "

The door slid open and a waitress appeared with a tray. She set out the usual things, the chopsticks and small dishes of food, but this time there were two sets.

"I'm breaking rule," Peggy said. "I'm not supposed to touch food when I'm at work, but I want talk to you."

A sense of compassion for the girl touched Seaton. "I'm very glad you did, I would feel very awkward if you had not."

"That's what I figure. Now, from now on what we talk is classified, okay?"

He remembered that her boyfriend was in the United States Air Force. "You don't mean really, do you?" he asked.

"I mean you keep big mouth shut and I do the same."

"Agreed."

"Okay, because if you spill on me, I'm busted; I go to work for Mitsubishi making transistor radios."

217

"You have my word."

"Okay, here goes. Do you remember first night you meet Masayo?"

"Yes."

"Well, you start something. Japanese guys don't treat us like Americans do, mostly we get the brush-off. Masayo, she is a pro, right to her fingernails."

"I know that."

"You threw her a curve, you offered her some soup—remember?"

"Yes."

"I looked up the word—that was 'considerate,' she not used to that. So you score in the first inning. She give you her phone number."

"She's in business, isn't she?"

"Yes, but you supposed to call geisha house to get her. Now understan', geisha house have her like maybe a ballplayer. If he belongs to the team and you want him you buy—right?"

Seaton nodded.

"Anyhow, when Matsumoto Company hire her for you she have no choice, she have to go in and pitch."

"I understand that. And if it will make you feel any better, she was good, she fooled me completely."

"No," Peggy said. "You fool her."

He took time to try the food and waited until she too had had a few mouthfuls.

"I fooled her?"

"Yes, you take her for serious and she not used like that. But more, she begin really like you."

"Very kind of her."

"Seaton san, what your first name?"

"Dick."

"Okay, Dick, now the straight goods. You go to Kyoto. She get paid, yes, because she belongs to geisha house and for her they get top prices."

"I found that out, to the penny."

"Well, you think she go off to Kyoto with any Tom, Dick or Shingiro? Like Willie says, hell, no. And when you treat her like classy girl she really is, you score. You know that—she take your picture, have a blow-up make, and keep on her dresser. One and only."

That was news and he received it as such.

"She want see you own time, but she have no own time; twenty-four hours she geisha, no relief, no chance for TDY. So she no stick Matsumoto with bill, geisha house ran up the tab."

Seaton tried to be fair and just. "All right, if I judged her too harshly, I'm sorry."

Peggy ate and despite the mask of makeup over her face managed to say something with her eyes. "Now listen, and hang onto you hat. Can I talk straight?"

"You can."

"In Japan is what is called 'pillow geisha.' Lower class and not a real geisha, just use the name, see?"

"Yes, I see."

"Well, Masayo she *never* pillow geisha, and when I say 'never' I mean—get it?"

"Not entirely."

"One time she was maiko. She came from poor family up north and they sell her."

"Sell?"

"Cash on the line. Not like me, I'm free agent, I can quit. She couldn't. When she fifteen her owner sell her for one night, you get meaning? She have no choice, she must. She think she go to sing and entertain, she go really to get rape."

"Good God!" Seaton said. He swallowed hard and tried to blot the visual image out of his mind.

"So she lose virgin, but she can't help. Now dig this: all the time she hate men mostly, but she become top-rank geisha. Then you come. You take her Kyoto and not try any monkey business. So she kiss you good-night because in Japan almost same thing. Do you see the light?"

"Just a little."

"Okay, now comes Atami. If I tell you something, you believe me?"

He considered that. "If you say so, then I will."

"Okay, Dick, now listen good. For Atami, Matsumoto get no bill. On the house."

He shook his head. "You just told me that geisha never have a day off, no free time of her own."

"Oh, geisha house collect all right. They collect plenty.

Geisha costs high because must new expensive kimono every month, much other overhead. Girl must pay your money maybe fifteen thousand dollar year just to stay in business."

"That I didn't know. I see in part why the prices are so high. But if Matsumoto didn't pay the bill for the weekend at Atami, who did?" He thought for just a moment and made his confession. "It would be a high bill."

She nodded. "I dig you, but you got a shock coming. You all set?"

"I'm set."

"Geisha house charge about thousand dollar for their share. They get the money. You know who pay? Masayo."

His forehead wrinkled in doubt and disbelief. "Do you mean she paid the geisha house for her own time?"

"On the money. From her saving, she pay."

He was stunned.

"Okay, Dick, now I give it to you straight. I know what happen. She give to you herself, for first time any man her choice. You are number one."

Seaton looked at the white blank of a face and decided that she was old enough to be told. "I give it to you straight, Peggy, for me it was the first time too."

"I know. She know. You now get message in the clear?"

"I think so."

"You better think, Dick, because she love you, don't you dig?" She swallowed visibly. "Not suppose to happen geisha, but you make happen, foreigner and all. If you want, you got yourself one damn fine wife."

Seaton took off his glasses and brushed his eyes.

"How do you know all this?" he asked. "Does everybody?"

"No, not everybody. Only me. She my sister."

Chapter Twenty-One

$\mathcal{T}$he night was uncertain, restless, and contained very little sleep: Seaton tossed and turned as conflicting emotions spun and collided in his mind. When it was at last seven he got up, dressed and with his briefcase in hand descended to the lobby. He had his usual breakfast and then climbed into a cab to go to work. He was halfway to the Matsumoto plant before he noticed a difference in the traffic and realized that it was Saturday.

When he arrived he found to his surprise that he was expected. A call had been made to his hotel to ask if it would be convenient for him to stop by. The desk clerk had reported that Seaton san had been observed leaving with his briefcase. His arrival at the plant was therefore anticipated.

The production personnel and most of the office people were not in, but Reiko was there along with Shig Fujihara, Messieurs Yamaguchi and Futaba, and Matsumoto san himself, who was in a rare mood; in fact he was composing a poem.

News travels with remarkable speed in Japan; he was therefore already aware that the trade press on Monday would announce the triumph of his firm in accomplishing the impos-

221

sible design for the U. S. Air Force. As soon as this information became general, which would be within a matter of minutes, the phone would begin to ring and the treasured opportunity would be given to talk business.

On the wall of his office he had mounted a copy of Seaton's drawing. He could not understand even the smallest part of its complexity, but he regarded it as he might have viewed an exquisite piece of calligraphy—one of the most admired arts in the Orient. He was now attempting to frame a tribute to the flight of genius which had created this remarkable work. He could view it in no other light.

He picked up a brush, drew it carefully across the inkstone, and began to paint characters on a piece of soft fibrous paper. When he had finished he viewed his handiwork and felt a glow of satisfaction. Haiku was a form he much admired—the three short lines made up of imaginative, eloquent imagery in precisely seventeen syllables. This one, he felt, possessed some slight merit.

> *Great storm come*
> *Mighty Bird fly in*
> *Sun break through*

He looked again at the intricate engineering drawing and knew as a practical man that it was no ordinary effort. Even if it described something which would not work, it was still a great accomplishment. However, Fujihara san had told him that there was a very high probability that it *would* work. He too agreed that Setanu san was a genius.

At that point Reiko san arrived to inform him that the American engineer was on his way and should arrive shortly. After delivering the message she went out to the lobby so that she could meet him as soon as he came in.

When he arrived she gave him a happy smile and a bow. He returned the courtesy and then put an affectionate arm across her shoulder. "I'm glad you're here," he said.

"Me too, Dick chan."

He sat down and motioned for her to join him for a moment. "Reiko, in Japan is it possible for two young ladies who are sisters, and both unmarried, to have different last names?"

"Oh, very easy, Dick chan. Many times family have no daughter, relative give baby girl for present. Also sometimes boy. This way keep family name going, most important."

"I see, that clears up a point."

"Good. Matsumoto san, he want see you if you time."

"Of course I have time to see Mr. Matsumoto, whenever he wishes. Is Shig here today?"

"Shig yes, he wait you engineering department."

"Then please tell Mr. Matsumoto that I'm here and await his pleasure. And, oh yes, Reiko chan . . ."

"Hai?"

He took both her hands in his. "Thank you for taking care of me. I'll never forget it."

She let him feel the pressure of her fingers. "Much pleasure to do."

"You're a wonderful girl, do you know that?"

"Not so, Dick chan."

"Oh yes it is." He stopped there because he could not go on. He remembered acutely what she had offered to do for him and for a few moments she was very dear to him. Then he stood up, helped her to her feet, and went back into the plant.

As soon as he had spoken his good-morning greetings in Japanese, which he could do now without having to stop and think of the words, he was handed something to examine. It was the redesigned Mercer and Doyle component, beautifully made and finished. When Reiko appeared with the tea things Shig was able to converse. "I checked it out last night," he reported. "It works like a poem. Forgive me for praising my own work in small part."

"You've got it coming. It was my job, you did it for me."

"Speaking of jobs, we have already started building a prototype for the Air Force. What you did is revolutionary, but I am sure it will work–I know it."

"I hope so. I went on a real binge. I've already thanked Reiko for taking care of me. Thank you too."

Shig smiled. "For this we have friends. Drink your tea and then we will go and see Matsumoto san. He wants to talk to you."

Ten minutes later there was a small gathering in the front office. Sitting loosely around the president's desk were Seaton,

223

Reiko, Shig, and the still functioning hospitality team of Yamaguchi and Futaba. Before Matsumoto could speak, the phone rang, he picked it up and received congratulations on the triumph of his company in designing the impossible. He accepted like the gentleman he was and then turned to the group which awaited him.

In Reiko's translation he spoke with his full dignity.

"We have now finished our work on the new component for Mercer and Doyle. We regret that this event will take from us our now good friend Seaton san; none of us wish to see him go."

Seaton turned to his translator. "Reiko, how do you say 'good friend' in Japanese?"

"Yoi tomodachi," she answered.

He recognized the words; they were the ones Masayo had spoken to him at Atami. At that moment he very much did not want to go home either.

"Domo arigato, yoi tomodachi," he said.

Matsumoto san continued. "While suffering from great pains of distress, our good friend relieved himself by studying a problem which was beyond our powers. By enormous effort and great genius he has produced the answer and I say also it is possible that he has saved our company."

He produced an unsealed envelope from his desk. "A very small return," he said and handed it to Seaton. "Now it is my turn to insist that you accept."

Seaton looked inside and saw the check he had written to cover the geisha fees. It was a great overpayment for the work he had done, but he saw the justice and appropriateness of it all; he bowed his thanks from a sitting position and put the envelope into his pocket.

"Now I think we all agree that in only a short time Setanu san has become one of us. I wish this to become so. I know he has position of great worth and importance with Mercer and Doyle, but I make offer anyway. Because of what he did for us, much new business will come to make us strong. And only among us Reiko can speak the perfect English. So I now invite Setanu san to honor us by considering offer to become vice president our company for sales and engineering. I think maybe he like some things here Japan. Also we are closer

224

coming to United States, even though Socialist Party not like, and maybe someday we have international electronics firm. Matsumoto and Seaton. More better sound maybe Seaton and Matsumoto."

He stopped. In the sudden quiet Messieurs Yamaguchi, Futaba and Fujihara bowed their way out leaving their president and Seaton alone with the necessary interpreter.

"It is understood," Matsumoto continued, "that if you accept us, you must first make farewell from Mercer and Doyle, We are not rich American company, but we can offer three things. First, monthly salary."

He handed Seaton a small folded slip of paper. The American opened it and read the figure: four hundred thousand yen.

"Second, very important in Japan, expense account. If it bring in business, almost no limit. You entertain American customers, you hire best quality geisha. Travel first class.

"One more thing, if we make success, end of year is a bonus and stock option. Maybe also four five year, maybe less, you become partner, see name up in light. Not can read, maybe, but still there."

Seaton noticed that the quality of Reiko's translation was beginning to slip; perhaps the importance of the discussion was distracting her.

"I hardly know what to say," he responded.

Reiko did not translate that, instead she said, "That all right, I answer for you." Then she turned and rattled off a considerable speech in Japanese.

At once Matsumoto san registered the greatest pleasure. He bowed from his chair, then rose to shake hands.

When the interview was concluded Seaton took Reiko by the hand and led her into the conference room where he shut the door.

"Please, for heaven's sake, tell me what you said to him!"

Reiko smiled. "I say for you first very much honor to have offer from such wonderful company."

"Great, that's fine—what after that?"

"I say you must returning with new part because nobody else smart enough to put in and make work."

"Oh, no!"

"That okay, Dick chan, *I* say no one else so smart is."

"That's better, now watch yourself and get your verbs in the middle."

"Ah, so yes. I say you must consider, think, and consult most famous fortune-teller. Then you make answer."

"Fortune-teller?"

"Fortune-teller very important in Japan, always good business to ask. You ask lawyer, we ask fortune-teller, maybe not so different. Sometime both guess."

He thought for a moment. "Reiko, since the assembly is finished, and my job is done here, at least for the moment, I must go home."

"I know, Dick chan. I not want, but I understan'."

"Reiko chan, I'll be honest: I don't want to go either."

She brightened at once. "Then you work here? Be my boss?"

"I'll think about it," he promised.

After he had said his good-byes all around, had shaken hands especially warmly with Shig, and had kissed Reiko very thoroughly in the otherwise unoccupied lobby, he went back to his hotel.

He made two calls. The first, with the assistance of the desk clerk, produced the information that Fujikoma had gone to the country and would not return before Tuesday. In shattering disappointment he realized that he could not wait that long. His second call was to Japan Air Lines.

Despite the fact that the big DC-8 jet was eating up the distance at the rate of a mile every six seconds, he had plenty of time to think as the hours dragged on across the vast Pacific. The atmosphere of Japan was preserved within the aircraft, but every minute that passed seemed to be restating the fact that to Seaton the United States in general, and the conservative environs of Boston in particular, was where he belonged.

Masayo, of course, was much in his thoughts, but now he was trying to decide how much of his interest in her should be regarded merely as infatuation. As the plane continued to knife its way through the sky, the seemingly endless water underneath underlined the vast separation between Japan and the United States. He was an American, he could not deny that, and the natural resistance to change cautioned him against any rash move.

A pretty and well-mannered stewardess offered him an oshibori with which to refresh himself. "Domo arigato," he said automatically, and having expressed his thanks wiped his face and hands with the wet towel. In his luggage he had safely packed away the thing he had been sent to fetch. Now he could go back to Mercer and Doyle to resume the even tenor of his life.

Only there would be no striking Norma Scott whom he might call up for a date, no warm-hearted Reiko Watanabe to put his interests before hers—and no Masayo.

Since he had hours of time with nothing to do, he thought about her and let the devil's advocate take over for an inning.

"Remember," the voice said, "that she is a professional. It is her trade to please men—she is probably doing it right now. She has undoubtedly excited hundreds of men by fluttering her fan and making eyes at them at the same time. And face the blunt fact; in her trade sexual partnership has little meaning."

"Yes, but she herself paid the bill at Atami," defense counsel retorted.

"That's what Peggy says, but she is part of the *mizu shobai,* the hard-cash entertainment industry, herself. How much would you believe a bar hostess's story, her flattery, or her promises? After the Matsumoto people found out that you knew Masayo had been hired, of course they wouldn't let you see the bill for her services at Atami. And, if she liked you so much, why didn't she tell you she was being paid?"

"I held her in my arms," Seaton said silently on his own behalf, "and we were like one living thing."

"So you were—she's a skilled professional, remember? Who is she with right now? It must be somebody, because that's her business. Is he kissing her? Are they having dinner together? Are they making love?"

The stewardess smiled and deposited a luncheon tray on his lap. With it was a knife and fork, and he picked them up. It would be ridiculous to use chopsticks on a plane half filled with other Americans.

As he ate he tried to think of other things and of how good

it would be to find himself back again where he knew he belonged.

"Why, Mr. Seaton!" the receptionist exclaimed, obviously surprised. "I hardly recognized you."

He smiled at her and caught himself in time before he started to bow. "Hello, Elsie, how've you been"

"But what happened to your glasses?"

"My old ones? I don't wear them much any more?"

"Well, it's quite a change, I must say. I'll tell Mr. Williamson that you're here. How was Japan?"

"Most interesting; it was quite an experience."

"I bet it was. My husband and I hope to travel together some day." She plugged in a cord and flicked the ring lever. "Mr. Williamson, Mr. Seaton has just returned—he's in the lobby now."

She listened for a moment. "Yes, sir, I'll tell him." She looked up. "Mr. Williamson says he will see you in about half an hour, probably in Mr. Mercer's office. He just came back this morning from a business trip to New York."

"Thanks," Seaton said. "I'll be in the engineering department."

He pushed his way through the familiar doors which led into the plant, turned left, and went down the corridor past every well-remembered nick in the plastered wall, past every dog-eared exhorting poster. As he walked once more into the room where he had spent so much of his unspectacular lifetime, he saw Herb Fineman look up from the drawing board over which he was hunched, as always. "Well hello, Dick!" he exclaimed, and came forward to offer his greetings. "What the hell happened to your glasses?"

"I switched to contacts."

"Where did you get them?"

"In Japan."

"Well I'll be damned—come on over and tell me all about it."

"Before I do," Seaton said, "I want to put you wise to something you ought to know. I know that Williamson rushed the hell out of you to get that drawing finished for Matsumoto."

228

Herb spread his hands. "Not really. Nobody ever really rushes around here; they can't make up their minds fast enough."

"All right, then let me put it this way—there was an error in the design. It didn't follow the mock-up and consequently when we got it built, it wouldn't check out."

"Oh my God!" Fineman said.

"Relax, you're covered. There's a helluva sharp engineer at Matsumoto, Shig Fujihara. We worked on it together, actually he did most of it, and he not only fixed it, he worked out a way to make it perform one more function and cost just a little less."

"Then I'm for him, Jap or not."

That disturbed Seaton and he said so. "Herb, calling a man a Jap is like calling him a wop."

"Or a kike," Fineman finished.

"Exactly, you've got it. He's a friend of mine and a damn good engineer. Of course I'll tell Williamson that Matsumoto came up with a 'suggestion' to improve the component and that I bought it when I found that it would represent a saving."

"That kind of language he'll understand. Dick, behind this I get the general idea that you saved my hide for me—thanks a lot."

"Forget it; if you ever meet him, thank Shig. Meanwhile I'd suggest that you pick up any stray copies of our original blueprint. Williamson can't read it, but he has a sharp nose."

"I get you. Now tell me about Japan; did you run into any of those geisha girls?" He dug a friendly elbow into Seaton's ribs.

"Yes," Seaton answered.

Fineman leaned on a desk and beamed. "Well, come on, tell me all about it."

Mercifully the phone rang. Fineman picked it up and took a message. "Williamson wants to see you right away. You're to bring the component from Matsumoto with you. It's to be in Mercer's office—he just got back from New York."

"Okay," Seaton answered. He picked up his briefcase and departed to answer the summons.

Basil Mercer did not appear to have moved since he had

seen him last. He was again sitting behind his desk, looking ninety percent a human being and ten percent a blowfish, ready to preside. Williamson, as small, neat, precise, and dusty as ever, had taken up his station at the side of the desk where he could nurse some additional status from the authority it represented. Seaton was welcomed with the exact amount of cordiality which the situation required; it was agreeable, but without a trace of familiarity or camaraderie. Such enthusiasms were kept carefully bottled up for the annual meeting of stockholders.

"I am very glad to see you back in good health," Mercer began. "I trust you have not had an accident with your glasses."

"No, sir, I was recently fitted with contact lenses. I find it quite a bit more convenient and efficient." By putting it that way he shot down any implication that personal vanity had been involved.

"I see. In Japan?"

"Yes, sir."

"I was not aware that they had advanced to the point of contact lenses."

"I believe, sir, that they invented them." It was a horrible blunder and he knew it the moment he had spoken. To correct Basil Mercer in his own office, and in the presence of a subordinate, was unthinkable. He saw a thin way out and took it. "I believe, sir, that it was you who first told me about that."

The dangerous pressure which had immediately started to build up eased off. "I may have done so, I don't recall at the moment. Did you have any trouble locating the Matsumoto people?"

"No, sir, the head of customer relations and the executive vice-president met me on arrival."

"The executive vice-president!" Williamson interjected.

"I believe that any representative of our firm would be so treated," Mercer said. "I am a little surprised that Mr. Matsumoto did not see fit to be there himself."

For the first time in his life Seaton lied with ease and a clear conscience. "At the time he was in conference with some of the top people in Air Force procurement. The United

States Air Force, that is. We did have dinner together that evening."

"What was your, ah, impression of Mr. Matsumoto?"

Seaton was careful this time. "I believe that your selection of Matsumoto and Company as our Japanese suppliers was very astute. The best direct answer to your question that I can give you, sir, is that he heads what is obviously a successful technical organization and one which is handling very responsible work. They are building a prototype now for a very advanced radar system for the Air Force which several American firms were unable or unwilling to produce. Of course this is not in our line, but Matsumoto and Company is most capable over a wide spectrum. Their ethics are also impeccable."

"You were well treated?"

"To the highest standards, both professionally and personally."

Mercer leaned back a little to allow Williamson his turn.

"Did you bring their assembly back with you?" Williamson asked.

Seaton opened the first of two boxes in his briefcase and set the beautifully made component on the desk. Both men bent over it intently, although neither was in a position to appreciate its subtleties. When they had inspected it for perhaps twenty seconds, Seaton took it upon himself to speak. "There is something quite interesting I should tell you about this. The chief engineer of the Matsumoto Company is a Mr. Fujihara; he is a man of very superior ability."

"I presume then he was trained here," Williamson interjected.

"I didn't ask him concerning that," Seaton answered. "When the production of the first prototype was well advanced, he proposed a suggestion concerning its design. I studied it very carefully and then authorized a change."

The effect was electric, as he had known it would be. "*You* authorized a change?" Williamson demanded, his voice even dryer and more impersonal than usual.

"Precisely; I did not believe that the company would invest in sending me that far except to represent its interests to the best of my ability. As it is, Mr. Fujihara's brilliant suggestion

231

accomplished two things: it will give our tester an additional mode of operation which it did not previously have, and it will reduce the net cost approximately two dollars and eleven cents per unit."

Williamson's face underwent a change. "Do I understand that by adopting this suggestion we could effect a saving of more than two dollars on each unit that we purchase?"

"That's correct. My thought was that during our first production run of one thousand units we could recover in full most or all of the expenses incident to my trip to Japan and might show an additional profit in the bargain. So I authorized the change."

Williamson looked at his superior to be sure that the pronouncement he was about to make would have been the necessary endorsement. He looked at Basil Mercer's passable imitation of the Great Stone Face and read nothing to the contrary. "Then under those circumstances, it is my opinion that your action was *probably* justified."

"Thank you, sir. I have one thing more to add: I have the highest confidence in the Matsumoto Company, but you will recall that Japan is a land of earthquakes and I foresaw a possible inconvenience to us if the Matsumoto plant were to be seriously damaged or destroyed. I therefore looked into a possible second source should we ever require one. This is their product." He opened the second box and set George Sakamoto's entry on the desk. It received the same scrutiny as before, but for a few seconds less.

"How much did you pay for it?" Williamson asked.

Seaton lifted his eyebrows at him. "Nothing, of course. The firm asked to bid and on their own initiative made up a sample."

Williamson tightened down a little. "What are their prices?" he asked like a judge of the Inquisition.

"To have obtained an exact price on the modified and improved version I would have had to stay another three days," Seaton answered, a touch of coolness in his own voice. "I did not consider it necessary or a good investment—we can obtain the estimate by mail. They are competitive pricewise with Matsumoto."

"They could be, possibily, a little less," Williamson persisted.

Seaton accepted the challenge. "Possibly, but after Matsumoto developed the saving for us, which can amount to several thousand dollars according to our sales forecasts, I could not conceive that Mr. Mercer would authorize transferring their effort to another firm. I lined up a second source because it seemed to me to be good business."

Basil Mercer elected to speak. "On the whole I believe that you acted prudently. I realize that considering the distances involved, you could not readily approach us for a decision. Under those circumstances you did not exceed your authority."

Williamson cleared his throat and looked at his superior.

"Oh, yes," Mercer went on. "During your absence a most significant change has taken place within our organization. You will be glad to know that Mr. Williamson, in recognition of his fifteen years service and outstanding capabilities, has been elected to the office of assistant vice-president."

The subject of that remark managed without visibly moving to preen himself like a peacock, which was something of an achievement.

"Congratulations, sir," Seaton said.

"Thank you," Williamson intoned dryly. Then he ignored Seaton for a moment. "Do you wish to discuss the Callahan matter with him?"

Basil Mercer put the tips of his well-cared-for fingers together, and, since he was not an Oriental, instead of contemplating his navel, stared off into space. "That might be advisable," he said finally.

Williamson assumed his new authority. "The Callahan Company, with which I presume you are acquainted, is quite anxious to develop a Japanese source themselves. Since they are not in direct competition with us, they presumed to ask who took care of our needs. I would like to caution you that you are not to discuss the Matsumoto Company by name in any way outside the office and with as few people as possible within the company." He did not need to state that the request had been refused, it was automatic; there was a possible future competition for Matsumoto's production time which could not be risked.

"I have a suggestion," Seaton said. "Since Matsumoto is on firm ground, quite literally, we could very conveniently get off the hook by giving them the name of our alternate source. They would then have no further interest in our affairs."

Williamson looked at Mercer for a decision.

"A very sound thought," he said. "It occurred to me a few minutes ago."

That, thought Seaton, was even-Stephen with a lie apiece.

"I happen to know some of the people over there," Seaton said. "We have been to the same professional meetings. I'll take care of it for you."

"I prefer not," Williamson said.

"Sir?"

Williamson glanced at Mercer, like a batter checking with the third base coach, and then delivered himself. "I realize fully that you have been away, to a foreign country in fact, and have therefore temporarily lost sight of certain protocols which are observed in more civilized society."

"I don't quite follow you."

"Because we found it convenient to send you to Japan does not imply that you have been advanced to membership in the management group. Perhaps I am being unnecessarily blunt, but if anyone calls the Callahan Company, I will. Their request originated on the management level. It would be out of place for Mr. Mercer to concern himself personally, equally so for yourself for perhaps the opposite reason. Am I quite clear?"

"Entirely so," Seaton answered. "I lack the necessary stature within the company."

"Precisely." The word was clipped with the snipping precision which made Williamson what he was. "And I will add that while you made the correct decision in the matter of the modified design, it would have been more suitable if you had notified us at once and requested confirmation."

"Did you receive my expense accounts?" Seaton asked.

"Yes, I did."

"Did you find them in order?"

"On the whole they were moderate; I am not fully acquainted with the cost structures in Japan. I trust you have all necessary supporting receipts and invoices with you."

"Certainly." He turned to Mercer himself. "I hope, sir, that you are satisfied with the results of my visit to Matsumoto."

Speaking directly to the president that way was not called

234

for since no question had been asked, but Mercer overlooked it, which required his new assistant vice-president to do so as well.

"If the component works properly, and all liaison arrangements are in order, then I would say that you have conducted yourself creditably."

Seaton rose to his full height and for a very brief moment surveyed the office. "Thank you, sir. And now, since everything seems to be in order, let me thank you for your confidence and submit my resignation. I have a pay check coming which I will ask you to accept in lieu of two weeks' notice."

"I suggest you reconsider that," Williamson snapped. "Using my own career as an example, there is a future to be found here. Industrial discipline is something which everyone has to learn to accept, I thought you understood that."

"Industrial discipline has nothing to do with it," Seaton answered him. "I've been here enough years for you to appreciate that. It simply happens that while pursuing my duties in the Far East I was offered a position, without my in any way soliciting it, which I would be poorly advised to decline."

Mercer looked at him for a moment; when he spoke a mellowing of his tone could be detected. "Would you care to tell us what that position is?"

"Certainly, sir, in confidence for the moment. I have been offered the post of vice-president for engineering and sales with the Matsumoto Company. So it will be my pleasure to continue our association."

Williamson did not like that part about "our association" and showed it. "And may I ask what kind of salary they offered you?"

Seaton looked at him. "About double yours," he answered.

He cleared out his desk with no trouble at all; few personal things were there. He invited Herb Fineman to join him for dinner, then he shook hands with half a dozen people and ·informed them that he was leaving. At last he headed toward the lobby and the free unmetered air which was waiting for him outside.

235

Elsie was watering her plants, a major concession she had been allowed as long as it was at her own expense. She was bent over, administering the last few drops of the water ration as Seaton walked past. Her inviting posterior beckoned to him and he responded. With the flat of his hand he smacked her plump curvatures, not hard enough to cause any discomfort, and said, "So long."

"Why, Mr. Seaton!" she exclaimed and pursed her lips in a coy smile.

Chapter Twenty-Two

$\mathcal{T}$he next three weeks flew on leaden wings. Now that his decision had been made, Seaton resolved to follow it despite the constant voices of habit and inhibition which told him that he was a lunatic. Whenever the pressure of doubt grew too strong, he reminded himself that he was at last free of Williamson's picayune interferences, an annoyance which time after time had kept him from doing any original or creative work. Despite long-standing opinion to the contrary, there *was* a form of civilization west of the Hudson River and the focus of the universe was not necessarily within a mile of Boston Common.

On the first afternoon of his freedom he had an idea and picked up his telephone. Within a minute he was informed that a call to Japan cost only twelve dollars plus tax for the first three minutes and that Japanese time was nineteen hours ahead of his. A quick calculation told him that it was midmorning tomorrow in Tokyo; he gave the Matsumoto Company number and asked to speak to Miss Reiko Watanabe.

In less than ten minutes the operator called him back with the succulent words, "Go ahead."

"Ohayoo gozaimasu, Reiko chan," he said, and then waited to hear if the connection had really been established.

Back came the familiar voice which gave him a sudden stab of pleasure. "Dick chan, where are you?"

"I'm in the United States," he answered. "Reiko, is Matsumoto san in today?"

"Hai. Yes he be."

"Please tell him I have made my decision—I will accept his offer. You understand?"

"Oh, Dick chan, so wonderful! You come be with us. Matsumoto san, I know he most happy this wonderful news. Dozo."

For almost a full minute the line was apparently dead at trans-Pacific rates, then Reiko was back, slightly breathless. "Dick chan, you there?"

"Hai," Seaton answered.

"I speak you now Matsumoto san's office. He most much happy you come. U. S. Air Force Colonel Klein much excited your design, say most wonderful."

"I'm glad to hear that. Give Matsumoto san my regards."

"So yes. Dick chan, when you come?"

"I have to arrange a lot of things, I'll need three weeks."

"I tell now Matsumoto san what you say." There was a pause and then the voice of Matsumoto himself came on the line. He spoke in Japanese, of course, for a few seconds, then Reiko came back on to translate. "He say much new business already for what you do, so he want company will pay you ticket to come back Japan. Expense account, yes?"

Seaton said, "That's too generous," and then took a deep breath before he asked his question. "Have there been any calls?"

"No, Dick chan, she no call, I sorry. You want me maybe do something?"

"I guess not, Reiko. If she does call, you might tell her I'm coming back."

"Of course, Dick chan, I understan'. Where you live, please, so can write maybe?"

He supplied his address, said "Sayonara" with real regret, and hung up. Girls like Reiko didn't turn up every day.

Immediately he realized that a subconscious worry had been stripped from his mind—the possibility that he might have

238

gone all the way to Tokyo only to find that there had been a misunderstanding or that the offer had been withdrawn. The conversation, brief as it was, brought back to him all the warmth and friendship he had felt at the Matsumoto plant; as soon as he learned the language, communication would be closer still.

He wound up his affairs more easily than he had thought, did the final packing of his technical books and other things he would need, and then, at the appointed time, took the limousine to the airport. He had a bad moment when he climbed on board the big jet; there seemed to be an almost irresistible force pulling him back, telling him to stay where he belonged and to find a girl somewhere among his own people.

He defeated it by using his engineer's mind. Almost half of his life had already been spent here and what did he have to show for it? A little money in the bank, no especially close friends, and the memory of a job which, in retrospect, he could see had been a dead blind alley. He could have worked his life out in that engineering room and his reward would have been the ability to pay his modest bills, some additional savings, and perhaps a pin to wear when he had completed twenty-five years of service. Now he was shortly to become the vice-president of an expanding company in his chosen field. Vice-president before he was thirty-five—almost unheard of in New England unless you were born to the company or to the money behind it.

While spending a few hours in San Francisco he had the happy thought that he would be coming back often in search of new business. He wanted to very much, because he dearly loved his own country. Come to think of it, a West Coast branch office might be a sound idea.

Shig and Reiko met him at the airport when he landed in Tokyo. They had been advised of his arrival time and beamed wide smiles of welcome. A Matsumoto plant car was standing by as suited the dignity of the new vice-president; as soon as he was through customs they ushered him to it and superintended the loading of his luggage in a flow of Japanese instructions and comment. When everything had been safely stowed and they were settled inside, Reiko did the talking for them both.

239

"We got you nice place to stay. Shig find for you and make rent for month. If you like, keep, if not find new place. Not much big, but only hundred yen taxi to office and one block railroad station."

"That sounds great," Seaton said.

"Is little bit Western-style house, was belong to major U. S. Air Force who just go Alaska. Maid can cook, so she make you everythin' you like."

"Maid?"

"Oh, sure, Dick chan, everybody have maid. This one she work long time Air Force people, she speak 'nuf English you understand sometimes."

His entrance into his new quarters was a minor adventure for Seaton. He found that he had the second floor of a two-story wooden frame house which had been Westernized to a degree. The space was limited, but there was a welcome breeze which could flow in any one of the four sides. Furthermore there was the promise of heat in the wintertime, a luxury still reserved for the limited few in Japan. The maid proved to be of indeterminable age; she bowed repeatedly and in proud English said "Welcome new master" at least a half-dozen times. The major who had lived here before had even constructed a corner bar and had built a niche for a television set in the side of the bedroom.

"This is great," Seaton assured his friends, "I can't tell you how much I appreciate your finding this for me. Let's go have dinner."

"No thank," Reiko answered promptly. "I understan' for you now morning so maybe sleep a little, take bath. Tomorrow come plant. You no got telephone yet, but we try. Pretty soon, maybe."

Seaton *was* tired and the bed he had inherited looked inviting. He shook hands again with Shig, unabashedly kissed Reiko in his presence, and despite the bright daylight prepared to at least nap. He experimented with the window shades of his room, walked around in his stocking feet in search of the bathroom, and then attempted to inform the maid he had inherited that he intended to sleep for two or three hours. Miraculously she understood. He turned in with the rare feeling that life was just about to begin and that he was one of the first in line.

240

Miss One Thousand Spring Blossoms

When he awoke the maid had his dinner ready; she served it with a knife and fork, but with a pair of ohashi at hand if that proved to be his preference. When he had finished, he sat back and decided that so far he very much enjoyed living in Japan and that it was wonderful to be a vice-president.

In the morning he was welcomed back to the Matsumoto Company with appropriate ceremony. Matsumoto san himself met him in the lobby and after an enthusiastic greeting personally escorted him to his new office. It was not a large one, but by Japanese standards it was more than ample and an air conditioner hummed in the window. The whole thing gave Seaton an enormous lift; it was visible, tangible proof that he had not cast himself adrift on the seas of commerce, and that his new status as an executive was valid. He was still inflating his lungs with the air of fulfillment when Yamaguchi arrived to shake his hand and present a young woman he had with him. "Meeting, please Mrs. Yamada," he struggled out. "Hisho."

"Good morning, Mr. Seaton," she said. "What Mr. Yamaguchi means is that I am to be your secretary. That is, if you approve of me."

Seaton looked at her, collecting himself. He had not expected a secretary, let alone one whose English was obviously so excellent. He could not imagine where they had found her. "I'm most happy, Mrs. Yamada," he answered. "May I say immediately that your English is wonderful; you don't have a trace of an accent."

She laughed, lightly and pleasantly. "That's not to be wondered at, sir," she answered. "I'm American. My husband works for the Army over here; he's a civilian."

"I beg your pardon; do you by any chance also speak Japanese?"

"That's about all we talked at home, both of my parents were born in the old country."

"Surplise," Mr. Yamaguchi inserted.

"Hai," Seaton agreed.

Mrs. Yamada became professional. "I have one message for you: Lieutenant Colonel Howard Klein of the Air Force procurement office would like you to get in touch with him after you've settled in. He is the officer handling the proposal we have made concerning a new radar system."

241

"I know about that," Seaton said.

"Good. I should tell you that I've been instructed to translate for you any documents in the company files you'd like to see. One more thing; Mr. Matsumoto has created what you might call an English-speaking department under your direction; Miss Watanabe will therefore be working for you. For the time being everything which comes in English will be routed to us for handling, and translation if necessary."

Seaton seated himself, a little self-consciously, in the stiff new chair which had obviously been obtained for him, looked at the top of his virgin desk, and wished that Williamson could see him as he was now—well, someday he might. Then he had an intense urge to begin work, to dig in solidly and prove that he was worthy of all this consideration which had been shown him. He looked at the telephone on his desk and thought of the number he wanted most to call. He would, as soon as he was decently able.

"By the way," his new secretary said, "my name is Ellen and I'd be pleased if you'd use it."

"Thank you. Will you help me with my Japanese?"

"Of course, whenever you wish."

"I'd like you to do one thing for me now: please see Mr. Matsumoto and tell him for me how very much I appreciate the pains he has gone to to prepare all this for me. I'm extremely pleased in every way."

"I'll take care of it right away, Mr. Seaton. I should tell you that it was actually Mr. Yamaguchi who made most of the arrangements, shall I thank him too for you?"

"By all means."

He looked again at his new desk as soon as he was alone and discovered a small pile of correspondence in the neat teakwood box set to one side. This gave him something to do and he grasped at the opportunity. He forced himself to remember that Masayo worked in the evening and it would be inconsiderate to call her until lunchtime at the earliest. He thought about her and clenched his teeth. As soon as he had looked at her face once more, he knew, his contentment would be complete.

At three-thirty, while his secretary was absent and he was again alone, he dialed the number with shaking fingers. There was one ring and then a high-pitched voice told him something in Japanese. He tried it again with the same result, looked up, and saw Reiko waiting respectfully in the door of his office.

He beckoned her inside. "I can't get my number," he said simply.

She understood. She dialed quickly, from memory, and waited. Then she hung up. "Telephone disconnect," she reported.

"Could you try the geisha house for me?" he asked.

Reiko hung her head. "Already I did, Dick chan, yesterday, I want make you great surprise. Masayo san, she no more there. I ask where go and they no say. I tell them from Seaton san, then they say very sorry but can no help."

"Do you think they know where she is?"

"Oh, they know, Dick chan, she belong them. But if they no tell Matsumoto san, they no tell anybody."

"Matsumoto san?"

"Hai, when I can no find he try, but geisha house make excuse. Not so good, Dick chan."

For the moment he accepted the verdict, but only as a slight setback. He could not call her immediately; beyond that single fact he would not concede a thing.

The evening was a happy one; he had dinner with Shig and, of necessity, Reiko to interpret. They talked about many things including learning each other's language. Seaton went to bed still happy with his decision and the way in which it was working out.

The following afternoon he looked up from the new blueprint he was studying, thought for a few moments, and then asked Ellen Yamada if she could get Mr. George Sakamoto for him.

"Sakamoto is quite a common name," she responded. "Is he a Nisei? With a first name like 'George' it seems likely."

"That fooled me too," Seaton admitted. "He's Japanese, but his English is better than mine. He does business with a lot of American firms."

"Then he's undoubtedly in the English-language Tokyo phone book. There is one, you know. I'll check it right away."

Three minutes later she had George Sakamoto on the line.

243

"Good afternoon," Seaton greeted him. "I owe you a dinner; I called to see how soon I can have the pleasure of your company."

"You don't owe me a thing, but of course I'd be most happy to get together with you. Very sincere congratulations on your new job, by the way, I'm certain you'll never regret the step. Let me see—my calendar is full this week and most of next, after that I'm leaving for the States for a month. The only time open, or at least partly so, is this evening. Would that be too soon?"

"Not at all," Seaton assured him. "Since I don't know the city yet, would you be kind enough to select a spot and brief my secretary on how to get there?"

"Of course, if you wish. Suppose you put her on the line."

That took care of that. For the rest of the afternoon he worked over the blueprint on his desk, finally circling one small area where he felt a design improvement might be possible. Satisfied with what he had accomplished, he went home, bathed, dressed for his appointment, and took the train into town.

George Sakamoto was on time to the minute, which in Japan is phenomenal for anything but a train. After the proper greetings they sat down to dinner and discussed the political happenings in Southeast Asia. When he felt that the conversation had developed to the proper point, Seaton switched to a new subject. "I showed your component to Mercer and Doyle. They are very interested in your ability to offer a second source should they ever require one."

"Very considerate—thank you very much," George said.

"Another thing: there is a company in our area—I mean in Mercer and Doyle's area—which is looking for a prime source. I'd like to get the business, but for ethical reasons, and a purely personal one which is also valid, I don't feel that I can. Perhaps you'd like to look into it."

"Absolutely, do you care to give me their name?"

"It's the Callahan Company, I don't have the address offhand, but it's good-sized outfit and easy to locate."

Sakamoto took out a pocket notebook and made a careful entry. "I'll call them tomorrow. May I mention your name?"

"It wouldn't mean anything to them, but go ahead if you like."

"Thank you. This is a very valuable lead and I want you to know that I appreciate it. If we get together by phone, then I'll stop in and see them while I'm over there next month."

Seaton accepted a cup of coffee and stirred in a spoonful of sugar. "Now another matter," he began. "This is an entirely separate thing and bears no relation to our conversation up to now, is that clear?"

"Entirely," Sakamoto sipped his coffee black and leaned back to listen.

"We have discussed Miss Fujikoma before, if that's the proper way to refer to her. Despite the fact that she was compensated for the time we spent together, I still regard her as a friend."

The Japanese showed a touch of embarrassment. "Frankly, Mr. Seaton, I still haven't forgiven myself for speaking so carelessly in your presence. Every time I think of it I could kick myself."

Seaton waved a hand in the air. "Please, forget it—as it worked out it was for the best. There were—certain compensating factors. In confidence, I learned that not all of the time we spent together was paid for by the Matsumoto Company."

George looked up. "Frankly, you surprise me."

"Unless I was badly misinformed, and I don't believe that I was, I have some justification for considering her a personal friend. At any rate, I know that you know her and I thought it possible you might be able to tell me where I might find her now."

There was a pause of several seconds. "Mr. Seaton, because there is nothing in your country like the geisha system," Sakamoto said, "I wonder if I presume to fill you in a little. In this instance I believe that it might be of some value to you to know the score."

"Please do."

"All right, then, to begin properly I have to explain that Japan is a country very deeply steeped in tradition. I know that you come from New England, but even the traditions there are no comparison for those in this country. Take the tea ceremony, for example. In all of the several schools every motion is rigidly formalized; a Russian ballet is no comparison. Furthermore, the exact manner in which each gesture is performed is also important. This may strike you as going to extremes; the viewpoint here is that it has been refined over the centuries and must be done precisely as the old masters set down."

"In our country," Seaton commented, "a tremendous amount of fuss is made in Washington over who sits exactly where around a formal dinner table."

Sakamoto nodded. "Then perhaps I may bring up another parallel. In the United States several persons may 'own' part of a prizefighter. In the literal sense of the word he is not their slave, but they direct who he will fight, when, and where. They participate in his earnings. In some cases of unreasonable contracts the fighter does all the bleeding and his manager makes all the money. Or others who share in his contract.

"The geisha system is a very ancient tradition with its roots far back in the samurai era. While there have been some changes, largely to adjust to modern living practices, the basic structure remains unchanged for the past several hundred years. So it's a formidable institution.

"Now a geisha 'belongs' to her manager or geisha house in the same manner that a ballplayer or a fighter belongs to the organization that holds his contract. Only to a much higher degree; in some instances very poor families have literally sold their daughters in times of severe distress to be trained as geisha."

"It's shocking," Seaton said.

"When a girl enters the geisha establishment she is taught certain skills and a great deal about entertaining and pleasing men. When she is old enough she becomes a maiko or student geisha. After a few years at this level, when she is sufficiently mature, she is given a geisha name and put to work. She may remain a geisha then for as much as fifty years. When she starts out she is usually almost hopelessly in debt to the geisha house, since all of her room, board, and training will have been charged against her account. Is all this too much for you?"

"No," Seaton answered. "I'm intensely interested. Please go on."

"Sometimes a girl will enter the geisha ranks of her own accord—because the work appeals to her, because she wants to be part of the glamour world, or because she is related to a successful geisha. Fujikoma has a younger sister in that position."

"I've met her. Peggy."

George nodded. "Now here the going gets a little rough and you'll have to forgive my bluntness. Sometimes a maiko's virginity will be sold for a very high price to some rich man; for all practical purposes the girl has no say in the matter. Similarly, a geisha can be put to work wherever the establishment that owns her wishes; if she is very good, then she may become, in time, a geisha of the first class. Then she commands higher fees, but her overhead also goes way up.

"Now I realize that you are interested in knowing whether or not a geisha can, let us say, be married. Normally that is difficult, that is, unless her proposed husband is in a position to pay off her debts in full, add a substantial bonus to the geisha house, and then support her in the manner to which she is accustomed. It has happened, but it isn't too common.

"What is much more likely is that she will find a patron—someone to support her, pay all of the costs involved in her being a geisha, and who will take her for what is commonly called a second wife."

"In actuality a concubine," Seaton suggested.

"More or less, yes. The exact relationship is another of those complicated things; sometimes the young lady will continue to work as a geisha, but with her patron having first call on her services. And an intimate relationship is presumed in such cases. A considerable number of geisha go this route."

"Are you aware how Fujikoma became a geisha?"

"Not precisely. It is possible that she is a geisha by her choice, in which case her obligations would be much less and she could be in a position to quit when she wanted to. The geisha people would certainly try their best to prevent this as she is one of the very best we have right now—she is extraordinarily attractive, and very popular. In other words she is money in the bank to them and they don't want to lose her."

Seaton tried his coffee again and found it cold. He put down the cup and then began the question that was on his mind. "She's gone from the area—at least her phone has been disconnected and when Mr. Matsumoto himself tried to locate her, not at my request by the way, the geisha house refused to supply any information. Considering the extent of your connections, could you, or would you, be able to help me find her?"

George Sakamoto pushed his coffee cup aside, drew a deep breath, and let it out slowly. "Mr. Seaton, at this precise moment I am not able to promise you anything. I understand your interest and I am fully convinced that it springs from the highest motives. It is most unfortunate that you chose a geisha to honor with your attention; unless you are thinking of her in very serious terms I would suggest making some further acquaintances among young ladies of good family who, I am sure, you will find to be very charming companions. To be perhaps rudely abrupt, have you considered the possibility that at least part of your interest in Fujikoma is based on her attraction as a well-bred and properly mannered daughter of Japan? That sounds a little more flowery than I had intended—what I am trying to say is that Japanese girls are generally regarded, in this country at least, as very superior and Fujikoma is a fine example of what I mean."

"My friends call me Dick," Seaton said.

"Fine, Dick, I'm George."

"Now that that's cleared away, George, it was a good try, but no cigar. I'm no longer a starry-eyed adolescent." He took a sip of water. "I admit freely that I have never been a great hand with the ladies, Norma can tell you that, but geisha or not, my interest is in one Masayo Kanno, simply because she is the person she is. I know another Japanese girl for whom I have a very genuine feeling, but it's no go. I also know Norma, not nearly as well, of course. She is certainly most attractive; she's got about everything a girl can have, and we have a common heritage and language. Two months ago the prospect of a date with a girl like Norma would have sent my head spinning. Now it's Masayo; if she fell off a bridge and had to spend the rest of her life in a wheelchair, it would still be Masayo."

"That much?"

"That much."

"All right, let me see what I can do."

Miss One Thousand Spring Blossoms

"Thank you."

They parted company a little after nine when Sakamoto dropped Seaton off at the railway station. Then, as he was driven home, the Japanese executive leaned back to review the knotty problem he had been given.

Finding the girl was not the difficulty; he was confident he could do that easily enough. He was much more concerned with the moral question as to whether he ought to try. He remembered again the old Japanese proverb: "A man should look close to home to find his wife."

There were too many negative factors for his business-honed mind to accept them without a careful appraisal. The girl was a geisha, a fact which had much more meaning for him than it did for the American. Not all of the geisha life was made up of pretty kimonos and happy, carefree parties. If they were to marry, it would probably be years before they could communicate properly in either English or Japanese; only his extensive foreign residence when he had been a boy accounted for his own exceptional bilingual capability.

The world was changing, he acknowledged and accepted that, but knowing firsthand the still great differences which separated the cultures of Japan and the United States, he had serious reservations. Finally, there was the question of race. He largely dismissed that—a person was either cultured or not.

Now that Seaton was a more or less permanent resident in Japan, the geisha house had clearly taken precautions. It was his informed guess that arrangements would be made to secure a patron for Fujikoma without delay.

Chapter Twenty-Three

$\mathcal{E}$arly in the following week Seaton left for the Philippines. He had never been there, but as he sat in the big aircraft passing the four hours plus of the flight, he remembered that a few weeks ago he had never been to Japan. Now he was a ranking officer in a Japanese company. If he could accomplish that, he would get along in Manila.

Actually the way was paved for him from the moment he stepped off the aircraft. Someone had been appointed to see him through customs and into the main terminal where he was met, greeted in excellent English, and then taken to lunch at a fine club overlooking Manila Bay. This was a new experience in his life, being received as an industrial executive and treated accordingly. Before the luncheon was over he had already determined that the chief problems in the past had been generated by a lack of communication combined with a certain feeling that the Matsumoto Company was on a downgrade.

He took corrective action, carefully and without any display of eagerness or attempts at salesmanship. The fact that the Matsumoto Company had taken on an obviously expensive American vice-president was eloquent in itself. Although he was not experienced in sales work, he had the good sense to realize that new ideas take time to sink in and that old ones are sometimes hard to eradicate. He therefore took three full days to complete his visit with one afternoon off to visit the Rizal Shrine and take the hydrofoil ride across the bay to Corregidor. One of the three days he devoted entirely to the former customer's engineering department. While there he was able to make one pertinent suggestion relative to production technique which was immediately appreciated and put into effect.

That, perhaps, was the most significant thing he accomplished during the time he spent with the company and its English-speaking management. When he shook hands at the airport before his flight back to Tokyo he had nothing tangible to hold in his hand, but he knew that the reservations had been erased and that orders would again begin to flow in at the proper time.

He had passed Okinawa on the return trip when an idea came to him. It appeared, full-blown, from somewhere back in his subconscious; unless a piece of extraordinary bad luck intervened, he knew how to find Masayo.

Just because he did not want to take any chances, he pulled out a pocket notebook and wrote down a name while it was still fresh in his mind.

That evening he spent alone in his quarters; after he had eaten he sat down with a magazine for a little while, but then his mind digressed from circuitry and he looked out over the lower rooftops from his second-floor vantage point and studied the face of Japan. Quietly, and without announcing itself beforehand, a certain rich and satisfying emotion began to develop within him until it reached the point where little quivering sensations began to run down his spine.

This was life, and this was living. He had dared to break out of the mold, the formalized shaping of his life that had been done for him so that he would conform and adhere to the Pattern. He was to have been an engineer, changing jobs perhaps after a few years in order to have a little better environment and a little more salary, but he was never scheduled to rise much above that level.

All he had had to do to effect his escape was to make one decision and then stick to it. To be willing to do an unconventional thing when it made good sense and to take a certain calculated risk without which no one can really get anywhere. The price of security, he decided, was mediocrity, and even when it had been paid there was no guarantee that the desired benefit would follow. Management could always make decisions which like a tidal wave could sweep people aside, even when they thought that their foundations were most secure.

He realized that by refusing to be cautious one time he had promoted himself from a pawn to at least a knight, and possibly a bishop. He had seen that the gambit was a good one and thanks be to heaven, he had not been afraid to take it! In the morning, after he had communicated the results of his trip, he asked Ellen to get Colonel Klein on the telephone.

"Howard," he began, "I want to ask a favor of you, if I may, which has nothing to do with procurement."

"Shoot," Klein responded.

"I want to locate an airman who is on duty somewhere in the Tokyo area, I don't know precisely where."

"What is his duty specialty?" Klein asked.

"I don't know that either, all I have is his name. But it's an unusual one and for that reason I hoped that you might be able to track him down. It's Millsup; I have an impression that his first name is Willis, but I'm not at all sure of that."

"There can't be too many Millsups," Klein agreed. "I'll have a go at it and call you back."

"Thanks much."

"No sweat." The colonel hung up.

Approximately thirty minutes later he was back on the line. "There is an airman first named Millsup who is a radar maintenance technician over at Tachikawa," he reported. "First name Willis; does that do it?"

"It most certainly does," Seaton answered, trying to keep his voice even. "I certainly appreciate your trouble."

"No problem at all. Did you want to talk to him?"

"Very much so, if it can be arranged."

"Are you going to be in this afternoon?"

"Right."

"Then let me see what I can do. It may not be exactly sanitary, but since you're working on a radar project for us, it

252

might be in order for you to talk to one of our bench maintenance people as a matter of good business. Call you back."

Seaton was in conference with Matsumoto san when the call came in, but Ellen took the message. When he returned to his desk he found a memo that Airman Millsup would be at the plant at two-thirty and would wait until Seaton had the time to see him.

An Air Force vehicle manned by a Japanese driver pulled up on the small parking lot beside the garden three minutes early and delivered a young American airman to the plant. Seaton sent Ellen to bring him in.

He looked with unusual interest at the young man, hat in hand, who came in the door. He was rail thin, redheaded, and his fingers would not stay still. His uniform was perfectly pressed, indicating that he had put on a fresh set of 1505's before keeping his appointment. His shoes were models of military glisten. Despite the according-to-regulations perfection of his appearance, however, he was charged with a kind of energy which seemed almost to flow out of the seams of his uniform.

"Sit down," Seaton invited. "Tea? Or, if you prefer, the English-speaking department carries a stock of ice-cold Coke."

"That sounds great," Millsup said.

Ellen disappeared to produce the refreshments. After his guest had settled himself like a coiled spring, Seaton looked at him pleasantly and inquired, "How's Peggy?"

Millsup reacted sharply, then he revolved his hat in his fingers for a few seconds before he replied. "*You* aren't going to try to talk me out of it too, are you, sir?"

"Not at all," Seaton answered. "I've met her and I'm quite impressed."

Millsup brushed a hand across his forehead. "That's a relief," he admitted, then the light dawned. "Say, I think I know who you are. I'm sorry, sir, no lack of respect, but didn't you date her sister?"

"Right," Seaton said.

Ellen arrived with the cold drinks in tall glasses and excused herself as soon as she had served them. She closed the door behind her as she left.

The two men who shared a certain common interest enjoyed their drinks for a few moments before the conversation continued. "Masayo," Seaton began, "is a pretty exceptional girl."

Millsup bobbed his head to indicate agreement. "You're damn right—I mean yes, sir. I go for Peggy myself, but that sister of hers is something."

"I'm not trying to be personal," Seaton continued, "but have you seen Peggy recently?"

Millsup looked around him as if to be sure he would not be overheard. "Last night, but keep it to yourself; the geisha house is getting real sticky lately."

"I know, which is why I thought it would be nice to get together."

"It's fine with me," Millsup agreed. "I could use a little backing up right now. I've got plans for Peggy as soon as she graduates and gets her name. But I'm not an officer, you see. . . ."

Seaton raised a hand to stop him. "Don't worry about all that, we have the same problem. Only mine is a little worse. I don't know where Masayo is."

"Call the geisha house. It might cost you, but it's sure worth it."

"That's been tried, they clammed up. Her phone's been disconnected. They won't tell anybody anything."

"Peggy would know," Millsup volunteered.

"That was my thought," Seaton said.

"Okay, I read you five square." The airman leaned forward and assumed a position where he looked like a rocket set to blast off at any moment. "You know, sir, this geisha system needs some overhauling, it's past due. Maybe we ought to operate on it a little. I have trouble seeing Peggy now, they want to keep her tied up all the time. I don't go for that."

"We might just do that," Seaton agreed. "Meanwhile, if you do see Peggy, will you ask her for me? I have a hunch she might be in my corner."

Millsup leaned still further forward and became confidential. "I might just be able to get to her this afternoon. I don't have to report back to work and I've got a couple of friends around. Don't ever sell the Air Force short, you know."

"I won't. If you get any results, will you let me know?"

"On the double. Can I call you at home?"

"I don't have a phone yet, it takes time over here. You can reach me here, probably until about six." He passed over one of his new name cards which Ellen had ordered for him while he had been away.

"How about your address, just in case anything drastic breaks," Millsup suggested. "This might develop into something."

Seaton wrote the information on the back of the card and returned it to his guest. "Good hunting," he said.

"Right, sir. If Peggy can come through, I know she will. These Japanese girls have something."

"All girls have something, it's a question of degree. We have some fine ones at home too."

"Oh sure, there's some, no doubt about it. The ones who don't read the fashion magazines maybe." He stood up. "I better be going, sir. I'll touch base as soon as I have anything at all."

"Thank you, Millsup; any expenses are on me, of course."

"Don't let it worry you, I might just bring your girl back. Anyhow we'll try."

"Give my best to Peggy."

"Right, sir. Good-bye."

The scene remained calm until a call came in just at five-thirty. Ellen piped it in and nodded her head to indicate that it was personal.

"Dick, this is George," came over the line. "Since our conversation last night I've been looking into matters a little bit. Concerning the young lady, all that I can tell you right now is that she is out of town and isn't expected back in the near future."

"At least that eliminates Tokyo," Seaton answered.

"I can give you a little more than that. I want to level with you as far as I am able. In the first place, I know the lady quite well myself—professionally, that is. She is one of the very best in her line of work and I do a great deal of entertaining, so I could say that we are friends."

"Excellent," Seaton commented.

"To a point, perhaps. I must confess that I knew she had left; I called for her two days ago and I was frankly told that she had become emotionally involved with a client and had been transplanted until she could get over it. My compliments—someday, if you care to, I wish you'd tell me how you did it."

Seaton had no answer to give and could think of nothing to say.

"Now there is one more thing which I hope won't prejudice our friendship, but I feel obligated to tell you about it. Before she left I happened to see the young lady for a few minutes and we discussed certain matters. I told her that in my opinion your interest was based, to a degree at least, on the glamour that she represented and to the exotic aura which surrounds her profession. This was, of course, previous to our meeting last night. I advised her, therefore, to try and put the matter out of her mind and to go back to work."

That was a blow which left Seaton numb, but he still remembered that he was a gentleman. "It's very decent of you to tell me this," he said, "and considering the circumstances as you saw them, I can see why you advised her as you did."

"You have given me cause to change my mind," George went on. "I have, therefore, notified the geisha people that I would not be pleased if they put any further obstacles in your way. I am just about their best customer and I have a very close friend whose bill is, if anything, larger than mine."

"I'm permanently indebted," Seaton said.

"Not at all, as a matter of fact I've talked twice to the Callahan people to whom you referred me and they are airmailing over some blueprints for estimates. So if anything, I'm in your debt. One more thing: I didn't ask the geisha people where the lady is, because that would be applying undue pressure and interfering a little too deeply in their affairs. I did ask them to pass on a message which they promised to deliver. In it I stated that we had had a further meeting, as a result of which I had revised my viewpoint. That's the best I can do at this time, I hope it will be of some help."

"Very much so, I'll express myself more fully when I see you."

"That may have to wait until I come back from overseas, but the best of luck in the meantime. By the way, I'm losing Norma."

"What happened to her?"

"She's engaged and plans to be married shortly."

"That's a surprise."

"For me too. She met the gentleman only a comparatively short time ago. He's quite a bit older than she is, but he's very sports minded—a Texas millionaire type."

English failed Seaton, but he found a phrase which expressed matters perfectly for him. "So desuka."

Sakamoto laughed. "Precisely. I called the best employment agency in Tokyo for a new English-language secretary; they told me they had had one crackerjack, but that she had just been hired for you. That's how I got the word on your new status, which is richly deserved, by the way. It's no secret that you are the genius, and I use the word advisedly, who did that radar design that no one else could handle. So you deserve the best and I suspect that you have your eye on her right now."

When the conversation was over Seaton looked up to see Reiko standing in the doorway to his office. "Come in," he invited.

"You still want me call you 'Dick chan'?" she asked.

"Always," he answered.

"Dick chan, I have friend who is cousin to girl who mother run geisha restaurant. She say she try find Masayo for you."

Seaton beckoned her closer. "Reiko, listen, I want you to understand something. I don't know what makes human beings think and act the way they do; I don't understand myself most of the time. I don't know why I feel about Masayo the way that I do, I only know that I can't help it."

"I understan', Dick chan."

"One thing I do know," he went on. "I think the world of you, I don't ever want to lose your friendship, and you're going to be very dear to me for as long as I live."

She burst into tears. "Dick chan, you make me so most happy. I never think nobody like me so much." She covered her face with her hands and cried. Then she wiped her eyes and smiled. "Dick chan, you make me new girl," she said, and went out.

"Damn," Seaton said to himself. He packed up his work and went home.

He ate the dinner that had been prepared for him and so far forgot himself that he stuck his chopsticks into a cube of ice cream before he realized it.

At seven he had visitors—the first who had come to his new home. The maid ushered them in, took their shoes, and bowed them into his presence. Airman Millsup and Peggy came in a little hesitantly for fear that they might be intruding. Seaton welcomed them cordially and noted that his maid had already gone to the refrigerator to start preparing refreshments.

"Hey, this is real classy place," Peggy said. "May I look see?"

"Go right ahead," Seaton invited.

Walking with the peculiar and yet graceful manner of a Japanese girl with only socks on her feet she made short work of exploring the premises. "Real good," she announced when she had completed her inspection. "Masayo will like very much, I think." She leaned over the sill and peered down out of a window. "Even place for the kids to play."

"What kids?" Seaton asked.

Peggy stared at him. "Your kids. You want Masayo give you some kids, don't you?"

Seaton sidestepped that one. "Mostly I'd just like to find her."

"You got it made," she assured him. "Mamasan at geisha house teld me I'm fired if I tell you where she's at, so I promise I won't do that."

She sat down and studied his features. "Without glasses you handsome guy," she said. "You kids, I think, come out nice and tall. Me, maybe I get redheaded Japanese babies—could happen." She intensified her scanning of his face. "You look tire," she went on. "New job too much hard I think. You need vacation, nice place like Shimoda."

"Not right now, I'm afraid," he answered.

Peggy became impatient. "I still think good idea you go Shimoda for nice rest."

His brain finally reacted. "Maybe I should do that, over the weekend anyway. Do you happen to know a good hotel?"

"Hoteru not matter, but I think you much like big summer festival, happen right away. You ever hear Kurobune Matsuri?"

"No. Tell me about it."

"I can fill you in," Millsup cut in. "Festivals are a big deal over here. This one has something to do with commemorating Townsend Harris's arrival in Japan, you've heard of him.

258

Once a year they put on a big show with ondo dancers, all kinds of stuff."

"Better you make reservations real fast," Peggy advised. "Shimoda not such big place, many people want to see festival."

"How long does it take to get there?" he asked.

"Maybe three hour, take New Tokaido Line to Atami, then East Coast Line to Shimoda. Best you go Friday, same night so many pretty girls all dance same time in kimono, big deal."

"I'll go," Seaton announced. He looked carefully at Peggy. "If anybody asks me, I'll explain that my secretary told me all about it and thought I would enjoy it."

"Incidentally," Millsup interjected, "I don't think you've seen Peggy since you came back to Japan."

"Of course not," Seaton agreed. "I haven't even spoken to her on the telephone. The only way I know to reach her is through the geisha house—I didn't keep her number."

The airman touched the tips of his forefinger and thumb together and held his hand in the air. "We'd better be going now, Peggy has to work tonight. Tell your maid we'll take the tea next time."

Seaton showed them out, then sat down to think. Oddly enough, his mind turned to Norma. So she was going to be married! To an older man with money. In a certain sense she had accepted her patron; he found it difficult to believe that to a girl of Norma's disposition true engulfing love had come so rapidly. Perhaps all girls were something like geisha—they were to a certain extent for sale, especially if money or position were involved. Norma, for all of her independence, was an American geisha.

As far as Masayo was concerned, he knew little about her family except for Peggy, but he didn't care. She was what she was and that was the way he wanted her. He had never believed in dowries and things like that; he was now well established in a far better than average job with excellent prospects. He could support his own wife very comfortably without any outside assistance.

The efficient Ellen Yamada made the reservations for him promptly the following morning. A few minutes later she had an appointment to brief Matsumoto san on any interesting

mail which might have come in in English. There were three
such communications, one of them from the Philippines. It
contained a message of sincere appreciation for the visit of Mr.
Seaton who had made a most valuable suggestion concerning
production methods. Heartened by this stimulating news Matsumoto san thought again of the great bird which was the
intellect of his new vice-president. While in this expansive
mood he showed such evident approval that Mrs. Yamada
made a fast decision. She informed him that Mr. Seaton was
interested in attending the Kurobune Matsuri and asked if she
should suggest that he leave early to catch a more convenient
train.

This happy thought was at once endorsed and recommended. As a result of it Seaton left the plant shortly after noon,
picked up his overnight bag, and headed for the railroad
station. With its customary efficiency, the Japan Travel Service had everything in order for him, even a car to meet him
upon arrival and take him to his hotel. It was another
Japanese inn, the Western-style facilities being already sold
out. A guide, whose English was as fragile as a soap bubble
and as likely to pop apart at any moment, offered his services.
It was the typical reception for a wealthy American tourist.

Seaton declined the guide's assistance and instead asked the
way to the bath. Since in Japan the bath and the toilet are
two separate entities, the inn management was immediately
impressed with the fact that this was no ordinary foreigner; a
maid was rushed to prepare the facilities for him and another
to deliver hot green tea and bean jelly cakes to his room
without delay.

Already a mardi gras atmosphere overlaid the little seaside
city: the hard clatter of geta on the pavement, the occasional
call of vendors, the sounds of many people moving about.
Seaton drank his tea and munched on the cakes as he got out
of his clothes and climbed into the yukata which had been
provided for him. Barefoot, because the inn had no slippers
which would fit him, he made his way to the bath facilities
and there after washing soaked himself in the steaming hot
water. When a maid appeared to provide him with towels, he
was hardly aware of her presence. The wooden tub had about
it a friendliness that Western porcelain would never be able
to match; when at last he climbed out he decided that the

Japanese bath was not only superior to the American variety, it was also a great protection against ulcers.

He ate alone in his room; the dinner was served early because of the festival. He tried to eat calmly and enjoy his food, but outside the sounds were growing more insistent. The event itself was not the attraction, but the fact that somewhere—on one of the streets, in one of the houses, was Masayo. She might even be within a few hundred feet of where he sat on the tatami, perhaps eating her dinner alone or with a group of friends. Or possibly she was entertaining professionally at a party. That last thought was a bitter one, because if that were the case his chances of finding her were greatly reduced. If there was a geisha area, he could go there and inquire.

When he had finished eating he retied his yukata well below the waistline in the correct manner, and slipped his wallet into his sleeve. Then he went to the lobby to find out where the festival was being held and if there was a geisha district in the city. The amount of English available at the front desk was extremely limited; after he had repeated the word "geisha" several times his intentions were misunderstood. He fortunately sensed that and waved his hand in the air to indicate that casual feminine company was not his desire.

When all else failed the willing man behind the desk took a sheet of paper and drew a map. Since addresses in Japan are uncertain—many houses being numbered according to the year in which they were built—drawing maps is an almost continuous occupation. The clerk indicated the location of the inn, the directions in reference to the shoreline, and the street where the main parade could be seen. Satisfied that this was the best he could do, Seaton bowed his thanks and went out on the street.

Mercifully the geta he had been given were both new and built lower to the ground; he found he could walk in them with much greater ease than in those he had had in Atami. Soon he was striding along almost at his usual pace, although the folds of the yukata held him back almost as much as the unaccustomed footgear.

The carnival mood was now fully in command. Nearly everyone was in some form of Japanese dress, the Western business suits and blue and white street dresses were replaced by kimonos and yukatas; the few Occidentals he saw were de-emphasized by clothing like his own. The pages of time had been turned back and old Japan had risen, like the engulfed cathedral, out of the sea.

As he walked he looked into all of the faces that he could, a quick glance just in case. Bright, vivid splashes of color surrounded him, kimonos worn by an increasing number of young women, all with their obis tied with careful perfection behind their backs. Occasionally someone would bow to him, and on each such occasion he tried his best to bow back without being too awkwardly Western about it.

He came to a corner and saw at once that he had found the principal route of the festival parade. People three and four deep were already lined up, silently and patiently, along the curb while others flowed in steady streams of human traffic behind them. Overhead paper lanterns were strung in low rows, a profusion of reds and yellows with characters printed on their sides.

As the daylight became dimmer the brilliance of the floral kimonos grew in intensity. The movement of countless thousands of fans added to the illusion of a river of humanity with uncounted ripplets on its surface. There were some foreigners, but they too had been swallowed up in the traditional dress of this ancient country; an occasional light-colored head of hair was like a bit of substance floating along on the surface of the water.

From somewhere the deep voice of a Japanese drum sounded, the beats coming at studied intervals, each one a separate stroke like the striking of a huge and sedate clock. Because of his height, Seaton could see over the heads of the spectators who were lined up awaiting the coming of the parade. He hurried on, not sure where he was going, but intent on the idea that he must cover as much ground as he could; the more people he saw, the better the chance that he might somehow, in one blinding moment of realization, find the face he sought.

Presently he had to slow down, the pressure of many other bodies all around him grew in density until almost all traffic had been slowed to a thin winding stream. Then he felt a stir in the crowd and saw that the tempo of the swaying fans had picked up visibly. He looked and saw that far down the street the parade was coming.

Darkness was almost complete now; the gentle glow of the lanterns made everything softer. It was indeed the time of the black ships, when Townsend Harris had stepped ashore onto the soil of Japan as the first, and uninvited, diplomatic representative of the United States of America. He had come to open this island kingdom to trade. In that he had, in his way, succeeded and those who had come after him had carried on what he had begun. But tonight Japan had returned to what she had been, so that she would in some part always be. The paper lanterns swayed gently, untroubled by the transition in time. The boom of the Japanese drum punctuated the air, sounding the note which summoned back all the spirits of the ancient noblemen, the samurai, and the humble people who in long rows had bowed before them. The drum boomed again and the message was changed; it was no longer a summons to those long gone, but rather a recognition of their presence.

The drum boomed again and with it this time came a thin hint of melody. Just within audible range musicians were playing, giving rebirth to songs which echoed the patina of centuries. The sounds rose and fell in a minor key as though nature herself had first set them down and spun out the thread of their flow. The drum boomed louder and the spell of the music hung more thickly in the air. Heads turned and watched as the parade came closer and the figures of people could be seen carrying banners covered with intricate characters.

An intricate, massive, model shrine carried on poles supported by dozens of bearers resolved out of the darkness; ahead of it a Shinto priest walked with stately dignity. Behind came a float with more people and the figure of a fairly tall Japanese dressed in old-fashioned Western clothing, the personification of the man who had come to this place in a sailing ship from across the ocean.

The drum boomed, its voice clear and authoritative. The drummer could be seen now, riding on the upper platform of a float, a cloth tied around his head, concentrating on his work. He remained motionless for a second or two, keeping time invisibly in his head, then he swung his beater against the horizontal drum with exactly the right amount of force at the precise instant that the sound had to be heard.

Behind him came a small sea of children, uniformly clad in matching kimonos and marching with grave, expressionless faces, tiny flags held in their hands.

Another float came slowly advancing; it was covered with motionless figures in ancient costumes from the days of old Edo when the shoguns ruled Japan with feudal authority. They were people of the past, but now only the very recent past. The ancient warriors rode by, timeless and mute, part of the living heritage of the land.

Behind them a group of young men, forty or fifty of them, with workingmen's cloths tied around their heads, were carrying something on poles; it appeared to be a small doll's house of some kind. Their motions were erratic, they would run with their burden close to the people on one side of the street, then turn away and dash across in the other direction.

A flower-covered float followed; on it a dozen lovely kimono-clad girls stood against a background representing a woodland glade. Seaton clamped his teeth in sudden expectation and looked carefully at each of the pretty faces, then he slowly let his breath out again.

The sounds of more music came; a row of flute players, each with a wicker basket covering his head, walked slowly behind the flower float. They held their bamboo instruments straight down in front of their invisible faces, like creatures from some ancient legend or fairy tale. Although they appeared as musicians, they were making no sounds; the music came from somewhere behind them.

A long pattern of marchers followed, men carrying banners by the hundreds, some with vertical rows of characters, others with patterns and designs. They moved with studied precision, advancing step, pausing, then moving forward once more.

The music came nearer, this time a song with the definite throbbing rhythm. It had to be a song, since the melody seemed to have been created solely for some human throat to produce at a time of gentle happiness. A float bearing the musicians came slowly past, its wheels turning as though they had an indefinite amount of time at their disposal and no particular place to go.

As they at last rolled past there came behind them a

spectacle of mass color, grace, and movement which made Seaton catch his breath. Six long rows of young women in exquisite red and black kimonos were dancing, all in unison. With open fans in their hands they advanced a few steps, paused, bent sideways, turned, stepped backward, lifted their fans, turned, and then slowly formed a new pattern with their arms. Every movement was in perfect unison, timed to the throb of the music and to the measured beat of another drummer who was keeping precise pace with the one far ahead of him in the procession.

The rhythm and movement of the dancers were compelling; they personified the inexpressible grace of a deeply rooted tradition in which the lovely, the delicate, and the poetic were essential ingredients. The kimonos were cunningly designed so that when the dancers were facing forward they were a panorama of red, when they turned they became a spectacle of black and white. The music pulsed through the air, its sharply throbbing beat emphasized by the uniformed movement of the feet of the dancers and the sounds of their soft geta against the pavement. Time after time the simple pattern of the dance was repeated, but it flowed with unbroken smoothness and the music kept up its unvarying melody.

No one could have watched such a sight unmoved; to Seaton it was an enchantment straight out of the exotic world he had once believed had never existed. He drank in every movement of the ondo dancers, marveling at the flawless grace of each flowing gesture. It was perfection multiplied by perfection, something which his eyes saw, his ears heard, but which his mind could hardly grasp. He responded to it emotionally, realizing that it was one of the experiences of his life—a world unknown to him before.

The dancers swirled and became black and white, then they turned and were transformed into red again. It was almost intoxicating to watch them, and to hear the music which was so hauntingly different, and so magically potent.

Then he saw her.

He had been so swept up by the spectacle his senses had refused to admit anything else, until he looked at the second row and one face riveted his attention. She was moving, like all the others, with immaculate grace, tipping her head, maneuvering her fan, bending her knees as she turned. Her

265

features were quietly composed as she made herself one with the whole ensemble.

The crush of people was at its densest now; he could hardly move from where he was standing without stepping on someone's feet but he managed. Quietly and inconspicuously he paced the slow procession, keeping her opposite him, never taking his eyes from the graceful movements of her body.

Then after it had seemed that it never would, the music stopped. The girls paused and rested, fanning themselves with quiet dignity as they waited in place for the parade to continue. He was tempted to try to attract her attention, then he decided against it. Instead he stood back and waited until the drum started things again with a single echoing beat; the dancers lifted their arms in front of themselves, holding their closed fans horizontally in both hands, and then swung into movement as the music began once more.

For almost an hour he paced the parade, keeping her always in sight, marveling at her ability to dance for so long with undiminished grace and beauty of movement. Near to the end of the long street the parade moved around a corner in its full splendor and then, out of sight of the tens of thousands of spectators, began to disband. The heavy miniature shrine rested on the ground at last, its weary bearers sitting around it, regathering their strength. Parents were rounding up the children, still clutching their little flags in their chubby fingers. He did not stand on ceremony then, he simply walked into the midst of the red and black kimonos, took her by the hand, and led her away.

When he found a tiny spot where they could stand together he turned to her, drank her in, and was overwhelmed.

"Konban wa," he said. He did not remember where he had learned to say "good evening," but the words came mechanically to his lips.

She looked at him steadily for a few seconds as though she were trying to catch hold of herself. When she finally spoke, it was with difficulty. "How you find?" she asked.

"Easy," he answered. "I came to Japan and looked."

Her lips moved before she spoke again, as though she were saying something silently to herself. "Why?"

"You know that. I told you—remember?"

She lifted her arm and fitted it around his waist for a brief

266

moment, then she dropped it and backed a step or two away. "I must go," she explained. "This kimono not mine."

He was still holding her hand and he did not let it go. "For how long?" he asked.

She shook her head that she did not quite understand. "I want you back," he said.

"But so many things . . ." she began.

"Change your kimono if you must, then come back—understand?"

She gave in. With her fan she pointed gently toward the direction of the ocean. "If you want, I come back one hour. We talk little while. Nice place by water."

Seaton looked at his watch in the darkness and tipped its face until he could see the hands. "One hour. You promise?"

"I promise, Dick."

He let her go then and she disappeared into the midst of the many other dancers. He walked away without looking back. He had time to kill now; he filled it by making his way slowly through the crowd, looking at the decorations, and studying the wares of the many vendors who were out in force. He listened to the sounds of Japan—the talk of the geta against the pavement, somewhere an unseen player bringing dry, pungent music in strict rhythm from the strings of a samisen, the meaningless chant of an old man selling hot soba noodles. Time was banished from this place, robbed of its relentlessness, except for the dispensation of measuring off one single hour. A beautiful girl in a purple kimono loomed in front of him, he stepped aside to let her pass. As she bowed her thanks, he tried his best to return the gesture, knowing that she would take the will for the deed.

He caught a snatch of conversation in his own language. ". . . so I was right there on the phone when the big board opened and I got in for thirty-two and five-eights . . ." He did not turn to look who was speaking; he did not want to see the face of the intruder here, the kind of person insensitive to anything but the petty harsh realities of his own limited world. Let him have it. Let him go back to his own century and make a pest of himself there.

A red banner lettered with white Chinese characters he could not read told him that he need not worry—all was well.

He saw a torii gate, faintly illuminated by a long row of stone lanterns which had been lit for the occasion, poised silently, inviting those who wished to do so to pass underneath and be purified. There were a few steps and at the top a Shinto priest stood gently fanning himself. They saw each other at the same time and bowed their mutual greetings. There was an unspoken communication between them—the priest recognized the foreigner but made him welcome nonetheless; the American did not subscribe to the priest's faith, but he offered it his respect. The two men who would never meet again each gave a little of his dignity to the other, and gained in the process.

A child selling little ornaments held one up in front of his face. It was a small salmon-colored fish made of paper and suspended from the end of a stick. Seaton had no coins with him or he would have given the little boy one. In lieu of that he rubbed the close-cropped head in friendly salutation. The boy looked up at him and smiled.

There was forty minutes yet to go. He slowed his pace and tried to look at everything that was to be seen. He had stopped searching the faces around him; now he looked at the lanterns, the little displays of merchandise, the kaleidoscopic colors and patterns of the kimonos and the darker hues of the men's yukatas all blended into a strange and yet harmonious whole. If Townsend Harris had seen all this when he had stepped ashore, what an overwhelming adventure he must have lived.

For a moment a doubt hit him that he was wasting away an hour while she was packing and making her escape. Then he remembered that she had given him her promise; the demon of doubt was banished and ran gibbering away.

Twenty-five minutes.

He began to walk toward the water and the little parklike place that she had designated. She might be early, perhaps as much as ten minutes early; one hour was, after all, only a rounded-off unit of time. When people spoke of an hour, they seldom meant precisely sixty minutes—it was plus or minus.

Pacing himself in his geta, which had adapted themselves now to his feet, he made his way calmly in the hope that he could consume a full ten minutes in covering the short distance. Overhead the sky was still dark, but an almost full

268

moon hung low in the east, tracing a long, tapered, shimmering path across the water.

When he reached the place where she had said that she would meet him, there were many others about. He was used to that, there were crowds of people everywhere in Japan except on the slopes of the steep mountains which encroached on so much of the land area. He found one little place that could be theirs and then looked all around very carefully to be sure that she had not already arrived. He had no idea what color kimono she would be wearing and in the darkness it was not easy to see people's faces.

He sat down on the grass and tried to keep his mind from working so that the minutes would pass by unnoticed until she came. He remembered the last time he had waited for her, on the train for Kyoto, and how she had appeared as she had agreed to do. Of course on that occasion she was being lavishly paid for her time, but she had come nonetheless.

By moonlight he read his watch—there was only five minutes left to go.

He sat, his back to the water, facing the little city, patiently waiting. He did not look at his watch, but he knew when the five minutes must have passed and there was no sign of her anywhere.

To expect her to appear on the exact minute was too much, he therefore tried to attune himself to the timelessness of everything about him—the ocean, the moon behind him, even the ageless characters visible on the signs and banners.

When he thought that it was fifteen minutes past, he looked at his watch and saw that it was only twelve. He had made his decision, he would keep his trust in her, and wait. The probability that she would appear slipped with each passing minute, but he refused to abandon his belief in her—any one of a dozen different things could have happened to delay her; he had been late himself many times against his will.

He turned for a moment to look at the water and to take for himself some of the endless patience that it represented. It was always there, always in a pattern of some kind of movement, yet never conscious of anything which might distract it from its contemplation of eternity.

Against the moonlight he saw a standing figure silently

269

watching the water. Fire raced within him as he got to his feet, wondering how long he had kept her waiting. As fast as he decently could he made his way toward her, stepping around the many other couples and families who were silently sharing this place with him. She saw him coming and lifted her hand shoulder-high in recognition.

She had found a little place too where they could be almost alone. Together they sat down, quite calmly, beside each other. Then she leaned back and turned on her side facing him. When he was beside her, separated by just a little bit, they could talk without being overheard, together in this little bit of private world.

"Akiko," she said softly, "she tell me you come."

"Akiko?" he asked.

"Her friend make her name 'Peggy,' but she really Akiko."

"What did she say?"

"She say you come. Also mamasan has find me patron to marry."

"Who?"

"I not know yet. She very anxious I marry quick."

"Second wife?" he asked calmly. She was here now and he refused to be disturbed by minor matters.

"I think yes."

He knew that this was conversation and nothing more.

"He wants the geisha Fujikoma."

"Hai."

"I don't," Seaton said.

She lifted herself on one elbow and looked at him.

"I have no time for Fujikoma, or any other geisha," he went on. "Only for a girl, Masayo Kanno. Do you know her?"

"Sometime'," she answered.

"You know what?" he said. "I know Fujikoma, I went to Kyoto with her." He gave her time to absorb that. "That's the last time I saw her."

She let her head slide down until it rested on her arm. Lifting his weight onto his elbows he turned onto his back, stretched out his own long arm, and offered it to her. She accepted, putting her head on it like a pillow so that there was physical contact between them at last.

"Dick, I tell you something. You remember Atami?"

"Yes," he answered.

"What I do, never for money. Once, but I cannot help. That pay my debt, can no make me do again."

"I'll tell you something," he countered. "First time."

She rolled her head to look at him. "Why?" she asked.

"Because I never wanted to before. Not really. Sometimes . . ."

He decided to try again. "Listen, Masayo, some men have lots of girlfriends. Not me."

"You very nice man."

He changed the tack. "Let's not talk about it, it's all in the past anyway." He turned his head sideways so that he could look at her. "Masayo, would you like to be my wife?"

She teased him gently. "First wife?"

"Only wife."

She grew more serious. "Very difficult, Dick. Geisha house make terrible trouble. They think me worth much money, they must be pay."

"I've got a friend who's looking into that. He is a very important man and I think he will succeed. Let someone else become Fujikoma, they have lots of girls."

"Your friend is maybe Sakamoto George?"

"Yes."

She moved her head on his arm as though she were caressing him with the back of her neck. "If he say let me go, they have very hard time refuse."

"I think so. You didn't answer my question."

She moved her body so that she was a little closer to him. "Many ploblem, Dick. You know."

"I know, and I don't care. I'm going to learn Japanese anyway, you can help me."

"You not understand."

"I understand perfectly well, Masayo. You're a Buddhist. You're a Japanese national. You're tied up with the geisha house." He reached out and took hold of her hand. "But I don't care about any of these things. Go to church where you like. Stand up when they play the Japanese national anthem— if there is one. George, I think, can handle the geisha angle; if you owe them money, I'll take care of it one way or another."

271

"Dick." She moved so that she was very close to him now and could speak very softly. Face to face they were alone in a private world. "What maybe my babies look like me?"

She was too close to resist so he kissed her. "They couldn't be that lucky," he answered.

She turned her head a little so that she could look up toward the sky.

"Dick, you see moon?"

"Yes, of course."

"Some say in very old time sun god have grandson become first emperor Japan. Moon god also very nice person, I think."

"She's often admired," Seaton agreed.

"Moon god look down, see everything. Sometime maybe boy with girl. Family not let marry, so she say, 'I make you married anyway.' So they happy. You like?"

"I like," he agreed. Carefully he eased his arm out from underneath her head and got to his knees, then he helped her to her feet and stood beside her. He remained there for a few moments, looking first at her and then at the moon whose unexpected authority had just been revealed to him.

"Come on, Mrs. Seaton," he said, and led her back toward the city.

Made in the USA
Middletown, DE
19 November 2019